Fanny Newcomb

&

The Irish Channel Ripper

By Ana Brazil

Fanny Newcomb

&

The Irish Channel Ripper

By Ana Brazil

New Orleans
Friday, April 26, 1889

1.

FANNY NEWCOMB SUCKED THE BLOOD from the knuckle of her right thumb. Her fingers were stiff and reddened; her nails were torn. Her cuffs were rolled up to her elbows and she'd undone the top three buttons of her bodice. She dabbed the glow from her forehead with her crumpled handkerchief and surveyed her opponent. The battle had just begun.

The Hammond typewriting machine was not entirely uninjured. The A, P, and W keys were snarled tightly and buried deep in the carriage well. The typewriter was immobilized.

Fanny's pride was bruised but her spirit was unbowed. "You're just a machine," she sneered. "Wires and plates and copper and keys. I'm smarter than you are. It might take me a while to figure you out but I'll do it."

But Fanny needed to master the machine *now*. If she couldn't teach her students how to create perfect correspondence on the typewriting machine by next Wednesday, all hell would break loose. All hell in the grand personage of Sylvia Giddings, Founder and Principal of the Wisdom Hall Settlement House. Sylvia

Giddings's outlook, authority, and decisions were absolute. She did not allow her employees to fail her. And Fanny was entirely in Sylvia's employ.

Four months ago—when she answered Sylvia's newspaper advertisement for a woman to teach business courses—Fanny had consummate confidence in her abilities. After all, Fanny had managed her father's law office for ten years. If Fanny could file papers, keep accounting ledgers, and take shorthand, she could teach younger women to do so also. Fanny excelled at every office chore; she just had never seen a typewriting machine before.

But four months ago Fanny was at the end of her resources. Lying to Sylvia was her only option. Like Sylvia, Fanny was a spinster. But unlike Sylvia, Fanny's prospects had shriveled to almost nothing after her father's death a year ago. Since then, Fanny had both lost her livelihood at the Law Office and failed as a ladies' companion. Teaching at something as new as a settlement house—especially one in New Orleans' roguish Irish Channel—appealed to her as interesting, useful work. And Fanny was definitely qualified to teach. Well, almost.

Fanny dug her hands into the carriage well only to prick her fingertips again. "Damnation!"

Her fidgeting was interrupted by a resounding thump. And then another, both echoing from the third floor and down to Fanny's first floor classroom. Even at eleven at night, Sylvia's carpenter was still hard at work, building a staircase from the new third floor up to the roof. The work of turning Wisdom Hall into a glorious edifice of immigrant education—Sylvia's *Grand Plan*—never ended.

"Go home, Karl!" The carpenter had disrupted both of Fanny's classes tonight with his noise. "Give me a moment of quiet!"

Fanny dabbed her forehead and neck with her handkerchief again. Although it was only April, New Orleans was choked with a sudden heat that was worthy of summer and the early evening breaks of rain only intensified the humidity. Closed-up in the classroom, Fanny was drenched in frustration.

Still, she carefully unglued the keys from each other and examined the machine to make sure she had not permanently injured it. She reviewed the diagram of the keyboard pinned on the easel and commanded her fingers to press each key with equal strength and rhythm. She'd almost completed typing the date when the 8 and 9 keys jammed.

The paper was smeared and unreadable. Fanny ripped it from the wheel, enjoying the harsh whir she forced from the machine. She picked up the machine—ready to shake it into submission—and then thought better of it. Sometimes a mean machine really needed a sharp kick. She set the machine on the floor and aimed her boot at it. But before she could discipline the keys, the infirmary night bell rang out from the front gallery.

Fanny was out of the classroom and into the main hallway in seconds. Only Sylvia's sister—Dr. Olive Giddings—or the doctor's assistant Thomas were supposed to answer the infirmary bell but it was still ringing frantically when Fanny arrived at the front door. And there was no sign of Olive or Thomas.

Fanny gave a thought to buttoning up her bodice. Despite the roar of spring heat, despite her frustration, she should never have aired her neck until she reached her bedroom. But the collage of blood and ink on her fingertips had already left vivid stains on her skirt, and this was her best bodice.

Two sturdy black dogs rose from their beds at the back of the hallway and galloped toward the front door. "Ready to break the rules again?" Fanny asked Cain and Abel as she pulled the doorknob.

Liam O'Donnell, all twelve years and eighty pounds of him, stood at the threshold, feet planted firmly apart, as if he were in the boxing ring. Through his thin cotton shirt Fanny could see his narrow chest heave up and down. He gulped for air but managed to blurt out, "Doctor Olive's needed at Conner's Court."

Fanny stooped down to meet his dark wet eyes. "Why? What's happened?"

The boy wiped his hand under his nose and then on his pants. "Someone's been murdered in the Irish Channel!"

FANNY HURRIED THE boy through the dark halls toward the back of Wisdom Hall. She barged through the Infirmary door to find Olive looking up from behind a table of dark apothecary bottles.

"Well," the doctor asked sharply. "What is it?"

Fanny put her hand gently on Liam's shoulders, "He sa—"

"Murder!" The boy honked like a trumpet. "A girl's been murdered in Conner's Court!"

"Murdered girls don't need doctors." Olive scowled at Liam and returned two of the bottles to the cupboard behind her. "Even you should know that."

"They *said* she was murdered...but somebody screamed for a doctor."

Fanny pressed forward gingerly, having been told more than once that the Infirmary was Olive's sacred soil, and entrance was by invitation only. "If there's any chance she's still alive, we must—"

"Of course we must." Olive took a key from her pocket and turned the lock on the medicine cupboard. She grabbed her medical bag and passed the lantern on her desk to Liam. "Well, what are you waiting for?"

THE SULTRY FRIDAY evening had enticed the inhabitants of the Irish Channel out of doors, and young Liam gamely maneuvered between men, women, donkeys, and dogs as he led Fanny and Olive through the soft darkness. Fanny had never been in this direction from Wisdom Hall, and quickly inventoried the new landscape: the battered old mansions that were as large and imposing as Wisdom Hall; the tall brick warehouses that were built almost into the streets; the slight shotgun houses that seemed to sink into the soft soil; and...was that a church steeple?

After five blocks and one near-miss with a pair of drunken roughs, Liam pointed toward a swelling of light coming from between two saloons. "There!"

As Liam led the women forward, Fanny saw dozens of men and women crowded together, staring into the dimly lit space between the saloons. Just beyond the crowd, the doors and windows of both saloons were pinned open to the warm evening. Lights bounced from lamp to mirror in the saloons, illuminating tables of card players, drinkers, and the women who entertained them.

Conner's Court, New Orleans, America ~ Irish Only was painted in broad strokes on a wall. Even from the calmness of her father's downtown law office, Fanny had heard about Conner's Court, a well-known enclave of New Orleans' depravity. Could it really be as evil as it was reputed to be?

Liam grabbed Olive's arm and plowed through a hole in the crowd. Fanny followed, but Olive turned and commanded, "Not you; this is doctor's work."

FANNY JAMMED HER hands into her skirt pockets, embarrassed by how absolutely Olive had dismissed her. Despite all of Fanny's hard work at Wisdom Hall, Olive and Sylvia still treated her like a simple-minded employee.

Fanny turned toward the growing crowd that began to envelope her. Were there fifty, sixty people here now? She inspected the men and women closest to her. *Something* had happened here. Something made that pregnant woman wipe her sleeve on her eyes; something made that man lose his dinner against the wall. *Something* was wrong here.

At five feet and six and a half inches, Fanny was the tallest woman in the cluster. If she'd taken time to put on a hat and cape, she would have been taller than most men here tonight, a thought that helped her remove her hands from her pocket and straighten her posture. Fanny felt eyes turning toward her and she met them unflinchingly. Her warm, golden hair and calm complexion marked her as an outsider amongst the freckled, flame-haired Irish. And her unfashionable clothes—even her ink-spotted skirt—were better made than the grimy rags worn about her. Even in the darkness, Fanny could not pretend she belonged in the Irish Channel.

Whispers cascaded throughout the court: *Mother of God!...poor wee thing...what type of monster...I'm going to be sick meself.*

More people collected behind her, immersing her in the odors of alcohol and the heavy, stale scent of Mississippi river. Fanny felt warm stale breath close to her ear and turned quickly. A thin woman offered a crooked smile.

"What happened here?" Fanny demanded.

"There's blood everywhere. Blood, blood, blood, and blood," the woman's litany continued. "Everywhere."

Fanny caught sight of the dried blood behind her own fingernails and remembered her failed attempts at mastering her typewriter machine. A shadow of responsibility and guilt hovered over her. She should be back at Wisdom Hall. She should be training herself on that accursed machine.

Instead, Fanny stretched to her full height and steeled her eyes into the darkness of Conner's Court. If someone was murdered blocks from where she lived, Fanny Newcomb wanted to know all about it.

2.

DR. OLIVE GIDDINGS TOOK THE LANTERN from Liam's hands and walked toward a knot of people bent over something. Just ahead of her Liam pushed into the tangle of trousers and skirts. "Doctor's here."

The men parted to reveal a young woman who looked as though she had slumped down against the wall to have a short rest. She wore a lightly shaded dress and short cape but no bonnet. Her dark hair was held back in a tidy knot, almost in mirror image of how Fanny pinned her golden hair.

"You," Olive commanded a man standing a few feet from the body, "hold my lantern."

With the girl illuminated, Olive stooped and placed her fingers on the girl's wrist. The man brought the lantern closer and Olive glanced up at the girl's head. She saw the dark imprint of something—fingers? rope? sash?—around the girl's pale neck. Strangled. Must have been. Even so, Olive searched for a pulse for over a minute.

Olive sat back on her feet and inspected the girl's body. If she had been strangled, why wasn't her face bloated and her eyes bulging? Even in this light, shouldn't her face be tinted blue? Olive lifted the girl's eyelids. In both eyes she saw a large red mass created by a broken blood vessel. Peering closely, she saw the other blood freckles that marked the girl's face. Severe hemorrhage and marks around the neck. *Now*, any doctor would agree with her: death by strangulation.

Although Olive had little expectation that the police cared about a murder in Conner's Court, she expected that the Charity Hospital ambulance had been called. Would John Remington arrive with the ambulance? Although he was the chief surgeon at

Charity Hospital, he often went on ambulance rounds at night. If John managed the ambulance tonight, Olive might be able to assist with the post-mortem medical examination.

It might take the ambulance an hour to get to Conner's Court and so Olive settled in to watch over the body, not trusting the bystanders to guard this girl. They might go through her pockets, strip off her clothing, even cut off her hair to sell. Olive pulled her leather bag toward her, knowing that the alcohol, medicines, and equipment she carried might tempt the thieves in the crowd. She paid well to have quality equipment and she did not want to lose it.

She also congratulated herself that she had not brought her assistant on this call. Although Thomas usually accompanied her on late night medical calls, Olive could not tell how this crowd of Irish might react to the presence of a well-spoken, authoritative colored man.

Suddenly, the lantern light above Olive wavered and then went dead. Other lanterns took its place, as a flurry of footsteps arose behind Olive.

"Back off everyone," ordered a raw Irish voice. Someone grabbed Olive's right shoulder. Olive shrugged off the hand and hunched protectively over the dead girl.

"Police business," crowed the man at Olive, as his hands came down on her shoulders. "Everyone out."

A second policeman pushed through the crowd, shoving people aside as though they were empty bottles. "That's right. Back off and let the doctor through."

Two policemen pulled Olive away from the dead girl, lifting her into the air and dropping her a few feet away. Before she could recover and protest, another man strode up to the dead girl.

Dangling a doctor's bag, he waved loosely in Olive's direction. "Get this woman out of here," his high-pitched Yankee accent pierced the low rumble of Irish murmurs, "and let me do my work."

FANNY WATCHED AS two policemen, both sporting enormous handlebar mustachios and looking as similar as bookends, emerged from Conner's Court carrying a body on a stretcher. One of the policemen stumbled slightly and the blanket shifted about the body, exposing a pale forearm and hand adorned by a crisp white cuff. Fanny held back a sudden instinct to take the dead fingers in hers and guide them back to the woman's breast.

The police placed the stretcher in the ambulance. A white-coated man emerged from the court carrying a medical bag. He shut the ambulance door, walked around the carriage, and climbed up to the driver's box. Within a few seconds, the ambulance left Conner's Court.

Olive emerged from the court, staring at the spot where the ambulance had waited. Fanny went to her and asked, "What happened in there?"

Olive scowled. "What are you still doing here?"

"Waiting to see what happened," Fanny stood her ground. "Who was that ambulance driver?"

Olive's scowl deepened, as though realizing that Fanny would not quit her questions. "I don't know, but the way he handled that body was shameful."

"Was she murdered?" asked Fanny.

"She certainly was."

Fanny saw the dark markings of handprints on Olive's shoulders. "Olive, are you hurt?"

Olive rolled her shoulders back as if to shrug off the handprints. "I'm going back to the Infirmary."

Then Fanny saw Olive's carriage approach. "It's Thomas."

"I don't need a—"

The colored man cut Olive short as he yelled down from his perch. "Herr Kasper sent word that his wife's real bad off. Something's wrong with the baby."

Without asking for more information Olive handed her leather bag to Thomas and joined him in the carriage.

"Get in, Fanny. You can keep the children quiet. And you, Liam O'Donnell." Olive pointed her finger at the boy. "Get back to Wisdom Hall and tell Sylvia where I went."

Fanny joined Olive in the carriage. Thomas skirted the vehicle around the crowd and as he turned the corner, Fanny heard a woman's shrill scream pierce the dark night.

"Jesus! Joseph and Mary! It's Jack the Ripper! Here in New Orleans!"

3.

OLIVE DID NOT LEAVE FRAU KASPER's sickbed until late Saturday morning. She returned to the infirmary soon after, glad that it was located in the rear of Wisdom Hall so that she might have some privacy and rest before opening the infirmary in an hour. She plopped into one of the white wicker benches lining the outside gallery, too exhausted to object to the sounds of Sylvia's carpenter pounding away on the third floor. She rested her eyes on the herbal garden that Thomas had planted and, as the air wafted about her, she caught the soothing fragrances of mountain mint and lemon balm. On the bench she found a small red ball left behind by some child. She rolled it between her palms, ran it through her fingers, balanced it on the top her hand. Ever steady, ever ready, as a doctor's hands should be. Olive arched the ball into the air, turned over her hand, and with sudden energy caught the ball swiftly in her palm.

It always came down to hands, didn't it? At least for a doctor. Her hands were her mother's hands and Olive had always regretted them. Out of proportion, short and broad, with stubby fingers, these hands should be hidden in lace gloves. They were not the hands a physician would choose. Despite how she had trained them to doctor, Olive cursed her hands daily. How often she had prayed to have hands like her father's, the hands she had so often watched in surgery: long and flexible hands, with fingers as nimble and fluid as a concert pianist, even at seventy years of age. Hands that worked miracles. With her father's hands, Olive could have saved the life of Frau Kasper's baby last night.

"Dr. Giddings? Olive Giddings?" A thin, plaid-suited man lifted his hand to his derby, raising the hat just high enough to reveal his bald head. "Clarence Halloway with the *New Orleans Nightly Sensation* newspaper." He pressed his business card into Olive's hand. "I heard you attended the murdered woman in Conner's Court last night."

The business card was smudged with a glob of seeded strawberry jam and Olive handed it back to the reporter. He held it for a few seconds, as though savoring the memory of breakfast, and then dropped it in his vest pocket.

Olive crossed her arms. Although she sometimes felt like a local curiosity—*See for yourself, gents! A gen-u-ine female doctor!*—she would not become one. She certainly would not grant an interview to the *Sensation*. She stood up stiffly, her fingers running down the front of her dark doctor's smock, confirming that each button was tidy in its buttonhole. "I have nothing to say to you, sir."

"But you were first on the scene, weren't you? Before the ambulance doctor got there?" Mr. Halloway steeled his eyes as though he were trying to draw an important fact from the back of his mind. "With your sister Sylvia, wasn't it? She runs the show at this place, doesn't she? With that other one. Fanny Newsom."

Olive had not thought about the dead girl once since leaving Conner's Court. And she did not want to think about her now. Olive turned toward the front door but Halloway was there before her, holding a long notebook and pencil.

"What did you see when you arrived?"

Olive reached behind him to open the door but his foot was firmly against the bottom. He scribbled away saying, "The police told me straight out her throat was cut. But some others...they're saying that her abdomen was ripped to shreds. That her intestines were thrown all over the place."

He looked up at Olive for confirmation. Already, this reporter's inability to get his facts correct irritated her: Sylvia had not gone to Conner's Court; Fanny's last name was Newcomb; and most importantly, the victim had not had her throat cut.

"Was her throat cut all the way through? Was her dress pulled up?" The reporter's pencil scrawls kept pace with his questions. He pointed his pencil at the stains on her smock. "Is that her blood all over you?"

What nonsense was this reporter making up? Olive grabbed the screen door handle again, this time with both of her hands—her short stubby hands that couldn't save a baby's life—and pushed him from his perch. Halloway tripped and sprawled on the porch; two apricots rolled out of his pocket and into the yard.

The reporter grabbed the stair post and stood up slowly. As his clothes settled about him, he turned a page in his notebook and began scribbling. "Did you know her? Was she one of your patients?"

Olive walked into the infirmary and slammed the screen door. The leathery odor of the carbolic soap she kept by the door reminded her that this was *her* infirmary and she drew the latch on the screen door sharply against the reporter.

"You know what they're saying all over town, don't you?" Clarence Halloway stopped writing and looked up at her darkened image behind the screen. "They're saying she was savaged by Jack the Ripper. He's already written a letter to my newspaper to prove it. And he says he's going to kill again. Soon."

4.

ALTHOUGH FANNY NEWCOMB AND HER employer Sylvia Giddings rarely saw eye-to-eye on anything, they did admit to a mutual affection for reading newspapers. Any newspaper from anywhere. As long as it contained *news*.

Saturday afternoon Fanny and Sylvia were at opposite ends of the Wisdom Hall dining table. Each woman had her own pot of coffee and her own pile of newspapers. In addition to the New Orleans and Baton Rouge papers, there were papers from Natchez, Jackson, and Memphis. Normally, Fanny would ask Sylvia to exchange the papers, but Sylvia's most elegant ivory cane was hooked on the arm of her chair, a clear indication that Sylvia would not yield to anyone else's requests.

Fanny read all newspapers (just as her father taught her) for information about bankruptcies, lawsuits, irregular court proceedings, unpaid taxes, and contested wills. And although Fanny had not admitted it to Sylvia (or to her father, even in the last months of his life, when she confessed almost everything to him), Fanny also read newspapers for details about jealous lovers, suspicious suicides, robberies, kidnappings, and murders.

In fact, a newspaper advertisement had brought Fanny to interview at Wisdom Hall. And before she accepted the position of Business Teacher, Fanny sought out a stack of very old newspapers in the attic of the courthouse.

Without the old and slightly damp issues of the *Daily Picayune*, Fanny would never have known the sad details about the tragic carriage accident that maimed Sylvia's right foot and ended her engagement. Or that after her long recovery, Sylvia had rejected all other romantic suitors and dedicated herself entirely to Good Works and her Grand Plan. Or that Sylvia created Wisdom Hall after an "extraordinary and enlightening" visit to London's Toynbee Hall Settlement last summer.

Fanny had long known about Sylvia, of course. The eldest daughter of esteemed surgeon Philip Giddings and his wife Jeanne, Sylvia had been celebrated for her Grecian profile, fine blue eyes, and pale complexion. More than a few strands of silver covered Sylvia's pale blond locks and her fine skin was marked by finer lines. But who really believed that the elegant Sylvia Giddings was 37 years old? She certainly didn't look 12 years older than Fanny or Olive.

And although Olive Giddings—dark-haired, round-faced, and ruddy-cheeked—looked nothing like her sister, Olive did share Sylvia's autocratic and superior attitude. Olive's accomplishments had also been recorded in the *Daily Picayune* pages. "*Destined to the medical life from the cradle*," Olive was educated in London and Berlin, conversant with the latest medical techniques and equipment, and the Physician-in-Charge at the Wisdom Hall Medical Infirmary.

But although Fanny had learned about both Giddings sisters, neither sister seemed to know much about her. Fanny preferred it that way, of course—keeping her true talents and interests to herself. Although occasionally, she wished the three women could talk honestly. Or laugh. Or hug. Or hold hands. Fanny missed her father and his busy law office and investigations and clients very much. And, Fanny admitted to herself as she finished the last of her newspapers, she very much missed Lawrence Decatur, her father's young law partner. Sylvia and Olive had each other at Wisdom Hall, but Fanny was on her own.

Olive's bold boot steps pounded along the hallway that connected the Infirmary to the dining room and Fanny sat back as Olive burst into the dining room. Olive lingered at the sideboard, as though Aunt Esther—their cook and housekeeper—would magically appear with a plate of fresh sandwiches. Finally, Olive poured a cup of coffee from a pot on the sideboard. As she plopped down at the table, her sister nudged a newspaper across the table toward her.

Fanny saw the headline plainly: *Murder in the Irish Channel!!! Jack the Ripper Stalks New Orleans!!!*

Olive settled her cup on the table and picked up the reputable *New Orleans Daily Picayune,* which was edited by Sylvia's good friend Eliza Nicholson. Olive read aloud, "The Scourge of London has landed in the South's Fairest City and is visiting his wrath upon New Orleans' prostitutes. Last night in Conner's Court, our ugliest and most shameful den of iniquity, the Ripper claimed his first American victim."

Fanny watched as Sylvia's celebrated complexion turned distinctly ashen.

"Is this possible?" Sylvia asked her sister. "Has Jack the Ripper followed us to New Orleans?"

Olive scowled at the newspaper and reached for her coffee cup.

"Has he Olive? Did he murder that girl last night? Fanny said you were both at Conner's Court last night." In an instant, Sylvia's cane was in her hand and she rapped it against the floor. "Olive Giddings, answer me."

Olive cast a stern look at Fanny before taking another gulp of coffee. "Of course he hasn't come to New Orleans, Sylvia. Last night had nothing to do with the Ripper, and nothing to do with our visit to London last summer."

"But Eliza says the girl was...Eliza says it *is* the Ripper."

"And so do all of the other newspapers." Fanny realized for the first time that Sylvia's visit to Toynbee Hall last summer must have coincided with the gruesome London murders. How truly thrilling that must have been. "And one of them is even calling him the *Irish Channel Ripper.*"

Fanny shuddered slightly at the sound of her own voice. *Irish. Channel. Ripper.*

"*Jack* the Ripper," Olive responded with precision, "used a knife to slit the throats and bodies of prostitutes. Last night's victim in Conner's Court was *strangled.* And I'd be very surprised if she was a prostitute."

"You're sure?" Sylvia asked. "Absolutely sure?"

"I know what I saw. All this," Olive nodded to the headline, "is just something to sell newspapers. It happened in London too. According to their newspapers, Jack the Ripper attacked and slashed at least one woman every night."

"But Eliza Nicholson is an editor of great integrity," persisted Sylvia. "She would not print something that was not true."

"I don't know how the newspapers got their misinformation, but the girl was strangled." As Olive surveyed the front page of the *Nightly Sensation*, she quickly detailed her recent run in with Clarence Halloway to her sister and Fanny. "I plan to talk to the police about all of this. Just as I will talk to John Remington about his ambulance driver. Rude and shameful."

As Olive sipped from her cup something fell on a floor above them. And then a roar of German profanity echoed throughout the house. Olive plunked her cup to the table. "Sylvia, you must make that man work more quietly. I've never known a carpenter to make so much noise. He frightens my patients."

"Karl is almost finished," said Sylvia, who was sensitive to any criticism of her Grand Plan for Wisdom Hall. "He worked until eleven last night and finished fifteen balusters in as many hours. I had to force him to go home. The sooner he finishes, the sooner the noise ends."

"He's not going to work tonight, is he?" asked Fanny. "Olive's right about the noise. And my students have worked so hard on their Waxworks tonight, that it wou—"

"Not tonight, of course. Tonight, Wisdom Hall will be full of our students and their families." Sylvia's eyes brightened. "No one works tonight, and everyone must have a lovely time. For the first time we'll have all of our students together. We'll have their families and friends too, and everything must be perfect tonight. Everything *will* be perfect tonight."

"But Sylvia—" Olive was cut short by a knock on the dining room doors. Without waiting for an answer Aunt Esther slid back one of the pocket doors.

"Miss Sylvie," the housekeeper wiped the bottom corner of her apron over the door's brass fittings as she spoke, "I know yer still reading and all but there's men come to front door and they's ask for you."

"Tell them to come back later."

"I already tried that, you know, that's the first thing I done," Aunt Esther nodded agreeably. "But Miss Sylvie, they said they had to talk to you and right now. I put 'em in your office."

Sylvia lifted an eyebrow. "And who is in such a rush to speak to me?"

"Why didn't I say, Miss Sylvie? It's the police."

FANNY FOLLOWED THE sisters into Sylvia's office, which was strategically placed at the front of Wisdom Hall. Large bookcases, constructed to Sylvia's demand and dimensions, dominated the walls. Bright yellow wallpaper embellished with life-sized magnolia buds peeked from between the cases. An important Wooton desk was tucked against one wall and half a dozen mismatched chairs attended each bookshelf. This was Fanny's favorite room in Wisdom Hall, and in a surprisingly generous gesture, Sylvia permitted Fanny to read any book in her collection.

Two uniformed policemen, almost indistinguishable in appearance, lumbered out of a pair of cushioned chairs. In mirror image, they smoothed their bushy handlebar mustachios.

Fanny was surprised to see that Sylvia held one of the many canes that she had secreted in her library. As sharply pointed as a sword, this cane was as treacherous for walking as Sylvia's bustles were for sitting. But it was an excellent tool for intimidating wayward students. And male visitors.

A caged-coyote look momentarily froze on each patrolman's face. Fanny wondered if Sylvia and Olive were enjoying this moment as much as she was.

That's right, Officer. We're women. The words resonated so loudly in Fanny's mind that she was sure Sylvia and Olive and the patrolmen could hear them also. *Spinsters. On-the-shelf.*

Out of the corner of her eye, Fanny realized that Olive's arms were folded assertively across her chest. Fanny folded her arms also.

And we're equal to any challenge that blocks our path.

Beads of sweat perched on the brows of both policemen as they raised their fingers to their caps in salute.

"Gerald O'Casey," said one. "Patrolman with the Sixth New Orleans Precinct. Good day to you."

"Eamon O'Casey," said the other. "Also with the Sixth."

Brothers, Fanny concluded. Or cousins. Or, given the incestuous nature of the New Orleans police department, perhaps brothers *and* cousins. Suddenly, Fanny realized that these men had carried the stretcher of the dead girl last night. She glanced over to Olive to see if she had also made that connection.

"Patrolmen?" Olive frowned. "They sent patrolmen to discuss a murder? I have important informa—"

"Oh, we haven't come for the *murder*." Gerald O'Casey gave an extra emphasis to the word, as though he could not say it often enough. Then he thrust his large hand into the knapsack strung over his shoulder. "But it *was* Detective Crenshaw who sent us." In sudden triumph Gerald O'Casey's hand emerged holding a trio of red leather-bound books.

Sylvia settled her cane against a table and took the books from the policeman. "My *David Copperfield!*"

"Sure, an' they are yours, then." The policeman brightened with achievement. "Crenshaw suspected as much. Saw the plates and said they must be yours. Said you can't be too careful in this neighborhood."

Fanny stifled a snicker. The patrolman's own accent suggested that he was born and bred in the Channel.

"My students would not steal my books." As Sylvia opened the cover of the first volume, Fanny noted the gold-bordered bookplate emblazoned with Sylvia's large signature and her parents' address: *St. Charles Avenue, New Orleans*. Not much detection done here. All this Crenshaw had to do was discover that Sylvia no longer lived with her parents.

"Where did you find them?" Fanny asked.

"Oh, we couldn't tell you that, Miss. Police business, it is."

"But I must know," Sylvia demanded.

Returning stolen goods had never been a hallmark of the New Orleans police, and Fanny wondered why the police had even brought the books back to Sylvia. But Fanny did know how to get them to tell where they had found them.

"I know you gentlemen can't accept a reward for your good deed. That would be against police regulations, wouldn't it?" Fanny watched the policeman's upturned mustaches droop perceptively. "But could you accept a contribution to the Policeman's

Welfare Fund?" She smiled broadly at Sylvia, hoping that she understood.

Sylvia did. "The Policeman's Welfare Fund. What an *excellent* idea. There's nothing wrong with helping widows and orphans." She walked over to her roll top desk. With one key from her chatelaine she unlocked the lid. With a second key she unlocked the center drawer. When she turned, she held her pocket book.

Gerald O'Casey's fingers flew back to the edge of his cap. "Yes, Ma'am, thank you, Ma'am. We couldn't say no to the poor widows and orphans."

"But it does seem a shame not to know who took my books," a hint of disappointment shaded Sylvia's voice as she opened her pocket book. "So that I could beware in the future."

Gerald looked at Eamon, who nodded in agreement. "The God's truth of it is, we hauled in so many goods this morning, we couldn't exactly say where it was found or who took it."

"We're rousting the entire Channel," said Eamon. "Every card room, crib, house, and saloon."

"Because of the murder at Conner's Court?" asked Fanny.

"Of course. The murderer's somewhere in the Channel and we'll get him soon enough."

"You're going to find Jack the Ripper?" Sylvia asked suspiciously.

"Of course not, Sylvia," Olive inserted herself between her sister and the men. "And as I've been trying to say, the girl last night was not—"

"Don't worry, ladies," Gerald held up his hand for order, as though it was bad business when two women talked at the same time. "There'll be an arrest soon enough. The Commissioner promised the Mayor a new prisoner in the Parish Prison by suppertime. And when the Commissioner makes a promise, he keeps it."

"Who told the newspapers that the girl had her throat slashed?" demanded Olive.

Gerald opened his mouth as if to speak but Eamon cleared his throat so loudly that Fanny almost pointed him to the cuspidor in the hallway.

"It would put our minds at ease to know more." Fanny spoke directly to Sylvia's pocketbook, as if a leprechaun's fortune was inside.

"That," Gerald said almost sadly, "we cannot tell you."

Olive bristled out of the room, and Sylvia—always a woman of her word—gave a dollar coin to Gerald O'Casey. "Thank you for returning my books. Give our regards to the widows and orphans." With another salute from their caps, the men jaunted past the women and out the front door.

Fanny followed in the patrolmen's wake and stood in the open doorway. She watched as Gerald O'Casey tossed the coin to his crony.

"The Commissioner promised the Mayor a new prisoner by suppertime," Fanny mimicked in an almost perfect Irish Channel accent. "And I'm sure that he will," she slipped into her own voice. "But will it be the real murderer or an easy scapegoat?"

FANNY CARRIED THE newspapers to the classroom that she and Sylvia shared throughout the week.

Once the rear half of a large double parlor, the room was furnished with shelves and cupboards along the walls and papered and painted in rich tones of gold and peacock blue. The broad oak desk was centered at the front and just to the right was the broad easel on which an exact replica of the Hammond typewriter keyboard was drawn. Three long worktables, accommodating fifteen students and typewriting machines, faced the desk like pews before a pulpit. Fanny's own machine sneered at her from atop her desk, blood from her fingers still stuck to the keys. She arranged one newspaper over the typewriter so she would not have to look at it anymore.

Last summer and autumn as the Ripper rampaged through the Whitechapel area of London, Fanny had read every newspaper she could find that had information about the murders. She had been entranced by these sordid doings, although she hadn't been able to determine exactly what had aroused her interest. Pity for the desperate women forced to prostitute themselves? The heinous brutality of the Ripper's knife? Or the evil soul of the murderer himself? Like people everywhere—like Sylvia and Olive, it turned out—Fanny had wondered what type of man would mutilate a series of solitary women and what motive he might have.

Today's New Orleans newspapers read much like the newspapers of last year. The *Daily News, Morning Chronicle,* and *L'Abeille* all printed grisly details of the murder. And the *Nightly Sensation*—a publication scorned by every sensible person in New Orleans—suddenly made good sense by warning their female readers to look out for evil in the Irish Channel. Of course, no newspaper yet carried the most vital information—that Dr. Olive Giddings could swear that the girl's neck was not slashed to the bone nor her innards thrown across her body.

The door to Fanny's office jutted open and Aunt Esther poked in. "Miss Sylvie wants you out on the gallery right now."

Fanny sighed; couldn't Sylvia decorate the gallery by herself? Fanny took a minute to restack the newspapers on her desk and consider her next actions. Although she and Sylvia would be spending the day preparing Wisdom Hall for this evening's Grand Event, Olive was headed to Charity Hospital, where she was sure to find out *something* about what happened in Conner's Court last night.

And somehow, Fanny would get Olive to share that information.

5.

CHARITY HOSPITAL WAS CAPABLE OF housing five hundred patients and towered an imposing three stories over Tulane Avenue. True to its name, the institution provided medical assistance to anyone who came to its doors and over the years Charity had become the dumping ground for the city's aged, insane, and impoverished. The most likely place to bring a nameless murder victim from the Irish Channel.

Olive paid the visitor's entry fare for admittance to the hospital. During her internship in Berlin she had traveled many a hospital corridor and, as she walked through Charity, she felt incomplete without her smock and pockets of instruments. Her reticule, hiding her notebook and pencil, was a sad substitute for her medical bag.

Someone called from inside one of the rooms along the corridor. "Doctor! Doctor!" Almost as if someone had rung a bell for Mass, three Sisters of Charity, their determined faces framed by their dark starched mantles, appeared and scurried toward the calls of distress.

While the nuns provided nursing and administrative care, the hospital was run by a surgeon, John Remington. Although the board of Charity—like the boards of all of the other local hospitals—had refused to hire Olive, Remington had become her friend. He had not flinched when she had shown up at Charity, introduced herself, and requested to assist him on his study of the possible causes of yellow fever. On the contrary, Olive thought he had been rather impressed with her nerve. *She* had been impressed with his intelligent administration of the hospital and his tireless interest in solving the city's ever-present yellow fever threat.

There was no response when Olive knocked at Remington's office door, but she entered with confidence, sure that since the door was unlocked, Remington would either be in his laboratory or examining room. The glowing reading lamp and remnants of burnt bacon confirmed that Remington had been working here *sometime* today.

The office was a large square with doors on both sides leading directly into two private examination rooms. The back wall had three windows, each of which looked onto one of Charity's small gardens. The door of the room on the left was closed and the room appeared unlit. The door to the room on the right was open slightly and Olive entered into it. Three tables lay before her, each with a sheet-covered body on it. She lifted each sheet hoping that the Conner's Court victim was among the trio. She was not.

The Charity Hospital Death Registers, she noticed quickly, were on their appointed ledge on the bookshelf under the window. Although she had not shared her thoughts with her sister, Olive had been unnerved by the newspapers' assertions that the girl had had her throat cut and been disemboweled. Even though Olive had been close enough to shield the girl's body was it possible that she had missed slashes to other parts of her body? Olive reached for the last Death Register and thumbed through it backward, realizing that none of the entries were in John Remington's handwriting.

George Brown, dockworker, died in hospital, Saturday April 27; Miss Jemina Cable and newborn son, died in hospital, Saturday April 27; Anton Schotz, sailor, died on the ship Loomis, Friday April 26. And then: *Unknown woman, found at Conner's Court (Irish Channel) Friday April 26.*

Olive set the Register on a small table. She opened her own notebook and wet the pencil against her tongue. Running her index finger beneath the short description in the Register she copied them into her own. *Red marks around throat.*

She scrutinized the shapes of the dead bodies on the tables and wondered if the dead woman's body was stored in Charity's ice room. She returned to the brief notes in the Register: *No outward signs of distress or other injuries. Death resulted from strangulation.*

The few sentences in the Death Register vindicated Olive, but she needed to see the full post-mortem (if one had been conducted) to understand the sensational claims made by the newspapers. And Olive had a duty to make sure that the women in the Irish Channel knew the truth and were not pulled into the fearful expectation of another murder by Jack the Ripper.

A crisp Yankee voice ripped through Olive's thoughts. "What are you doing in here?"

Olive looked up. The person before her wore a doctor's smock and carried two large syringes in his pocket. His head was dotted with flecks of dead skin. As he crossed his arms, his arrogant stance was vaguely familiar. But Olive had done battle with so many arrogant men in her practice that she could not place him.

As the man repeated himself, his arch Yankee accent brought her back to Conner's Court. He must be Charity's new ambulance doctor.

He looked her over also and Olive wondered what he made of her. She had surprised her sister by dressing more carefully this afternoon, ensuring that her cuffs were clean and that her short hair was brushed back so that she looked almost ladylike. Olive slipped her pencil and notebook into her reticule, careful to avoid looking at the Death Register that lay open and in full view.

To her relief, he did not notice the Register. Instead, he screwed up his lips and considered Olive intently. "Have we ...?" Suddenly he nodded his head, much as a hungry cat would address a cornered mouse. "Yes, I've seen you before. You were at Conner's Court. Fussing over that woman." He chuckled suddenly, a laugh that turned into a spasm of coughing. He ran his cuff across his mouth. "Well, what is it you want here? Have you come seeking some trinket from the Irish Channel Ripper?"

Olive recoiled at the gruesome name, which the man delivered with the hint of a smirk. She was ready to give him a smart lesson about exactly what happened on Friday night. And then she would report him to John Remington for spreading misinformation and sensationalism.

"Dr. Adams, you're needed in surgery immediately," one of the Sisters of Charity stood at the door. "Dr. Remington's asked for you."

"Thank you, Sister. I'll be right there." The man leaned forward and placed his hand under Olive's elbow, pushing her towards the door. "As soon as I see this lady out."

A FEW HOURS later, Sylvia Giddings stood at the bottom of her grand Wisdom Hall staircase, silently surveying her kingdom. Working with Fanny and her parents' servants, she had skillfully transformed the first floor rooms from a schoolhouse to a theater. Sam and Joe had even constructed a narrow wooden stage and moved Sylvia's piano from the hallway to the side of the stage. Close to the piano was a double semicircle of chairs for the musicians. Countless rows of chairs provided seating for over sixty people. The refreshment table was positioned close to the dining room. A table of beverages—including a barrel of beer—was on a table on the side gallery.

Sylvia took a moment to congratulate herself: what an incredible feat she had achieved. All by herself and despite her infirmity.

In creating Wisdom Hall, Sylvia had followed the same plan advocated by the university students who founded London's Toynbee Hall: she had bought an old building in the most destitute part of town, outfitted it with classrooms and a free library, and hired a teacher. Sylvia had done Toynbee Hall one better and built her sister an infirmary at the rear of Wisdom Hall and outfitted *that* with the best equipment in the business. No one could say that Sylvia Giddings was not dedicated to the social settlement ideal of educating the working poor.

Yet...Sylvia was almost paralyzed with fear tonight and wished that she had taken her dose of laudanum earlier. For although she had embraced the Irish Channel with her heart and soul, the Channel had not embraced her.

Despite her many invitations to her impoverished neighbors, her books went unread, her French classes unattended, and her wisdom unsought. A wave of apprehension shook Sylvia to her bones and she leaned upon her cane for real support.

Would anyone attend her Waxworks and soirée musicale tonight? Could she ever succeed in the Irish Channel? Or would she be forced to return to her parent's house on St. Charles Avenue and her life as a secluded invalid?

Then the heavy brass knocker sounded at the front door. All at once, as if they had decided it was safest to approach the fancy house of the wealthy American woman as a group, the Irish stood at the front door of Wisdom Hall. Sylvia hurried forward to welcome them. Ada and Ida, the Fitzpatrick twins, dressed in their Sunday best and hugging their fiddle cases like babies, introduced their parents, siblings, aunts, uncles, and cousins. The Fitzpatricks alone would fill a quarter of the seats.

Behind the Fitzpatricks came the O'Conner's, the Kelleys, the Ryans, and the O'Ryans. Following them were the Murphys, the Mealeys, and the Meaneys. So many families arrived *en masse* that Sylvia could only point her cane towards the parlor.

Each family took a moment to look around Wisdom Hall and Sylvia was gratified, for she had made the Hall as artful and welcoming as she could. The William Morris wallpaper had been purchased in London, the masses of camellias were clipped (furtively) from an uptown garden, and over a dozen gas sconces illuminated the rooms. Sylvia's clever work *must* bear fruit.

Yet, Sylvia wished that the Channel's German neighbors would participate in her classes and events, too. She had tried to recruit German children into her classes but parents had refused to allow their children to mingle with the shanty Irish. Although Sylvia was disappointed, she did not take it as a personal failure, for the German and Irish were so opposed to each other that two separate Catholic churches—just across the street from each other—had to be constructed to ensure Channel harmony.

There was only one German amongst the Irish tonight, the carpenter completing the balusters for the third floor. Karl Schultz looked distinctly uncomfortable as he stood at the bottom of the grand stairs, his eyes darting from Irish face to Irish face. He caught Sylvia's gaze and nodded to her as if to say *I'm here like I told you.* Sylvia was sure he would escape up the stairs as soon as he could.

As the youngest children ran down to the front benches, the older children and their mothers settled quickly on the hard, wooden seats. The men filtered out to the front gallery where Sylvia was sure a bottle of spirits was passed among them.

Amid the tinkle of children's fingers pounding at the piano keyboard, Sylvia released her apprehension with one sound breath. She would be successful tonight. She would be more than a jilted invalid. Sylvia had moved heaven and earth to make Wisdom Hall vibrant and useful, and she would allow her Grand Plan to continue no other way.

6.

WHEN SHE STARTED TEACHING at Wisdom Hall, Fanny saw her eleven students as one vivacious Irish gaggle. She could hardly tell the girls apart from each other. But over the eight weeks of classes, the girls had shown themselves as individuals and Fanny had learned to enjoy each of them for their talents as well as their temperaments.

There was Colleen, who led the class much like Sylvia did, through a combination of charm and combustion. There was Patsy, patently untalented with letters and numbers, and devout Cara, who seemed destined for a convent. There was Siobhan, who could make light of any situation, and Meggie, who preferred life to be moody, dark, and romantic. Kelly, Kathy, and Bridget were sisters so similar in appearance that Fanny still worked hard to tell them apart. Moira was a natural actress, while Molly was quiet and sweet-tempered (and, by Olive's guess, at least four months pregnant). And then there was Nora, Fanny's most promising student, whose ambitions to operate her own business perfectly matched her keen accounting talent.

As Fanny pushed open the dining room door at seven and two quarters on Saturday night, she was not surprised to see the girls circled around Colleen, who was reading from a newspaper. But Fanny froze as she heard Colleen's words.

"'Harlots of the Irish Channel. I'm coming after you.'" The words were dry, almost catching on Colleen's lips. Despite the melodramatic words, Colleen's tone was low and serious. "'You haven't heard the last of me.

I'm ready to rip the life from you.'" As Colleen lowered the newspaper to her lap, she made sure everyone's eyes were on her before she said, "It's signed *Irish Channel Jack.*"

Molly clutched her belly so hard her fingertips were white; Cara brought her rosary to her lips. The other girls sat quietly, too shocked to respond to the cold-blooded threat.

Finally, Siobhan put her hands on her broad hips. "Sweet Jesus! Would you look at yourselves girls? I'm not going to let old Jack scare me."

"Me neither," said Colleen. "That girl last night, she was probably a bad girl all along. She got what she deserved."

Poised at the doorway before her students saw her, Fanny wished that she could shield her students from this tragedy; that she could offer some pleasant fiction to assuage their fears. *This would never happen to you.* But Fanny could not lie to her students. Of course, the murder in Conner's Court affected them. Of course, they should be concerned. Of course.

Patsy lifted her tear-stained face, saw Fanny in the doorway and screamed. Colleen leaned over and slapped her sister hard.

Fanny knew the girls were waiting for her to say something but she hesitated, unsure of herself. She had grown up without sisters or brothers and had no experience in advising a roomful of fearful girls.

Not for the first time since coming to Wisdom Hall Fanny wished her father were here. Oscar Newcomb had been a Counselor at Law in the truest sense of the phrase and his good counsel had always soothed Fanny's fears and provided practical advice for her troubles. But a threat from Jack the Ripper was different from the agony of a stained dress or the shame of being too tall. A wave of protectiveness surged through Fanny's soul. These were her students and they looked to her for guidance. She could only start with the truth. "That's a very nasty letter."

"It's not the first, either," Patsy cried out.

"He's sending letters all over town." Meggie tossed her dark curls. "Says he's going to kill again! And soon!"

Fanny looked at Colleen, who answered, "That's right Miss Fanny. The Ripper's writing letters to all the newspapers. And the police and the mayor."

"He is?"

"Oh, yes Miss, they all say he's out to murder all us girls in the Irish Channel. In our beds or in the streets or as we walk about our business."

Fanny took a seat in the center of the ten girls, once more mindful that Nora was unable to attend tonight. She wiped a tear from Cara's eye and put her firm hand under Moira's quivering chin.

"According to my father, murderers are evil, evil men." Fanny extended her other hand toward the clutched hands of Kelly, Kathy, and Bridget. "But despite their evilness, the reason they murder is very logical. When one person has something and another person wants it, they often think the only way to get it is by murder. Every murderer has a very specific motive for their murder. It's a hatred for someone they know. Now, since I'm very sure that no one hates you...." Fanny brightened at her own words. It was true; no one could hate these girls. "None of you is going to get murdered. But that doesn't mean you shouldn't protect yourselves."

"Sweet Jesus!" cried Siobhan. "I'll get a knife as good as Jack's. And if he ever comes near me I'll let him see my blade."

Fanny winced at the image of Siobhan wielding a knife. "What I meant is that you should be careful about where you go. Be careful of who is near you."

"But if no one hates us why do we even have to do that?"

Before Fanny could reply Molly said, "Because a murderer might make a mistake, that's why. Maybe he's forgotten to wear his spectacles or he's too drunk to know you're the wrong person. And he doesn't know who you are. But if you have a friend along, you'd be safe."

As the girls paused to consider this response, Moira stood up. "It's getting on eight. We've got a show to put on and we want to be ready, don't we?" After a few seconds of silence, Moira decided for everyone. "All right then. Let's get into our wigs and costumes."

"MY GIRLS ARE ready," Fanny reported to Sylvia a few minutes later. "Ready to go home and hide under their beds. There's a hateful letter in the *Nightly Sensation* signed 'Irish Channel Jack'."

"Sometimes I think that people *like* to frighten themselves." Olive's voice faded as she surveyed the crowd: Liam wiping the snot from his nose with his hand, a man coughing black specks into his hand, a young girl scratching her head furiously with both hands. "Sylvia, before you start I'd like to make a few announcements about the Infirmary's services."

"Oh, no," Sylvia's eyes brightened with alarm. "You're not turning this evening into another lecture about hygiene. No one wants to hear anything about lice or mice tonight. I absolutely forbid it."

Olive frowned suddenly. "What's he doing here?"

Fanny followed Olive's hard stare. Seen in silhouette, one pencil scratching away at his notebook, another pencil perched behind his ear, it wasn't difficult to discern who Olive was talking about.

"Is that the reporter from the *Sensation*?" asked Fanny. "Is that Clarence Halloway?"

"I think he's slumming." Olive folded her arms across her chest before addressing her sister. "Looking for a little excitement in the rougher streets of New Orleans."

Fanny looked the reporter up and down. She watched as he filched an apple from a centerpiece and dropped it into his pocket. And then watched as he palmed a tangerine and added it to his other pocket. "Or he's looking for a free meal."

"Still," said Sylvia, "he *is* our guest."

"He's no guest of mine, and I suggest you all stay far away from him," warned Olive.

"Too late," replied her sister. "He's headed over here."

"We *should* talk to him," Fanny said. "He's got to know more than we do about what the police are doing to catch the murderer."

"His newspaper only prints lies," Olive asserted.

"You often need to know the truth before you can lie successfully." Fanny paused just for a second, not giving Sylvia or Olive any time to consider what she had just said. Or to respond. "Let me talk to him."

"If you must," Olive and Sylvia almost replied in unison. Olive turned to walk away. "I'll be in the Infirmary."

Halloway's eyes lighted on the trio. He watched as Olive collected Liam and dragged him toward the back of the Hall. Then he walked full steam over to Sylvia, as if drawn like a moth to her glow.

Halloway pulled a business card from his shallow vest pocket, offered it to Sylvia, and launched into a succession of questions. His questions ran together like a Baptist preacher's homily, to which Sylvia listened graciously. When he paused—for an exhale that reeked of fried oysters—Sylvia smiled, reminded Fanny that it was almost time to begin the waxwork tableaux, and excused herself. Graciously.

Fanny, who had never learned to do anything graciously, asked the reporter, "What really brings you here tonight?"

"I'm on the trail of the Irish Channel Ripper, ma'am."

"You won't find your murderer here, sir."

"Won't I? What better place to find the Ripper than in the Channel?" A smile glazed the reporter's lips as he squinted across the rooms. His eyes steeled as though he saw someone he knew. "Or here at Wisdom Hall."

Fanny fumed. It was entirely wrongheaded to think that one of the men here tonight could be the murderer...that her students might be in danger here...or that the police might descend upon Wisdom Hall. "Speculation like that causes more damage than good."

"I may write for the *Sensation,* but what I write is not speculation."

The reporter slid his pencil behind his ear and Fanny knew he was moving on. She wondered if she had managed to offend him and hoped she had. But as Clarence Halloway disappeared into the crowd Fanny was sure that the reporter knew more than he had told.

ACTING ON THE stage was not a suitable occupation for girls but amateur theatricals were quite acceptable. Waxwork tableaux—which required no other talent than to dress in costume and remain in a pose for a minute—were eminently respectable.

Fanny and her students had debated at length about which tableaux to create for tonight's entertainment. Fanny suggested someone patriotic, like Varina Davis, the former first lady of the Confederacy. Or someone literary, like Shakespeare's Juliet or even someone modern, like newspaper editor Eliza Nicholson. But the girls decided in one voice that they wanted to portray ladies from the Bible. So biblical ladies it was.

As Bridget played piano, Fanny's students took their poses: Mary learning she was carrying the Christ child; Mary struggling to find a place to give birth; Mary smiling down on baby Jesus in his crèche; and many Marys more.

Finally, the girls took one last pose: Mary watching her son die. The girls froze into place, gazing up over the heads of the audience as though looking at three crosses. Almost as one, the audience turned from watching the girls and looked up at the ceiling. Then the audience turned back to the girls and applauded. The girls broke their poses and stood in a row at the front of the small stage. When the applause stopped, the girls stepped down from the stage and ran to sit with their families. Sylvia's students rose from their seats, came to the front of the room, arranged their chairs, and took up their instruments. The sweet twang of guitars and fiddles launched into popular songs.

Fanny retreated to the front gallery and leaned against one of the fluted columns, enjoying the broad spread of lawn and trees that separated Wisdom Hall from the bustle of Annunciation Street. She heard the screen door open and close behind her and turned to watch as a few older folk sought chairs on the broad gallery.

Suddenly, Fanny was glad she had allowed her students to choose which waxwork characters to portray. Her students' every day choices were few and their lives were hard and limited. Shouldn't Fanny make their schooling as pleasant as possible?

From inside Wisdom Hall, Fanny heard the guitar and fiddle strings blend into buoyant *Dixie*. The southern homage plucked at Fanny's deepest emotions for her father. If only Oscar Newcomb hadn't died last year, Fanny would have a family roof over her head and days filled with meaningful legal work.

And her friendship with Lawrence Decatur would be intact.

Some days Fanny wasn't sure whom she mourned more: her father or his charismatic and handsome law partner. Lawrence had joined Oscar in business over ten years ago and quickly developed a successful career in criminal and commercial law. Fanny had assisted him in every way possible, and he had returned her favors by sharing his own tricks of the trade, legal and otherwise.

It had all been so perfect until it wasn't. Oscar died suddenly, Lawrence took over the law firm, and instead of giving Fanny her due for her own legal expertise and cunning, he banished Fanny from the law office.

But only after he asked her to marry him.

From inside Wisdom Hall, the string band launched into a jaunty rendition of *If Ever I Cease to Love*. Fanny smiled grimly. *If Ever I Cease to Love* was one of New Orleans' most popular Mardi Gras tunes. It was the first song that Fanny and Lawrence had properly danced to and the song that Lawrence hummed throughout the day as he worked. Fanny could hardly separate the song from her love for Lawrence, but tonight, remembering his unemotional offer of marriage, the lyrics ran a dagger through her heart.

Suddenly, a parade of dark shadows emerged from Annunciation Street. A pair of policemen marched toward her. She recognized them immediately; it was the Patrolmen O'Casey from this morning. Puffed up and self-important, buttons and belt buckles glinting in the torch light emerging behind them, the patrolmen were nothing like the deferential public servants who had accepted Sylvia's money earlier in the day. Behind the O'Caseys was a line of men in plainclothes and behind them were uniformed policemen in a column that dissolved into the darkness.

There was only one reason for this massing of policemen: to arrest the Conner's Court murderer. Fanny's heart lurched. Who had the police come for? A Murphy? A Kelly? A Callahan? Could any of these celebrating fathers, brothers, or sweethearts be capable of murder?

Fanny walked to the front door, crossing her arms before her. Inside the hall, she heard the squeal of a concertina running up and down a scale. She knew that chairs and benches were being stacked against the walls and the rugs were being rolled up; girls were tightening their bootlaces while their young men removed their jackets before the dancing began.

The O'Caseys parted to allow the foremost of the plain-clothed men to walk up the stairs and onto the gallery. He stopped a few feet from Fanny and lifted his glossy bowler to her, his unoiled hair glowing like dark copper in the torchlight. He nodded towards the screen door behind her. Fanny followed his salute to see that Sylvia waited on the other side of the screen, biting her lip, one hand poised against the screen in front of her. Clarence Halloway stood just behind Sylvia and removed a pencil from behind his ear. He murmured a name between his teeth, a name that Fanny heard clearly but for the moment meant nothing to her.

"Detective Daniel Crenshaw, ma'am," announced the officer. "New Orleans Police."

Fanny looked straight into his dark eyes. "Who are you here for?"

"We'll be in and out in a minute," he replied. "If you ladies would wait here on the porch."

Fanny stood her ground and fought for the breath to speak. "These are good people in here."

The detective's sharp jaw rolled slightly and his eyes tightened. "Would you shelter a murderer ma'am?"

Fanny hesitated. Was it really possible the Conner's Court murderer was inside Wisdom Hall?

7.

DETECTIVE DANIEL CRENSHAW ENTERED Wisdom Hall quickly. Fanny slipped in behind him, dislodging a sergeant sporting a nose that had been broken more than once. The sergeant looked sharply at Fanny, as if irritated that she had usurped his place behind the detective. Crushed against the detective's green hound's-tooth suit coat, Fanny saw the grimy stain along the rim of his tall stiff collar. She wondered if it was dirty from the day's frustration.

Inside the wide central hall, Crenshaw signaled to his men to enter the rooms leading from the hallway: Sylvia's office on the left; the double parlors on the right. He nodded at them to continue down the hall and to spread up to the floors above. The policemen carried lanterns as they went up the stairs and Fanny heard them stumble and curse in the darkness.

"No one is up there. The doors to all of the rooms are locked," said Fanny. The detective spun around, clearly irritated by Fanny's nearness. She stepped back as much as she could and felt compelled to explain. "Aunt Esther always makes us lock up when we open the house."

"Afraid the Irish will steal your silver, is that it?" Daniel Crenshaw turned towards the stairs. "Your Aunt Esther is a very wise woman."

A patrolman ran down the stairs and, in a low tone, reported to Crenshaw. Still unaware of the presence of the police, the fiddlers launched into a boisterous song.

Fanny turned toward Sylvia, who had been pushed to the side of the hall as the police entered. "Olive's alone in the infirmary," Fanny heard Sylvia whisper to herself. "I must go to her." In an instant, Sylvia swept past Fanny and through the policemen, who parted to let her pass.

Clarence Halloway sidled up to Fanny, scribbling in his notebook as he attempted to peep around Crenshaw's broad shoulders. "Had no idea they'd bring so many men."

"You knew the police were coming here?" Fanny grabbed his arm and heard his pencil rip his paper in half.

"Rumors are out there. It's my job to listen for them."

Crenshaw stepped forward into the parlor. Fanny followed. The room chilled with silence. Open-mouthed, wide-eyed, fearful, the Irish neighbors and students stared at the detective and the ranks of uniforms behind him. The detective stopped suddenly, a quartet of gray-coated patrolmen on either side of him.

"Karl Schultz." Crenshaw's voice reverberated throughout the double parlors. "You're under arrest for murder."

FANNY SAW KARL standing against the refreshment table, holding a plate of cake in one hand and a fork in the other. His wide eyes were fixed on the uniformed police approaching him.

Karl dropped his plate and fork and ran across the parlor and into the classroom, sweeping chairs, children, and musical instruments to the floor. The Irish began yelling: "Catch him!"

"Murderer!"

"Cut him off!"

Karl rushed to the room's side door, which was guarded by a lone patrolman. With no time to draw his stick or gun, the patrolman braced himself. Karl knocked the man to the ground and pushed open the door into the central hallway.

Crenshaw doubled back to the hallway, halting at the foot of the great staircase. The broken-nosed sergeant appeared at his right. Fanny was close on his heels and realized that Clarence Halloway kept in step with her.

"He's got a knife!" someone shouted.

In the middle of the great stairs, the glint of polished silver reflected off the heightened gaslight. Karl crouched against all comers, wielding a short knife like a lance. A few steps below and above him, the police stood back. With the police crowded against the side of the staircase, Fanny knew Karl could not escape.

Crenshaw stepped forward, his eyes riveted on Karl, although Fanny was sure that the detective was aware of every other person around him. "Come with me now," the detective said, "or I can't guarantee what will happen to you. Right now, I've got enough men to get you safely to jail."

Karl's eyes swept over the crowd as if looking for an escape. As his mouth opened in reply someone else yelled out, "Dirty German!"

"Murderer!"

"Monster!"

"Fiend!"

The curses catapulted from the Irish crowd and Fanny saw pure hatred in her neighbors' eyes. Despite the police guard, the Irish swelled closer to the staircase. Karl flicked his knife wildly in the air.

Fanny stood at the newel post looking up the stairs. All around her, police were forcing back the Irish. If the police broke, the neighbors would rush past her up to the stairs. What would happen to Karl then?

Crenshaw took another step towards Karl, speaking so quietly to him that Fanny could not hear him. As the crowds surged towards the staircase, Karl dropped the knife and raised his hands over his head in surrender. The crowd stilled. Fanny wondered if the Irish were going to raise a cheer to the detective but they remained silent. Fanny looked from the crowd to the sergeant, who stood just a few feet away from her at the bottom of the stairs obviously awaiting orders from the detective.

Crenshaw turned Karl's face toward the wall and brought his hands down behind his back. In one movement, he produced a pair of handcuffs from his pocket and slapped them over Karl's hands. The detective stooped to pick up Karl's knife and slipped it in the same pocket that had held the handcuffs. As the detective turned Karl around to walk down the stairs, the calm of the crowd shattered.

"String him up now!"

"Don't let him get out of here!"

46

Many of the voices were tinged with beer and spirits and, for the first time, Fanny was afraid. Sober men could be reasoned with; drunken men could not. Standing between Karl and the Irish, she felt the rage of their anger upon her. No, they didn't even see her. All they saw was Karl and they were eager to rip him apart.

"Jeee-sus."

Fanny turned, surprised to see Clarence Halloway still at her side. He swore once more and scribbled into his notebook. He smiled grimly at Fanny. "If Crenshaw doesn't get him out *now*, I'll have another murder to report."

Crenshaw turned Karl to face the bottom of the stairs and then addressed the Irish. "You'll have your justice, the American way. This man gets a fair trial." The detective looked about the crowd slowly. Then he caught the eyes of each of his men, as if trying to remind them that he would allow no accidental justice tonight. "Now back up, all of you."

The detective walked Karl down the stairs until he was directly in front of the sergeant. Karl stared down at the ground, sweat dripping from his face. Suddenly one of the younger Irish broke through the police line. He sliced a broad knife back and forth in the air and headed towards Karl. "This is for our poor girls."

Clarence Halloway jumped up the staircase toward safety, pulling Fanny up with him. Karl looked up, horrified to see the large blade slashing towards him. But the detective stepped in front of Karl and the Irish youth stopped short. Just enough time for the sergeant to grab and take the knife from him.

Without another look to the crowd, Crenshaw hustled Karl out the front door. Fanny followed after and watched him steer Karl down the walkway and into the police wagon. By the time the last of the policemen streamed out of the front door—with the irate crowd on their heels—the wagon was rattling down Annunciation Street.

A FEW MINUTES later Fanny, Sylvia, and Olive stood at the top of the gallery stairs, surveying the ravaged muddy lawn trampled by the police and Irish neighbors. Fanny could see a child's shoe on the walk, and a red ribbon a few yards down. Inside Wisdom Hall, Aunt Esther swept up the broken plate while Thomas and Liam rolled the piano back into place.

Fanny sat down on the top step, suddenly exhausted. "The police said they'd have someone arrested by supper time and so they have. But why Karl? I know the New Orleans police aren't troubled much by the truth, but even they wouldn't arrest a man without a good reason."

"Good reason?" Sylvia's voice flared to an unladylike volume. "Do you know how the police treated us when I opened Wisdom Hall? They had the nerve to barge in and ask if we were opening a house of prostitution. Even after a half-hour of assuring them that we were not, they couldn't even begin to understand what I was attempting to do in the Channel."

Sylvia anchored her cane on the step below Fanny and plopped down, completely crushing her bustle as she sat.

Olive sat down next to her sister. "I'd put nothing past our police force. Most of them are thugs and bullies, hired without any thought to civic duty and protection. The police are just one big happy Irish family and they take care of their own."

"That detective didn't seem like a bully," said Fanny. "He was determined, yes, but once he cornered Karl on the stairs he seemed fair enough. And if the police just had to make an arrest to save face, why didn't they arrest a colored man? That's what they usually do when a white woman's attacked."

Sylvia and Olive looked at each other and then clasped hands, as if just realizing how risky life was for a colored man like Thomas.

"Fanny's right about that," Sylvia said softly. "Maybe Karl really is guilty."

"Or," her sister replied, "the police needed to make an arrest and they did."

"But why did they have to arrest Karl at Wisdom Hall?" Sylvia's voice strained with frustration. "Before the police came, we were such a success! All of the girls played their roles perfectly. Everyone was enjoying themselves. It was a such triumph, until...people couldn't get out of here fast enough."

The infirmary bell rang out from the back of the house and Olive stood up wearily. "Don't worry, Sylvia. Your students will come back. If the Ripper events of London indicated anything about human nature, it's that we are fascinated by evil. And right now, no man in New Orleans is more evil than Karl."

Olive offered a hand to help Sylvia stand up. "Who knows? You might even gain a few students from this evening."

8.

SYLVIA SIPPED HER COFFEE AS SHE READ the Sunday edition of the *Daily Picayune*.

She read the Society Section; she read the Shipping Section; she read the International, National, and Parish sections. She read all of the advertisements. And then she reread them. Finally, there was only the local news to read.

With a quick glance at a stray coffee ground in her cup, Sylvia turned past the department store advertisements on page one and folded the newspaper over to reveal page two and the headline:

Conner's Court Murderer Captured at Wisdom Hall Settlement House

She stared at the headline for so long that she did not realize Fanny and Olive had joined her in the dining room. As if on cue, a large tray poked through the kitchen door, followed by Aunt Esther. In short order, Esther placed an urn of fresh coffee, a pitcher of warmed milk, and three covered platters on the sideboard. Olive poured her cup of coffee and went to stand over her sister's shoulder.

"What do the papers say?" Fanny sat back in her seat. She dug her chin into her chest, as if resigned to a long listen. "Best to hear the bad news as soon as possible and get it over with."

Sylvia glared at Fanny and passed the paper to Olive, who read "German carpenter Karl Schultz was arrested late Saturday night at the Wisdom Hall Settlement House for the brutal murder of Nora Keegan, a known prostitute."

Fanny's chin lifted. "Who?"

"Nora Keegan," repeated Olive. "A known prostitute."

Fanny chest tightened as leaned towards Sylvia and Olive. "Did they have an address for her? An age?"

Olive ran her finger beneath the text. "She was seventeen." Olive traced her finger through the column silently. "It says 'Miss Keegan arrived in New Orleans from County Limerick, Ireland, within the past year. She resided at 1021 Basin Street.'"

Fanny bounced from her chair and through the dining room door. Sylvia and Olive heard Fanny rummaging through the cupboards in the classroom. Fanny returned with a stack of papers. She shuffled through the sheets swiftly and then pulled one from the pile. Only then did Sylvia realize that Fanny was holding her student applications.

"1021 Basin Street." Fanny fell back into her chair, the application falling from her grasp and drifting to the floor. "But it can't be." Fanny turned to Olive. "What did the dead girl look like? Nora was small and dark haired, with brilliant brown eyes."

"Your description is accurate," Olive replied quietly.

Fanny sat stunned. Finally, a glimmer of defiance edged her voice. "But Nora wasn't a prostitute, she was my best bookkeeping student."

"I'm sorry Fanny. It says here that Nora Keegan's body was identified by Mrs. O'Sullivan, her landlady. There doesn't appear to be any question about her identity," said Olive. "And Basin Street...that's just across from the Spanish Fort Depot, isn't it? That part of town is rife with houses of prostitution."

Sylvia scowled at her sister. "How would you know that?"

Oblivious to Sylvia and Olive's conversation, Fanny took the stack of papers and walked out of the dining room. Sylvia and Olive heard her enter the classroom and close the door.

Sylvia rested her head on her hands. "This is worse than I thought. Not only is the murder suspect under my employ and arrested at my settlement house but the victim is one of my students. I can just see the next headline: *Wisdom Hall Settlement House: A School for Prostitutes*."

"One of Fanny's students," corrected Olive, her attention still directed toward the classroom. "Fanny's always so steady and businesslike. I've never seen her upset before." Olive read the rest of the article as she finished her coffee. "But it does not say Nora Keegan was a student here. I think Eliza must have been watching out for you—if she knew."

"Even though she's editor of the newspaper, Eliza may not know," said her sister. "Perhaps no one knows. And if we can keep it that way—keep it a secr—."

Aunt Esther poked her head through the kitchen door. "Thomas says it's getting on time for church, Miss Sylvie. You need to get going."

"You certainly need to get to church today, Sylvia." Olive tossed the newspaper to the table. "Because you'll need a miracle to keep that information secret in New Orleans."

NORA KEEGAN HAD not just been Fanny's best student, she had been something of a kindred soul. She had showed real promise early in class and Fanny had eagerly taught her, guided her, praised her. And now Nora was dead. No, *murdered*.

Fanny left Wisdom Hall. Her first steps took her toward Conner's Court but then she turned around, not yet able to revisit the place where Nora had been murdered. Instead, she walked toward Canal Street. Just ahead, a streetcar took on passengers but Fanny passed it by. The New Orleans streetcars were the quickest transport across the city but today their mule-drawn cars were too fast for Fanny. She needed to walk; she needed to think; she needed to mourn.

She marched from the working class Channel, into the commercial blocks, and past the grand residential estates. She was barely aware of brightly dressed women and children, smelling of verbena and rose-water. Or of families entering church and cathedral. Or even of the mules as they dropped their pungent manure along streetcar route.

She reached Canal Street glowing with exertion. She turned onto Canal, aware that the usually bustling street was oddly quiet. She walked along the broad commercial street until she reached Basin Street.

The newspapers had called the building at 1021 Basin Street "Mrs. O's Palace of Pleasure," but Fanny found no palace; no confection of gingerbread trimmings, no elegant iron fencing, no flower boxes at any window. Instead, there was a two-story brick commercial building of the most ordinary kind, with no business signage. Only a black mourning wreath hung upon the crimson door suggested that someone who lived there had died.

Two girls with long unbound hair walked past the building and looked toward the door. They clutched each other's hands and giggled, as if the sight of the mourning wreath excited them. The shrill of their nervous laughter drifted to Fanny's ears and she stifled an urge to lecture them. If they'd known Nora as Fanny knew her, they wouldn't be laughing.

Nora was Fanny's most gifted student, a natural woman of business, and would have succeeded anywhere a woman was given a chance. Fanny had high hopes for Nora's office career. But instead of succeeding at a decent job, Nora had the most indecent job of any kind. Fanny cringed. Fanny knew nothing about the business of prostitution and had a hard time picturing the intimate details of it. Fanny wondered what Nora had to endure at Mrs. O's and had great difficulty envisioning Nora bending her strong will to please strange men. If only Fanny had known about Nora's real life, she could have found her a decent job immediately. She could have saved Nora.

A nearby telegraph pole across from the building was plastered with broadsides, many with the name *Jack the Ripper* written in large type. Fanny pulled down one broadside; it was the same letter that Colleen had read to the girls last night.

Fanny stood across the street from Mrs. O's Palace of Pleasure for over an hour. But no one—man, woman, child, servant or master—went in or out. Finally, Fanny caught the streetcar bound for Conner's Court.

THROUGH THE GATHERING rain clouds, dim patches of sunshine filtered between the tightly cramped buildings at the edge of Conner's Court. Here, Fanny was one of a large crowd of people, each one vying to see exactly where Jack the—no, the newly proclaimed *Irish Channel*—Ripper killed his first American prostitute. Although no alcohol could be sold in New Orleans on Sunday, the odor of beer permeated the crowd and twice Fanny had to walk over drunken men slumped against walls. There were people who looked like they had not yet gone to bed (and not because of honest labor) and women and children who were dressed cleanly for church services. No police were about and Fanny was glad for it. After last night, she did not want to see a policeman for a very long time.

As Fanny entered the Court, a gaily-suited man described what he saw The Night the Ripper Stalked the Channel. "Black Jack gutted her where she fell and cut out her liver and kidneys and took them home to cook for his breakfast. Her head was almost slashed clean through. The doctor had to fight to keep it from rolling off her body and down the street."

Fanny stood at the site of Nora's murder for so long that she heard the man's description three times. Each time he embellished it even more. "Blood by the glassful dripped from her throat. There was so much blood that women dipped their handkerchiefs into it for souvenirs. If you look closely into the gravel, you might be able to still see it." As the crowd surged toward the stain, Fanny was pushed forward. There was something indeed dried and red mixed in the dirt and she shuddered at the thought of Nora's blood on grisly display. She jumped back awkwardly, angry with herself for letting the hubbub of Conner's Court carry her common sense away. But from the wide eyes of the men and women around her, she realized that other people enjoyed the sensation, enjoyed the horror and terror of reliving the Ripper's rampage.

The dark gray sky hovering over the Channel shrugged. It began to rain and the bloody color that marked the spot of Nora's murder dissipated into the dirt. The crowd at Conner's Court evaporated into the back doors of the saloons and damp alleyways until Fanny was alone. She looked away from the bloody spot and studied the old buildings, the sagging doors, ripped awnings, broken windows. What had Nora been doing in Conner's Court? It was not on her route from Wisdom Hall to Basin Street and it was not a place for a casual visit. Had she gotten lost? Was she meeting someone here? A chill ran through Fanny's damp body. For the first time, she had to consider another possibility—Nora and Karl might have met at Wisdom Hall. Any meeting could lead to a relationship and any relationship could lead to murder. Or so her father had always said. Was it possible the police were correct? Did Karl murder Nora?

But why would Karl be in Conner's Court? Sylvia said that, like all Germans, Karl had been very cautious about where he traveled in the Channel. He stuck to the blocks occupied by German immigrants and avoided the blocks occupied by Irish. He had agreed to work at Wisdom Hall only because the streetcar stopped right in front of it. Conner's Court was for Irish only.

No, Fanny could not envision Karl Schultz in Conner's Court. Ever.

RAIN FELL IN torrents as Fanny reached Wisdom Hall. Although she wanted to retreat to her bedroom and remove her wet skirts, something compelled her to trudge up to the third floor and visit Karl's domain.

Wisdom Hall's third floor was one large space, strategically supported by stout posts. Sylvia planned to install a large skylight in the roof and use the floor as an auditorium or workshop. The flat roof would become an observation deck and Sylvia had Grand Designs for setting up a telescope once the roof was completed. Sylvia had hired Karl because of his experience with large windows, but the skylight was slow to arrive, forcing Karl to turn his skills to single-handedly crafting an elegant spiral staircase connecting the third floor to the roof.

Although the framing was in place, much of the roof was unfinished and covered with tarpaulin. And when it rained—as it did almost every afternoon and evening—much of Karl's time was spent positioning buckets under the leaking tarpaulin. Fanny inspected the buckets quickly finding only one full. She emptied the bucket out one of the back windows onto the roof covering Olive's infirmary. She returned the bucket to the top of the spiral stairs and sat beside it on the step, surveying the vast unfinished third floor. Cluttered with lumber, framed windows, and odd baskets and boxes, the floor looked more like a stall at the French Market than a schoolroom.

Fanny's eyes lingered on the boxes of Karl's carpentry tools. She had not known Karl well—her German was as weak as his English—but she had admired his skills. And despite their language barrier, Karl had proudly displayed his new balusters to her only hours before Nora was killed. Fanny ran her finger—still sore from tussling with her typewriter machine on Friday night—along the smooth baluster at her side. Yes, that was right: while she was battling her machine, Karl was crafting his final balusters.

Fanny's fingers closed around the baluster and she clutched it tightly. She thought harder about Friday night, Karl, and his balusters. She counted the number of balusters on the spiral staircase. And she counted them again. Aloud. And then she went in search of Aunt Esther.

THE MOMENT SYLVIA and Olive returned to Wisdom Hall, Fanny ushered them up to the third floor. "Karl couldn't have killed Nora. He never had enough time."

Olive could not mask her eagerness. "How do you know?"

"I came up here just before class started at seven, to see if I could get Karl to stop hammering during class. When I was up here he showed me the balusters for the spiral staircase and said he had completed a dozen of them. All on that day, working from seven in the morning until seven at night. He didn't even stop for lunch."

Fanny stopped short, realizing that the tone of her words was familiar. She could clearly see her father in court: how he would walk back and forth between the jury box to the witness box, spinning the jury or judge into his web of truth. And then she realized that she needed to be entirely honest with Olive and Sylvia. "At least I think that's what he said."

"What?" asked Sylvia.

"My German isn't as good as yours," replied Fanny. "But I think I understood him correctly. Karl had three more balusters to finish that night, which he did. You told me that, Sylvia."

"I did?"

"Yes, at breakfast yesterday, you said that Karl showed you fifteen finished balusters Friday night." Fanny nodded to the balusters, knowing that Sylvia and Olive were counting. Fifteen. And then recounting them. Still fifteen.

"So?" asked Olive.

"I just spoke with Aunt Esther. She said that she always made Karl enter and exit the Hall through her kitchen door so she could contain his mess. Friday night Karl left at seven, when the bell rang for classes, and he returned an hour later. If he started working on the balusters at eight and by eleven he had three more bal—"

Olive took up Fanny's thought. "If it took Karl one hour to complete one baluster and if he was gone from the hall from seven to eight and if he finished three balusters between eight and eleven and if Nora left Wisdom Hall at 10 o'clock after class and she was murdered before eleven, then Karl could not have murdered Nora."

"Yes!" Fanny smiled.

"Karl is innocent," Sylvia spoke softly to herself. "His arrest at Wisdom Hall was a gigantic mistake."

Flushed with her triumph, Fanny answered "And we need to let the police know as soon as possible."

9.

FANNY LED SYLVIA AND LIAM TO THE central police station on Monday morning. As the ladies entered, Liam—who had seen the harsh interior of a police cell more than once—waited outside.

Inside, a crush of people—wildly gesturing men, beer-soaked women, and fast-talking boys who should have been in school—crowded into the large waiting room, each vying for the attention of the lone uniformed policeman who sat behind a tall desk. One word echoed around the room: *Ripper. Ripper. Ripper.*

Fanny searched the room twice for Olive, but who planned to meet them? Olive was nowhere to be found, but Fanny did see *Nightly Sensation* reporter Clarence Halloway across the room, hunched down and listening to a bleary-eyed woman at his side. The reporter looked up as if someone had shouted his name and was obviously surprised to see uptown ladies like Fanny and Sylvia amidst the raffish crowd. He disengaged himself from the woman at his side and headed toward Fanny and Sylvia.

Fanny grumbled at the reporter's approach but Sylvia was glad to see him, and at her request the reporter escorted them to the front desk.

Flanked by Fanny and Halloway, Sylvia announced to the policeman, "Miss Sylvia Giddings to see the Commissioner of Police."

The policeman crossed his arms. "No one is getting in to see the Commissioner today."

"The Under Commissioner then," countered Sylvia, tapping her cane on the floor.

The sergeant shook his head.

Fanny stepped forward. "Detective Daniel Crenshaw? Is he available? We have important information about the murder at Conner's Court."

The sergeant shrugged. "So does everyone else."

Fanny turned to look at the bickering Irishmen, ranting Germans, and half-drunken sailors of every nationality. Was it possible that any of them knew anything?

"Let's leave," Sylvia decided. "Liam can wait here with a message for Olive."

But Fanny pulled away from Sylvia. Across the room from her, standing at the station entrance stood a tall man in an ivory suit. His prematurely silvered hair and whiskers glistened like a beacon through the well-worn police station crowd. He held Fanny's gaze from a distance and removed his hat before crossing the threshold.

"Not just yet Sylvia, please." Fanny resisted the urge to rush toward her shining white knight. "I'm sure the Commissioner will see us now."

LAWRENCE DECATUR STRODE through the agitated crowd with the confidence of a trial attorney who forever had the judge and jury secured between the folds of his fine cotton handkerchief. He reached Fanny and Sylvia and escorted the women to a quiet place. He scowled at Clarence Halloway and the reporter backed silently into the crowd.

"Good Lord, Fanny! You don't know how relieved I am to see you out here in the waiting room. From your message, I thought you were locked up in the Ladies' Prison. Or is that just what you wanted me to think?"

"I knew you'd get here faster if you thought I was in trouble." Fanny emotions were suddenly active and she resisted an urge to kiss the only smooth spot of

Lawrence's cheek that was not resplendent with whiskers. "It's good to see you too, Uncle Lawrence."

"Oh, Good *Lord*. When you call me *that* I know you want something special. It's bad enough I haven't seen you since September but to hear you call me *Uncle* again!" Lawrence moved to clutch Fanny towards him, but instead held her at arms' length. "Well, what is it?"

Fanny hadn't anticipated how glad she'd be to see Lawrence again, and she certainly couldn't have anticipated that greeting him by his pet name would almost undo her. (But she had dressed her hair with special care this morning and she had worn her best gown. She had even gone into Sylvia's room and dotted a few drops of *eau de lavender* on her wrists and throat.)

Fanny had a lot to prove today—to herself and to Lawrence—and she steeled herself to continue unemotionally. "I *do* need a good lawyer and you're the best in New Orleans. Someone we know has been arrested for murder."

Sylvia offered her gloved hand and her most charming smile as she introduced herself. Although she and Lawrence were of an age and same family social circles, they had never met before. Sylvia returned a solid handshake as she said, "And Fanny's discovered that he's innocent."

Lawrence turned to Fanny. He seemed nonplussed that she should be playing at the law again. For a second, she thought he was about to call her *Goldenlocks*, his favorite pet name for her. Instead, he said, "Fanny Newcomb, you're your father all over again."

"I'll take that as a compliment, of course." Fanny slipped her hand easily through Lawrence's arm, comforted by his familiar firmness. "But back to our problem. The police have wrongly charged an innocent man and now they don't want to hear the facts of his innocence."

"The man at the desk said that the Commission would not see us," said Sylvia.

Lawrence chuckled, almost against his will. "But the Commissioner would never refuse to see Lawrence Decatur. Is that it? Fanny, my dear, you still know how to get around an old man."

Fanny was silent. Despite the sheen of his silver hair, at thirty-seven years of age, Lawrence Decatur could not be called old. In truth, he and Sylvia were the same age. Was Lawrence actually trying to elicit a compliment from her? He held her eyes a little too long and his crystal blue brilliance glinted with a shade of doubt. Her friendship with Lawrence had always been based on candor and she did not want him to think that she would attempt to charm him with minor falsehoods or outright lies. Well, not *too many* falsehoods or lies. She said quickly, "You'll feel as strongly as we do once you've heard our story. You *can* get us in to see the Commissioner today, can't you?"

Lawrence raised his eyebrows directly at the man standing at the front desk. "We'll be sitting in his office within the hour."

WITHIN THE HALF-HOUR Olive—anointed by the sweet fragrance of carbolic disinfectant—slipped into the Police Station. A few minutes later, Lawrence escorted the trio of women into the office of the Under Commissioner of Police.

Fanny presented her evidence that Karl Schultz could not have murdered Nora Keegan in Conner's Court. In simple words that even the police could understand, she explained that she had said goodbye to Nora at ten o'clock that night and had been alerted to the need for a doctor at just one hour later. Therefore, Nora must have been killed between ten and eleven o'clock. Fanny then explained that during that hour she and Sylvia Giddings had heard Karl Schultz working away on the third floor. And it had to have been Karl

Schultz working because Esther and Thomas Giddeons had been watching all of the other doors. In addition, Fanny had physical proof that Karl had been working during that hour.

The Under Commissioner asked no questions, made no comments, showed no interest. The sergeant took no notes. Then the Under Commissioner stood, a clear indication that he was dismissing them. Fanny stood also and repeated her initial argument. The Under Commissioner was silent.

Even when Olive rose to her feet, insisting that Nora Keegan had been strangled, not slashed to death, the Under Commissioner said nothing. Finally, he thanked the women for their civic concern and asked the sergeant to escort the ladies from the office. As Lawrence watched the ladies leave the room, he made arrangements to meet the Under Commissioner for lunch at the Choctaw Club.

Out in the hallway, Lawrence bristled at Fanny. "If you had told me who *your friend* was earlier, I could have convinced you to save your breath."

"But Karl's innocent!" Fanny bristled back, "and the New Orleans police are up to their old tricks."

Lawrence squared his shoulders. "If they are, you and I both know that there are better ways to outwit them and ensure that justice is served. Confronting the police outright is not one of those ways. Have you forgotten everything I taught you?"

Fanny huffed like a bull considering its next run. She stepped up to Lawrence as though she was going to take him by the lapels and shake some sense into him. Instead, she straightened his gleaming white cravat, just as she had hundreds of times before. "I know you'd never let the police railroad an innocent man."

As Fanny pulled away, Lawrence grabbed her hands and held them within his own. "You made your case to the police eloquently, Fanny. I was proud of you. If your words didn't sway them, someone else must have already convinced them otherwise."

But Fanny would not let Lawrence deter her with compliments and she quickly loosened her hands from his. "Karl is Sylvia's carpenter and Nora was my student. We've got to do everything we can to make sure that Nora's murderer is found."

Fanny nodded toward the Under Commissioner's office. "Now go have lunch with that man and see what you can find out about Karl. We all need some time to think this through."

FANNY, THE SISTERS, and Liam huddled together at the back of the streetcar traveling up St. Charles Avenue bound for the lush environs of prosperous Americans—Tulane University, Audubon Park and Zoo and the site of the World's Cotton Exposition four years earlier. Liam pulled a small bag of tobacco from his shirt pocket. As he lurched forward to seek a light from the driver's pipe, Fanny said, "We must find more information to convince the police that Karl is innocent."

Olive shook her head. "The police have their minds made up. Karl is guilty, and nothing we tell them will make them change their minds."

"Olive's right," said Sylvia. "No amount of evidence could have convinced the Under Commissioner that Karl is innocent. We'll just have to wait for someone to come up with real proof about who killed Nora. Perhaps even now, one of those people from the waiting room is identifying the murderer to the police." She sat back as the streetcar rounded Lee Circle. "Perhaps the police will believe *them*."

Fanny shook her head. "But if we can show them that Karl didn't kill Nora, they'll have to admit he's innocent. And they'll be forced to find Nora's real murderer."

"We don't need to show the police anything," Sylvia replied. "Graduation is a few days away. Your students need all of your attention right now."

Fanny sat back. She had hardly thought about her students since learning that Nora had been the Conner's Court victim, and now their faces, their goals, their needs, crowded her thoughts. They had lost a classmate. They would be afraid, even paralyzed with fear. She would need to reassure them that there was no Ripper at large, that they were safe.

But as long as the murderer was free to walk New Orleans, was anyone safe? "Still Sylvia, if we could prove Karl's innocence to the police—"

"And if we can't? What will you do then? Go after the murderer yourself?" Sylvia halted, suddenly aware that Fanny and Olive were staring into each other's eyes, communicating silently.

Fanny asked Olive, "Do you think—"

"I wasn't serious," said Sylvia. "You can't think that—"

"Of course we *could.*" Fanny's shoulders set squarely against the wooden seat. "Why not? What does it take? We're intelligent women. We know New Orleans. We know the Channel. We could find out information. Probably in a way that wouldn't stir up anyone's concern."

"Absolutely not." Sylvia responded bluntly. "You're a business teacher not a Pinkerton detective."

"What other choice do we have? *We know* that Nora's murderer is out there." Fanny gazed out the open window upon a group of working men eating lunch under a tree and realized *one of them could be the murderer.* "He could kill again. He could kill another one of our students."

"No," Sylvia persisted. "We cannot step in and do the police's work." A sudden suspicion crossed Sylvia's mind. "You haven't done this before, have you Fanny? Your father and Lawrence didn't have you out playing detective, did they?"

"Of course not," lied Fanny. For on more than one occasion she had assisted her father or Lawrence in collecting and evaluating evidence in a case of murder, and those investigations were among the happiest days in her life. "My father did teach me," Fanny continued truthfully, "that innocent men should not go to jail."

Liam returned from the front of the car and sat next to Fanny, the pungent gray smoke firing from his cigarette. Sylvia breathed deeply, as though she could inhale the cigarette's entire tobacco. Fanny knew that Sylvia secretly enjoyed an occasional fragrant smoke and wondered how desperate she was to have one now.

Fanny was the first to see that the streetcar was approaching the Giddings mansion. It was time to sharpen her arrow. "If Karl is convicted of murder...if everyone in the Channel despises Wisdom Hall because of what Karl did to a student...I suppose that you'll shut down Wisdom Hall and return home to your mother and father?"

Sylvia's eyes popped open as she followed Fanny's gaze toward her parents' extravagant Greek Revival marvel. All of New Orleans might admire the fluted columns, Corinthian capitals, and generous balconies, but to Sylvia it was a prison. Now that she had finally escaped, she could never return.

Sylvia slid silently into her seat. Only after the mules had walked past the house did she speak. "Say something Olive. Please."

"Don't worry, Sylvia," replied her sister. "I think I know how to find Nora's killer."

"What?" asked Fanny.

"I've already solved one murder," said the doctor.

Sylvia rose from her slouch. "I've never heard this before."

"I didn't think you'd want to know."

"You're right, I don't."

"But I do," said Fanny. "I want to hear all about it."

Liam leaned towards Olive, as if saying, *Me too.*

"It happened when I was studying in Berlin," began Olive. "The wife of one of my professors was murdered."

"Go on," said Fanny.

"Doktor Hertz had invited some of his students to supper at his house. His wife, the hostess, was kept upstairs with a teething child. When he went to get her, he found her lifeless on the bed. While we were discussing knives and scalpels in the parlor, she was dying. We never would have known she had been murdered if it weren't for one of the other students. He was a young internist—not invited to the dinner party—and the next day he dissected Frau Hertz."

Sylvia clutched the seat in front of her. "He what?"

"He cut her up for study. When he was questioned about it, the internist said he'd never met Frau Hertz and thought the body was of one of the indigent women donated to the dissection lab. He conducted tests on her organs—just for practice, he said—and proved that she had been poisoned with nicotine."

"But even..." Fanny lowered her voice, "...even undressed, wouldn't a medical student be able to tell the difference between a doctor's wife and an indigent? Even a student has enough common sense to discern *that*."

"That's what the police thought also. And that's when they discovered—after talking to Frau Hertz's maid, housekeeper, and sister—that Frau Hertz and the student were not strangers. They knew each other very well and in fact," Olive made no attempt to lower her voice, "they were on intimate terms. The internist confessed that he was in love with Frau Hertz and also confessed to dissecting her deliberately because he suspected that she had been murdered."

"So the husband knew his wife had a lover?" asked Sylvia as easily as if she were discussing the plot of a romantic novel. And she took no notice of Fanny's reaction to how easily she said *lover*. "He killed her because he was jealous?"

"That's what the police said when they arrested Doktor Hertz."

Liam could contain himself no longer. "This is better than a story from the *Sensation*. What happened next?"

"Nothing." Sylvia turned Liam around in his seat and as the car came to its next stop, she led the group from the car.

As they made their way toward Wisdom Hall, Fanny walked next to Olive. "That's not the end of the story, is it?"

"No." Olive replied grimly. "It was hard for all of us to reconcile Doktor Hertz's grief with murdering his wife. He had always seemed so fond of her."

"Perhaps that's what he wanted you to see."

"It wouldn't be the first time a charming man dissuaded you," added Sylvia, who had come abreast of Olive and Fanny and was trying to push Liam out of earshot.

Fanny furrowed her brow. "He wasn't the murderer?"

"Of course he wasn't, and I had to do something to help him, so I tested her organs for nicotine again."

Liam skidded around Olive. "Was it poison?"

"Oh, it was poison all right but not nicotine, which is a very quick poison. It was arsenic, which could have been given to her gradually for many days before she died."

"So someone else besides her husband could have poisoned her," Fanny stepped in front of Olive to avoid two dogs fighting over a bone. She walked backwards as she said, "Someone who may not have been at the dinner. Someone else with a motive. Like a maid or a sister or a lover."

Fanny had never said the word *lover* before and she let it linger at the tip of her tongue. Then Lawrence Decatur's image flashed through her thoughts. How well he looked today: gleaming and glorious; carefully clipped and scented by his barber. His hair had silvered slightly more during the past months but it only reinforced his authority and confidence. And when she put her arm through his, she'd caught the fragrance of his tart lemon soap. Fanny clamped her lips in a grimace and forced Lawrence from her thoughts.

"It *was* the student," said Olive. "He confessed quickly when confronted with the scientific evidence of his misidentification."

Liam almost tripped in front of Olive. "You solved a murder!"

"Medical science solved it; I brought all of the evidence together."

Sylvia leaned firmly on her cane for a few seconds when they reached Annunciation Street. "I don't see how medical science can help us find Nora's murderer. I don't see how we can do anything but what we've already done."

"A murderer needs motive and opportunity," said Fanny. "That's what Law—, my father told me. And Karl did not have an opportunity."

Sylvia started down the path to Wisdom Hall. "How could you prove that he had no motive?"

"That's obvious enough," replied Olive. "We need to find out if Karl and Nora knew each other."

Fanny stood on the first step of the staircase. "I'll ask my students."

"No, you won't," Sylvia tilted the bottom of her cane at Fanny. "I forbid it."

"But they knew Nora. She could have told them—"

"Our students cannot be pulled into anything concerning Nora or Karl and that's final, Fanny Newcomb."

"But Syl—"

"That's final."

Fanny and Olive watched as Sylvia walked carefully up the steps and into Wisdom Hall. As the door closed behind Sylvia, Olive said, "She's thinking only about the school, but the infirmary is already suffering from Karl's arrest. Not one person came in yesterday; they'd rather suffer in pain than seek me out. I have to do something to restore their trust before it's too late."

"There must be other ways to find out who murdered Nora," replied Fanny. "And I'm going to find all of them."

10.

H AVE YOU EVER BEEN INSIDE A HOUSE OF prostitution before?" Fanny asked matter-of-factly as she and Sylvia waited inside the foyer of the brick building where Nora Keegan had lived.

"Fanny Newcomb! Of course, I haven't. Never. How could you even ask?"

Fanny enjoyed Sylvia's discomfort, although she was surprised that Sylvia had agreed to visit Nora's residence at all. A good, proper woman of Sylvia's social standing—no matter how much she had shocked New Orleans society by opening a Settlement House—was not supposed to visit a house of prostitution, even for charitable purposes. Of course, Fanny was a good, proper woman also, but as a lawyer's child she had been privy to a number of improper things.

But after a good night's sleep, Sylvia had made it clear that she would do whatever was necessary to keep Wisdom Hall open. And today, what was necessary was a visit to a house of prostitution. Still, Fanny was amused at seeing the elegant and starched Sylvia Giddings reduced to a fluster.

Fanny leaned forward and whispered, "I stood outside one once. I was waiting for my father, who *was* inside. On legal business, of course."

Despite her lighthearted exchange with Sylvia, Fanny was abashed to be in a house of prostitution. There was little charm to the entrance foyer and the drab green walls were drearily reminiscent of a boarding house that Fanny lived in last year. Compared to the bright floral wallpaper, fresh paint, and elegant oil landscapes that adorned Wisdom Hall, this house was a cheap cousin.

Noiselessly, a door off the entrance foyer opened and closed and an older woman stood next to Fanny and Sylvia. With a curt nod, she dismissed the porter from his front door perch, as if she wanted no one to overhear her conversation. The landlady had a sharp jaw, and despite her copper-colored hair, her skin was without freckles. It was also free of powder and cosmetics. Dressed in severe black broadcloth from collar to boot and festooned with a large broach of intricately woven blond hair and three black onyx rings about her fingers, the short, stout-figured woman looked more proper than an undertaker's wife.

Her voice had a broad lilt as she said, "I'm Rose O'Sullivan. Which one of you is Miss Newcomb?"

"I am." Fanny did not offer her hand. The newspapers had portrayed Rose O'Sullivan as a harsh, money-hungry woman. Someone who plucked pretty girls from their parents' houses, forced them into prostitution, and threw them on the streets when their beauty faded.

"This is Miss Sylvia Giddings, Principal of Wisdom Hall," Fanny continued as politely as if this visit were a proper funeral call. "Nora was our student."

"Yes, one of the girls told me she was getting schooling somewhere."

"I was her teacher," Fanny faltered on her rehearsed speech. "And I...I—"

"We wanted to let you know how sorry we are about Nora's death," said Sylvia.

"Yes, I suppose you would," replied Mrs. O'Sullivan. "Seeing that she wouldn't even have been in the Irish Channel if you hadn't lured her there."

"You think we had something to do with her murder?" Fanny sputtered. "Because she came to classes at Wisdom Hall?"

"Nothing could be farther from the truth," Sylvia spoke in her most authoritative tone. "We had no idea that Nora frequented the Irish Channel. And we certainly never knew that she lived here and worked for you."

"Yes, this is no grand and wise hall for learning, but my girls are good girls," Mrs. O'Sullivan's voice rose, as though she wanted her testimony to reach the rafters. "And Nora didn't deserve what happened to her."

"Of course she didn't," Fanny agreed softly. "We can all agree upon that. And we—"

"We have given you our sincere condolences," said Sylvia not so softly. "And now we will give our goodbyes."

"And you'd go before seeing her room?" asked the landlady. "Are you sure about that...ladies?"

Fanny and Sylvia exchanged looks of surprise. After the heated words blasted at them by the landlady, had they heard correctly?

Fanny did not wait to be asked again. "No. No, we wouldn't leave before seeing her room."

The landlady lifted her skirts and, despite her girth, daintily mounted the narrow stairs. Sylvia and Fanny followed closely behind. The landlady placed a hand on the doorknob to the first door on the right. "We're all brokenhearted, every one of us. Nora was such a favorite here." The landlady opened the door with a flourish, as though showing the rooms of murder victims were a specialty of hers. "Well, here you are then. Nora's own."

Sylvia and Fanny peered in from the hallway. The furniture was plain and pale: a broad bed with a small square table beside it, a narrow chest of drawers, and an armoire. Close to the bed was a washstand with basin, ewer, and several cakes of soap. On the bottom shelf of the stand was a covered chamber pot. Two wooden chairs against the wall and one cushioned chair with two layers of antimacassars—clearly showing the imprint of men's hair oil—completed the furnishings. The room smelled of soap and disinfectant, much like

Olive's infirmary. Indeed, it was almost clinical, lacking emotion or color or any sense of Nora Keegan.

Fanny's father had told her—that day long ago—about the business of a house of prostitution. She had understood little of his explanation then but the prominence of the bed provided her with more understanding today. She had a sudden memory of a summer picnic with Lawrence—also long ago—where after a feast of fried chicken they each fell fast asleep with Fanny awakening with her head resting on Lawrence's thigh.

"I've tidied it up, of course. What with everyone wanting to see it." The landlady swept into the room and lifted the window blinds, allowing a soft light to ripple through the room and bounce off of the polished furniture.

Fanny released her remembrance of that afternoon with Lawrence and returned to the present. "You've been showing Nora's room to people? You mean the police?"

"They were up here an hour after I identified the poor child. It took me and the girls a while to clean up after the officers went through her things. And then the others started coming round. I'm only charging a dollar for each person." She looked sideways at Fanny and Sylvia, as if to gauge if they had brought that amount of money with them. "It's not often someone gets to see where one of Jack the Ripper's whores slept."

Fanny and Sylvia recoiled at the landlady's coarse language. *Prostitute* was sad and desperate enough. *Whore* was deliberately low and filthy. Fanny looked from the pillows on the bed to the chamber pot to the cakes of soap. This was all she would ever see of Nora again and she forced back a tear.

"I know, dear." The landlady's voice softened as she looked at Fanny. She smoothed the scarlet bed coverlet. "It's all too much, isn't it? Such a sweet child and for her to end up as she did." The landlady pulled a white cloth from under her cuff and blew her nose. "May Karl Schultz rot in Hell!"

Fanny had been hoping for this moment, the mention of Karl's name, and she rallied herself from her sorrow. "Did you know him? Did Nora know him?"

"Never heard of him until the police knocked at my door."

"He never came here to visit Nora?"

"Certainly not. Rose O'Sullivan never opens her front or back door to German riffraff."

As Fanny considered her next question a high-pitched whistle broke the silence.

"That'll be the wine merchant." Mrs. O'Sullivan rushed out of the room, stopping briefly at the door. "You ladies just come downstairs when you're ready."

FANNY CLOSED THE door after the landlady and went directly to the large armoire. Without hesitation, she turned the small black key in the lock. She opened the door slowly, as if anticipating a creak to betray her. Although Mrs. O'Sullivan was downstairs, what if there were other women in the house? Fanny would need to be careful.

"Quick Sylvia, go lock the door."

"Why? What are you doing?"

Fanny patted down the soft piles of white cotton undergarments as if she were an expert in finding secrets. "I don't believe anything that woman told us. There's got to be something here that tells us more about Nora." Fanny's voice sobered. "Or who might have wanted to kill her." She pulled one of the wooden chairs over to the armoire and stood on it to look onto the top shelf. Fanny sifted through a pile of straw hats, three pairs of black cotton gloves, and a white blanket with blue edges.

Sylvia spoke from behind Fanny's shoulder, like a prickly conscience. "You shouldn't be doing this."

"I don't like it any better than you do," Fanny lied. Actually, she was beginning to enjoy herself. After her father's death and before she came to Wisdom Hall, Fanny had worked as a lady's companion for a month. Her employer had been rude and nosey and Fanny had rectified her own unhappiness by searching through her employer's baskets, drawers, and boxes. "But is there another way to know more about Nora?"

"I thought we were going to ask questions, not search through her things."

"We'll do both," replied Fanny. "Are you going to help or not? We'd better be quick about it."

As if enticed by a bright blue feather boa that hung on a hook, Sylvia joined in the search, riffling through the bodices and skirts that hung on the armoire hooks. "She didn't have many clothes."

Not every woman owns as many outfits as you do, Fanny wanted to say. Instead she replied, "Why don't you look in the drawer in her bed table?"

Sylvia pulled out the drawer and reported. "A deck of cards. A pair of broken spectacles. A bottle of patent medicine. A bible. Pamphlets. Another book. *Lives of Our Lady Saints and Martyrs*. Really, Fanny, how is any of this supposed to help?"

Fanny closed the armoire, returned the chair to the wall, and considered the narrow bureau. She leaned over to look under the bureau. Nothing. She opened the bottom drawer. Empty. She began to doubt if this was really Nora's room. Perhaps it was just an empty room in which a few things had been thrown. "The man who murdered Nora had a reason. He had some connection to her and I'm looking for that connection. Nora learned to read and write when she was a child and was quite good at it. I thought she might have kept a diary of some kind. That's what I'd really like to find."

"A diary that identifies who wanted to murder her?" Sylvia glared at Fanny. "You and your working girls have been reading too many gothic romances."

Fanny opened the drawer second to the bottom. A stack of pillowcases and table napkins of Irish linen, each monogrammed NAK. A pair of matching embroidered slippers. Nora's bridal dowry? "If you don't think there's anything to find up here, you can go downstairs and keep Mrs. O'Sullivan from coming up."

"No," Sylvia replied. "I'll stay."

Fanny opened the drawer second from the top. At last, boxes. Sure to hold something personal, something important. Fanny opened each box, only to find layers of cardboarding. No, there was something at the bottom of one box. Fanny saw the top half of a photograph; a confident Nora gazing directly into Fanny's eyes. Fanny's pulse rose. She glanced at Sylvia, who stood with her back to Fanny, and slipped the photograph into her pocket.

"We need to talk to the other girls who live here." Fanny closed the drawer gently. "They knew Nora best. They must have something to say about her."

Fanny opened the top and last drawer—the drawer that usually held all of the small, immediate things needed by women, the drawer where Fanny kept her own diary. But Nora's drawer was empty.

Sylvia hovered over Fanny. "Finished? Satisfied? Then let's go. The sooner we're out of this house, the better." Sylvia pulled Fanny from the room and down the narrow stairs. As they reached the first floor, Mrs. O'Sullivan popped in from the long hallway, as if she had been waiting for them. Everyone paid admission to Mrs. O's house.

Sylvia removed two dollar pieces from her purse and handed them to Fanny, as if she could not give them directly to the landlady.

Mrs. O'Sullivan accepted the money easily and asked, "But you're not leaving without seeing Nora, are you?"

"She's here?" Fanny asked.

"Yes, of course, dear. We got her earlier this morning." Mrs. O'Sullivan put her hand on the knob to the double leaf parlor doors. "With the funeral tomorrow where else would the poor girl be but at home?"

MRS. O'SULLIVAN'S PRIVATE parlor was crowded with potted palm trees, heavily carved furniture, fringed pillows, and large brass spittoons situated by each overstuffed chair. In the back corner was an entire table covered with bottles, decanters, and glassware. A large painting of a trio of naked women spanned the wall over the fireplace mantle. Other paintings of unclad women dotted the flocked red wallpaper. The carpet was thick; the windows were covered with velvet drapery; a polished piano presided over the back wall.

Fanny was strangely satisfied. Now *this* was a house of prostitution.

Sylvia grabbed Fanny's hand as they entered the room. As Fanny moved forward, Sylvia stumbled over the carpet, knocking into a table with a vase of lilies, their indulgent fragrance almost overwhelming the airless room. Fanny glanced back. Sylvia's eyes were closed tightly against the sight of Nora's dead body. Fanny knew without asking that they would remain closed until they left the dead woman's presence. She felt a small satisfaction that Sylvia had a weakness, although it was irritatingly inconvenient just now.

"The photographer left just a bit ago," said the landlady.

The coffin was settled on a low table in the center of the parlor with the top half open. Fanny walked forward, but Sylvia yanked Fanny back toward her. From the distance of a yard Fanny could see nothing of Nora. She clutched Sylvia around the waist. "Walk with me just a little and I'll have you out of here in a minute. I promise." With Sylvia stiffly at her side, Fanny moved toward the casket.

Fanny leaned into the coffin until she was inches from Nora's face. Dressed from chin to wrist in dove gray, Nora was an angel at rest, her dark brown hair plaited around her head like a halo. Her arms crossed solemnly over her breast and a crucifix was entwined within her pale fingers.

Fanny's eyes were drawn to Nora's high collar. Olive said that Nora had been strangled and if Fanny could lower Nora's high collar, she could see for herself. At least she assumed that strangulation marks would still be evident. But how could Fanny get her fingers inside Nora's collar?

"Mrs. O'Sullivan, is it possible...." Fanny fumbled, until she saw the mourning brooch of woven hair on Mrs. O'Sullivan's black collar. "Could I have a lock of Nora's hair?"

"Yes, of course. Just let me get my scissors."

As soon as Mrs. O'Sullivan closed the door behind her, Fanny put a finger into Nora's high collar. But Sylvia, her eyes shut tightly and a handkerchief to her lips, pulled Fanny back. Fanny's finger slipped from the collar.

"Sylvia, stop it. I just need to see one thing," Fanny tugged her hand from Sylvia's grasp and put her two index fingers on opposite sides of Nora's collar. But the collar would not budge, no matter how firmly Fanny tugged. It remained pressed to Nora's neck, as though it had been glued on. Determined to find something, Fanny ran her fingers along the shoulder of Nora's dress, feeling for scars or stitching or anything unusual.

Sylvia grabbed Fanny's waist, pulling her from the coffin. "Let's go. Now." Waving aside the porter, Sylvia opened the front door, rushed into the fresh air and ran down the steps. With a last glance at the crimson door and the mourning wreath, Fanny followed.

The women passed the telegraph pole where Fanny had seen a broadside of a letter from Jack the Ripper on Sunday. A new broadside was positioned below it, the words *Nora Keegan* in bold lettering. Fanny tore the paper from the pole and jammed it into her pocket. She caught Sylvia's hand in hers and they marched toward the streetcar stop. Sylvia did not release Fanny's hand until the streetcar turned away from Basin Street.

11.

OLIVE ARRIVED AT THE OFFICES OF THE *Daily Picayune* newspaper around noontime to find editor Eliza Nicholson and her business manager husband disagreeing with each other. Eliza's voice—as always—was the loudest. "The public must be warned about the dangers of those dead animals rotting in our streets. Especially as summer approaches. I don't care who my editorial offends, it is our duty to provide honest information."

Eliza's husband shook his head in response, but lit up when he saw Olive at the doorway. "Dr. Giddings. What brings you to the offices of New Orleans' finest newspaper?"

From behind her desk, Eliza leaned forward and thrust a typeset page at Olive. "Here. Read this. Tell me what you think."

Olive had known Eliza most of her life and was not surprised at the editor's unconventional greeting. In fact, she enjoyed Eliza's abrupt discourse. Olive read the three paragraphs quickly and said, "Everything you write here is true. Horses and mules are whipped, starved, and dying all over New Orleans. But how can you expect people to feed their animals when they cannot even feed themselves? Many people in the Channel eat less in a week than a horse eats in a day."

Both Eliza and her husband exchanged glances as if to say, "I told you so." Then her husband took the paper from Olive's hand and left the room.

Eliza Nicholson had a reputation as an honest newspaperwoman, and Olive liked her immensely. Many years ago Eliza had married her first husband, the owner of the *Daily Picayune*. Upon his death, she was advised to close down the debt-ridden newspaper but had chosen to keep it going. Through her articles, whispers of society scandal, and some say, her marriage to the *Picayune's* talented business manager, she had made the newspaper solvent. Which meant she had as many enemies as allies.

A short burly man lunged into the room and dumped a pile of letters and envelopes on Eliza's desk. "More Rippers." Without further explanation, he barged out of the room. When he was out of earshot, Eliza said sarcastically, "Thank you very much, Mr. Shaunasey."

Eliza nodded to stacks of letters planted about her desk and then studied the new arrivals. "We get about ten letters a day. All from people claiming to have killed that poor woman and promising to kill more. Of course they're cranks. We even got one mailed from Memphis and that writer claimed he would murder a prostitute in New Orleans that very night."

Olive gazed at the papers on Eliza's desk. "That's why I'm here. Nora Keegan was not killed by Jack the Ripper. I was the first physician to see her. I'm here to tell you everything I know and I'm ready to talk to your reporters. Unless you'd like to write this story yourself."

"Close the door and sit down," Eliza nodded to the empty chair by her desk. "Tell me what you know."

"First," said Olive, "Tell me who told you that Nora was murdered?"

"John Remington told us. Haven't you been reading our series of articles?" Eliza fixed her eyes to the distance and Olive turned to follow Eliza's gaze. Shaunasey's pudgy features were pressed against the window in the closed door. Olive and Eliza both heard him say, "Detective Crenshaw is back."

"All right. I'll be with him in a minute," answered the editor. But instead of hurrying Olive out, Eliza leaned back in her chair, as if all the time in the world were hers. "How is your dear sister Sylvia doing these days?"

Olive was surprised by Eliza's change of subject but answered readily. "The best she can, considering. Nora was our student. Karl was our carpenter. Both of them are very much missed." A sudden thought struck Olive. "What else do you know about Karl that you have not printed?"

"We know where he lives and where he was working, but not much more," said the editor. "The Germans are very tightlipped. No one is allowed to talk to him at the Parish Prison. The first time we might get any comment from him will be at his trial." Eliza looked away from Olive and at the door. This time Daniel Crenshaw stood on the other side. Eliza tapped the collection of papers and envelopes on her desk. "This may take a while. But I want to hear what you have to say. Can you come back later?"

Olive agreed reluctantly; so much must be done. By the time Olive reached the Infirmary, she had decided her course. Just as Fanny and Sylvia had seen Nora's lodgings, Olive would convince Sylvia to help her seek out Karl's.

AFTER OLIVE CLOSED the infirmary for the afternoon—and after Sylvia recovered from the shock of being inside a house of prostitution—the sisters walked a few streets uptown from Wisdom Hall.

Karl's address proved to be one of the larger three-story wooden buildings on the street. At Olive's knock, the door was opened by a young woman using the corner of her apron to wipe soot from her eyes. Olive took advantage of the girl's distraction and pulled Sylvia and her cane across the threshold with her, closing the door behind them. They were in a very narrow central hallway and Olive could smell that someone had recently washed the walls with strong soap.

The girl pulled the apron away from her eyes. She was not pleased to see two uptown ladies who obviously were not here for boarding. She wailed, "Mutter!"

A thin, older woman emerged from an upstairs room and rushed down the steep stairs, brushing her hands toward Olive and Sylvia like a broom, as if to shoo them from the house. Before she could speak, Olive asked in German, "Is this the home of Karl Schultz? I have money owed to him."

Taken aback by Olive's perfectly spoken German, the woman replied in equally well enunciated English, "Herr Schultz lives at the Parish Prison now." Then she pushed the girl toward the dark end of the hallway as if to shield her from the conversation.

"Yes, we know," said Olive. "But before he was arrested he was doing some carpentry for my sister. And we are bringing his wages today."

A gruff male voice spoke in broken English, "Vee do not vant...want his monies. Und vee...do not want... you here." A large, hulking man—or perhaps a talking bear?—emerged from the room at the end of the hallway. The girl blessed herself with the sign of the cross. As the man lurched toward Olive, she wondered if she should do the same.

Olive knew that every lodging house employed a ferocious man as its "peacekeeper"—making sure that people paid on time, that no one snuck into a bed without paying, that all rules of the house were kept— but she had never encountered one before. As the man neared the women, the enormity of his stature became clear.

Olive nudged her sister, and Sylvia knew exactly what Olive expected of her. Sylvia raised her chin elegantly and extended her hand regally toward the bear. "Good day, sir."

The man stopped short within a few feet and looked at Sylvia's gloved hand as though he had never before seen anything as clean and respectful. Sylvia smiled. "Karl Schultz was in my employ at Wisdom Hall. I have the monies from his last week with me and I would like to give them to you to hold for him." Sylvia and Olive had discussed all of this earlier at Wisdom Hall: they did not care what Karl's landlady did with the money—for Sylvia would recompense Karl generously when he was released from the Parish Prison—and they hoped his landlady would take the bait.

The scrawny woman seemed to know exactly what Sylvia was offering. "You think we're like the Irish and we'll take this money for ourselves? You think we steal from our own?" Suddenly she waved her hand toward the hulking man and ordered, "Take them upstairs then. Make them put the money in his bible. Make them see that we are honest."

Sylvia and Olive followed the man up to the third floor where, just like at Wisdom Hall, there were no walls or doors. Instead, there were stacks of large, narrow wooden shelves, built about two feet from each other. Sylvia saw a grey woolen blanket on one of the shelves and then saw something move underneath it. Sylvia realized these shelves were all beds. She had never seen anything so lonely in her life and could not imagine what sleeping in one of these bunks might be like. Sylvia reached for her sister's hand.

The girl came up the stairs and led them to one of the shelves in the far corner near a window opening devoid of glass or curtain. Olive asked, "Is this where Karl slept?"

The girl reached under a thin, odorous mattress and pulled out a book. It was a small, palm-sized Old Testament bound in cheap black paper. She gave it to the man, who presented it to Sylvia, who looked through it casually, checking the flyleaf and front section for anything written in ink. And then she found a small card. She removed it, not surprised to see a photograph of Karl seated between an old man and woman.

"His grandparents?" asked Sylvia.

"Parents."

Sylvia had estimated that Karl was close to Olive's age. In this photograph, he looked much like he did when Sylvia hired him. But his parents—Sylvia asked the girl to confirm that these were his parents? *Ja, ja—* looked extremely aged, almost three times his age.

"Karl had no sweetheart?" Sylvia looked half-heartedly at the girl. After all, she had known just where Karl's bed was and where his Bible was kept.

"A man with elderly parents has no money for marriage," said the landlady.

"Do you think Karl killed that girl?" Olive asked.

The girl answered quickly, as though she had been waiting to be asked. "We told them that Karl was in bed when that girl was murdered but they didn't believe us."

The sisters looked at each other, understanding why the police would not believe their alibi. Why should they, when someone else had provided a conflicting alibi?

Sylvia removed two paper dollars from her pocket and laid them against the pages of Karl's bible. Then she replaced the photograph between the pages.

12.

ALTHOUGH SYLVIA COULD NOT BEAR TO look at someone dead, she had a great fondness for funerals. Closed-coffin funerals, that is. And so at Wednesday noon, Sylvia accompanied Fanny to Nora's funeral at Metairie Cemetery, a racetrack-shaped burial ground located far uptown.

Indeed, before the war and the reversal of fortunes afterwards, the Metairie Cemetery property had been a popular racetrack. The cemetery managers had retained the oval shape of the track, cut broad avenues around and through it, planted oak and magnolia trees, and provided benches and other amenities for visitors. Large and elaborately sculpted tombs were fashionable in Metairie—the larger the better, for generations of dead might rest here—and with a population of gazebo-sized tombs, white stone avenues, and shade trees, Metairie was a very fashionable neighborhood for the New Orleans dead. Just a week after Easter, the cemetery was still decorated with impressive tributes of colored ribbons and bright flowers, soggy from last night's rain.

Fanny had found no announcements of Nora's funeral in the papers and the only detail she had was from the broadside she ripped from the telegraph pole on Basin Street. It had not mentioned a church service but stated that interment at Metairie would take place after noon.

Just inside the cemetery's stout brick gates, Fanny and Sylvia sat in the carriage, with Thomas and Liam on the driver's seat, watching Nora's procession enter Metairie. The hearse was an elaborate confection of ebony and gilt, drawn by six black horses. Behind the hearse came no less than four large carriages, each with their cover collapsed down, ensuring that all occupants could see and be seen.

Mrs. O'Sullivan occupied the first carriage, highly visible as the chief mourner. She was dressed in the same dark broadcloth and mourning jewelry worn the day before and clutched a large black book between her hands. Within the other three carriages were clusters of females, uncountable from a distance because their black dress and bonnets seemed to blend together.

As the carriages drew closer, Fanny inspected the occupants: a dozen girls of Nora's age, a few well-composed women, and two young girls with hair as golden as her. "If only I could talk to those girls, I'm sure they'd tell me something about Nora."

"Those children should be in school," Sylvia said firmly as she scowled at Liam. "And you should not stare at them."

Sylvia was in a foul mood, and to her surprise, not even a funeral could lighten it. Last night had been the first time that Wisdom Hall had been open for classes since Karl's arrest, and none of Sylvia's students had shown up for her Reading Circle. Sylvia had been livid at first, but as the evening wore on, she became transfixed with worry; without students, she would have to shut down Wisdom Hall. And without Wisdom Hall, Sylvia Giddings was a complete failure.

Fanny studied the worry lines that creased Sylvia's pale forehead and she was equally concerned. Tonight was Fanny's turn to teach, and her students must come to class. For if Sylvia closed Wisdom Hall, Fanny would be unemployed. And homeless.

"In school," Sylvia repeated as one of the girls stood up in the carriage and blew a kiss to a group of men standing nearby. "And not living in a house of prostitution." Then she looked at Liam who was trying desperately to follow Sylvia's command to ignore the girls in the carriages. "It's going to rain in a minute."

As Sylvia sat back into her seat, Fanny looked from the hearse and mourners' carriages to the other people in attendance. There must have been at least sixty people standing about, including Clarence Halloway, who kept pushing around a rotund man balancing a large camera on a slender tripod. Fanny also identified Detective Daniel Crenshaw and his broken-nosed, note-taking sergeant. But who were these other people?

As Fanny's eyes darted amongst the men in the crowd, Sylvia's mood improved slightly. "I know what you're thinking, Fanny Newcomb. But you didn't really think the murderer would be here, did you?"

Fanny was surprised that her thoughts were so transparent. "He could be here. Any man who hated

Nora enough to kill her might find satisfaction in making sure she's buried."

"And just how did you expect him to identify himself? Perhaps he'd raise his hat to you?"

"I didn't really think the murderer would make himself obvious but I rather thought that *he*," Fanny nodded toward Detective Crenshaw, "might watch one man more than another."

"And has *he*?"

"No, but there's still plenty of funeral remaining. If the police believe they've caught the murderer, why is Crenshaw here at all?" Fanny nodded to Crenshaw's sergeant. "And wouldn't you like to know what his sergeant is writing down?"

"What we need to see is what he wrote in his notebook before Karl was arrested," replied Sylvia as she accepted an umbrella from Liam and opened it with a swoop. "He's probably had a bird's eye view of the police investigation and knows exactly why Karl was arrested."

As Mrs. O'Sullivan and the others stepped down from their carriages and walked over to a large stone mausoleum, Fanny had to pinch herself sharply to keep back tears. Shaped like a child's playhouse, with its sleek stone façade, gable roof and gothic arched entranceway, Nora's mausoleum in Metairie was exactly like Fanny's father's mausoleum in Greenwood Cemetery. The only difference was that a large stone cross-topped Oscar Newcomb's tomb.

As a quartet of men removed Nora's coffin from the hearse, a light rain began to fall. Within a minute the drops of rain turned into large pelts and everyone scattered for cover. Soon rain fell in a downpour.

"Everyone is leaving." Sylvia nodded to Mrs. O'Sullivan who had gone back into her carriage and was yanking up the cover. Nora's casket was unceremoniously shoved and locked into the mausoleum by the hearse driver. "Liam, sit down. Thomas, back to Wisdom Hall."

A FEW HOURS later, Fanny obediently followed Sylvia into the infirmary. Sylvia disliked all details of medical practice as much as Olive relished them, and although Sylvia had directed the construction of the infirmary, once it was operational she all but refused to enter it. If Sylvia voluntarily entered the infirmary, Fanny knew that her foul mood would get only worse.

"It was a complete waste of time! A fool's errand!" Sylvia strode to the table where Olive was squinting at a label on a small bottle. "Olive! Are you listening to me?"

"Everyone can *hear* you, Sylvia," replied her sister as she raised the bottle toward the window light. "I'm sure they can hear you all of the way to Metairie."

"A complete waste of time!"

"You've said that, Sylvia."

"Our priority is getting our students back in class. Not attending funerals and going to" Sylvia lowered her voice, "houses of prostitution."

"You *are* the Principal, Sylvia," Olive looked from the label to Fanny, who stood awkwardly a few feet from the open door. "I'm sure Fanny will go along with whatever you say."

Sylvia turned to Fanny. "Speak, then. I'm sure that you have an opinion."

Fanny scowled. Sylvia had fumed silently during the return ride from the cemetery and, with great effort, Fanny had managed to bite her tongue and remain silent. As much as Fanny wanted to find out who killed Nora, and as much as she wanted to free Karl from the Parish Prison, Fanny had to keep her job at Wisdom Hall. The small legacy from her father had been spent months ago, and Sylvia provided room and board and allowed Fanny to read freely from her library. And although neither Sylvia nor Olive was exactly friendly to her, Fanny felt a growing regard for them; she respected the depth of Olive's medical knowledge and appreciated how difficult it was for Sylvia to succeed at building a settlement house and school. Fanny thought that she could build a life here at Wisdom Hall, but she needed to tread carefully.

"I'm very sorry," Fanny began. "It really did seem—"

"'Cuse me, Miss Sylvia." Liam's head popped through the infirmary's hallway door. "I got something here you'd like to read."

Sylvia turned regally from Fanny to Liam. "Later, Liam. We're busy right now."

"But Miss Sylvia! You'll want to see this."

"Is it a special edition?" Fanny tried to see if the boy held a newspaper. "News about Nora or Karl?"

"It ain't a newspaper." Liam entered the infirmary cautiously, having been banished more than once for bumping into bottles. "It's a notebook, Miss Sylvia. I got the Sergeant's book."

"Sergeant who?" asked Sylvia.

"Why Flynn, of course."

"The one who works with Detective Crenshaw?" asked Fanny. "The one with the broken nose?"

"One and the same." Liam pulled a cloth-covered package from inside his shirt. "It's his notebook I've got. But it's only for a little while. I've got to get it back soon."

Sylvia looked Liam directly in his eyes. "Liam O'Donnell, you promised you'd stop stealing."

"But you said you wanted to see what was inside Flynn's notebook. You said so at the funeral. And I need to return the damn thing—'scuse me, Miss Sylvia—so we don't have a lot of time." Liam unwrapped the book to hand it to Sylvia, but Fanny grabbed it from his hands and eagerly ran her fingers along the pages, flipping them rapidly.

"There's only one problem," she mumbled.

"It's in Irish?" asked Olive.

"No," replied Fanny. "It's coded."

Liam drew out a chair, turned it around and sat, his forearms settling over the back of the chair. "That's what I thought. Only it's not a code I've ever seen."

Fanny winced at the understatement, knowing that despite Sylvia's numerous attempts, the boy could still neither read nor write.

"Bet you can read it, Miss Fanny, can't you?"

"Now just a minute." Sylvia protested. "As far as we know, the good Sergeant may have followed Liam and will be knocking at our door in a minute. If the police find the notebook here, they'll haul us off to jail for petty thievery. And that be the end of Wisdom Hall for good."

Olive ignored her sister's exaggeration. The police would never arrest any one of Philip Giddings' children. "Go on, Fanny. Tell us what it says."

Fanny's mouth puckered. "It's not Gregg shorthand. And it's not Pitman either. It's something else entirely. I don't know how to read it."

"It can't be too much unlike Gregg or Pitman, can it?" asked Olive, who knew absolutely nothing about shorthands of any type.

"Yes, it can. There are at least ten different types of shorthand used in business today. And many people create their own." Fanny flipped through the book. "Liam. How much time do we have?"

"Yes, and how did you get this book?" asked Sylvia.

Liam put his hands on the top of the chair and leaned back leisurely, as if all danger of suffering Sylvia's disapproval had passed. "I found out Flynn eats lunch at O'Reilley's saloon. Half an hour after lunch he takes his jacket off and hangs it on a peg, goes into a room off the kitchen, settles down in a chair, and falls asleep."

"And today the notebook fell out of his tunic?"

"If you say so, Miss Sylvia."

"When does the sergeant wake up?" asked Fanny.

"In an hour."

"I can't do anything with this in an hour. Whatever his code is, his script is awful. I'll never break it. I don't see how anyone could...although there are some words in here."

"Gregg words?" asked Sylvia.

"Pitman words?" suggested her sister.

"No, English. Or at least most of them are. I do that myself, when I'm writing too fast but can't think of how to write a proper name. I write it in longhand English so I don't make any mistakes. I lose time but I make it up later." Fanny pointed loosely at Sylvia. "Just give me a piece of paper and a pen I'll see what I can do. Liam, watch the clock and alert me to every quarter hour."

OLIVE TAPPED HER pencil nervously on the first of the long tables facing Fanny's school desk. "Out with it, Fanny."

Fanny was still transcribing her own quickly scribbled notes. In three-quarters of an hour, she had been able to go through the Sergeant's entire book. Her concentration had been complete and now her body bore the brunt. Her right hand was cramped and black with ink, her shoulders ached, her golden hair had escaped from its bun, and her eyes were strained and dry. But mentally, Fanny was fully awake and keen to continue. And never would she trust her typewriter to record such important information.

Despite Olive's eagerness to hear Fanny's transcriptions, Sylvia had demanded that Fanny could not begin her report until they were sure Liam had safely restored the notebook to the Sergeant's tunic. And now, Liam sat in a chair behind Sylvia, as if waiting for another opportunity to serve her. Almost in mirror image, Thomas sat behind Olive. Fanny wondered how she should present the information. She knew that Olive would appreciate a more scientific method, the exact number of pages in the notebook and the progression of information, an overview which Fanny herself preferred. But Fanny could also go straight to the heart of the matter—which Sylvia would clearly prefer—and discuss the information that appeared to be the focus of the police investigation.

"From the dates in the notebook, it seems clear that Flynn wrote in it just before the Conner's Court murder. Since the notebook had a few blank pages at the end, it seems logical that it is his entire record of the investigation so far." This was the first time that Olive and Sylvia had sat in Fanny's classroom and Fanny was flattered, realizing that the quartet seated before her were indeed her students right now.

"Nora's name was written in longhand and after her name there were about forty-five others." How she wished she could be more accurate. She knew that Olive was a stickler for exactitude and Fanny even felt Thomas's meticulous mind judging her. He scowled, as though irritated he had not added shorthand to his own considerable skills. "Some of the names are grouped together, some have their own pages with information. But I think the most important names are the ones that have stars by them. There are six names with stars next to them and each of them has at least a couple pages of notes. Since Karl's name is one of the six, I believe that the names with stars are the police's primary suspects." Fanny paused, ready for Sylvia or Olive to challenge her assumptions.

"The other names, the ones with no stars, might be earlier suspects?" asked Olive.

"Some of those names are checked off and have a paragraph or two so they may be. Since many of the names are women's names, I think it's more likely that they were witnesses. Or people who just knew Nora Keegan. For example, Mrs. O'Sullivan's name is in the notebook." Fanny realized that while she had been talking, Olive and Sylvia had outfitted themselves with notebooks of their own and had their own pencils poised to write.

Sylvia said, "Let's have the names, then. The ones with stars."

"All right." Fanny swallowed hard. "Karl Schultz."

"Top of the list and the first arrested," replied Olive. "No surprise about that one. Next."

"Gabriel Boylan."

"Not him!" Liam slapped his cap against his knee. "He's in the seminary. Going to be a priest. He runs the boys' school at St. Mary's. If his brother ever found out about the Sergeant writing his name in his book...he'd have Flynn's badge for certain."

"And his brother would be?" asked Fanny.

"Father Boylan of St. Alphonsus," replied Liam, in the same tones reserved for names of saints.

"And his Christian name would be?" Fanny asked.

"Terence," answered Sylvia. "I've locked horns with him many times although I've never met the man. He's the reason we don't have classes or functions at Wisdom Hall on Sundays. He made it clear—through mutual acquaintances of ours—that if we did anything to conflict with his church days, he would blacklist us among the Irish neighbors. And I'm sure he would."

"Is that the man we almost met in London last fall?" asked Olive.

"That's right." Sylvia looked to Fanny. "He'd been in Ireland and was in London before sailing home. The Davises had taken a house outside London and thought that since we were all from New Orleans we should meet each other."

Fanny pressed forward. "Did you?"

"No."

"Have you met his brother Gabriel?"

"No."

"Pity, because Father Terence Boylan is suspect number three. The Sergeant wrote four pages about him."

Sylvia began to fan herself with her notebook. "I can't believe the police would even consider him."

"Because he's a priest?" asked Olive.

"Well, yes, of course. And because he's lace curtain Irish. The Boylan family is tied into everything. They're on the Sanitary Commission, the Streetcar Commission, the Public Works Commission, *and* there's one or two of them in the Police Department. Suspecting a Boylan is like suspecting one of *our* cousins. It just isn't done." Sylvia set down her notebook with authority. "Who's next?"

"Pierre deVille. Six pages of notes after his name."

"Liam?" asked Sylvia.

"Dunno, Miss Sylvia. Don't sound like a Channel name to me."

Olive looked over at Thomas, who replied in his precise even tones. "Many deVilles are from an old Creole family. Some still live in the French Quarter. However, I am not familiar with the Christian name Pierre."

The infirmary bell rang harshly through the classroom. Olive scowled and rose from her chair. But Thomas was up a second sooner. He adjusted his coat jacket and walked toward the infirmary. Olive followed after him.

"Just a moment Olive," commanded Fanny, as she did with any student who attempted to leave her class without permission. "There are two more names on the list and you'll want to hear them. The first name is John Remington."

Olive plopped into the nearest seat, as though she'd been punched in the stomach. "John? A murder suspect? I can't believe it."

"It's true." Fanny referred once more to her notes. "Dr. John Remington and Dr. Lester Adams are the last two names with stars."

"But the police could never suspect John of murder."

"If a priest could be suspected," asked Sylvia, "Why not a doctor?"

Olive looked at her sister sharply. "I can't believe that we are even discussing this. John Remington is a physician with a highly respected practice. He'd never murder anyone." Olive rose from her chair. "I think we've all been fooling ourselves that the Sergeant's notebook had any information we could use. Or could have used, if we could have read all of it. This method of assuming partial truths from information is unscientific and is getting us nowhere. This is not the way to prove Karl's innocence." When neither Fanny nor Sylvia responded, Olive scowled. "You're determined to take this list seriously, aren't you? But just tell me this: were any of the names with stars crossed out? Or was there anything to indicate that Flynn had thought better of them and they weren't suspect?"

"No." Fanny looked from sister to sister. "Only the fact that one of them was arrested. The only way to find more evidence supporting Karl's innocence is to find evidence against someone else. And these men seem the most likely suspects. This list is our best hope." Fanny stared at Olive as though she was a disobedient student and to Fanny's satisfaction, Olive sank back to her chair.

At that moment, Thomas burst in. "There's been an accident at McClennan's. You've been called." Thomas' nose turned up slightly at the name of the Channel's largest slaughterhouse. "I'll get the buggy ready for you."

Olive's scowl softened. The awful suggestion that her mentor could be guilty of murder faded into the background as she began to mentally prepare for the possible injuries awaiting her at McClennan's. But she couldn't leave yet. "Just what do you want me to do?"

"Find out if John Remington or Lester Adams knew Nora." Fanny nodded her head approvingly. "And then find out if they had any reason to murder her."

WHEN FANNY ENTERED her bedroom that night she was not thinking about Sergeant Flynn's shorthand or the six suspects. Nor was she thinking about the failed evening at Wisdom Hall, as she waited for an hour for her students to show up for class. (They did not.) Nor was Fanny thinking about Sylvia's dour expression and wondering if Sylvia would shut down Wisdom Hall and make Fanny find another job and a new place to live.

No, Fanny would think about those worries tomorrow, because tonight, Fanny was thinking about Liam O'Donnell.

Sylvia had found Liam camping in the Talbot mansion when she purchased it. The boy had latched onto Sylvia quickly and she did not have the heart to turn him out on the street. If allowed, Liam would follow Sylvia as closely as the dogs Abel and Cain. It did not surprise Fanny that if Liam thought Sylvia wanted the sergeant's notebook, that he would get it for her.

But it amused Fanny that both she and Liam had the same ability to steal away with the belongings of others. When the milkman delivered sour milk and refused to replace it, Fanny took fresh milk *and cream* from his cart. When the dressmaker grimaced at Fanny's unfeminine height and wild golden hair, Fanny absconded with a paper of pins. When the subscription librarian refused to allow Fanny to check out *Madame Bovary*, Fanny took home both *Bovary* and *The Grandissimes*, hidden inside her petticoat pocket. Yes, Fanny and Liam were somewhat kindred souls.

Fanny flung open the door of her armoire and pulled out the skirt she had worn yesterday. She dug deeply into the pocket to retrieve Nora's photograph. Last night she could not bear to look at Nora's smart eyes and determined chin; but tonight—knowing that she might be able to identify Nora's murderer—Fanny was ready to face Nora.

Fanny dusted the photograph against her skirt and held it up to the gaslight. Yes, there were Nora's intelligent expression, her bright eyes and outthrust chin. There, too, was her dark hair, not only tumbling across her shoulders but—as Fanny's eyes widened in surprise—curling across the tops of her breasts, around her nipples, and down along the rest of her naked body.

Fanny had never before seen a photograph of a woman's naked body—she had barely looked at herself completely naked—and the image of Nora absorbed her entirely. Fanny was mesmerized by Nora's pale breasts and strangely dark nipples, by her small waist and the graceful bend of her hips. Finally, Fanny was drawn to the inky-black patch of hair on Nora's lower regions. Fanny knew she should turn away but couldn't. Nora's posture was striking and proud, commanding Fanny to admire her, and reminding Fanny of the proud Amazonian figures fashioned in one of the murals at the Centennial exhibit a few years back.

But just as Fanny basked in Nora's majestic glow, she recalled other types of photographs of naked women. Photographs that her father had railed against from both his law office and pulpit. Photographs that lead men and women down the path to Hell and Damnation. Photographs that were sold to men in darkened saloons and alleyways. Photographs that men—and even boys—displayed in their masculine domains.

From beyond her bedroom door Fanny heard Sylvia calling out her *goodnights*. In quick response, Fanny hid the photograph under the linens in her bottom drawer, knowing she would look at it in the daylight, searching it once more for a studio name or inscription or address.

Nora's naked image haunted Fanny as she fell asleep. Was it an immoral image designed to satisfy a man's sexual urges? Or was it a classical pose, a model for a mural or statue? Fanny reached no decision before she yielded to sleep and was completely surprised in the morning to remember that her dreams were about her own naked body.

13.

ALTHOUGH THEY SHARED A LAW OFFICE for ten years, Oscar Newcomb and Lawrence Decatur had hardly a single thing in common. Fanny's father had been forgetful of comb, razor, and soap; Lawrence was always consummately groomed, carefully manicured, and fashionably suited. Father had forgone alcohol, tobacco, and gambling; Lawrence embraced all three. Oscar Newcomb offered free legal counsel to the poorest citizens of New Orleans; Lawrence Decatur's clients came from the best and most prosperous families in New Orleans. And he charged them accordingly.

Despite their seventeen-year age difference, Oscar and Lawrence had been fast friends and honest partners. For as long as Fanny could remember, the Law Offices of Newcomb & Decatur had been her second home. Oscar Newcomb's humble rooms above the law offices had been her first.

And now, almost a year after Oscar's death and eight months since Fanny had moved out of her room upstairs, she stood at the open doorway to Lawrence's office. Although he had always been particular in his own appearance, Lawrence gave no thought at all to his office's outfitting. Over the years, Fanny had organized his papers, shelved his law books, proofread his legal briefs, and made sure that his bills—especially his restaurant bills—were paid on time. Since her absence, Lawrence's office had suffered: dust lingered upon every surface, newspapers were stacked haphazardly, and empty bottles of wine were left to roll on the carpet like bowling pins. And just what was that wretched odor? Soured *lait*? Gumbo remains? Both?

In the middle of his chaotic office, Lawrence slept soundly in the plush cushions of his leather chair; his feet anchored on his desk, his head thrown back, his mouth wide open, his snores so ferocious that Fanny had heard him from outside the main office door. And despite his well-known sartorial splendor and his elegant appearance at the jail on Monday, Fanny could see that he was beginning to take on the shopworn semblance of his office: stained cravat, frayed collar, and—could those be?—holes in the bottom leather of both shoes.

Fanny winced to see Lawrence's personal and professional disorder but knew he deserved it. She would have taken care of everything for him if he had respected her professionally and paid her the salary she was worth. Instead, he had tried to romance her into working for no wages. Fanny removed her glove and rapped sharply on the unshut door.

Lawrence awoke in mid-snore, snorting in rapid succession like a bewildered bull. He opened his eyes briefly, closed them, and then put his hands up to his eyes, rubbing them deeply. Fanny waited as Lawrence lowered his feet from the desk to the floor, slowly acknowledging her presence. She entered his office careful to keep her skirts from toppling the towers of books and papers.

"*Good Lord, Goldenlocks*! You could give a man some warning!" Lawrence's voice betrayed the natural softness of someone just awakened. He looked around his office in careless apology. "If I had known you were com—"

"But Uncle Lawrence," Fanny replied sweetly, surprised at how much she enjoyed Lawrence calling her *Goldenlocks*. "You knew I'd be back."

"I did?"

"Certainly. I've come to find out what the Under Commissioner told you about Karl."

Lawrence shook off all appearances of sleep and sharpened his eyes in displeasure. "Good Lord Fanny, you're not still poking into this mess, are you?" When Fanny did not answer, he said, "This is not like the time you terrorized the neighborhood to find out who took your rabbit." When she still did not answer, he added, "Or the time when you chased that boy who grabbed your hat. Through the Quarter. For six very long blocks."

Finally, he said, "This is murder and the police are involved. Dammit girl, you're dealing with things you don't understand."

"Then explain them to me. Explain everything to me." Fanny removed a box of cigars from the client chair and sat, ready to keep her silence until she was answered. But to her surprise Lawrence was also silent. So silent, that she wondered if perhaps he had fallen back asleep. With his eyes open.

Then slowly, he leaned over his desk, opened the box, and pulled out a crisp cigar. Fanny groaned inwardly; once Lawrence started a cigar, he rarely spoke before finishing it.

"All right then, here's what *I* think," she said. "My best student was murdered within an hour of leaving my classroom. Dr. Olive Giddings—who was called to the murder scene immediately afterward—says that Nora was strangled. But the police and the Chief Surgeon at Charity claim that Nora died by having her throat slashed. And that she was disemboweled. The newspapers even go so far as to claim that Jack the Ripper murdered her. Sylvia's carpenter—who clearly has an alibi for the time of Nora's murder—is arrested at Wisdom Hall and the police have no interest in hearing anything about his innocence. And now you...." Fanny stumbled for a second. She had adored Lawrence for most of her life, but returning to the Law Offices today put her feelings in a tumble. How could she describe him? "The best damn lawyer in New Orleans," Fanny said with a flourish, "is siding with our corrupt police force. Have I missed anything?"

"Yes, you have." Lawrence jerked the cigar from his mouth. "Not only did Karl Schultz murder that woman but he is suspected of killing more."

Fanny chilled, suddenly uncomfortable in the chair. "The Under Commissioner told you that?"

"No, the Commissioner."

"Did he give you reasons?"

"He did. Reputable citizens of New Orleans have sworn that Karl Schultz had been following that woman for a few weeks. And he's been seen with other women of her type."

As Lawrence stuck his cigar in his mouth and sat back in his chair, Fanny asked, "Can you get me in to see Karl?"

"No, I cannot."

"Just one visit?"

"Just one? Will you swear to it?"

"On a stack of Bibles." Fanny looked amongst the piles of books as if she expected to see a stack of Bibles awaiting her.

"I was thinking more of your father's grave."

"Really, Lawrence! Father would be the last person to want me to swear an oath on his grave."

"If your father could see his daughter now—too stubborn to listen to me even when she knows that all I want is her happiness." Lawrence looked soulfully at Fanny as if his sad eyes could persuade her to agree with him.

But Fanny was immune to Lawrence's pleadings; she had plans for today and would not let Lawrence jeopardize them. "Let me know when I can talk to Karl."

"When sheep heads grow on apple trees," Lawrence quoted his favorite line from *If Ever I Cease to Love*. "That's when I'll let you talk to that murderer!"

Fanny resisted the desire to place a farewell kiss on Lawrence's cheek and exited from the room with as much grace as she could manage. Fanny surely loved Lawrence Decatur, but *Damnation*, how he vexed her.

WITHIN HALF AN hour, Fanny was once again inside Mrs. O'Sullivan's Palace of Pleasure and feeling none of the awkwardness of her last visit. She watched as the landlady's finger traced the blue ink along the flyleaf of the small hardback book in her hand. "That's Nora's signature, to be sure."

"I found the book underneath some of my typewriting lessons. Nora must have left it there accidentally." Fanny lied. This was her own copy of *William Shakespeare's Love Sonnets* and instead of eating breakfast, she had spent an hour copying Nora's signature from her school application. Only then was she confident enough to forge Nora's name into the book.

Although it was after noon, Mrs. O'Sullivan wore an emerald dressing gown and her hair hung loosely about her shoulders. As she watched the landlady, Fanny wondered which of her sides Mrs. O'Sullivan would show first—the kindly mother figure or the single-minded business woman—and which would provide Fanny the most information.

The landlady shook her head. "I knew she could read, but love poems? What got into the girl?" From the top of the stairs, Fanny heard a man's voice bellowing, "More shaving water, dammit. And hot this time." Almost before his yell faded, a small colored boy clasping a creaking bucket ran down the stairs. He turned toward the back of the house from where Fanny caught the tempting fragrance of strong coffee.

"Romance is always very popular with girls," said Fanny truthfully. "And when I saw the book, I was sure that her family would want to have it. I thought you would be able to pass it on to them." *And it was the only way I could think of to talk to you again.*

"Oh, there's no family here in New Orleans. They're all still in the old country. Nora was the first to come over, all by herself."

"Nora's entire family's in Ireland?" Fanny was deflated. The people who knew her best could tell Fanny nothing. A sudden thought struck. "They know what's happened, don't they? Someone wrote them?" Even as Fanny asked, she realized that no letters would have reached Ireland in the week since Nora's death.

"Didn't have to write anyone. Her murder was published in newspapers all over the world, just like all the other Ripper's victims. Her name was all over Dublin almost as soon as it was in New Orleans and her da sent me a cable telling me where to send her money."

Fanny flinched. Money. Of course Nora had money. After all, it was *why* girls prostituted themselves. But how much could she have? And was it enough to matter to anyone?

"But there wasn't any money to send home." offered the landlady. "Nora spent it all. Frittered it away, just like all of the others."

Fanny repressed an objection; Nora was not the type to fritter anything, although her funeral at Metairie Cemetery certainly cost *someone* a pretty penny. Was that where Nora's money was spent? "I'd like to send a letter of condolence to her parents. May I get their address from you?"

"It's upstairs dear and I'd be glad to get it for you but can't just now."

Fanny was sure that if the landlady wanted her to have the address, she could have sent someone up for it. She didn't want Fanny to get in touch with the Keegan family. Mrs. O'Sullivan *was* hiding something.

Suddenly, a man—stout and swarthy—burst from an upstairs room. He was without a shirt and his pants hung low on his hips. His suspenders looped to his knees. He roared like a lion at the zoo, "Millie! Where the hell are you?"

From the back hallway came a pale girl in a pink negligee, her long strawberry-blond hair scattered about her. She quickly took the man's arm and tried to turn him back into the room but he fought her off. He wobbled unevenly and then raised his hand as if to slap her. But the girl deflected the hit and deftly pulled the man back into the room and shut the door.

"Italians," Mrs. O'Sullivan growled dismissively.

"Mrs. O!" A woman's voice reverberated throughout the house so loudly that Fanny was unsure where it came from. "Mrs. O, now!"

Despite the urgency of the voice, the landlady remained calm and walked Fanny toward the front door. "If you give me Nora's family's address," Fanny tried one last time, "I can send the book back to them."

"There's no need for that." Mrs. O'Sullivan opened the door, took Fanny's elbow, and pushed her expertly across the threshold of the crimson-colored door. "I'll give it to one of the girls; as a memento of Nora."

FANNY SAT ON the end of the wooden bench outside Mrs. O'Sullivan's house, thinking about money. Could the motive for Nora's murder really be so straightforward? But how much money could a seventeen-year-old girl have? And which of the suspects needed money enough to kill for it?

Terence and Gabriel Boylan came from money and besides, what would a priest and a seminarian need money for? Sylvia had mentioned that Terence was responsible for raising funds for new stained glass windows at St. Alphonsus but would someone really kill a girl to buy a window?

Fanny knew nothing at all about the incomes or reserves of John Remington or his nephew Lester Adams. She imagined that a doctor of Remington's status should be well-established financially but if Remington's disinterest in money was similar to Olive's, he could be a pauper and in need of money. Of Adams, Fanny had no idea.

Fanny's reverie was interrupted by a low feminine voice. "Why can't you leave Nora alone?"

A girl eased onto the other end of the bench, keeping her distance from Fanny. From the bright tone of her hair, Fanny realized that it was the girl from Mrs. O's who had stood up to the half-naked man. Fanny tried to remember the girl's name. *Millie*, was that it?

The girl crossed her arms in front of her, molding the filmy negligee to her body. "I said, wh—"

"Because Nora was one of my students."

"I know *that*. But what are you doing here again?"

Just across the street, a train whistle shrilled and Fanny suddenly wondered if Nora had ever wanted to take that train somewhere beyond Mrs. O'Sullivan's. Looking down the street, Fanny realized that there were many other red doors among the houses and wondered if they were all houses of prostitution. And if a woman sitting at a streetcar stop in a pink robe and negligee was acceptable behavior for this neighborhood. Perhaps it was Fanny, dressed in severe, solid brown, her mind crammed with knowledge of accounting, typewriting and the law, who did not belong on this street. Fanny responded, "The first time I came here—"

"On Tuesday," interrupted Millie.

"I came to pay my respects."

Millie almost sneered at Fanny. "But you were at the cemetery the day after that. And now you're back here today."

Fanny wondered suddenly if instead of wanting something from her, Millie wanted to give her something. Perhaps if Fanny helped the girl along, she would tell Fanny everything about Nora's life at Mrs. O'Sullivan's.

"Although everyone knows who killed Nora," Fanny winced inwardly as she condemned Karl as a murderer, "we don't know why. And that puzzles me. You see, I know Karl and I know Nora. And I just don't know why Karl would kill her."

Millie's lips pursed in clear disapproval. She dug into a pocket of her robe and drew out a silver cigarette case and a box of matchsticks. With a feminine grace that rivaled Sylvia's, Millie withdrew and lit a pastel papered cigarette. She turned her head to look at Mrs. O'Sullivan's front steps and Fanny followed her gaze. Millie turned back to Fanny, snorting rough smoke in her face.

Fanny did not flinch as the smoke assaulted her eyes. *You sat down next to me. What do you want to say to me?*

"There are some other men who may have killed Nora," continued Fanny. "If I tell you their names, will you tell me if Nora knew them? If they ever visited her here?"

Millie shrugged her shoulders. Fanny took it as acquiescence and asked, "Pierre deVille?"

Millie looked through the haze of smoke at the houses across the street. Her long eyelashes appeared to flutter but said nothing. Fanny thought of the portrait of Nora nude. "Did Nora have her photograph taken at his studio?"

A door slammed behind them. Fanny turned around to see the boy in front of Mrs. O'Sullivan's red door, desperately seeking someone. He spied the woman and girl on the bench and ran down the steps toward them. Fanny would have to hurry.

"What about Terence and Gabriel Boylan? Terence is a priest at St. Alphonsus; his brother Gabriel is a seminarian?"

Millie licked a dried ash off her bottom lip.

"What about John Remington and Lester Adams? They're doctors. Perhaps there was a medical emergency and they were called here. Lester Adams runs the Charity Hospital ambulance."

Millie turned suddenly toward Fanny but Fanny realized that Millie's gaze was focused on the boy as he ran up to them. "Miss Millie, Mrs. O'Sullivan says to get in the house this instant."

Millie dropped the cigarette to the ground and leveled her gaze at Fanny. Her voice was so low that

Fanny strained to hear her. "What makes you so sure that Karl didn't kill Nora? If you'd seen the way he looked at her...."

Fanny grabbed at Millie's shimmering pink sleeve, suddenly aware that the robe was made of much finer material than anything she owned. "Karl knew Nora? You saw them together?" Fanny made the only connection possible. "He visited her here?"

Millie pulled away from Fanny without answering. She ran down the gravel path and up Mrs. O'Sullivan's front steps, where the door opened before her just as she reached it. Fanny realized that the large black ribbon of mourning had been removed from the crimson-colored door. Business as usual.

Fanny exhaled sharply, only faintly aware that the boy had picked up Millie's discarded cigarette and gleefully drew it to his lips.

14.

OLIVE WAS INTENT UPON MAKING SHORT work of Fanny's suspicions regarding John Remington and so on Thursday morning she located the doctor behind his desk at Charity Hospital. Although the window behind him provided ample light, a small oil lamp burned on his desk, glowing over his stack of open books.

Olive sat in the wingchair directly across from Remington's desk before saying, "I came by Sunday morning to see you."

Remington took out his pouch of tobacco. "Sunday?"

"I wanted to discuss Nora Keegan, the girl who was killed at Conner's Court."

Remington leaned back in his chair until he almost rested against the wall behind him. "Yes, I thought you'd be here sooner or later about her. I assumed that you were the 'rude, bossy woman' hampering the ambulance surgeon's work." He began to prime his pipe. "Tell me, was the girl a regular patient of yours?"

Olive wanted to tell him that Nora had attended classes at Wisdom Hall but Sylvia had forbid her to do so. Instead, she said, "I never saw her before that night." But seeing John Remington serenely drawing air into his pipe rankled her. "What about you?"

He answered readily, as though he had anticipated her question. "We never saw her at Charity." He puffed and continued, "Under that name, at least. And I arrived at Conner's Court after the ambulance started its return."

"You were at Conner's Court?"

"I go to many ambulance calls. Does that surprise you?" Remington looked over at Olive, his face clouded by the smoke. "When I hire a new ambulance surgeon I must check the quality of his work. But by the time I arrived only the police and the gawkers were left. What was it that you wanted to know on Sunday?"

For the first time, Olive had to give some credence to Fanny's assertion. Since Remington had been at Conner's Court, it was possible that the police could see him as a suspect. But Olive knew that if she probed deeply enough this morning, she could clear Remington of Fanny's accusation. "Everything, starting with the cause of death."

"Cause of death was a deep cut across the throat. Straightforward. To the point. Much like Jack the Ripper. Which, unfortunately, is just what the newspapers wanted to hear."

"But that's impossible." Olive pulled forward in the wingchair. "When I saw her, she was still warm. It was clear that she had been strangled."

Remington looked at her cautiously. "I performed the post-mortem myself Saturday morning. Her neck was cut straight through."

Olive sat straight in her chair. This was all wrong. John Remington was supposed to tell her that he had never been to Conner's Court and confirm that Nora had been strangled. Instead...but no, Olive could never believe that Remington would lie to her. Someone must have lied to Remington. Most likely it was that sniffling, arrogant man who had challenged her on Sunday morning.

"Dr. Adams."

Olive jumped slightly, alarmed that Remington read her mind. Yes, that was the rude doctor's name. A second later Olive caught the professional inflection in Remington's voice and realized that they were not alone. The formal, stiff Remington—no intimate to female physicians—had returned. Hidden within the confines of the tall chair, Olive turned her head toward the door and saw Lester Adams, framed by globes of the hallway gaslight. She turned away, hoping that Remington would not introduce them. She was not afraid to face Lester Adams again nor be judged 'rude and bossy' by him. But she was not eager to see him.

Adams stayed close to the door, seemingly respecting Remington's private consultation. "The meeting is starting. Your absence has already been noted."

"I'll be there in a moment." Remington closed the books on his desk, stacking them upon each other as he stood up. "You'll relay my message?"

"As you wish, Uncle. But they don't look like they want to wait for long." Adams shut the door.

Remington thumbed through a stack of papers on his desk and handed a crisp single sheet of hospital stationery to Olive. "Here's my post-mortem report on Nora Keegan. You should find what you're looking for here."

WHAT IS THIS? Olive closed her eyes and rolled back in Remington's desk chair. She rested her head against the wall, hoping to shake the information into something logical. Nothing made sense.

The Death Register entry she had read on Sunday clearly stated that Nora Keegan died from strangulation. Yet Remington's post-mortem report—written in his own hand—stated that in addition to having her throat slashed, Nora had multiple lacerations to her lower regions and that parts of her skin had been cut away.

Had Olive pulled the wrong Register or read the wrong entry on Sunday? Had she overlooked *pages* of information? She turned up the watch brooch on her bodice and adjusted her eyes to the small numbers. Ten-twenty. Remington had said he would be in meetings until after luncheon time and Olive needed to open the infirmary at 2pm. She could leave him a note but what could she write? "Your post-mortem report entirely contradicts the entry in the Register. Why? Is it possible you recently examined the corpses of two women named Nora Keegan?"

Olive brightened at this last thought. Although two Nora Keegans were unlikely, in a city with so many Irish, it was possible. She placed the post-mortem report squarely in the center of Remington's blotter. She looked once more at her watch and realized that she had read it wrong a few minutes ago. Eleven-twenty. There was no time to write Remington. Just as well, for she needed more time to think this through. As Olive reached the door, it rolled into her, forcing her back a few steps.

"You again?" Lester Adams stood before her. Through the long thin hair that crisscrossed his almost bald head, Adams scratched at his patchy scalp. "I thought I got rid of you on Sunday."

Olive had ignored many men in her life. She had looked through disapproving cousins, walked past bullying medical students, and closed her ears to degrading professors. In fact, Olive had ignored most of the men in her life; it was the only way she could get her work done. But from the moment he had dismissed her at Conner's Court, from the moment he had ordered her away from Nora Keegan's limp body and *Olive had obeyed*, she found it hard to ignore Lester Adams. She sensed that his rudeness toward her was not the result of mere ignorance about the abilities of women to practice medicine but something else entirely. Something deeper.

What's more, Olive did not want to ignore Lester Adams. She wanted to set him straight about her abilities as a doctor. But as the granddaughter and niece of two of Louisiana's finest soldiers, Olive had learned the art of picking her battles and she knew her confrontation with Lester Adams was not to be today. She would not allow him to distract her from her purpose.

Olive walked past Adams and into the hospital corridor. He followed and silently began walking alongside her. She picked up her stride but he was taller than she and kept pace easily alongside her. Another smock-coated doctor attempted to get Adams' attention but he shook him off. Olive continued along the hallway and turned the corner into the main lobby. She passed the front desk with Adams at her side, dogging her steps. Nervousness, an old unwelcome emotion, began to creep through her veins. How much farther would he follow her?

The guard opened the front door and Olive descended the steps. Lester Adams was at her side, a line of sweat on his forehead collecting the patches of skin that fell from his head. Olive realized that she was perspiring also.

The streetcar had already left its stop and was coming toward her. Olive knew that if she signaled it, the driver would stop the mules and let her board. Almost as if he anticipated her successful escape, Lester Adams stopped directly in front of her. He leaned toward her, his face inches from hers, the scaly red scars glowing in the sunlight. A slight breeze stirred up along the street, gathering Olive's skirt. Thin flakes of skin drifted from Adams head to his shoulders. There was only one thought on Olive's mind.

"Psoriasis."

Lester Adams' stance shifted as though he'd been nudged from behind. "What did you say?"

"Psoriasis. It's the Greek word for a skin condition such as yours." Olive waved her hand at the streetcar conductor and watched with satisfaction as the driver pulled his mules toward her.

"I know what psoriasis is. I *am* a doctor."

And so am I.

As Olive entered the car, Adams stood on the walkway, his small eyes squinting at her. Not until she sat on the hard bench did Olive feel rid of him. Minutes later she recalled that Lester Adams' name was also on Fanny's suspect list. Olive's battle with Adams would have to be sooner rather than later. But the next time she would be prepared to face him.

FANNY MET OLIVE'S streetcar at Wisdom Hall. "Well? What did you find at Charity?"

Olive steeled herself. Since she had met Fanny four months ago, Olive had come to admire Fanny's good sense and reasoning, her almost intuitive understanding of people, as well as her ability to endure Sylvia's regal dictates. But sometimes Fanny's persistence was irritating. This was one of those times. Still, there were a few facts that Olive would share with Fanny.

"Dr. Remington said he was at Conner's Court after Nora was murdered," Olive announced. "He was there to review his ambulance surgeon's work."

Olive walked up the front steps and entered Wisdom Hall. Fanny pursued her through the halls to the infirmary doorway. "Did you ask him if he knew Nora?"

She wanted to answer *Of course not* but knew it would raise Fanny's ire. Instead, she said, "I had almost no time with him before he went to a meeting and then...Lester Adams showed up."

"Dr. Lester Adams," said Fanny. "Suspect number...well, we didn't really number them, did we? But meeting up with Adams was an excellent opportunity. What did you find out from him?"

As Olive unlocked the infirmary door, she explained her encounter with Lester Adams, from his hostile voice in the doorway demanding to know her name, to his aggressive pursuit of her to the streetcar.

"He knows exactly who you are," Fanny decided quickly. "He was just taunting you."

"Yes, he was."

"But...you had one of the suspects right in front of you and asked him nothing about Nora Keegan?"

"No, I had two of the suspects right in front of me and asked neither anything. I'm a doctor, not a detective. I don't enjoy prying into people's lives." Olive folded her arms, attempting to defend herself against Fanny's enthusiasm. "But *you're* enjoying this, aren't you?"

Fanny seemed to understand exactly what Olive meant and answered honestly. "Yes I am. I wish all of this had never happened but I do find it challenging to seek out the truth. I've never been able to use my intelligence, my full intelligence before. And I like it."

"I can understand that certainly," Olive replied just as honestly.

"I knew you would. You must use your intelligence to heal people everyday."

"But I learned from books and studied with great doctors. You...well, you learned how to think all this through, how to investigate, on your own. Or did your father teach you all of this?"

"He taught me some but I really learned from watching him and Lawrence make mistakes. And they made a lot of them." For a moment Fanny was silent, overwhelmed with longing for her father. And surprisingly for Lawrence, although she could not really describe those longings. She pulled a cloth-covered object from her pocket and unfolded it to reveal her photograph of Nora. "I wanted to show you this."

Olive looked at Nora's face and then quickly swept over her unclothed body. She turned the photograph over, just as Fanny had, looking for any photographer's inscription. "Yes, that's her. Where did you get this?"

"At her landlady's house."

"She gave it to you?"

"No, I found it."

Olive studied Fanny, as if trying to understand exactly what she meant. "What did Sylvia say?"

"I haven't shown it to Sylvia." *And I don't know if I will.* "What do you think it means?"

"It's called pornography but I'm sure you know that. Many girls pose for these. It's often the first step toward prostitution. Posing for such pictures must be part and parcel of a prostitute's life."

"Pierre deVille is a photographer. It's possible he took this photograph of Nora. And maybe he killed her because of it."

Olive shrugged. What response was Fanny looking for? "Anything is possible."

Obviously unsatisfied, Fanny took the photograph from Olive's hands and slid it back into her pocket. From another pocket, she pulled a folded piece of newspaper. "I thought you'd want to see this also. I showed it to Sylvia already. It was in the *Nightly Sensation.*"

Olive took the paper from Fanny. It was an advertisement, large enough to take up a quarter page of the newspaper.

**Jack the Ripper revealed!
Jack the Ripper caught in the act!
Villainy exposed!**

Photographic Exhibit opens Saturday evening at the St. Charles Hotel, 7pm, until the New Orleans public is satisfied.

Admission $1.00.

**Pierre deVille, Photographer and
Master of the Magic Lantern**

Corner of Canal and Royal Streets

"If Pierre deVille was near enough to photograph the murderer, he was near enough to be a suspect. I'm going to his studio this afternoon and I'm going to ask Sylvia to go to St. Alphonsus to question Terence and Gabriel Boylan." Fanny pulled the paper from Olive's hands and pushed it into her pocket. "But we've still got to find out about Lester Adams."

"Don't expect me to do it. I can't stand the man and he's made it plain that he detests me." Olive looked at her hands and the fresh black newspaper ink that was smeared all over her fingers. "And don't think you'd be any good with him either. You and I are cut too much from the same cloth. I'm not sure if Lester likes ladies but I know for certain that he hates women."

"Well, if it's *ladies* he likes," Fanny smiled slyly, "we'll have to find some way to send Sylvia to question him."

15.

BY MIDAFTERNOON FANNY WAS AT PIERRE deVille's studio located on the top floor of a professional building at the corner of Royal and Canal Streets. Fanny was very familiar with Canal Street—the Law Office of Decatur & Newcomb was just a few blocks uptown—but she had never been to this building. Nor had she been to a photographer's studio, although she and her father had their photograph taken at the 1884 Cotton Exposition.

A young boy answered her knock and let her into a small room where framed photographs set from chair rail to ceiling on every wall. The boy walked through a pair of long draperies and left Fanny alone. She surveyed mothers with babies, boys with dogs, men with cigars, young men with horses, and innumerable photographs of caskets with tiny infants bundled inside. As Fanny reviewed the mass of photographs, she became aware that something was wrong with each one of them: half of a face was cut from the picture; a boy's cowlick was not smoothed down; eyes were colored with thick blobs of paint.

Fanny carried with her the photograph of Nora naked. Although she had searched the city directory and knew that twenty photographers advertised studios in New Orleans, she couldn't help but feel hopeful: Nora had had her photograph taken and one of the police's suspects was a photographer.

Fanny walked back and forth on the hardwood floor, bringing her heels down heavily, hoping to remind the boy that she was waiting. When a few more minutes passed and the boy did not return, she walked through the long drapery and then through another set of dark heavy curtains.

The room she entered was awash in sunlight and reflection. From every angle of the room, radiance assaulted her. One wall was completely paned in window glass. Two skylights opened up to the full brightness of late spring. The sunlight reflected in a series of mirrors and magnified throughout the studio. Fanny squinted, then closed her eyes entirely. She heard the sound of canvas falling and the light dulled. The fragrance, almost a stench, of bay rum floated toward her and she opened her eyes slowly. A different sharp odor—as pungent as anything in Olive's infirmary—stung at her like an angry bee.

A man—older than Fanny by a few years—stood before her. He was without jacket, vest, or cravat, and his white sleeves were folded up above his elbows. His hands and forearms were flecked with white patches of something like dried soda. His complexion was so light, he might be Creole, he might be American. His hair was inky black—blacker than any hair she had seen before— and it grew stiffly around his round face. Even his thin moustache was vibrantly black.

The room overflowed with chairs and rugs, half columns and pedestals, children's toys and plump cushions, broad feathered masks and elaborate Mardi Gras costumes. Feminine accoutrements were everywhere: boas, hats, strands of paste jewels, trays of what Fanny recognized as lip and cheek rouge.

Everything was carelessly deliberate in its enticing artistry. Yet as she looked more closely, she saw that cobwebs hung everywhere, captured savagely by the full light shifting through the windows. Behind a rack of colorful costumes, a tower of dirty teacups balanced under a three-legged chair. Dead flies collected on the windowsill overlooking Canal Street and water stained the artfully draped curtains. Business cards mingled with receipts on the floor. Everything was so out of order that it would take Aunt Esther a week to clean up.

Finally, Fanny saw the business of the studio: the large wooden box camera balanced on its tall tripod; a black box with glass slides beside it; the sitter's chair, poised about eight feet in front of the camera; a wide canvas backdrop of a spreading oak tree behind it.

Just beyond Pierre deVille—for it must be him— Fanny could see an open door with a ruby-colored light glowing from within. She had seen a similar darkened room at the Centennial and knew that glass slides would become photographs inside that room.

What images was deVille developing today? Bridal couples in their wedding finery? Politicians in front of

City Hall? Young Christian Men saluting the Henry Clay statute? Naked girls?

Had this man photographed Nora naked? Had he photographed her murderer? Or was he the murderer and were the advertised photographs of Jack the Ripper an attempt to point attention away from him? But why bother pointing a finger at another when a suspect was already in jail? Why allow yourself to be publicly scrutinized if you were guilty of murder?

Fanny shivered slightly and then remembered: if his advertisement were accurate, he just might have a photograph that could free Karl and identify Nora's real murderer.

"I'm sorry," said Fanny, "but I thought you called me. I have a message for you from Dr. Giddings of St. Charles Avenue. You are the photographer Pierre deVille?" Fanny was gratified that Sylvia and Olive's family was so prominent and was pleased with herself for using the Giddings name.

The photographer nodded.

"Dr. Giddings' daughters operate a settlement house in the Irish Channel called Wisdom Hall. I'm a teacher there. We offer self-improvement classes for our neighbors. Throughout the month, we have a series of lectures organized to provide educational enlightenment. On Saturday nights, we host the neighbors for light entertainment. I have heard from many people about your splendid magic lantern show and wanted to engage you for a show this Saturday night."

"That will be impossible." His voice held no hint of accent, no trace of where in the city he lived.

"It doesn't have to be this week. Next week would be just as fine or the week after. The neighbors are always eager for entertainment."

"If it's entertainment they want, invite them to my new exhibit." The photographer looked around the room until his eyes lit on a stack of broadsides. He picked off the top one and gave it to Fanny. It was an enlargement of the *Picayune* advertisement. "Nothing is more entertaining than Jack the Ripper."

Fanny recoiled, remembering Nora's lifeless body in her casket. How could this man think murder was entertaining? How could he find a madman slashing at innocent women amusing? As she stared at the photographer, she realized that at least one person might find Jack the Ripper entertaining: the madman himself. Emboldened by the memory of Nora's life cut short, Fanny questioned the photographer deliberately, as if he were a well-raised child who would answer truthfully. "Did you murder Nora Keegan?"

The photographer's forehead rose in alarm—at least she thought it was alarm—and his entire hair and scalp lifted in response. Only then did Fanny realize that his unnaturally stiff and ebony-colored hair was a toupee. But the photographer did not answer and Fanny realized her bold effort would not work. She smiled as if embarrassed by her earlier question. "I mean, did you really see the murder of Nora Keegan? That's what I really meant to say. How could you even see anything that night? When it was so dark?"

"Darkness was what I craved. Master photographers have long been able to capture night tableaux with adequate amounts of flash powder," he replied as though from rote. Fanny wondered if he had rehearsed this speech for the police or his Saturday night audience at the Hotel St. Charles. "That night I was testing my own flash concoction."

"But why test in the Irish Channel? Why not here on Canal Street?"

"Canal Street is awash in electrical lights; the Channel courtyards are very, very dark. To truly see if my new flash powder was successful, I had to photograph in total darkness."

Fanny could almost accept deVille's explanation. Canal Street was brightly illuminated with electrical lights and even when she arrived at Conner's Court after Nora's murder, the inner court was close to pitch

118

black. Hadn't Olive said that? But close to midnight, wouldn't an interior windowless room—like deVille's own front parlor—be just as dark as Conner's Court? "May I see your photograph now?"

"Not even the police have seen the photograph." The photographer fixed his dark eyes on her. Once more the photographer's forehead creased, causing his toupee to creep forward. "The entire city will see the photograph for the first time on Saturday night."

Fanny attempted to replicate one of Sylvia's most charming and demanding pouts. "But I have classes to teach Saturday. Can't I see it now?"

"Absolutely not." He stepped toward her sharply. Fanny stood firm but was prepared to run if he touched her. "I can almost understand why you are so persistent about my photograph...living so close to Conner's Court but if I didn't know better, I'd almost think that you had been sent here by one of the newspapers to question me. And that I cannot allow."

He led Fanny through the double curtains and the waiting room door, out of the studio and into the building's hallway. As he locked the door from inside the studio, Fanny pressed her back against the door. She was alarmed that he removed her so quickly from his studio, and even more alarmed that she had learned nothing from him.

Her thoughts were so fixed that she did not notice the man walking along the hallway. With his bowler hat and green checked suit, he looked vaguely familiar. Not until he stood directly in front of her could Fanny identify him. Police Detective Daniel Crenshaw.

The detective looked toward her for the longest minute. No, she realized, he was looking *above* her, trying to read the door sign. She stepped aside, sliding past him and down the four flights of stairs to the street.

FANNY WALKED ALONG Canal Street to the river. Usually, she could watch the busy river for hours, entertained by the ships and sailors, the exotic cargoes, and even the muscular roustabouts. But today she crossed to the other side of the street and walked back down Canal Street finally stopping across the street from Pierre deVille's building. The gold foil letters of his business sign glinted across a pair of windows. One of the windows opened and Daniel Crenshaw leaned out of it, knocking ashes from a cigar onto the ledge.

After criticizing Olive so soundly this morning, Fanny could not return to Wisdom Hall without information. Across the street, four stories above her, was one person who might be finding out just what she wanted to know. Fanny sat down on a streetcar bench, waiting for Daniel Crenshaw.

There were many questions in Fanny's mind as she watched Crenshaw exit deVille's building and walk to the streetcar stop in the middle strip of Canal Street. Why had the police believed deVille innocent? What image—if any—had deVille captured during his midnight photography? Despite Olive's claims, was it possible that Nora had been murdered by Jack the Ripper?

Fanny crossed Canal Street going toward the narrow streetcar median, watching the detective's broad back as he waited at the streetcar stop. Beneath his hat, his copper-colored hair ran down the back of his neck, ending in a slight curl. Crenshaw's very real hair reminded her of the photographer's artificial toupee and she looked up at his fourth-floor window. For a second, she thought she saw someone watching her from behind the large gilt letters of the window but then the image was gone.

Crenshaw stepped into a streetcar. Fanny entered behind him. She followed him through the narrow aisle as if they were traveling together. He stopped short at an unoccupied bench and turned toward her.

"Window or aisle?" he asked.

The streetcar lurched forward as the driver coached the mules. Fanny ground her boots into the wooden flooring to keep her footing and gripped the back of a seat. She looked around the car, seeing that all of the other benches had at least one person on them.

"The aisle, thank you." She had been boxed into the window seat on many streetcars, unable to move or leave, and today she would use the aisle seat to her advantage.

In the few days since Daniel Crenshaw arrested Karl Schultz, Fanny had thought about the detective many times. She had read about him in the newspapers and heard no less than three conflicting descriptions of how he tracked down Karl Schultz. In her mind, she had discussed suspects with him and inundated him with questions. His image had even haunted her the night she viewed Nora's photograph. But right now, she had just one question for him.

"Did you see the photograph?" Fanny spoke before turning and was surprised to see that the detective was staring out the window. She tilted her head toward Crenshaw and spoke in a voice she knew only he would hear. "The Ripper photograph?"

Crenshaw ground his jaw sideways, much like Sylvia's dog, Cain. "You're a long way from Annunciation Street."

Fanny looked past Crenshaw through the open window and into the street beyond. The streetscape of five- and six-story embellished commercial buildings along Canal Street was eroding into two-story, darkly painted structures accented by rusty iron railings. She had no idea what streetcar line she was on but clearly, she and the detective were traveling away from the heart of New Orleans.

For the first time, Fanny realized that Crenshaw held an envelope on his lap. "Is that the photograph?"

Crenshaw put his hand on the envelope. "It is *not*."

"But did you see it at least? What did it show?" Fanny asked him as casually in person as she had in her imagination. And then she asked the other question she'd asked him in her mind, many, many times. "What did you tell Karl to make him go with you? It wasn't the mob that scared him into giving you his knife. You told him something that...inspired him."

Crenshaw's index finger tapped lightly on the envelope before he turned to Fanny. "I told him that he might not get hurt but there were women and children who might."

"That's what made him drop the knife?"

"That's what I said to him. There was no telling what was going on in his mind. I was lucky that night. He could just as soon as run up the stairs or jumped over the stairs and plunged into the crowd."

Fanny thought to place her hand on the detective's lower sleeve—something that had always made Lawrence respond favorably—but she stopped herself. Instead, she leaned as close to him as she dared and asked, "Do you really believe that a man who would protect women and children from harm would murder a woman?"

"That investigation is closed."

"But if Pierre deVille was close enough to take a photograph of the murder, how do you know he wasn't the murderer? Doesn't this photograph raise some questions?"

"Not to me, it doesn't. It's shameless sensationalism, that's all it is. And I would think that a woman like you would know better than to give into it. Miss Sylvia and Dr. Olive Giddings should know better, too."

"You seem to know a lot about us at Wisdom Hall."

"You and the Giddings sisters have made yourselves well-known throughout the Channel. Only a deaf man would never have heard of you."

Although Fanny's temper grated at the detective's words, she deliberately misinterpreted his statement and replied, "Of course, Sylvia has had to advertise Wisdom Hall. How else would people know about us? There's never been a school like it before. We teach young women the skills to find good jobs. Or are you one of those men who think that women should not be educated at all?"

"Women," Crenshaw flexed his jaw once again, "will do what they want to do."

"And they want to work." Fanny persisted, not really knowing why it was so important to press her point. "They need education to make a living wage."

"You can educate every blessed rat in the Irish Channel but it won't make a difference. No one leaves the Channel and all of your classes and books and schoolmarming won't change that."

"Of course it will. The Channel is just the beginning for these Irish immigrants."

"The Channel is a sewer. Infested with vermin, thieves, rapists, and murderers who will never come clean no matter how hard you scrub them. You and the Giddings sisters are on a fool's mission and you're lucky you haven't already been murdered in your beds." The detective's face flushed. "Good day to you, Miss Newcomb." In one movement, Daniel Crenshaw deftly maneuvered himself past Fanny and walked off the streetcar.

Fanny slid over to the window seat and gazed out, surprised that the two-story red brick buildings were familiar to her. Crenshaw stopped at one building and wiped his boots on the bottom step of a short stairway leading to a crimson-colored door. He entered Mrs. O'Sullivan's Palace of Pleasure without knocking. As the door closed behind him Fanny enjoyed a new and welcome sensation of satisfaction. Either Daniel Crenshaw often visited houses of prostitution as a customer—a sordid thought that filled her with unexpected disappointment—or else the detective had lied to her and the investigation into Nora's murder was not concluded.

16.

SYLVIA GIDDINGS ANCHORED HER CANE AT the corner of Constance and Josephine Streets and glared at St. Alphonsus Catholic Church. The church's square, twin towers thrust upward and broke into the graying sky like the presence of God Almighty himself. Just beyond the massive and somber brick church, Sylvia could define the other buildings of St. Alphonsus parish. The Boys' School, the Girls' School, and St. Katherine's College were all easily identifiable with their broad expanses of red brick and clear, open windows. Somewhere behind the school buildings was the Convent for the Sisters of Mercy, and across the street from the church was the Rectory for the Redemptorist Fathers, who had organized the St. Alphonsus parish for the Irish almost thirty years ago.

The property holdings of the Redemptorist fathers were vast and Sylvia had heard that the city's communities of Catholics owned at least a quarter of New Orleans. Not only orphanages, schools, churches, and convents, but blocks of buildings and empty lots that might become future orphanages, schools, churches, and convents.

Sylvia turned to glare at St. Mary's Church, an equally monumental sanctuary that was created solely for German Catholics. Sylvia sighed. It bode ill for the neighborhood when German and Irish Catholics would not worship together. And now a German had been arrested for the murder of an Irish girl.

Sylvia entered through the center door and was immediately in the sanctuary looking down the main aisle. She had only been in a Catholic Church once in her life and it was the dark and slightly sinister St. Louis Cathedral. She was not prepared for the lightness and beauty of St. Alphonsus. Although the exterior of the church was red brick, the interior was painted white and trimmed in gold. From the pews that spread across the ground floor, to the balconies that hung on the sides of the church walls, the sanctuary seemed large enough to hold thousands of parishioners. On the ceiling directly above Sylvia was a grouping of intricately painted frescoes. She recognized the Twelve Apostles and the Ascension but the other figures were unknown to her. The elaborate main altar rivaled any monument erected at Metairie Cemetery: fluted columns, kneeling angels, Greek molding, and classical embellishments. Flanking the altar were a pair of huge rounded arch, stained glass windows, and Sylvia could tell by the change in the color of plaster about them that the windows had been recently hung.

A robust melody floated down from the balconies. Not the majestic pomp of the monstrous church organ but the rich texture of a solitary cello. Sylvia set her hand on a pew, overwhelmed by the church's jewel-like radiance and the lyrical warmth of the cello rehearsal. Part of her own mission in opening Wisdom Hall had been to provide the Irish with an introduction to beauty, an access to paintings and sculpture and artistry, and she was suddenly ashamed at herself for not understanding the majesty of her Irish Channel neighbors' own church. Sylvia turned toward the left aisle, sure that she would find the church offices somewhere at the end. She was confronted by life-sized statues in the alcoves and rows of candles flickering before them. Sylvia knew they were Saints but wanted to know their names and their reasons for sainthood. Suddenly, she wanted to know more about this exotic faith that stirred the souls of her students.

Sylvia had arrived at St. Alphonsus with no appointment, no list of questions, no methodology, and no suitable plan of introduction. The only advantage Sylvia had was that Terence and Gabriel Boylan had been pointed out to her once by Liam. She remembered them only as almost mirror images of each other.

Dressed in similar black suits and hats and free from all beards, mustachios and side-whiskers, they looked like twins, rather than elder and younger brother. Could either of these men really know anything about the murder at Conner's Court? Was it blasphemy to even consider that a priest or seminarian could be involved in a murder?

After many refusals, Sylvia had finally agreed to Fanny's plea for information about the Boylan brothers. (At least Fanny had not asked Sylvia to return to Mrs. O'Sullivan's house of prostitution!) Of course, Sylvia would do anything to keep her Grand Plan alive, but she was irritated by Fanny ordering her here and there.

An unreasonable nervousness caught Sylvia by surprise. She would have gladly stuffed every coin in her purse into the church's poor box to avoid having to question the Boylan brothers. But she was a Giddings. She was *Sylvia* Giddings. She had opened Wisdom Hall. She had stood up to policemen, streetcar conductors, and drunken Irishmen. She would not allow a mere man of the cloth to intimidate her.

Sylvia passed the side altar, an elaborate profusion of candles, flowers, and chalk-white plaster. She exited through the door into a corridor. As she had anticipated when she entered the church, the back hallways were similar to her own church. Sylvia found a dark paneled door with the word OFFICE stenciled in white.

Just inside the office, hunched over a dark table, was an old man with a green shawl around his black-suited shoulders. He did not stop as Sylvia closed the door behind her but continued at his task: pulling pennies into a pile and counting silently through his lips.

"Terence Boylan, please," Sylvia said with more confidence than she felt.

The old man stopped, as if he might have heard something. He counted out four more coins and then squinted up at Sylvia. "Got an appointment?"

"No, I haven't." Sylvia stood solidly, giving the man plenty of opportunity to inspect her. At least she hoped he was inspecting her and was duly impressed by her silk gown and Paris bonnet. "But I have very urgent business."

"Father Boylan is a very busy man."

"And so am I."

"Would you like to make an appointment for later in the week?"

"I only need a few minutes of his time. Isn't there some way that I could meet with him this morning?"

"And just what's so important that I should disturb Father while he's preparing to report to the Bishop?"

"My name is Sylvia Giddings. I'm the principal of the Wisdom Hall Settlement House." Sylvia waited for some recognition somewhere from his small, tired eyes and was pleased to see the man tilt his head intelligently. "Yes, I can see you've heard of me. The truth of it is...I need to see Father Boylan today, because...because...." Sylvia looked beyond the man to the crucifix on the wall. Suddenly, a reason occurred to her but did she dare use it? Yes, she did. "Because I've decided to convert to Catholicism."

TERENCE BOYLAN WAS curious about Sylvia's visit. At least she thought it was Terence Boylan who casually entered the office, like an actor crossing a familiar stage. He tossed a straw boater gracefully onto a hat rack, extended his hand toward Sylvia, and directed her from the outer office into what appeared to be his private study. "My secretary said that you were interested in converting to the Catholic faith?"

Sylvia raised a quick prayer to her own church for her apparent betrayal but deep down she knew that Fanny would be impressed by her subterfuge. *She* was proud that her ice-blue gown highlighted the pale perfection of her complexion and made her hair glow beneath her flower-sprigged hat. Even a priest must enjoy the company of an attractive woman.

"As you may know, my sister and I have opened up the Wisdom Hall Settlement House and Infirmary." Sylvia sat in the seat offered her, surprised at its plush firmness. The small study was an artistic extension of the main church, with elaborately carved furniture, plaster statuary on the walls, and a row of arched stained glass windows. Despite the lush religious ornamentation, Sylvia was very much at ease in Boylan's study; it was very much like her father's study, even down to the burgundy upholstery and bottle-green carpet.

"I have the pleasure of knowing your father. Doesn't your family attend Christ Church Episcopal?" He retrieved a pouch and pipe from inside his jacket pocket and began to pack the pipe. Two of the fingers on his left hand were bandaged and they slowed him, causing him to spill tobacco on the desk.

"Since my sister and I have been living in the Irish Channel, we have become immersed in the lives of our students, who are primarily of the Catholic faith. Of course, I had never considered Catholicism. Until recently." Sylvia looked down modestly at her folded hands. She was jarred to see dark brown stains on her right glove and looked accusingly at the priest's hands. Yes, he had dark stains on his fingers and bandages.

"What spurred your interest?" he asked.

"The murder in Conner's Court." Sylvia knew at once that she had his interest. "It was just terrible. And then, as you may have read in the newspapers, the police arrested the murderer at Wisdom Hall." When the priest did not respond, Sylvia said, "I was completely taken in by Karl Schultz. I hired him to install a staircase and windows at Wisdom Hall. He came highly recommended. In fact, he had a letter of recommendation from St. Alphonsus."

"Not from St. Alphonsus himself, I'm sure." The priest smiled calmly.

"No, of course not." Sylvia smiled just as calmly, remembering how much men enjoyed correcting women who made mistakes. "The letter said that Karl had worked here and had done an excellent job. As I as remember, Father Boylan, the letter of recommendation was signed by you."

The priest's smile faded. "Your memory is faulty, Miss Giddings. I signed no such letter. Nor have I ever met the man."

"Never? But didn't he attend St. Alphonsus?"

"Only the Irish attend St. Al's. The Germans attend St. Mary's," the priest explained as if to a child. "But how does the murder persuade you to seek out the Catholic Church?"

"The Irish have taken such comfort during these dark days." The image of a full mug of beer—the most common kind of Irish comfort—crossed Sylvia's thoughts, before she continued, "Comfort from the Church, I mean. The Catholic Church seems to be a great solace to them and I couldn't help but wonder at the strength of their faith. And if it wouldn't be right for me also."

"So you are considering conversion to the Catholic faith based on one murder?"

"But didn't St. Paul convert because...." Sylvia left her question unfinished. Biblical history was not among her talents and she needed to steer this discussion away from holy writ and toward Nora's murder.

"Miss Giddings, although God's ways are mysterious and His hand is capable of turning every evil into something good, I must doubt—"

"But how can you be so sure that this murder isn't a sign from God?"

"Because I was in Conner's Court that night, and from what I witnessed, God's hand was not at work. If anyone was working that night it was the devil himself."

"You were at Conner's Court?" Sylvia had not expected this admission. "Called there because of that poor girl?"

"Unfortunately, more than one woman died in the Channel that night."

Sylvia clutched the arm of the chair. "There was another murder?"

"No, not at all. One of my parishioners died giving birth. I was at Conner's Court to hear her last confession and administer last rites."

Sylvia lowered her head. As a doctor's daughter, she understood exactly what he did not say. "And the baby?"

"Baptized and died that same night." Boylan sighed, as if the revived memory of death was painful to him. "Yes, my brother and I were quite busy that night."

"Your brother?"

"Yes, Gabriel is also in the Church's service and has been assisting me in the Channel."

"Then you were both at the murder?"

"We were both at the deathbed of our parishioner," the priest corrected her. From somewhere in his study a clock chimed the hour and within seconds the man with the green shawl was at the study threshhold. Terence Boylan stood up, "My apologies Miss Giddings, but I have another appointment."

Sylvia anchored her cane and rose slowly from the chair. Once upright, she took the priest's arm. "You and your brother were both at the deathbed of your parishioner— But you were going to say more, weren't you? Before we were interrupted?"

"There's nothing more to say," the priest responded matter-of-factly. "By the time we finished with our work and arrived at Conner's Court, the ambulance had taken that poor murdered woman away."

"That poor murdered woman brought me to you, Father Boylan." Sylvia took the priest's hand in farewell, disregarding any damage to her gloves. "Perhaps God really does move in a mysterious way."

17.

OLIVE STABBED HER LONG FORCEPS deeper into the water boiling on the infirmary stove and gave the instrument a sudden and forceful poke with her wooden tong. Fifteen minutes ago, when Sylvia started describing the previous day's visit to Father Boylan, Olive had been attentive. But it was almost eleven and now she was behind on her infirmary chores. She looked at Fanny and Thomas, who both appeared restless and asked, "Did you talk to his brother?"

Sylvia twisted her lips slightly. She had brought her knitting with her, concentrating as much upon her stitches as her story. "No, but he said he and Gabriel arrived at Conner's Court after the ambulance was gone."

Fanny drummed her index finger on Olive's desk. "It doesn't matter where they were *after* the murder but *before* it."

Olive looked at her watch brooch, counted out five more seconds and then removed the forceps from the boiling water and laid them on the clean toweling. "You didn't talk to the brother at all?"

"No," Sylvia mumbled into the tunnel of the sock. "Since I've already talked to Father Boylan about converting I've got no real reason to see his brother."

"Whatever made you think of telling him you wanted to convert?" asked Fanny.

A sly smile played upon Sylvia's lips. "It was wicked, wasn't it? But it was worth it. It worked, didn't it?"

"I wish it had won you some information we could use." Fanny sighed, her attention turning to Thomas, who stood at one of the infirmary's side windows. His long fingers separated the closed wooden blinds so that he could look outside but not be seen. Olive joined him at the window and Thomas stepped aside, his fingers still holding open the blinds. Olive had to stand on the tips of her toes to look through the opening and into the side yard of Wisdom Hall.

A stranger dressed in a light gray suit and holding a walking stick paced the dirt walkway that connected the infirmary to the street. His face was shadowed from under a brown straw hat but from the way he scratched his ear, once, twice, three times, Olive knew exactly who was trampling the side yard of Wisdom Hall.

"Lester Adams." Olive's hiss rivaled the boiling spit of water on the stove.

Fanny joined Olive and Thomas at the window and widened the blinds slightly. "So that's the man. What's he doing here?"

"Over the last five minutes he's walked back and forth from the street twice." Thomas reported as if he had been waiting for permission to speak. "He sneered at the front door of the infirmary twice and got close enough to read the sign and ring the doorbell. And then he walked back toward the front of the house and then back here again."

Olive watched as Adams scratched the back of his neck. "He must be looking for me." But what did he want with her? Had John Remington sent him?

Adams turned around and headed toward the street. Olive, Fanny, and Thomas shifted in front of the window to watch Adams' progress until he disappeared from view. "Perhaps he's..." Thomas was interrupted by the ring of the front door bell, "gone around to the front door."

"Just as well." Fanny turned to Olive. "We did want Sylvia to talk to him, didn't we?"

But Olive did not want Sylvia interviewing Adams without full preparation. In fact, Olive had already determined that Sylvia would have an opportunity to question Adams at the dedication of Charity Hospital's new ambulance.

Aunt Esther's face appeared in the glass window of the door connecting the infirmary to Wisdom Hall proper. She entered without knocking. "You got a caller, Miss Sylvie. I've put him in your office."

Sylvia collected her knitting. "Thank you, Aunt Esther, I'll be right in to see Doctor Adams."

Esther shook her head. "There's no Doctor Adams, Miss Sylvie. The man waiting in your office is named Gabriel Boylan."

SYLVIA EYED THE bundle of books on her office table. From underneath the sober black ribbon that tied the books together, she read two of the titles, *History of the Catholic Church in North America* and *Christ in America: His Catholic Church, Goodness and Evil.* "You brought these books for me?"

Gabriel Boylan placed his hand on the top book as though he was declaring an oath in court. "My brother told me about your visit yesterday. He said that you were eager for information on the Catholic faith and he suggested I bring these around so that you could begin your studies. These are all glorious books that explain the tenets of Catholicism. I think that you will especially enjoy this one: *Lives of our Lady Saints and Martyrs.* You will certainly be impressed by the sacrifices of these ladies and by their humility and willingness to confess their sins and give their lives to God."

Sylvia did not think Gabriel Boylan looked very much like his brother. Terence Boylan had a commanding presence and the natural confidence of an elder brother and leader. His brother Gabriel was more like...Sylvia suddenly had an image of newsprint: the first printing off the press was always strong and clear, while the second printing was dim and a bit fuzzy in contrast. "Thank you, Father."

"Oh, I'm not a priest, yet. I'm a seminarian and acting Principal of the Boy's School. You can call me Mr. Boylan." He spoke confidently but his eyes wandered around the room passing over her collection of family photographs, stacks of newspapers, and stuffed bookcases. Finally, his eyes wandered out the door and into the hallway. He fingered the rim of his hat.

She was going to invite him to sit but thought better of it. "Would you like a tour of Wisdom Hall? We're very proud of our classroom, although it's quite small compared to any of yours." Without waiting for a reply, Sylvia discretely collected her cane and escorted him from her office into the central hall. She was leading him toward the classroom when he stopped at the foot of the stairs.

"Is this where the murderer was arrested?" He looked up and down the staircase, his eyes lingering in the middle, exactly where Karl had yielded his knife to the policeman. "I thought I'd know it if I ever saw it. The newspapers described it so well."

Sylvia rested her hand on the newel post, glad for its solidness. "The newspapers didn't capture what really happened at all. The police were all over the hall and everyone was frightened to death. Especially Karl."

"Really? From what I heard, he was boasting of his deed. And he strutted out of here like a cock in a henhouse."

"Oh, no." Sylvia shivered slightly. Saturday night was difficult enough but to have Karl so erroneously described was hurtful. "That's entirely untrue."

"But he ran from the police. That much is true, isn't it?" Boylan's voice grew louder. "An innocent man has nothing to run from and so he must be guilty."

Sylvia leaned on the newel post, resisting the desire to set him straight. No one was supposed to know that the women of Wisdom Hall had any interest in releasing Karl from jail by finding the real murderer. And so she said, "But you must admit, the police can make mistakes. And in that case, a man may protest his innocence by evading the police."

"You knew the murderer, didn't you? He was your carpenter?"

Boylan's tone was almost accusatory and Sylvia shrank slightly. Karl's arrest and imprisonment weighed heavily upon her and she didn't want to think or talk about Karl any more. Especially with Gabriel Boylan. If she was going to question the seminarian about Nora, she needed to get him away from the staircase and his absorption in Karl. "Would you like to see the rest of Wisdom Hall?"

The seminarian plucked at the narrow ribbon on his hat. "That would be very pleasant, Miss Giddings, if you have the time."

Sylvia did have the time and she always enjoyed talking about Wisdom Hall. "James Talbot built this house in 1838. It's a grand place. Ideal for my purposes. You see the central hall, of course, and there are rooms on both sides of the hall. On this floor we have my office, which is one of the original double parlors." Sylvia nodded at the room they had just exited. "And then at the end, the winter kitchen. And here's our classroom." Sylvia led him into the artistically decorated room. "Down the hallway is Olive's infirmary, built to her specifications."

Gabriel Boylan crinkled his nose and Sylvia wondered which he disapproved of: a female physician or the acrid odors drifting from the infirmary. She led him back to the central hallway, up the stairs to the second floor. "These are our private quarters. Olive has an office here and we have two rooms for storage."

Sylvia walked slowly up the stairs to the third floor hoping that the seminarian would appreciate the open space as much as she did. Despite the unsightly rain buckets, the clutter of carpenter's tools, and the mishmash of boxes and baskets, the uncovered windows flooded sunlight on the newly plastered white walls. Sylvia glowed in the reflection of light and once more envisioned a small auditorium or a workshop in the space. But Gabriel Boylan was not admiring the sunlight, staircase, or wide-open space. Instead, he stared at a pile of broken furniture and baskets of clothes that had been shoved into a corner.

"Those are from some of Mother's church friends." Sylvia explained. "When they heard I was moving to the Irish Channel, they thought I was opening up a missionary shelter and expected me to give these away."

"And are you?"

Sylvia's reply was cut short by Fanny, who appeared suddenly at the third floor landing and declared, "Don't mind me; I'm just going to check the rain buckets."

Sylvia was so glad to see Fanny that she completed introductions in record time.

"You're Oscar Newcomb's daughter?" asked the seminarian.

"Guilty," replied Fanny.

Sylvia tensed. In addition to being an attorney, Oscar Newcomb had been a famously eccentric preacher, who had been both respected and ridiculed by local churchmen. Sylvia wondered what the seminarian thought of Fanny's father. If he said one bad word about Oscar Newcomb, she would refute him immediately.

To keep Gabriel Boylan silent, Sylvia replied to his earlier comment: "It was never my intention to give shelter or food. There are plenty of places that offer charity. I want to provide an education that will lead to a good job and a future."

"I understand that you are charming our Channel girls into learning such vital subjects as French and German."

Fanny replied promptly. "As long as *your* schools stop educating girls at the sixth grade, Channel girls will need a helping hand."

"But a woman's job—as you put it—is to take care of her husband and children. She should never take employment away from a man."

"You know the war left the south without her men," Fanny replied. "There will never be enough men for women to marry and spinsters must work. And they must have an education."

"Is that one of your father's ideas?"

"It was," Fanny smiled. "But now it's all mine."

The seminarian continued his silent scrutiny of the third floor until his eyes lighted on the spiral staircase. Suddenly Sylvia blurted, "Karl was working on that when he was arrested."

The seminarian appeared to study every element of the staircase—the steps and risers, the balusters and handrail—even the sensuous curve of the stairs itself. "The man seems to have done a fine job."

"You talk as though you didn't know him," said Fanny.

"No, I've never met him."

"But he told me that he had seen you at St. Mary's."

"The man is not only a murderer but a liar."

"But he did work at St. Alphonsus," Sylvia persisted on Fanny's behalf.

"He didn't work there for long," the seminarian conceded. "And you would really have to ask Terence about him. He deals with the carpenters at both churches. Terence has been adding so many embellishments that we've had workers there night and day. Have to shoo them out each day to say Mass." He turned from the staircase and smiled at Sylvia. "My brother is leading the efforts to raise a subscription for seventeen more stained glass windows. And he's also looking for money to tile the sanctuary."

At the mention of a subscription, Sylvia relaxed slightly. She was used to dealing with people who wanted money from her. Had a donation to the St. Alphonsus building cause been Boylan's purpose all along?

But Gabriel Boylan did not pursue any subscription. Instead he removed his watch from his pocket and quickly snapped it open and shut. "I must go." He started towards the stairs to the second floor. "Mass is in a few minutes."

Although Fanny hung back, Sylvia pursued him to the top of the stairs. But the seminarian could not be deterred and headed down the stairs without Sylvia. At the second floor landing he turned upwards and said, "I hope you enjoy your reading, Miss Giddings. And when you are finished, perhaps you'll share the books with Miss Newcomb."

Once she heard Gabriel Boylan's footsteps reach the front door and was sure he had let himself out of Wisdom Hall, Sylvia turned to Fanny. "What do you think? Could he be Nora's murderer?"

"How would I know?"

"But how will we know when we've found Nora's murderer? He's not going to confess to us, not someone who would do something so awful. And not when his actions are being covered up by Ripper hysteria."

"We might not find the murderer at all." Fanny started downstairs. "We might just find information that incriminates the murderer and then hand it to the police." She thought of the stolen photograph of naked Nora in her bureau drawer; she still had not shown it to Sylvia. "We might also collect things."

"What type of things?"

"Oh, business correspondence, newspaper articles, diaries, photographs. Father and Lawrence sifted through everything they could—what they were told and what they collected—and reconciled it with what they knew to be true." Fanny had watched the men at their work but had never put their technique into words. "Father was a master at understanding how people really felt and he could discern when someone lied." She cringed as she remembered the lies her father had caught her at but then shook off the memory. "Sometimes I wondered if there wasn't something Divine about Father's ability to discover the truth."

As they reached the second floor landing, Sylvia asked, "You think God guided his hand?"

"Well, Father did claim that angels rescued him from prison during the war."

"Do you really think someone religious like Terence or Gabriel Boylan could kill someone?"

"Father was religious and he could have killed someone, I'm sure of it."

Sylvia put a hand on Fanny's arm. "Fanny, whatever your father did in the war was something that all our men had to do."

"I don't mean the war, Sylvia. I mean...when a religious man believes himself shrouded in righteousness, he will do anything he thinks needs to be done. At any time." Fanny looked down the stairs towards the central hall. "We must be very careful with the Boylan brothers. I know religious men and I assure you, they will murder when they believe they are justified."

"Maybe we're going about this the wrong way," said Sylvia. "Gabriel and Terence Boylan and these other men have no reason to tell us the truth. They might not even have told the police the truth. Instead of questioning them directly, perhaps we should question people who know them."

"But we don't know anyone who knows these men," said Fanny. "Do we?"

"What about Lawrence Decatur? Hasn't he sued or defended almost everyone in New Orleans? He must know something about these men."

Sylvia watched Fanny closely: was she smiling just a little at the mention of Lawrence's name? Sylvia had noted the affectionate undercurrent between Fanny and Lawrence at the police station and her curiosity had been piqued. She was honest enough to admit that Lawrence Decatur was an extremely attractive man, and knew that his public reputation as a litigator was matched by his enthusiastic reveling with Rex during Carnival. And wasn't he also celebrated for his magical card tricks? But after suffering her own romantic trauma, Sylvia had no patience with love or lovers, and if Lawrence De—

"We can't go to Lawrence again," Fanny shook her head firmly. "Not yet, at least."

"Perhaps we won't have to," Sylvia realized suddenly. "I might know the very person who can help us navigate the murky waters of New Orleans society."

"And who's that?"

"My very own Cousin Charlotte."

18.

THE STREETS OF THE FRENCH QUARTER led to the French Market and as Fanny and Sylvia walked down Bourbon Street they dodged wagons of vegetables, carts of cow carcasses, and bins of cackling chickens. Young Liam followed behind them, preparing to sneak an orange or banana from an unguarded fruit bin.

As Fanny gazed up at the pink and red flowers waving from between the black iron balusters, she remembered her youthful visits to the Quarter. She had watched the striking of silver dollars at the Mint with her father; eaten her way through the French market with Lawrence; and entirely by herself, bought a baby alligator at Dupree's Pet Shop.

But the Quarter had aged. The buildings were the same—brick and stucco structures slapped against the banquette and rising two and three stories—but they seemed greatly worn with time and the fences that met the banquette were rotted and colorless. Fanny had not remembered the giant cracks along the stuccoed walls or the ripped awnings or the lines of dingy washing hung from balcony to balcony. Nor did she remember the odors of outhouses and offal or the Italian-accented curses that permeated the streets.

As she and Sylvia neared the outer streets of the Quarter, Fanny urged, "Tell me more about your Cousin Charlotte."

"She's not really our cousin. She's father's sister, so she's really our aunt. But everyone has always called her Cousin Charlotte. She's been living in Paris. She's an artist, you see, and Paris was the best place for her after her husband died. Olive and I spent most of last year with her."

"And why is she back in New Orleans and why is she living in the Quarter?"

"Hardly the part of town for a Giddings, is it?" Sylvia replied tartly. "Fanny, you sound just like everyone who said I shouldn't move into the Irish Channel."

Fanny stopped short. "She's not running a settlement house, is she?"

"No." Sylvia halted in front of a broad iron lace gate and waited for Fanny and Liam to catch up with her. Sylvia had agreed to let the boy tag along this morning, but she would not introduce him to Cousin Charlotte; asking Charlotte to talk to Fanny was burden enough. "But she is thinking about opening an art school. To teach impoverished spinsters and widows how to decorate pots and pitchers and plates. She's in the Quarter because the rents are cheap and she needed space."

Looking between the iron rails, Fanny saw the large, sunny courtyard that was the envy of every Creole family. As Sylvia opened the gate, Fanny and Liam followed closely behind her.

Inside the courtyard, a dingy marble fountain gurgled a pitiful spray of dirty water. Beneath a wall patched with three different shades of ochre, a round table with a sloping top—almost perfect for an intimate *petit dejeuner*—was surrounded by a ragtag trio of battered chairs. Clearly, the courtyard furniture had seen better days.

But around the sides of the courtyard were wild tropical flowers brilliantly arrayed against pots of dark palms. Steep wooden staircases rose up to second and third floor balconies and each step was festooned with a lattice of flowers. All was quiet in the courtyard, except for the occasional drift of birdsong. It was almost like a children's storybook, where a single door led from the chaos of the street into a garden of paradise. Amid the fantasy of foliage was another door, held open by a rusted piece of broken cast iron. Tucked into the iron was a white calling card: *Mrs. Charlotte Blanchard Decatur Sutter.*

"But if she's been living in Paris, how could she possibly know anything that will help us?" asked Fanny.

"Because Charlotte has friends everywhere in New Orleans," replied Sylvia, as she commanded Liam to wait in the courtyard. "Even after all of these years abroad. And her friends have friends. And eventually, one of those friends will know what we need to know."

A BESPECTACLED WOMAN wearing a maid's apron smeared with several different colors of paint led Sylvia and Fanny through a warren of connected rooms and hallways, out one door, past an alcove that bristled with heat, around a courtyard and into another building, until they reached a large stuccoed room that smelled of fresh clay. Nailed to the walls were wooden shelves, each of them laden with the familiar forms of pots and bowls. The items were an unusual color of unpainted pink.

Fanny was drawn immediately to the potter's wheel. She had seen a wheel at the Cotton Centennial but had never seen a woman working at one; never seen a woman spinning the disk with her feet as she shaped the lump of clay with her hands. From the graying blond hair piled on her head and the admiration in Sylvia's gaze, Fanny was sure the potter was Cousin Charlotte.

Standing beside Charlotte was a bald man with a cigar in his hand. When Charlotte circled her hands around the mound of clay on the wheel, the man urged, "Keep your arms tight." When Charlotte caught the heel of her shoe on her skirt and the wheel slowed down, he shouted, "Faster, faster." When Charlotte dug her hand into the center of the rotating mound of clay, he cooed like a pigeon, "Slowly." And finally, as Charlotte's long fingers began to pull up the side of what began to look like a cylinder, he crunched the cigar between his lips and said nothing.

Fanny and Sylvia watched as Charlotte pulled the clay, steadily coaxing it to rise higher and higher. But the wheel jerked suddenly and Charlotte's hands ripped through the wall of clay. The cylinder collapsed back into itself. The instructor spat on the floor and shook his head, but Charlotte only laughed at her misfortune. With the back of her clay-encrusted hand she pushed a stray hank of hair away from her forehead and resettled a large pair of spectacles on her nose and ears. Only then did she see her niece. "Sylvia! What in heaven's name are you doing here?"

Cousin Charlotte extracted herself from the wheel and the bench. She removed her apron and glided over to a pitcher and bowl in the corner. As she scrubbed the clay from her hands she said, "They say that ladies don't have the strength to work up the clay or keep the wheel moving steadily, but I think it's just our skirts that slow us down." Charlotte dried her hands on a cotton cloth.

"Fair warning Mr. Weymeyer. Tomorrow, I'll take my lesson wearing trousers. It's not proper but it's practical. And this is my house."

Her hands dried, Cousin Charlotte came over to Sylvia and hugged her strongly.

"It's good to see you too." Sylvia exchanged kisses with the older woman and then introduced Fanny.

Charlotte looked directly into Fanny's eyes, and then stood back, as if surprised to find another woman with her own superior height. Then Charlotte took a moment to survey Fanny's face: the structure of her high cheekbones; the tobacco-colored eyes and golden hair; the critical wrinkle that settled easily between her eyes. Fanny stood silently, impatient to such scrutiny, but reluctant to challenge the older woman.

"Good Gracious!" Charlotte grabbed both of Fanny's hands and pulled her closer. "You're not Preacher Newcomb's daughter, are you?"

"Yes, ma'am, I am," Fanny replied softly, "Although he only preached on Sunday evenings. The rest of the week he was a lawyer."

"And a fine lawyer he was and a good soldier too. I heard that his funeral at Greenwood was something splendid."

"Yes, ma'am, it was."

"Partnered with Lawrence Decatur, didn't he? Stubborn men, both of them. And I suppose you're just as stubborn as your father?"

"Yes, ma'am, she is," Sylvia confirmed easily. "And it's because of Fanny that we need your—"

"You may certainly have my help." The older woman smiled at her niece. "But not before I have my cup of coffee."

FANNY, SYLVIA, AND Charlotte sat bravely in the ragtag chairs around the small round table, trying to keep their cups from spilling. The paint-stained maid hovered behind them with a palmetto fly-swatter.

Sylvia frowned over her cup; Liam had abandoned the courtyard and must be up to some mischief somewhere. Well Sylvia would show him; she maneuvered the latch so that Liam could not open it from the street.

Fanny was confused and intrigued by Charlotte Giddings Decatur Sutter and her living quarters. Was Cousin Charlotte reduced to poverty? Or did she truly enjoy the cramped quarters and noisy streets of the French Quarter? Or perhaps she lost her cook and depended upon the excellent Creole kitchens and coffee stands of the Quarter for her sustenance?

The moment that Charlotte set her empty cup on the table, Sylvia relayed the facts about Nora's murder. As succinctly as possible, Sylvia explained Olive's certainty that Nora had been strangled, Karl's arrest and evidence of innocence, the Under Commissioner's refusal to believe them, and finally, the necessary decision to identify Nora's real murderer. From the speed of her speech it was clear that Sylvia and Charlotte were longtime confidantes.

"You're sure that Karl is innocent?" asked Cousin Charlotte.

"Yes."

"And Olive's sure that Nora was strangled?"

"Yes."

"That's one bit of good news, unfortunately. Women all over the city are frightened to leave their homes and go about their business for fear that Ripper will be just around the corner. These Ripper letters will be the death of someone." Charlotte set down her cup and withdrew a silver box from her skirt pocket.

Cigarettes! A frisson of excitement fluttered through Fanny. Finally, Fanny was going to be offered her first cigarette. She suddenly liked Cousin Charlotte immensely.

But Charlotte held the box in her hand, and Fanny could tell that she fought hard *not* to open it. Charlotte said, "Tell me about Nora."

"But you must have read all about her," replied Sylvia. "I know you get the papers."

"Of course I've *read*. But I want to *hear* what you know."

"But it's the men—"

"Nora was in two of my classes," Fanny interrupted. "Office manners and bookkeeping. She was smart and quick and understood everything immediately. She was ambitious. She could have done anything she put her mind to. I was going to find her a good job on Canal Street. At a department store or a banking institution."

"What about her family?"

"I...don't know."

"Do you know *anything* about her family?"

"She worked as a prostitute and she called the landlady of her house her aunt, but I don't think she really was." Fanny studied the older woman to see if she would react to the word *prostitute*. (Charlotte did not.) "Sylvia and I went to the house where Nora lived. We saw her room and searched through her things. And we went to her funeral."

"They had it at Metairie," said Sylvia. "But..." Sylvia had not considered how to tell Charlotte about how she got the names from the sergeant's notebook, "...what I really want to ask you about are the various men suspected of murdering her."

"And how would you know *that*?" asked Charlotte. "Or do I not want to know?"

"That is a long story and I would prefer to not retell it. But we *do* know who the police suspect."

Charlotte traced her fingers over the silver cigarette box as Sylvia listed the suspects. When Sylvia finished, Charlotte said, "Your suspects are a respected doctor, a rude doctor, a Creole photographer, a Catholic priest, and a Seminarian. Is that right?"

"Each of the suspects was in the Channel and very close to Conner's Court at the time Nora was murdered," said Fanny. "Either before or after. The photographer even claims he was there exactly *when* Nora was murdered."

"You've got your work cut out trying to find out who killed Nora."

"But that's exactly why we came to *you*. You know everyone in town worth knowing," said Sylvia. "And someone you know has got to know which one of these men killed Nora."

"Do you really know Pierre deVille?" asked Fanny, somewhat doubting Sylvia's claim.

"The photographer on Canal Street with the bad toupee? I know *about* him. He keeps an apartment not far from here and can't keep a cleaning girl long enough to sweep the soot out."

"And Terence and Gabriel Boylan," said Sylvia. "You know *them*, don't you?"

"I knew their mother. Long ago."

"How about John Remington?"

"Everyone knows John. He's single-handedly brought Charity Hospital into the modern era of medicine."

"Lester Adams?" asked Fanny.

"That such a man as Remington should be burdened with a nephew like that!" Charlotte slowed slightly, as if expressing her disapproval. "I haven't met Adams but I've heard rumors about his doctoring. And it is quite unbecoming. I have a soft spot for well-spoken Yankees—Mr. Sutter was from Philadelphia, you know—but Lester Adams' reputation is *de trop*. Even for New Orleans."

Sylvia looked at Fanny, a hint of triumph in her eyes. "So you *do* know each of the suspects. Now, could you help us find out more about them?"

"What would you like to know?"

"Every—" Fanny halted as she saw Liam, who threw himself at the gate.

"Miss Sylvia! Miss Sylvia!" the boy clutched at the iron spikes as he shouted. "They're going to hang Karl!"

Fanny and Sylvia hurried to the gate with Charlotte close behind them.

"Somebody found a knife!" Liam was in tears as he pushed a handful of newspaper sheets through the gate.

As Fanny grabbed the *Nightly Sensation* special edition from Liam, Charlotte grabbed another. Sylvia opened the gate to retrieve Liam.

"He's right!" Fanny glared at Sylvia. "The police found the bloody knife that killed Nora early this morning."

"And," Cousin Charlotte announced sadly, "your Karl just confessed to her murder."

19.

PLEADING TO SEE IF KARL WAS SAFE, LIAM pulled Sylvia and Fanny to the Parish Prison. When the trio reached the street in front of the prison, they found dozens of men waiting outside, almost every man reading or waving a copy of the *Sensation* special edition.

Fanny abandoned her thoughts of inquiring about Karl. The protectors of the Parish Prison—the twenty or so patrolmen who lined up against the façade of the imposing brick fortress—had their club-wielding hands full.

"What's happening?" Little Liam peered up at Fanny, who was inches taller than Sylvia. "They won't lynch him, will they?"

"No, of course not," Fanny replied. "That was all newspaper excitement. These people are just curious. Like me and you." But even as she spoke, Fanny watched as groups of men joined the dozens already in front of the Prison.

Sylvia noticed the growing rowdiness also, and guided Fanny and Liam up the staircase and into the gallery of a building across from the prison. They could all *see* the prison now, but were still far from the mass of men that was forming. For good measure, Sylvia slipped her gloved fingers into Liam's collar; she would not risk losing him in the crowd.

Fanny couldn't even count the numbers of men—and were those women now as well?—who mingled in the crowd. And then it happened: the mass multiplied into a mob and a torrent of men, a few of them shaking lengths of rope above their heads, surged toward the prison, as if to barge inside and draw their nooses around Karl's neck.

"Ripper!"

"Lynch him!"

The phalanx of patrolmen lurched forward and rebuffed the crowd with their clubs. Fanny even saw one officer hit a man with the butt end of his rifle. The crowd backed up slightly, but the patrolmen did not retreat.

"I've never seen men this crazed before. Not even when Karl was arrested." Sylvia tightened her grip on Fanny and moved closer to Liam. "There must be three hundred men here and it's all due to the *Sensation*."

"It's all lies about Karl!" Liam spit on the ground.

As Fanny continued her surveillance of the broad area in front of the prison entrance, she identified a familiar form—the thin, plaid-suited *Sensation* reporter Clarence Halloway. *Had* he embellished lies to sell newspapers? Or had he told the honest truth? Was he walking amongst the angry rabble looking for honest truths, or had his words instigated this upheaval?

"It's possible that a knife was found," said Fanny said in fairness. "And it's possible that Karl confessed. We just need to wait for the better newspapers to print their papers."

Sylvia pointed her cane toward the front of the prison. A door opened slowly and the guards parted into two columns. A tall, barrel-chested man with slicked back hair stepped out from the jail.

"It's the Commissioner." As Sylvia spoke, the crowd regained its own voice and began to harass the police once more.

"Lynch him!"

As a rotten orange found its target on the Commissioner's broad lapel, the patrolmen moved closer to the crowd, their clubs raised high.

Suddenly Liam was at Sylvia's side, "We should go *now*, Miss Sylvia. No one's going to be too careful about who gets hurt here."

Sylvia lifted her cane defensively. A fight, a *riot* even, seemed a distinct possibility. "Liam's right. Let's go, Fanny."

"I'd like to stay."

"Suit your—"

High-pitched whistles shred the air and, from all corners of the street, patrolmen ran toward the prison. The rioters were encircled from all sides. Within a few minutes, the rowdies were either in the hands of the police or had scattered from the scene, their brutal nooses and shredded newspapers abandoned on the ground.

"Do you think they'll let us see Karl now?" asked Liam.

"They will not!" Sylvia took Liam's hand. "And you must never come back here again."

"Never? But—"

"Look, Sylvia," Fanny's gaze shifted from the crowd and back to the prison front. "There's a carriage. Someone's leaving the prison."

"Is it Karl?" Liam jumped up as he asked Sylvia.

"Of course not. I'm sure that it's—"

"It's what, Miss Sylvia?"

"Fanny, look there," Sylvia pointed her cane at the carriage. "The man in the clerical collar is Terence Boylan. And the man behind him is Lester Adams. What are those two men doing here?"

"I don't know." Fanny was just as confused as Sylvia. Until, steps behind Lester Adams, she saw the plaid-suited reporter hunched over his notebook. "But there's the man who might know something." She turned to Sylvia, "Well, why not? Halloway reported Karl's confession. I'm guessing that he knows a lot more than what he reported. Some of it might help us help Karl."

"Even if you're right," responded Sylvia. "How do we get him to talk to us?"

CREOLE PUNCH AND pickled oysters. Broiled pompano and potato croquettes. Roast filet of beef and *champignons a la Bordelaise*. Lettuce salad with remoulade dressing.

And in the kitchen, cups of bread pudding, a plate of chocolate cream bonbons, and an ice mold of lemon sherbet. (Little Liam was also in the kitchen, fast asleep from sampling too much food.)

As the clock chimed ten o'clock, Fanny could not recall when she had seen a table so laden with exceptional cuisine. Even Lawrence and his Choctaw Club cronies didn't dine this well.

"It's not often that a poor reporter is invited to such a feast." Clarence Halloway's knife and fork slashed across his fish. "But I guess you ladies knew that, didn't you?"

"Just a simple meal to help a hardworking man keep up his strength." Sylvia smiled, knowing that Clarence Halloway was aware of her true motives. Once the women had decided that the best way to Clarence Halloway's information was through his stomach, Aunt Esther had been cooking furiously. And what Aunt Esther did not cook herself, Sylvia had ordered up from two of New Orleans' finest restaurants. And how the man had eaten. "I see you've finished that side of pompano. Would you like another before Aunt Esther brings in the beef?"

"More potato croquettes?" Fanny slid a platter toward Clarence.

"Another oyster, Mr. Halloway?" asked Olive, as if secretly calculating exactly how much rich food the reporter could eat.

Clarence Halloway sucked down an oyster and fell back in his chair. "Yes, yes, and yes." He wiped his hands on the glossy white napkin covering his tie and shirtfront. "And while you're at it, why don't you tell me just what piece of information you're trying to squeeze out of me tonight?"

Sylvia's fingers wrapped around the green bottle, a claret highly prized by her father, and lowered the bottle over the reporter's glass. As the red liquid slid into the fine crystal she said, "We want to know everything you know about Karl Schultz's confession."

The reporter watched as wine rose to the top of his glass. "What I know is considerable."

"You really have information?" asked Fanny.

"Yes, ma'am, I do."

"From who?" asked Sylvia.

"Now you wouldn't expect me to give away my sources, would you?"

Sylvia's left eyebrow arched severely, a clear sign that *Yes*, she would.

"All right," Halloway said, relenting. "There is a saloon just by the prison. The police almost live there. The right amount of whiskey in a certain policeman's glass—sort of what you're doing to me right now—will usually get me the information I need."

"And you're sure your information is correct?" Olive asked.

"It's good. I heard the same information from at least three men, *before* they had too much to drink." Clarence tapped his finger on the fine linen tablecloth. "But that's enough about my end. Just what, ladies, are you offering in return for this information?"

Fanny flinched. The idea of a tit for tat beyond the extravagant late night feast had not occurred to them.

But Sylvia was prepared. "Nothing, Mr. Halloway, at least for now. I'm sure we'll be able to provide you with information sometime."

"My business is based on immediate transaction." Halloway belched aggressively into his napkin. "If you have nothing else to trade for, I would be hard pressed to share my information with you." The reporter belched once more and then his head slumped to the side. His complexion darkened and his eyes rolled from side to side as though he were seasick.

Olive leaned toward the man and realized he *was* sick, that his fragile frame was suffering from the excesses of his elaborate meal. "I have some bicarbonate of soda in the infirmary, Mr. Halloway. If it would help you talk to us."

Halloway tossed his napkin on his plate. "Ladies, I surrender."

AFTER THREE POWDERS of bicarbonate of soda, two glasses of water, and one dish of lemon sherbet, Clarence Halloway found his voice. "Last night the police found the bloody knife that killed Nora Keegan. It was hidden behind a brick at the back of Karl's lodging house."

Fanny frowned. "They found it last night?"

"Even I didn't find out about it until this morning. It seems that when the police want to keep information to themselves, they find a way."

"Or perhaps they really didn't find the bloody knife that killed Nora."

"Hidden behind a brick," added Olive.

"At the back of Karl's lodging house," concluded Sylvia. "I never heard of anything so contrived in my life! Even for the New Orleans police."

"Regardless," replied the reporter, "This morning Karl Schultz told the guards he wanted to confess. They had to wait until the Commissioner came in."

Fanny watched as Aunt Esther ladled rum sauce over a generous slice of bread pudding and set it in front of her. But Fanny had no appetite for dessert. She had no appetite for any food now that she knew there really *was* an actual bloody knife. She wondered if Daniel Crenshaw also provided Halloway with police information but did not want to distract the reporter from his story. "What did Karl say?"

"What I heard is that he said nothing. The Commissioner came down, dangled the bloody knife in his face, and asked him if he slit Nora Keegan's throat and ripped her to pieces. Then the Commissioner produced a piece of paper, Schultz made his mark, and it was over."

The women stared bluntly at each other. Fanny put their horror into words, "Karl really did confess to being the Ripper?"

Sylvia spread her long fingers in front of her on the table. "How did he look?"

Halloway had a ready answer. "Like he'd been pulling his hair out all night thinking about something."

"True?" asked Fanny. "Or something you made up for the *Sensation*?"

"True."

"What did he do after it was over?" asked Sylvia.

"Same thing he's done every day he's been in prison. Sat on his bed with his head between his hands. Doesn't even look up when he gets his food or has visitors. He's never left his cell and never said *boo* to anyone, although more than once the guards said they heard him crying. But not loud enough so that anyone could really hear him."

"Has he had visitors?" Fanny asked. "A lawyer?"

"That priest and his brother. That's all."

"Terence and Gabriel Boylan." Sylvia replied sternly, allowing no correction.

Halloway gazed at the plate of chocolate bonbons in front of Sylvia and then looked away suddenly. "Uh-huh, those two. They share the duty, each of them coming every other day."

Olive tapped the paper of bicarbonate of soda against the table. "What have they been saying to him?"

"I don't know. No one's ever gotten close enough to hear them."

Fanny wondered what Halloway's real relationship was with the guards at the Parish Prison. Did he just ply them for information when something happened or did he buy them beer at lunch and dinner, inspiring them to overhear conversations they might not usually listen to? And if he did, was it right or was it wrong? If such bribery could bring Nora's murderer to justice, it must be right. She asked, "We saw Lester Adams at the prison today. What was he doing there?"

The reporter shrugged his shoulders.

"You don't know what he was doing there or you don't want to tell us?"

"I don't know *yet*. And when I do and if it's important, you can read about it in the *Sensation*. Ladies, in the lingo of the Crescent City, it is time to bid you *adieu*." The reporter put his hands on the table and pushed himself up from the chair. Suddenly, anxiety clouded the reporter's thin face. "But before I go, Dr. Giddings, how about some more bicarbonate?"

FANNY ESCORTED THE reporter to the front door. She was beginning to like this scrawny man. Inside Wisdom Hall, she had almost wanted to tell him that Nora was strangled and not slashed. She wouldn't, of course. Only Olive had that right and she had not looked tempted to enlighten the reporter.

"A deal is a deal, Miss Newcomb," said the reporter. "I've been dined and you've been informed."

"But you know so much more, don't you?"

"I can't tell you everything, because then no one will talk to me. And if no one talks to me, I'm out of business."

"I have just one question." She reached into her pocket and produced a cotton napkin filled with melting bonbons.

"Oh, hell. I suppose one more question won matter."

"Good," said Fanny. "Who saw Karl last before he confessed? Gabriel or Terence Boylan?"

The reporter whistled sharply between his teeth as he took the napkin and gently placed it in his coat pocket. "That, Miss Newcomb, is something I do not know just yet."

20.

EVERY MORNING AFTER BREAKFAST Sylvia sat at her grand Wooton desk to command the daily tasks of Wisdom Hall. This morning—a morning that saw Sylvia drinking only *café au lait*, because after the Feast of Clarence Halloway last night, when would she ever be hungry again? —Sylvia's ritual was interrupted by Liam.

"'Cuse me, Miss Sylvia," The boy came boldly up to Sylvia. "Package for you."

"Where—"

"Porch, it was."

Liam lifted the paper and twine-tied package toward Sylvia and she recoiled slightly. There had been a "package" in London late last year. The newspapers reported that it contained a human kidney and was sent by Jack the Ripper. Fanny had wondered if the Irish Channel Ripper might also send something in a package, and although Sylvia had replied "No, of course not," for a second, she was not so sure.

Yet, as she glared at the package in Liam's hands, Sylvia could tell the contents. Books. Or more probably, pamphlets. Sylvia took the package from Liam, snipped the twine and paper with her scissors, and read the note on top of the pamphlets.

Dear Miss Giddings,

If you are to embark on a study of the Catholic Church, you will need some instruction. These books have been a great help to people seeking the truth. Please contact me when you are ready to continue our conversation.

Terence Boylan

History of the Catholic Church in North America. Christ in America: His Catholic Church. Good and Evil. Lives of our Lady Saints and Martyrs. Each title matched the books delivered yesterday by Gabriel Boylan. Sylvia swept both sets of books up into her arms and marched to the classroom. Empty. She walked down the hallway and into the infirmary where—to her surprise—Fanny and Olive sat together as thick as thieves.

"I just received these books from Terence Boylan." Sylvia held up the new books in one hand, their spines visible to Fanny and Olive. In the other hand she held up Gabriel Boylan's books. "And these are the books his brother brought me yesterday. The exact same titles." Sylvia put the books on Olive's desk. "Does it seem likely to you that Terence Boylan would send me two sets of the same books? It seems very unlikely to me."

"I was just telling Olive that I've gone through Karl's things," said Fanny. "The tools and boxes in the attic. I saw them today and thought...well, may—"

"You'd find something helpful? And did you?"

"Yes," Fanny handed a book-sized piece of board to Sylvia. "I found a photograph of Karl."

Sylvia studied the image. "It hardly looks like him. All cleaned up and dressed in a suit. Why would this be with his tools? Did you find anything else?"

"No." Fanny opened the flyleaf of one book. "You think Gabriel Boylan used these books as an excuse to come here? Without his brother's knowledge?"

"Perhaps," offered Olive, "Terence told Gabriel you were interested in converting and Gabriel took it upon himself to provide some instruction."

"He didn't seem very dedicated to converting me to Catholicism," replied Sylvia. "We spent most of our time going through the Hall. And he didn't need an excuse; I'm always eager to explain my work."

"But he couldn't have known that," said Olive.

Fanny rose from her seat and walked the short length of Olive's office. As she turned, she asked, "What exactly did you talk about before I met up with you?"

"The Hall. Education. Teaching girls. Karl." Sylvia's speech drawled lightly, as if she were thinking back. "He was very interested in the staircase where Karl was arrested."

"He could just be a sensation seeker," said Olive. "Just like everyone else stopping on the street to gawk at us."

Fanny studied the two piles of books, a small crease forming between her eyebrows. "Or maybe he wanted to know more about Karl."

"What do you mean?"

"Maybe he thinks Karl is innocent and came here to find out more about him."

"No, he's not in Karl's corner," said Sylvia. "Gabriel Boylan had already judged Karl guilty and sent him to the hereafter."

"Then if he isn't trying to help Karl he must be trying to help himself."

Olive picked up on Fanny's logic. "Or someone else, like his brother. Which could mean that we're close to the truth."

"I don't see how," said Sylvia. "Gabriel Boylan lied to me. And so did his brother. How can we be close to the truth when all we have is lies?"

"Maybe Lester Adams won't lie to you," Fanny bundled all of the books together as if she was eager to read them. "When you talk to him this afternoon."

When Sylvia did not respond, Olive said, "You are still going to talk to him this afternoon Sylvia. You must talk to him. You must find out why he was lurking around here. And why he left so suddenly once Gabriel Boylan arrived."

"But—"

"But nothing, Sylvia. Adams is hiding something and you're the only one who *can* talk to him."

"But—"

"*But nothing*. This afternoon," Olive checked her watchpin, "you will meet, flatter, and finesse Dr. Lester Adams into telling you what he was doing the night Nora was murdered."

"And," Fanny added, "exactly why the police suspect that he killed her."

THE DEDICATION OF Charity Hospital's new ambulance took place in front of the hospital on Tulane Avenue precisely at three o'clock. Over one hundred people attended, including a cadre of well-starched Sisters of Charity.

Sylvia surveyed the group of gentlemen assembled at the top of the hospital's front steps, obviously part of the group of speakers. As far as she could tell, Lester Adams was not among that august group. John Remington was, of course. And so was Sylvia's father. In fact, Dr. Philip Giddings was engaging Remington in conversation.

Sylvia caught her sister's gaze from across the crowd and glanced up at the front steps. She telegraphed her thoughts to her sister. *You didn't tell me father was going to be here.*

Olive's shoulders shrugged in response. *I didn't know.*

The sister's communication was curtailed when Remington stepped up to the edge of the hospital's front steps to address the crowd. "With this fully equipped ambulance we will be able to treat patients at the site of their injuries. No more will we need to transport them directly back to the hospital. No more will we risk further injury from dangers and flooded streets. We envision that many more citizens of New Orleans will enjoy longer lives due to the benefits of this fine ambulance and we would like to thank these gentlemen for their patronage in providing it."

Remington stepped back and immediately the shrill clang of an ambulance bell rang from the side of the hospital. As everyone turned to watch, the new ambulance turned the corner from Locust Street. Pulled by a double team of horses, the ambulance looked very much like an undertaker's wagon—long, sober, and entirely enclosed. The words *Emergency Hospital Ambulance* were written large on the side of the wagon.

The driver's perch was covered with a solid roof, sure protection against New Orleans' harsh sun and blinding rain. The lone driver secured the reins of the horses and jumped from the perch. He was dressed in a military uniform embellished with pairs of gold buttons and numerous large patch pockets.

Sylvia could feel the crowd disperse about her. Many of them rushed to inspect the ambulance. Lester Adams quickly accommodated each person by opening up the ambulance's back door and allowing them to stick their heads inside. He went around to the driver's perch and rang the bell. For an instant, Sylvia pitied Lester Adams. Listening to that bell regularly would drive any person mad.

As a flock of nuns glided away from the ambulance, Sylvia made her approach. *Sans* cane, today, for—unless she had a particular use for it—Sylvia disliked being seen in public with her cane.

The doctor greeted her politely and attempted to usher her to the back of the ambulance. Sylvia unbuttoned one of her gloves—pleased to see that Adams admired her elegant pale hand—and raised it to the lead horse's nose. Despite her carriage accident,

Sylvia retained a keen admiration of horses; it was the men who drove those horses—like Lester Adams—who forever gained her suspicion.

"This is a fine pair," said Sylvia. "You must be very proud of them. Are they fast? Yes, I'm sure they are." She ran her hand along the horse's side. "And you must be an expert driver. In fact, someone told me that you are the fastest ambulance driver in the city." Sylvia hesitated, wondering if perhaps Adams was the only ambulance doctor in the city. No matter, she forged forward. "I heard that you made it to Conner's Court in less than fifteen minutes. Very impressive."

Adams strutted toward the back of the ambulance. Reluctantly, Sylvia followed him. Olive had suggested that Adams would enjoy flattery and Sylvia planned to put her heart into it. She moved as close to Lester Adams as she could.

But he backed from her and stood to the side of the ambulance. He spread his hand over the inside. "I have everything I need to insure the safety and good health of my patients."

Politely, Sylvia looked inside. She saw metal instruments gleaming from the walls, wads of cotton and toweling, wooden splints, and a large wooden box that held tonics and medicines. A menacing saw hung on the back wall.

It was all too much like Olive's infirmary and Sylvia wavered with nausea. She perched delicately on the edge of the wagon. Only the familiar fragrance of sun-warmed cotton soothed her.

As if overcome with heat, Adams removed his blue cap. Flakes of skin followed after. As she watched the skin float down to his uniform, Sylvia asked, "You answered the ambulance call at Conner's Court, didn't you?"

Adams looked up at Sylvia as though she was a bright student. "Yes. Even though the dedication is today, we used this ambulance at Conner's Court." He surveyed Sylvia at length, as if evaluating her fair complexion and fine bonnet. "But this is not the type of information a lady like you should hear about."

As the heat of the ambulance settled about her, Sylvia swallowed. "Even though your horses are fast, you got to Conner's Court awfully quickly. I've heard that some people think you were already in the Irish Channel."

Adams lips curled slightly, as though he had been caught in a good deed that should not be mentioned. "I have heard that myself. Some people have suggested that I scared away the Ripper. Kept him from another *double event*, like the two...." Adams paused, as though he was going to speak of *prostitutes* in front of a lady like Sylvia. He continued, "the two he murdered on that one evening in London."

"You knew there was a murderer in the Irish Channel?" Sylvia asked sharply. "Someone wanting to kill that girl?"

"I didn't know he would kill her but I suspected that he would kill *someone*. I've been driving the Charity ambulance for a few weeks now and I have come across many, many women who have been frightened by men with knives. It took me just a little time to realize what was happening." He paused, perhaps for Sylvia to ask, but when she did not, he said, "Jack the Ripper was continuing his murderous rampage. This time in New Orleans. And because I am a doctor I realized quickly something else that no one knew."

"What was that?"

"Our Ripper is a doctor." Adams' eyes flashed brightly as he examined Sylvia's face. He seemed pleased to see her alarm. "Many in the London police force have long thought that the Ripper was a medical man. And from everything I've seen in New Orleans over the last few weeks, I must agree."

"He's a doctor? Just like you?"

"Not just like me, of course." Adams appeared lost in his own thoughts until he said, "If you're really interested in what happened last Saturday night...I put that girl right where you're seated."

Sylvia lurched from the wagon and was surprised to find herself caught in her father's embrace.

Philip Giddings released his daughter gently and offered Sylvia his cane, which she accepted quickly. If Lester Adams took one step toward her, she would clobber him.

"You must have some rare power to fascinate my daughter with anything medical." Philip looked from Adams to Sylvia as though he wondered if there was some actual attraction between the pair.

"Dr. Giddings." The name rolled slowly off of Adams's tongue. He glanced sideways at Sylvia, beyond her father's view and leveled his eyes at her.

Sylvia steadied herself with her father's cane and was suddenly appeased; no one in the New Orleans' medical world would lie to Dr. Philip Giddings. "Papa, Dr. Adams was just telling me about that horrible murder at Conner's Court. And how he believes that the murderer must be a doctor."

"Perhaps I overstated myself somewhat, Miss Giddings," Adams said, exaggerating her name.

"Certainly you did, young man. No doctor in New Orleans would harm a patient. And if he ever tried." Philip Giddings offered his arm to his daughter. "I personally would see him finished."

21.

SATURDAY NIGHT AT SEVEN, FANNY WAS AT the Hotel St. Charles in the company of three hundred other curious New Orleanians. She eavesdropped on the accents of Germans and Irish from the Channel; Italians from the French Quarter; French from the outskirts of the Esplanade area;

Americans from Uptown. Most of the audience was male, although there were a few young women and couples in attendance.

"Ladies and gentlemen," Pierre deVille roared from behind the podium of the hotel's largest drawing room. His right hand rested on a tall easel that was covered with a black cotton cloth. "Welcome to my exhibition and thank you for your patronage. I am immensely gratified that so many of you are interested in my photographic trophy of Jack the Ripper. Or, as he now likes to be called, the *Irish. Channel. Ripper.*

"Many people, including our fine New Orleans police, have asked me how I can lay claim to such a feat. Here is my story. Not only have I long been interested in studio photography—and I'd like to take the opportunity this very instant to invite you all to my studio at 520 Canal Street, fourth floor, whenever you need a photograph produced—"

"Get on with it!" a thickly accented Irishman yelled from the back of the room.

"In addition," the photographer's voice rolled on as though he had not heard the interruption, "I have long been interested in flash photography, which enables a photographer to capture images at nighttime. Flash photography is a tricky animal, my friends, produced by a combination of finely ground magnesium powder and potassium chlorate. Too little magnesium will produce no illumination at all; too much will blind you like new snow on a sunny day. Experimentation is the key to finding the correct dosage of magnesium. Now, after many months of experimenting at nighttime in my studio, I believed that I had discovered the perfect combination and I was ready to experiment outside in the street." The photographer retrieved a glass of water from inside the podium and sipped it leisurely.

Fanny stood near the front of the crowd and her feet were getting tired. She shifted each toe carefully; a bead of perspiration hovered on the top of her forehead. Fanny was warm all over from the press of bodies toward the stage and there was no relief. She was so warm she feared that if deVille did not reveal his photograph soon, if he did not stop drinking his precious glass of water, she might faint.

The photographer drained the glass. "Many people have asked me why I chose Conner's Court for my experiment, although the explanation should be clear. I chose Conner's Court because it is the darkest corner in New Orleans. Dark not just for its social evils, which are well known to every citizen of New Orleans, but for its total absence of electrical lighting. Yes, it's a den of thieves but I was not afraid. For if I was successful, if I had concocted the correct amount of magnesium powder, my discovery would have been useful to people throughout the world." The photographer leaned forward on the podium. "Now, I have been asked: When my magnesium flashed and this villain was revealed, why didn't I challenge the man then? Why didn't I raise the alarm?"

Fanny's focus tightened on the photographer. She had wondered that question from the very beginning. If he had seen a murderer, how could he let him go?

"Why didn't I yell for the patrolman?" The photographer seemed to read Fanny's thoughts. "Well, the answer is not very complimentary, but it is the truth: Ladies and gentleman, there was a spider underneath my lens cloth."

The audience laughed and the photographer laughed with them, his stiff black toupee rising slightly on his sweat-glossed face. "A spider that became known to me just as I closed the shutter. The magnesium flashed but my eyes were surprised by the spider and I did not see the man illuminated by my flash. I was so affected by the spider that I collapsed my camera and returned immediately to my studio to repair my vision. I did not know until the next day what image I had captured.

"When I developed the glass plate I was astonished to see, as you will be also, a man with a knife in his hand. At his feet lies a woman, her throat covered thickly with her own blood." The photographer paused and two burly men came forward, each standing at either side of the covered easel. "This photograph is not for the weak of heart. But now that you have been warned, I present you with the first known photograph of Jack the Ripper."

The photographer removed the black cloth from the easel and stepped back. Fanny could see nothing and had no idea of the size or image on the photograph. The entire audience quieted as the first person in line approached the photograph. No one spoke. No one moved. And then the orderly line disintegrated and everyone veered toward the photograph. Fanny pushed herself forward and, to her surprise, found herself in front of the photograph.

It was the size of a *carte de visite* and matted on hard muted gray board. The edges of the photograph were darkened and only in the middle was anything visible. Fanny quickly saw a side view of a man's body, from the bottom of what must be his chin whiskers to almost the top of his shoes. He wore a dark jacket and clutched a thick knife in his hand, as though he were going to lift it and cut away at a low tree branch. At his feet, just as deVille suggested, was the outline of a woman's crumpled body.

Fanny imagined how it all happened: the man grabbed Nora from behind, clutching her waist. Quickly, he anchored the knife on the middle of her neck and then sliced through her throat. He released Nora's waist and watched as she fell to his feet, like a puppet whose strings had been cut. Fanny shook herself. Jack the Ripper was not in New Orleans. Nora had not been killed by Jack the Ripper. This was not a photograph of Jack the Ripper.

Suddenly, Fanny was grabbed from behind. Someone pulled at her skirt and then let go. Fanny turned. A woman was slumped to the ground. Fainted. Two men kneeled down to assist her.

As Fanny bent to help them, deVille's voice pulled her back to the stage. "You've all seen the broadsides posted on the telegraph poles. Jack the Ripper plans to strike tonight. And when he does, I will be there to catch him." The photographer dug his hand into his jacket and came out with a sheaf of papers. He shook them at the audience and then waved his hand and flung the papers across the room. "Tomorrow morning, while the police are inspecting their next victim, I will have a new photo of Jack the Ripper."

Fanny scrambled to reach a paper, competing with others as though she were vying for strings of beads thrown from Mardi Gras floats. She used her full height, but could not get a paper. Finally, she stood over a pair of short women who gazed dumbly at the words and then up at Fanny. She read aloud for them:

I am about every night in the Channel, watching and waiting. Saturday night is mine. I will never be caught. No woman is safe. As you know me, the Ripper.

Fanny pulled the paper from the women and folded it into quarters and tucked it under her stiff cuff. She fought her way through the crowd and out of the hotel. If someone threatened to murder women tonight and if deVille was following him, Fanny must follow deVille. And Sylvia and Olive must join her.

AT FANNY's INSISTENCE, Thomas joined Liam outside Pierre deVille's studio at 11 o'clock.

Liam—who had followed the photographer when he left the Hotel St. Charles and had been watching deVille's studio windows for the last hour (also at Fanny's insistence)—leaned against the stuccoed wall of the Pelican Insurance Company watching as dark figures moved back and forth across the vivid light coming from the photographer's studio. "Looks like there's one or two people up there."

"Just as Miss Fanny predicted," Thomas replied softly.

"Miss Fanny sure seemed determined to come out tonight, didn't she?" Little Liam pulled a half-smoked cigar from inside his shirt. Shimmying up a lamp pole, he lit it off of the jet fire and jumped back to the banquette. He choked on the sudden intake of cheap tobacco but he was determined to settle into his tortured smoke, keeping one eye on the brightened windows of the photographer's studio. Liam considered offering Thomas a puff—no small thought for a boy from the Irish Channel to share his cigar with a colored man—but before he could decide, Thomas drew a leather cigarette case from his inside coat pocket. Inside were three perfectly rolled cigarettes.

Liam bent his cigar towards Thomas, who delicately lit a cigarette off of it. With one fume of smoke, Thomas' tobacco wafted sweet and full.

"Where'd you get that?" Liam held his cigar stump away and attempted to step into the sweet fragrance of Thomas's cigarette.

"Mr. Philip gave it to me."

"Hey." Liam looked up at deVille's studio. "Lights just went off." Liam and Thomas waited against the wall, finally rewarded as a caped man carrying a large wooden box emerged from the building's main entrance. A tall dark-haired boy, clutching a variety of objects, stumbled behind him.

"Is that him?" Thomas peered through the darkness. Fanny had described the photographer carefully but deVille's most obvious feature—his badly dyed, poorly groomed toupee—could not be seen from under his broad-brimmed hat. "He's got a camera in his hand."

"Looks like him. Must be him."

Thomas considered his cigarette before taking a final draw. "Then it's time to get the horses."

"We're gonna follow him?"

"That's correct," Thomas stepped out from the wall. "And if he begins photographing we go back and get Miss Fanny."

"And Miss Sylvia too? And Dr. Olive?"

"That depends," Thomas walked quietly toward the carriage, careful not to alarm the horses.

"On what?"

Thomas unwound the reins before taking his seat on the bench. "On just how persuasive Miss Fanny is tonight."

FANNY's POWERS OF persuasion proved surprisingly successful. It took an unexpectedly brief argument to get Olive to join the hunt for the photographer. And once Olive agreed, Sylvia demanded to come along to supervise everyone.

Fanny pushed the sisters into the carriage as soon as Thomas and Liam returned to Wisdom Hall. She sat on the front bench with Thomas and Liam as they drove through the darkened streets of the Irish Channel. She was not going to miss her chance tonight.

"Stop here!" Fanny put her hand out on the reins. "Now!"

Thomas halted the carriage and glanced at the signs on the buildings. "Fulton and Pleasant," he said softly to himself.

As Fanny leaned forward on the bench and searched the intersection, Sylvia cast a wary eye at a group of men leaning against the closed market stalls, their intentions shaded by the broad roof overhanging. Sylvia turned sharply as a woman's hysterical laughter rang through the intersection. The laughter had come from inside the Three Bells Saloon, and in short order a trio of men with gold-buttoned tunics slung over their shoulders swaggered out of the front doors.

"Well, it's good to know that if there is any trouble tonight, the police are already here." Olive's voice reeked with sarcasm as she nodded toward the trio. "But where is Pierre deVille?"

Ignoring her sister, Sylvia watched as the women swayed under the anemic gaslight with their arms around each other's waists in sisterly fashion. She knew they were prostitutes, even though the younger woman clearly did not have the determination—or was it resignation?—of the older woman.

"It makes me so mad," Sylvia almost growled. "That poor girl is scared to death."

Olive looked the girl over with the same type of detached precision she used for her patients: fifteen years of age; thin and lanky, probably from lack of nourishment. Despite her leanness, her young face was decidedly heart shaped and overwhelmed by painted crimson lips. She wore a low-cut blouse like those favored by the Creole girls at the French market and a short skirt appropriate for a much younger girl. Still, she had some semblance of decency: her long dark hair was pulled back in the same type of tight low bun favored by Fanny.

Without warning, the older woman tossed the girl at the drunken policemen. The girl landed upon the men with a soft cry. They did not release her.

Still looking at the girl, Olive spoke. "If we don't see deVille in the next—"

Fanny cut off Olive. "We couldn't expect him to wait for us, could we? We'll have to go out and look for him."

"This is a fool's mission, Fanny." Olive sunk back into her seat. Although Fanny's proposal to follow the photographer had made some sense earlier, Olive was entirely uncomfortable that only Aunt Esther was ready to answer the infirmary bell. It was time that Olive and Thomas returned to the infirmary. And time that Liam was in bed.

As Sylvia began to open the carriage door, Olive lurched from her seat and pushed her hand on the outside of the carriage door, holding it shut. "Just where do you think you're going?"

"You know exactly where I'm going." Sylvia met her sister's stern glare. "To talk to that girl."

"You'll just be wasting your time." Olive sighed but did not release her hold on the door. "You can't save that girl unless she wants to be saved."

"But look at her. I mean, really, really look at her Olive. She doesn't want to be out there. She's almost screaming for someone to save her. She needs me." Sylvia pushed against the carriage door, surprised at her sister's strength. "You should be ashamed of yourself, Doctor. That poor girl could use your help as well."

"If you want to save her now, you'll have to contend with the New Orleans police," Fanny interrupted. Everyone, even Thomas, turned to look. They watched as the girl walked between two of the policemen, her arms entwined easily with theirs. "And I don't think they're arresting her."

Sylvia stepped from the carriage, ready to do battle for the girl. But before she could reach the ground, the men escorted the girl into the saloon. As Sylvia started toward the saloon, Fanny followed after her and put her hand on Sylvia's arm. "What are you going to do?

"I'm going to save that child, of course."

"Not tonight, Sylvia." Fanny leaned closer to Sylvia. "Tonight we must save Karl. Let's just—" Fanny's plea was interrupted by a circle of bright light bursting against the side of a narrow alley. Fanny—who had heard of, but never seen a magnesium flash before—spoke triumphantly. "That must be deVille! That's the explosion from his flash tray. He's somewhere inside that alley." Fanny intertwined her arm with Sylvia's and then pulled Olive from the carriage. "We'll have to move quickly."

A DOZEN STREET boys were standing behind the photographer, watching as he unwound the camera pedestal and placed the large wooden box upon it. The women positioned themselves at the rear of the crowd. Liam stood even farther back.

Fanny had expected to follow the photographer stealthily through the Channel and was surprised to see him casually setting up his camera, as though he expected the Ripper to parade in front of him. Fanny moved to the side of the crowd, looking at what the photographer was preparing to photograph. Within the shelter of an arched door entrance, her head pushed against the raw wood, a woman slept, her loud snores marked by occasional coughing. A baby was clutched within her arms. Fanny tried to put a title to the scene. *A Life of Great Misery.* Or, Fanny thought more likely, *Abandoned and Alone.*

As Fanny continued to absorb the strange scene she explained the photographer's actions to the sisters. "That box by his feet contains his glass plates. He inserts the glass plate into the camera, closes the camera, clicks the shutter, and has his photograph. He'll have to remove the plate and put in another one."

Olive frowned. "But when we had our portraits done, we had to sit very still for four minutes. If that baby wakens or the mother coughs again the photograph will be ruined."

"He must have one of those special shutters," said Fanny, "then he can take a photograph of people in action. And if he's hoping to really take a photograph of Jack the Ripper, I'm sure he must be equipped with a fast shutter. Besides, the magnesium flash only lasts a few seconds so that's all the time he'll have."

Sylvia leaned forward. "But how—?"

Fanny put up her hand. "He's loading magnesium tray now, although he should have someone do that for him. I don't see how he'll light the tray and squeeze the rubber bulb." Almost as though the photographer had heard her whispered instructions, he put the bulb into the near corner of his pocket and patted it to make sure it was secure. "He said he was testing the magnesium last Friday night when he photographed the Ripper. Wait, it looks like he's ready to photograph."

As the crowd watched, the photographer stood three feet from the side of the camera and lit a match. He stretched his right arm to keep the magnesium tray away from his body and stretched his left arm to drop the match into the tray. At the same instant, as the chemicals exploded into a pouf of light, his hand slapped against the corner of his pocket. Although the light was brilliant, neither woman nor child awoke. Evidently satisfied with his photograph, the photographer collapsed the legs of the camera platform, leaving the camera still attached to it.

"Could you ever imagine," whispered Fanny, "being able to take a photograph in all this darkness?"

"When did you learn so much about photography?" asked Sylvia.

"Father and Lawrence went in on a camera a few years ago."

"And you took it over from them?" Sylvia replied harshly. "You learned how to take pictures and develop photographs yourself?"

"Oh no," replied Fanny. "I learned a few things but after a while we all got bored with it. Although the camera did make a very good doorstop."

Olive elbowed Fanny and not kindly. "Can you remind me what we were supposed to see tonight? Isn't deVille supposed to be hunting down 'The Ripper'?"

"Yes."

"But he's not."

"Maybe he is and this is his method," Fanny replied, "and even if he's not, *right now*, at least we're observing one of the suspects engaged in the same activity as the night the victim was murdered."

"And what *have* you observed tonight?" Olive barely hid her scorn. "Besides deVille's ability to take a photograph?"

"Nothing yet." Fanny watched as the photographer walked away, turning into an alley between a pair of two-story wooden buildings, toward Tchoupitoulas Street and the riverfront. "But right now, he's getting away."

OLIVE GRABBED HER sister's arm just as Sylvia began to follow Fanny into the alley. "It doesn't take three of us to follow a photographer. I'm going back to meet Thomas and I expect you all to be there in a half hour." Then Olive spoke directly to Liam who stood alertly at Sylvia's side. "Stay with Sylvia and Fanny."

Olive retraced her steps back to the intersection of Fulton and Pleasant Streets fully expecting that Thomas would be waiting. But neither Thomas nor the carriage was there, and Olive—trusting explicitly in Thomas's judgment—stood close to a shuttered storefront as she waited for his return.

Very little had changed at the intersection since she'd been gone. It became clear that the group of men who had lounged under the market's roof were involved in a fierce game of dice and the noise of the Three Bells was just as boisterous as before. An oyster vendor with his loaded cart had pushed his way to the corner but no customers clustered around.

The two prostitutes were back underneath their lamp; the younger one crying. Her hair was pulled out of her bun, her eyelids were lowered heavily, and the color of her lip had turned from crimson to blood red. Olive knew the girl had been roughed up and wondered if it were by a man or her female friend. There was not much Olive could do for the girl except offer her some ice for her swollen lip. As Olive dug in her pocket for a coin for ice from the oyster vendor the girl's sobs grew louder. The older woman slapped the girl's face. Once; twice; three times.

The wheels of a heavy wagon came to a sudden stop directly across the street from the prostitutes. It was the new Charity Hospital ambulance; the two pairs of perfectly matched horses snorting as if they wanted to race. Lester Adams dropped from the driver's perch. *Something is very wrong here.* Six years of education, two years of internships, and eighteen months in practice and Olive could only listen to the tingling of intuition pulsing throughout her body. Lester Adams was up to evil tonight. But was he up to murder?

FANNY, SYLVIA, LIAM, and the street boys followed as the photographer captured more images of the Channel: a girl of three or four years stumbling as she carried a bucket of beer; men sleeping in their own slop; cisterns crumbled and broken; doors without knobs or locks; a dead rat, swarming with flies.

Although she had started following the photographer with high expectations, each photograph cast a dark shadow on Fanny's spirit. She had lived in New Orleans all of her life, her father had taken her into every district and ward, but never before had Fanny seen such poverty and despair. Her heart grew heavier with every image until she thought only of the suffering of the photographer's impoverished subjects.

Sylvia was equally compelled by the images and had raised her handkerchief to her eyes many times, mesmerized by the sorrow. She followed behind the photographer like a trained sheepdog, watching as he sought his next subject. Suddenly, Sylvia's right foot hit something sharp in the alleyway. She tripped roughly and pitched headfirst into a stack of small wooden crates.

Fanny held out her arm to help Sylvia up, realizing that Sylvia had not brought a cane tonight. "Come on, Sylvia. He's moving on."

Sylvia rose to her feet eagerly enough but then fell back. She looked down at the expanse of skirt above her shoes and winced. "I can't walk! My ankle...."

Fanny huffed. Her only hope in finding something of value was to watch the photographer for as long as she could. He had to reveal something about himself tonight. *Something*. Fanny could not have been that wrong about him. She bent down to place her arms under Sylvia's legs. "Let me carry you."

"No!" Sylvia recoiled. "Just let me sit. Liam can fetch Olive and they can help me to the carriage. You go after your photographer."

Fanny was torn. It was wrong to leave Sylvia alone and both she and Sylvia both knew it. But if Fanny didn't, she would never catch up with the photographer. The evening's efforts would be wasted.

"It's all right. Really," said Sylvia. "I'd prefer it."

Fanny knew that Sylvia was being honest. She would prefer to be alone than to have to suffer Fanny's frustrations. Fanny touched Sylvia's hand lightly. "I'll be back in a minute. I promise."

Following the scent of spent magnesium, Fanny walked down one street, turned two corners, and negotiated underneath a series of cistern stands. But she could not find the photographer. Just as she was about to retrace her steps and return to Sylvia, a blaze of powdered light blew through the front doorway of a squat two-story wooden building. By the time Fanny reached the building, the entry way was empty. But the photographer had been there and Fanny would find him. Fanny heard shuffling on the second floor. There was no railing on the stairs and she hugged the wall as she climbed the steps. The steps sagged beneath her and she almost lost her footing in the rotten wood. But at the top of the stairs she found what she was seeking.

The crowd following the photographer was smaller now, only six boys. Fanny inched forward, walking through layers of paper and debris until she stood directly behind a thick boy her own height. She was only a few feet from the photographer's caped back and every nerve in her body tingled.

A sudden wind wailed from the river and the floorboards twinged beneath her feet. The room was entirely in darkness but the walls almost whispered, as though beetles scurried from the floor to the ceiling. Fanny stood still, expecting to be able to see the inside of the room once the darkness settled. The stink of poverty was abundant—urine-stained clothing, soggy rugs, spoiled meat, old lard and grease. There must be people in this room—people as poor, as desolate as any in New Orleans. But Fanny could not see them.

Suddenly, a man's raspy voice called out from the darkness on the other side of the room. "Who's there?"

The photographer did not answer. Fanny did not answer. Fanny felt the boys jostle each other with their elbows. A match struck suddenly and Fanny saw the photographer struggling to load his tray with a bag of magnesium.

Again, the raspy voice. "Is anyone there?"

As Fanny looked into the dark of the room, about to answer, a small flash emitted from the tray. But it had none of the strength of the earlier flash and did not illuminate the scene. One of the boys beside Fanny swore and she felt the group turn to leave, as though the low flash meant the end of their adventure. The photographer once more primed the magnesium tray. Fanny was alone with him. She watched as he took a pouch from his inside jacket pocket. He emptied its entire contents into the groove of the magnesium tray.

Almost without waiting to steady the tray he raised it high into the air, lit a matchstick and then the powder. The magnesium burst into a million specks of fire. Bright sparks showered down on the photographer, raining on his broad-brimmed hat, along his shoulders and down his cape. Fanny's eyes squeezed shut instinctively. Then, she forced them open.

She was horrified by the vision in front of her. Bodies were slumped against the back wall of the room, all of them with their eyes closed, as though they were sleeping. Men huddled side by side just like the fashion dolls lined up on Sylvia's bed. But there was nothing elegant or embellished about these people. They were draped in rags, from the cloths on their heads to the burlap covering the bottom of their feet. One body was so small and tightly bundled that it looked like a baby doll and the image of Nora composed in her coffin filtered through Fanny's mind. Around each person's neck was a chain and a metal square. Just as the powder settled to the floor and the light vanished, Fanny realized that the word **BLIND** was written on their metal tags.

Although the people were no longer illuminated, the firelight remained and the cloud of smoke hung in the room. The photographer stepped back sharply. Fanny realized that the flash tray was on fire. Sparks lit on the photographer's hat and cape and he dropped the tray to the ground. She watched as the photographer whisked the sparks from his body. But as the flames grew, the odor of burning cloth convinced her that he was failing.

Fanny watched in horror as the photographer struggled to free himself from the flames. Only then did Fanny realize that the sparks had caught more than the photographer. Small red beads lighted on her own skirt and smoke surrounded her. Fanny was on fire!

She fought off the sparks flying about her hair and clothes. Speckles of hot ash landed on Fanny's head and cascaded along her shoulders and dress-front. Her hair sizzled and she scratched at the heat, bending over to release the sparks of fire from her tight bun. Her gloved hands batted at the slivers of fire that fell on her clothing. She made a quick survey; her body was free of the fire.

But the photographer was still stamping fire from his clothes. He kicked at the wooden floor as though the bottoms of his boots were burning. Fanny looked closer. The photographer's boots *were* on fire. No, something on the floor was on fire and the flames spread quickly amongst the paper that littered the room. The photographer trounced at the short flames below him, his feet moving quickly as if dancing an Irish jig. His arms flailed about him, keeping Fanny at a distance. The flames flared for a moment, then died down. Within seconds the fire was out and the photographer's shoulders heaved.

The photographer took hold of his camera, tripod and slide box and jaunted out of the room. Fanny wanted to follow but she was frozen to the floor. Were there really blind people living in these awful conditions? Why didn't the raspy voice call out again? Could any of the other blind speak or was it possible they were deaf and dumb as well?

Fanny brushed the ashes from her face and licked her lips. She swallowed hard, about to ask the blind people if they were all right. Then she saw the red-hot mounds of fire and realized that the photographer must have upset the brazier of coals. The fire was not out. It had only gone dormant.

Fanny rolled back on her heels, horrified into silence as the thread of flames from the glowing coals scattered across the wooden floor, running into the waste that littered the room. Sparks erupted from each coal, with wisps of fire running along the floor and then up the oily walls of the room. She removed her shawl, twisted it up and beat it against the fire on the floor, following one stream of flame up to one wall and then another. She stepped on something. A broom. She picked it up and beat at the fire with the brush. Another stream of fire died down, but little fires engaged all over the room.

"Fire!" Fanny screamed. Despite the glow of the fires, she still could not see much of the room and was unsure of the location of the blind men. "Get up! The room is on fire."

Fanny expected the blind men to cry out, but she heard nothing. A sudden swish of air sent sparks flying. For a second the room glowed red with illumination and Fanny could see them frozen in place, their sightless faces stunned. As the heat closed in on them they began to stand up and press themselves into the walls as if they could dissolve into it and escape the fire.

With arms extended in front of her, slowly and deliberately, she walked forward until she felt something soft and human. "Take my hand," she said, her voice low from the smoke. A hand grabbed onto her hand and then a man's thick fingers grasped her own. "Take the hand of the person next to you. We'll all leave the room single file. Quickly!" Fanny felt the weight as the person's hand she held grabbed the hands of others and started moving.

Fanny lowered her head, her breath short and smoky. With her phalanx of blind men, Fanny stepped slowly forward, hoping the door was where she thought it was. And then she heard the door slamming shut.

22.

OLIVE HATED STANDING IN THE SHADOWS just waiting to see what Lester Adams was going to do. She knew that Nora Keegan had been strangled, not ripped to shreds. And she knew that the "Ripper letters" that had flooded the police and newspaper offices were written by perverts and sensation seekers; that they did not need to be taken too seriously. But Olive also knew that someone might capitalize on all of the publicity by replicating a Ripper-like murder. Instinctively, Olive felt it in her bones—as Aunt Esther would have said—that Lester Adams was evil. But was he a murderer?

If Olive was to catch him at his evil business she must remain unnoticed. And so she hid from him, knowing that if she waited long enough.... Well, she could only hope he would reveal himself tonight. Olive's thoughts were distracted by the heavy gulps of someone running hard toward her and she flattened herself against the wall to protect herself.

Liam pulled up short and heaved for air. "Miss Sylvia twisted her ankle!"

Damn. Not now. Olive whirled around to keep her watch on Adams. But in those few seconds he disappeared from her sight. Where was he?

Olive wondered if Sylvia had really hurt herself or if she had fabricated an injury in order to end the evening quickly. "How bad is she?" But before Liam could answer, she added, "Fanny knows what to do for a twisted ankle. Sylvia will be all right for a few minutes more without me."

"But Miss Sylvia's just a few buildings away. Do you want me to carry your bag?" Liam bent his knees and put both hands on his thighs.

"I can't leave. Something's going on here."

"But Miss Sylvia's *hurt!*" Liam pleaded. "And Miss Fanny said—"

"Sylvia will be all right for the moment. I promise." Olive pulled Liam out of the light and into the shadow.

Olive watched as Adams emerged from the ambulance and jumped down to check the pair of horses. He walked about the ambulance once clockwise, then again, counterclockwise. He stopped once more in front of the horses. He looked around carefully, his eyes seeming to peer into every dark crevice of the intersecting roadways. When he cast his eyes toward her stretch of darkness Olive shrank back into the shadows.

His gaze finally settled on the two prostitutes, who were passing a brown bottle between them, oblivious to his stare. Lester Adams removed something from his jacket pocket and pinned it to his lapel. It was scarlet and white and seemed to give him new confidence.

Liam planted himself squarely in front of Olive, forcing her to look at him. "We gotta go to Miss Sylvia now!"

Olive was softened by the youngster's devotion to her sister. Liam would do anything to help Sylvia. And Olive knew that he was right; they should go. Despite the intelligent anxiety that Adams' presence caused her, Olive's duty was to her sister.

Glancing out of the shadows again, she saw Adams walking purposefully toward the prostitutes. He moved in front of the women, obscuring them from Olive's view. She strained to hear him, but the only sound was Liam's whispered plea, "Let's go."

Angry shouts raged through the street and Liam and Olive turned to look. The older woman was yelling as loudly as she could, her drunken garbles directed at Adams. For good measure, she yelled in the direction of the saloons and began to wave her hands and fingers in rude gestures. She weaved away from Adams. She put up her arms in front of her face, mimicking the familiar stance of street boxers. Haggard as she was, the woman looked ready for a fight.

Adams turned and walked toward the ambulance. The two women watched him move on, stunned into silence. The older woman released her boxer's stance and put her hands on her hips, as though very satisfied with herself. Her chin rose in triumph. The younger woman leaned back against the lamppost for support.

Adams returned to the Charity ambulance, opened the double back door, pulled a lantern from the inner wall and lit it. He lifted himself inside and shut the doors. Olive could only wonder at Adams' behavior.

What was he doing in the ambulance? It wasn't possible that he had a patient in there, was it? Or had he been attempting to hire the prostitutes and planning to take them into the ambulance bed?

Olive's attention ricocheted back to the prostitutes. The older woman was laughing loudly, a fierce, almost hysterical laughter that drew the attention of a lone man emerging from the saloon. He stumbled over to the two women, coming just as close to them as Adams had, but garnering none of their scorn. He pushed his hand into his pants pocket and brought out a handful of coins, some of which fell to the ground. At the older woman's insistence, the young woman scurried to retrieve the coins. Taking the dropped coins, the older woman put her arm through the man's and led him towards the darkness between the saloons.

Olive's stomach caved. She knew all about the medical dangers of a prostitute's life and she knew of the social conditions that forced women to take on such a life. But she had no stomach for it—this acquiescence of a miserable, drunken woman to a strange man—and it saddened her deeply. Olive looked back at the ambulance and saw that the back doors were now open but there was no light within. She looked at the young girl at the lamppost. Lester Adams was at her side.

He shook his finger at her, as though he was a schoolmarm. The girl cringed. He beat his balled fist against his open hand, as if laying down the law. The girl shook her head. Olive could read the protesting words from her lips. *No. No. No.* Finally, Adams leaned into her, as if to whisper into her ear. Strangely enough she remained still for this address, absorbing his message.

Then Adams stepped behind the girl almost as if a dance instructor choreographed his moves. His right arm encircled her small waist. He squeezed her so tightly that she began to double over. A small scream seemed to burst from her mouth but then there was no noise. Could she breathe?

Adams jabbed his left hand into his pocket pulled out something white. A knife? No. His handkerchief? A sponge? Adams slammed it over the girl's nose and mouth. The girl reeled to the side. Her eyelids fluttered and sank closed and then her helpless body slumped into the doctor's arms.

Olive jumped from the shadows, determined to stop Lester Adams.

"Wait!" Liam yanked on Olive's medical bag. "I hear Miss Sylvia."

Olive halted. She looked back into the shadowy alleyway and listened carefully. Someone was shouting. Slowly, Olive watched as a figure limped toward her.

"Fire!" cried Sylvia, collapsing against a brick wall. "Fanny's caught in a fire!"

Olive knelt and ran her hands down Sylvia's legs. Her sister's left ankle was slightly swollen above her leather boot; at least Sylvia's more delicate right leg had been spared.

Sylvia whimpered with sudden pain and grabbed Olive's forearm. "Laudanum. Do you have it with you?"

Olive did, of course. She had everything she ever needed in her doctor's bag, but she also needed Sylvia alert and useful. "No."

Her thoughts still focused on Lester Adams, Olive weighed the possibility of sending Liam to follow the doctor. Suddenly, the high whinnies of the ambulance horses drifted over and Olive heard the heavy vehicle roll down the street. It was too late. Lester Adams had gotten away. And Olive was sure he had taken the girl with him.

"Can you walk just a little way, Sylvia?" Without waiting for an answer, Olive leaned over and grabbed her sister by her waist. She threw her doctor's bag on Liam's shoulder. "Take us back to Fanny."

INCHING FORWARD, CAREFUL not to break the chain of hands, Fanny waved her free arm in front of her. If she could reach a wall, she could feel her way toward the door. She stretched forth her fingers but recoiled at the heat on her fingertips. She was at the fire line. Still, there must be a wall nearby.

Fanny pushed her hand through the flame, her cotton gloves sizzling. Beneath her, the flooring swayed up and down. Within inches she felt a wall. *Which way was the door? Left or right?* She could only guess and stroked her free hand along the wall toward the right. "Keep close together," she yelled, her words muffled by the smoke. "Don't let go of anyone's hand."

With a few more strokes to the wall Fanny's hand hit a thin piece of wood. She ran her fingers up and down it; it had to be the door surround. She put her hand out and touched the wooden door. It was closed. She put her gloved hand on the doorknob but it would not turn. She clutched the knob with her entire hand and tried again to turn it but still it did not yield. She released the blind man's hand, grabbed the knob with both hands and tried to pull the door toward her. Could the photographer be holding the doorknob against her?

Behind her, the blind men choked against the smoke. As the smoke curled about her head, Fanny pulled her skirt up to her mouth to shield her throat. She looked around the door. It was ill cut, with a large space between the bottom of the door and the rotting floor. Smoke rolled from the room under the door and into the hallway. The photographer began to cough. Fanny reasoned that if he was holding one hand to his mouth, he held the doorknob with one only hand. With all of her strength, she tugged with both hands at the doorknob. But still the door would not give. She could hear the blind men falling to the floor, overcome by the smoke.

Fanny realized that the sooner she let go of the doorknob, the sooner the photographer would let go. He needed to get out of the burning building as much as she did. Fanny released the knob and slumped heavily to the floor, praying that the photographer thought she was overcome and could not breathe.

Within seconds the doorknob rattled loose. Moments later, Fanny heard the sounds of footsteps running away from the door and down the stairs. Fanny clutched the doorknob with both hands and pulled herself up. The knob turned and she pulled the door open. She turned around and began shaking the blind men, urging them on their feet.

"Hold hands again!" The words scraped from her dry throat, "We're almost out."

With the human chain secured, Fanny rushed out of the room, tugging the blind men behind her. She heard someone stumble, swear, catch himself from falling, and swear again. She kept tugging at the string of people, pulling the end of the chain from the smoky room.

The blind men stumbled about each other like puppies, bumping into each other, sliding into the wall, losing their footing, falling onto the floor. One stumbled backwards into the fiery room. Fanny grabbed him and flung him away from the open doorway. She needed to get everyone downstairs and out of the building. Where were the volunteer fire brigades? Where were the police? Where were Sylvia and Olive?

Fanny looked over at the men who had collapsed together in a lump against the wall. She counted their heads and bodies as best she could, but their filthy clothes all had a greasy dark sameness to them. Bunched together as they were, she could not be sure of the count. Seven? Eight? Nine?

Fanny shook the arm of the man on top of the pile. "How many of you were in there?" As she bent low to hear any response, the distant clank of a fire engine bell burst through. She looked back at the doorway to the blind men's room. From a few yards away, it appeared that some of the small charcoal fires had given up.

Fanny heard Olive shout from the bottom of the staircase, "Fanny! Are you up there?"

"Don't come up!" yelled Fanny but before she could add a warning, Olive negotiated up the rotten staircase.

Sylvia's thin voice called from below, "Olive? What's going on? Is Fanny all right?"

Olive called down the staircase, "Just stay down there!"

Fanny pulled one of the blind men onto his feet and said to Olive, "Get everyone downstairs before the floor goes!"

The sound of shattering glass rent the smoke-filled room. Slowly the smoke and fire swept out of the room and through the broken windows. She saw the sharp edge of a hatchet through the window opening. The fire brigade had arrived.

OLIVE SENT LIAM back to Pleasant and Fulton Streets where he found Thomas and the carriage waiting in the shadows; Olive had Fanny and Sylvia in the infirmary within minutes. Although Sylvia seemed to be in command of her swollen ankle, Olive knew that Sylvia's frosty determination could turn to hysterics at any moment. Olive gave her sister a firm dose of laudanum and then assigned Thomas to assist Sylvia with her ankle.

Olive focused on Fanny. Despite her ripped stockings and torn and melted boots, Fanny's lower limbs and feet were unblemished. Gently, Olive shimmied Fanny out of her bodice and removed her shredded gloves. She disentangled the remnants of Fanny's bonnet from her hair. Clearly, Fanny's head and hands had caught the fire's wrath.

Although Sylvia and Fanny were on beds only a few feet apart, Olive stood firmly between the women. Sylvia squirmed desperately, trying to see around

Olive. Thomas kept his back toward Olive and Fanny, determined to spare Fanny the embarrassment of being seen in her undergarments by a colored man. Liam, fighting Thomas for the privilege of swaddling Sylvia's ankle in ice and cushions, was oblivious to Fanny's bare shoulders and arms.

Then the gaslight wavered and dulled and Sylvia could not see Fanny at all. "Olive?"

Olive snapped at her sister, "For God's sake Sylvia, calm down. Just let Thomas hold that ice on your ankle. I've got to get more light." Olive took the last oil lamp from the infirmary cupboard, filled the oil well, and trimmed and lit the wick. The infirmary's back room illuminated quickly, creating harsh halos about Fanny and Sylvia.

Buoyed by the strength of the new light, Sylvia looked directly over at Fanny who lay propped up on a tier of pillows. Olive yanked a linen curtain between the two beds and from behind the curtain spoke tersely to her sister. "You're working yourself into a fit. I told you that Fanny's not hurt badly."

"It's all my fault." Sylvia's voice was slight and cracked. "If I hadn't let her follow the photographer alone, she wouldn't have gotten caught in the fire."

Olive took a large keyring from her apron pocket and tossed it to Thomas. "Get that bottle of whiskey out of the bottom of the medicine cabinet and give Sylvia a good strong dose. That'll calm her down for a while."

Liam took hold of the wrapped lump of ice on Sylvia's ankle while Thomas located the whiskey. With precise medical dispensation, he poured the amber liquid into a heavy glass and offered it to Sylvia. She took a deep sip, coughed harshly and then considered the contents of her glass carefully. "I'm impressed, Olive. How did you ever talk father out of his best spirits?"

Olive dipped a cloth into warm water and worked the ash from Fanny's face. "Father and I both understand the true medicinal qualities of alcohol."

Sylvia finished the glass and launched into a spasm of coughing. Fanny's eyes shivered open. Olive leaned toward Fanny and advised, "Don't speak unless you really want to."

Sylvia pushed out her arm and pulled back the linen curtain. "Oh, Fanny. I'm so sorry I didn't go with you." Sylvia's words slurred toward Fanny. "I'm so sorry you were stuck in that awful building by yourself!"

Fanny's eye's began to fully open and her forehead creased in thought, as if she were trying to decide where she was. Her eyes wandered around the room. Finally, she cocked her head and focused at Sylvia. Who had been being unusually pleasant. "You've been drinking."

"Olive made me." Sylvia hiccupped.

Fanny stiffened, realizing that she was partly unclothed and that her bodice and gloves and—was that her only bonnet?—were thrown to the floor. She inspected her exposed limbs and hands. They were clean but reddened. And they burned, hot and white.

Fire. She had been watching a fire. No, she had been caught in a fire and others caught with her. Unable to see, unable to breathe, unable to move. *And the photographer must have held the door shut against her.*

"Did everyone get out?" Fanny swallowed harshly.

"Yes," Olive's reply was sweet and soothing. She lifted a glass of water to Fanny's lips.

Sylvia tilted her empty glass toward Thomas, who added another finger full of whiskey. "*You* got them out. Don't you remember, Fanny?"

Fanny grabbed Olive's arm. "Did they stop the fire? The firemen?"

From his post next to Sylvia's feet, Liam called out, "They're gonna go stomp it to the ground! That's what they said."

Olive scowled at Liam who retreated under the bed. "They said they'd want to talk to you tomorrow to find out what happened."

"It was the photographer. He started the fire with his magnesium explosion. The blind men had nothing to do with starting the fire." Fanny settled back on her pillow, her already-reddened cheeks flushed with sudden fury. "They didn't even know they were in danger at first and then they were too frightened and didn't want to move. It was so dark in there and I couldn't breathe." Fanny recoiled, as if the smoke and flame were about her now. "They're really all right, the blind men?"

"Yes. John—Dr. Remington—has them at Charity." Olive paused for only a second to remember how glad she was to see Remington arrive moments after the firemen. "They're in very good hands."

"What about the photographer?"

"He should be thrown into jail! Leading you into danger like that...and then running away from the building. He didn't even turn when I called after him. Coward." Tears rimmed Sylvia's eyes as she gazed deeply into her empty glass. "If you hadn't been there, those people would have died. Those poor blind men!" She raised her glass awkwardly toward Fanny and said, "To our heroine."

Thomas, who was on the other side of the curtain from Fanny, tilted the bottle toward Fanny in salute. Olive looked at Fanny, then at the bottle, and told Liam to get four more glasses. Thomas filled Sylvia's glass halfway and then filled two glasses to the top. Olive poured water into Liam's glass and into half of Fanny's glass. Thomas topped Fanny's glass with whiskey. Olive, Sylvia, and Thomas raised their glasses to Fanny. Liam joined them.

"To our heroine," toasted Olive.

Thomas and Sylvia followed. "Our heroine."

Fanny sipped at her glass. The liquid burned as it went down but it was nothing like the smoke scraping her throat. She looked into the golden spirits in her glass and felt overwhelmed by the whole evening. She was a little embarrassed too. Not because Sylvia and

Olive had proclaimed her a heroine but because she felt like one.

She had fought her way out of a fire tonight. She had saved the lives of people who could not save themselves. She had prevented a tragedy. She had done it. She, Fanny Newcomb. She had changed people's lives for the better...just what Sylvia always boasted about doing at Wisdom Hall. And her father would be proud of her for rescuing the blind from the fiery furnace.

The glass weighed heavily in Fanny's hands and fell to her lap. Olive picked it up. "It's time for you to rest."

Sylvia, who was gingerly stretching out her swollen ankle asked, "Can you make it upstairs, Fanny?"

The tingle of whiskey surged through Fanny's limbs and she set her shoulders back, ready to stand at her full five feet and six and a half inches. "After tonight, I can do anything."

LIAM, THOMAS, SYLVIA, Olive and Fanny progressed from the infirmary, through the back hallway and into the central hallway. Just as they were about to ascend the central staircase to the second floor, a firm fist barraged the front door.

Olive was not entirely surprised to see Detective Daniel Crenshaw and Sergeant Flynn at the door. Something about the eagerness of Crenshaw's manner suggested that he was here about the fire but as she stood at the threshold, Olive told the detective, "Something terrible happened in the Channel tonight. I've got to get Fanny and Sylvia upstairs but come around to the infirmary in a few minutes."

The detective stepped across the threshold, looking to the hallway to where Fanny—clad in what seemed like a lady's dressing gown and a man's long cape—rested against the newel post. "Fire first, Dr. Giddings. I need to see Miss Newcomb now."

"But Fanny needs—"

The detective studied Fanny and then nodded at the open door to Sylvia's study. "A few minutes of her time is all I need."

Olive eased Fanny into the study's most comfortable chair. As Sergeant Flynn pulled a notebook from his inside tunic pocket, Olive slid a footstool beside Fanny's chair for herself.

The detective asked Olive, "Were you in the fire also, Dr. Giddings?"

"No, I was not."

"Then we have no questions for you at this time." Crenshaw nodded to the door leading into the central hallway, clearly indicating that Olive should leave. "We'll speak to Miss Newcomb alone. I assure you that she will be safe in our care."

23.

FANNY FOUGHT THE DROWSY EFFECTS OF Olive's golden whiskey. Her bandaged hands attempted to grip the chair arms but the pain was too fresh. "Did everyone get out of the building?"

"Thanks to you, apparently." The detective surveyed Fanny from the top of her flame-frizzed hair and the greasy ointment on her face and neck, to the bandages on her hands. "I'm sure when the news gets out about your—"

"No!" Alarm rang clearly through Fanny's voice. "I don't want anyone to know I was involved."

"The newspapers are already trying to ascertain the identity of the 'heroic Channel lass'."

"No." Fanny knew the detective could not understand her desire for anonymity, but it was essential if she were to discover who murdered Nora. She thought of one reason that the detective might accept, not that it was anything close to the truth, of course. "Having my name in the newspaper for everyone to read...no lady would like that." Crenshaw looked askance at Fanny's sudden modesty, but then she asked, "How did you find out I was there?"

"We have our ways, Miss Newcomb."

Sergeant Flynn sat by Fanny's side, ready to record her comments. She shivered slightly as he thumbed through his notebook. She had held that very notebook in her hands a few days ago and deciphered some of its secrets. That notebook had led them on the search for Nora's real murderer and it had led Fanny to follow Pierre deVille tonight and to get caught in the fire. How the night might have been different...how men might have died tonight...if she had never seen that notebook.

The detective leaned back in his chair, almost as though he were looking forward to a tale told by a great storyteller. "Miss Newcomb, why don't you tell us exactly what happened tonight."

Fanny spoke of the cloaked photographer, the blind men, and the accidental fire. She did not mention Pierre deVille by name. Nor did she mention that she thought he had held the doorknob against her, although she wasn't quite sure why.

She could not stop herself from watching Flynn's hand as it sped along the notebook pages. Fanny was familiar with at least two different types of shorthand and could read both upside down. But Flynn's shorthand she could not decipher and she hated knowing that his script was a closed book to her.

As Fanny described the arrival of the volunteer fire brigade, Crenshaw nodded to Flynn. "That's enough for now, Sergeant. I'll talk to Miss Newcomb alone for a few minutes." With Flynn out of the room, Crenshaw scooted his chair over to Fanny's and met her eye to eye. His nose twitched, as if he had—but could not believe he had—smelled the whiskey on her breath.

"The photographer started the fire?" he asked. "With magnesium powder from his flash tray?"

Fanny coughed, forcing Crenshaw to back away slightly. "Yes."

"And you don't know who this photographer was?"

Fanny held Crenshaw's gaze for a few seconds. She knew she should tell the detective the name of the photographer but she didn't want to. The photographer had started the fire by accident and no interview with Crenshaw could change that. Suddenly, Fanny clutched the chair arms with her bandaged hands. What if the photographer didn't hold the door against her? What if it was someone else?

"It was dark," Fanny winced in pain and slowly released her grip on the chair. "I never saw his face. I never spoke to him or heard him speak."

"You're sure, then? Because a man who starts *one* fire, there's no telling if he'll do it again. Burning down a building can hide a multitude of sins."

"But who do you think the photographer wanted to kill?" Fanny leaned toward the detective. "The blind men. Or me?"

"If he really wanted to kill you, I'm not sure the police could protect you," Crenshaw replied soberly. "And if he just wanted to scare you...well, I hope you've been scared. If I were you, I'd consider this a warning. No one likes other people looking into their business." The detective stood. "So if you cannot name the photographer, it's time I asked elsewhere."

OLIVE UNLOCKED THE inner door to the infirmary, surprised to see the two beds in disarray, dirty bandages on the floor, and the bottle of whiskey on her desk. Glad to have something to do while she waited, Olive collected the bandages and threw them into the hamper.

Olive heard a scraping noise from the infirmary entrance. Was it just Thomas going to his bed in the detached carriage house? Or was it one of the policemen answering a call of nature? She held still for a moment and the sound ceased.

Olive's gaze wandered toward the bottle and the empty glass beside. She heard the scraping again, although this time it sounded more deliberate and steady, something that needed to be attended to.

Turning down the lights, Olive went to the window and looked out on Wisdom Hall's back yard. From the porch floor to the row of young magnolias that held fast at the rear property line, she saw nothing but the darkness.

Scrape. Olive was sure that it came from her porch. She grabbed the poker that Thomas kept by the side of the front door, placed in anticipation of just such a need for protection. She opened the door and immediately saw that there was a person seated on the porch bench. It was so dark that Olive could not tell if it was male or female, child or adult.

"Are you in need of medical assistance?" asked Olive calmly, as her hands gripped the poker. Olive saw a sudden shake of fire and realized her nocturnal visitor was smoking. As she watched, the bowl of the pipe glowed with a sharp inhale, and as the man released his breath, the aroma of the tobacco rose to her nostrils. It was sweet and dense, ripened with aged cherry and apple wood, expensive ingredients imported from New York State. Olive knew only one man who favored that blend.

The poker relaxed in her hands. "John Remington, is that you?"

FROM HIS BLOODSHOT eyes to his clumsily tied cravat, Dr. John Remington seemed on the verge of collapsing. Olive brought him into the infirmary, faintly aware that underneath his fatigue was the sickeningly sweet odor of chloroform. Or was Olive just imagining it?

Remington quickly fell into the seat nearest Olive's desk. He had never been to the infirmary before and as much as Olive wanted to display her modern equipment and show off her well-stocked pharmacy, now was not the time. She took her own chair and with the desk between them, she was all too conscious that their usual roles were reversed.

To Olive's surprise, Remington had arrived on the heels of the fire brigade. As Olive tended to Fanny, Remington doctored to the blind men. He'd shown great concern over Fanny's burns, but Olive assured him that she could handle Fanny. But why was he here now? Did he want to check on Fanny? Or to check on something else?

Had he been worried about Olive's own safety? Once again, she eyed the bottle of whiskey sitting on her desk. She wondered if she should offer him a glass but decided against it.

"Fanny will be pleased to know you stopped by. Tonight, she appears to be in good shape. Tomorrow and the days beyond will tell the entire story."

"Good." Remington's eyes roamed away from Olive's face to the pharmaceutical case behind her desk.

Olive hoped he could see that she had everything categorized alphabetically and that the cabinet was double-locked, as a properly maintained pharmaceutical cabinet should be. If he looked closer, he could have seen that she had no patent medicines in her cabinet. She possessed nothing that promised to cure cancers, night vapors, or loss of male vitality. "The police are talking to her right now. Detective Daniel Crenshaw arrived just a little while ago."

Remington nodded even before Olive concluded her sentence. "That's all I really wanted to know." Although his muscles seemed to protest, Remington began to rise from his chair.

"Wait. I saw something tonight that you need to know about." But once she had his attention, Olive hesitated. "When I was in the Channel this evening—before the fire—I saw your nephew, Lester Adams."

Remington eased back into the chair. "That's not unusual. He *is* the ambulance doctor."

"He wasn't answering an ambulance call." Olive looked him straight in the eye. "He was abducting a prostitute."

Remington pulled out his tobacco pouch. Empty. He looked at the whiskey bottle and swallowed dryly. For the first time in their relationship Olive could tell that Remington was not in charge of a situation and the realization pained her considerably. He rested his eyes on Olive. "Tell me everything."

Olive explained what she had seen in quick order. Finally, she said, "I was about to intervene when I had to go to Sylvia."

"You're going to talk to the detective when he's through with Fanny. Aren't you?"

"Yes, of course. I wanted to tell you first. To warn you. Your nephew's actions are bound to reflect badly upon you. You know how New Orleans can be. Is there any reason why I *shouldn't* talk to detective Crenshaw?"

"You could have been mistaken." Remington did not look directly at Olive as he spoke. Instead his eyes fixed on the locked shelf of pharmaceuticals. "Is it safe to talk here?"

"Yes."

"Was he wearing a red carnation in his lapel when you saw him?"

"He could have been." Olive recalled the flash of scarlet against Adams' drab suit. And then realized that he was wearing a suit and not the ambulance doctor's white smock.

"Then there's a simple answer to your concerns." Remington returned the tobacco pouch to his coat pocket. "My nephew Lester is a Redeemer. He tries to rescue women from a life of prostitution. The carnations are their symbol. They wear them to show their mission and to ensure that they're not confused with other types of men."

"You mean there are more Redeemers?"

"There may not be any more in New Orleans but there are certainly more elsewhere. The organization began in Britain some time ago. You may have read that Prime Minister William Gladstone was a leader of an organization to reclaim fallen women."

Olive sat back in her chair, trying to make sense of what Remington said. Very faintly, she remembered some connection between a British politician and prostitutes; a connection that had garnered much laughter and ridicule. All right, Olive would go along with Remington's explanation for now. "What exactly do these Redeemers do?"

"They try to persuade women that they do not have to prostitute themselves. Their most favored method is to approach them while they are out looking for customers. Which is probably what you saw tonight."

"Your nephew wasn't *persuading* that woman. He was *kidnapping* her. He had a handkerchief dosed with *something* and he put over her mouth and nose. When she fell silent, he threw her into the ambulance."

Olive got up and came around to Remington's side of the desk and stood before him. "Your nephew's been in trouble before, hasn't he? Is that why you know what he does? Have you been protecting him from the police all along?"

"What he does is not illegal."

"Kidnapping must be illegal," Olive answered immediately, although she wasn't really sure. Was it possible that there was no Louisiana law against kidnapping women? Even white women?

"Lester would never do anything like that. He's assured me."

Olive stumbled at hearing Remington's last words. Adams' assurances meant that the men had talked about this seriously before. "Less than two hours ago your nephew assaulted a woman. I witnessed it myself.

I need to know that she is safe. The police need to make sure she has not been harmed." But even as she spoke, Olive knew that the New Orleans police did not care about the safety of a prostitute.

Remington sighed, a weary deflation she had never heard from him before. "Olive, we've worked together for over a year now. I suspect I know how you think. If you really thought someone had been harmed you would not have hesitated to tell the police as soon as they arrived here."

"I didn't hesitate; I had a burn victim to attend to. And besides, there's been enough hysteria since Nora's murder. I didn't want to add to it."

"Will you wait until tomorrow to tell the police? As a favor to me?"

In the silence that hung between them, Olive heard footsteps coursing through the hallway leading to the interior infirmary door. From the strained look on his face it was clear Remington heard them too.

Remington stood up slowly. "Tell me what she looked like and I'll find out about her."

The footsteps stopped outside the infirmary door. "Dr. Giddings," Sergeant Flynn's thick Irish accent cut through the door as well as any fist. "We'll be leaving now."

Olive opened the door to the sergeant and was not surprised to see Detective Crenshaw with him. She was surprised to see Sylvia's dogs Cain and Abel at the detective's side. The policemen looked equally surprised to see John Remington. Backing up, Flynn muttered, "We'll go out through the front door then." He started walking back down the hallway to the front door.

Crenshaw stepped forward slightly, although he did not enter Olive's infirmary. He looked at Olive and acknowledged Remington. "Doctor."

"Detective," replied Remington.

Olive felt herself leaning toward the detective, pulled toward his authority. Should she tell him now? Would he believe her?

"Miss Newcomb looks like she's ready for bed." Crenshaw turned, the dogs stood, and the three of them followed Flynn down the hallway.

With Crenshaw and Flynn out of sight, Olive turned back to Remington. They stood facing each other, both with arms crossed in front of their chests.

"I'll wait until noon to go to the police." Olive stared into the strained, bloodshot eyes of John Remington. "And I hope to God you know what you're doing."

24.

ON SUNDAY SYLVIA's ANKLE was swollen to twice its size and throbbed painfully at the slightest movement. Throughout the morning, she found no comfort on her goose-feather bed nor on the chaise in her study. Finally, Thomas carried her to the front gallery. With a glass of iced lemonade, an unexpected visit by Cousin Charlotte, and a bell to summon Aunt Esther, Sylvia breathed her first calm breath since last night. Even the snoring of Fanny, who slept in the chair next to her, did not disturb her peace.

A pair of mules led an empty streetcar down Annunciation Street. It was just noontime but the ordinarily lively street was as uninhabited as the streetcar. Sylvia suspected that her female Irish Channel neighbors were still in mass at St. Alphonsus' or St. Mary's and that their menfolk were asleep in their beds. But within an hour, Sylvia was sure that the Wisdom Hall neighborhood would be alive with neighbors enjoying their one day of rest.

Charlotte had arrived with the day's most important news: no woman had been murdered or assaulted in a Ripper-type attack last night. The taunting Ripper letters had been all hot air, for which Sylvia was very grateful. She had not been afraid that Jack the Ripper would murder last night, but it was possible that someone might imitate him and his methods.

Charlotte patted down the stack of pillows Aunt Esther had placed under Sylvia's ankles. "Now that you're settled, let's have a nice long talk."

"Must we?" sighed Sylvia. "I'm so tired today."

"I'm sure you are exhausted but I have information for you both." Charlotte nodded in Fanny's direction.

"We better wake up Fanny, then." Sylvia reached over to Fanny but hesitated to touch her. "She's been sleeping since we brought her out here. Even slept through Lawrence Decatur's visit, although he didn't so much visit, as rant about Fanny endangering herself."

"I'm sure he did," replied Charlotte. "How well I remember Lawrence's ranting. I'm sure Fanny will be glad she slept through it all. But she'll want to hear *me*." Charlotte reached over to Fanny's flushed cheek and stroked it softly. "Wake up, dear, won't you?"

Fanny breathed deeply, as if relishing the end of a pleasant dream. Her eyes opened slowly, adjusting to the bright midday sun. "Oh, Charlotte, it's you." Fanny turned uneasily in her chair. "I thought perhaps the detective had returned."

Charlotte settled into a wicker chair directly in front of Fanny and Sylvia. "I assume you mean Daniel Crenshaw, which is just as well, because I have something to say about him and I'll say it first. There's much more to the detective than you know. Did you know that he grew up in the Boylan household?" Charlotte looked from Fanny to Sylvia, gratified to see that they were appropriately surprised. "Crenshaw's parents were the Boylan's maid and stableman. Daniel Crenshaw was born in the attic of their house, the same year as Terence."

"They grew up together?" asked Sylvia. "But I thought you were friends with the Boylans. Why didn't you tell us before?"

"I was acquainted with Clara Boylan, dear," Charlotte bristled slightly. "Not her servants."

"Hmmm." Fanny wiggled in her chair.

"However," continued Charlotte, "that information is just a small tidbit about Detective Daniel Crenshaw."

"It is?" asked Sylvia.

"Yes. He has another connection to your Nora." Charlotte sat back in her chair but did not keep them waiting. "I've been told that Daniel Crenshaw is the nephew of Nora's landlady."

"Mrs. O'Sullivan?" Sylvia almost jumped in her seat. Instantly she recoiled in pain and looked down at her ankle.

"Rose O'Sullivan is the sister of Daniel Crenshaw's mother, who I'm told is deceased. As is his father. For all we know, she may be his only living relative."

"If Crenshaw knows the Boylans from childhood and if Rose O'Sullivan is Crenshaw's aunt, then it's possible that Terence and Gabriel Boylan also know Rose O'Sullivan. And if they know her," Fanny paused, as though what she was thinking was too good to be true. "It's quite possible, isn't it, that the Boylans knew Nora?"

"It certainly is," replied Charlotte.

"But then," said Sylvia, "there's Terence Boylan."

Charlotte nodded expressively. "And I've got some information about him also. He isn't the—"

"No!" Sylvia looked out on Annunciation Street. "I mean, *there's Terence Boylan!* He's walking down our street!"

Charlotte rose from her chair and stood by Sylvia's side. All three watched Terence Boylan. Dressed in a glossy black suit he paused every few feet to lift his hat to a woman, shake a man's hand, or place his fingertips under a child's chin. Finally, he stopped at the edge of the Wisdom Hall lawn and looked up at the trio on the gallery. Father Terence Boylan squared his shoulders and walked majestically toward the ladies.

Even before he climbed the stairs, Charlotte extended her hand and introduced herself, saying, "You may not remember me but I was a friend of your mother's."

Terence Boylan took Charlotte's hand and shook it strongly. He followed suit with Sylvia but halted when he saw Fanny's bandaged hands. "Miss Newcomb, I see you're injured." The priest discerned Sylvia's obviously swollen ankle from beneath her blanket. "And you also, Miss Giddings."

"My injury's of no consequence," declared Sylvia, "but Fanny's were won in a heroic deed."

Fanny cringed at the praise. Terence Boylan waited politely, as though he knew more information was forthcoming.

Sylvia did not disappoint him. "There was an awful fire in one of those old buildings on Tchoupitoulas Street last night. A group of blind beggars were trapped and Fanny pulled them all out to safety. Single-handedly."

Terence Boylan looked more closely at Fanny's bandaged hands and then to her blemished cheeks.

"That's what Sylvia says." Fanny's eyelids began to droop as though she might fall back asleep. "I don't remember much of what happened."

A sudden idea struck Sylvia. "Detective Daniel Crenshaw came by to question Fanny last night. Do you know Detective Crenshaw, Father Boylan?"

The priest looked at Cousin Charlotte almost as though he expected her to answer for him. The women's silence forced the priest to reply. "Yes, I know the man."

"He seemed very concerned about the fire," said Sylvia, who had actually heard very little about Crenshaw's visit.

"I could come back later in the week." The priest began to sidle toward the gallery stairs.

"The detective said that it was a wonder Fanny was alive. He said—"

Boylan slapped his hat against his leg. "I would think our Channel detective should have more to do than worry about fires."

"You mean he should be doing something about the murder at Conner's Court?" asked Sylvia, looking first at the priest and then to Fanny, confident that Fanny would be pleased at how well Sylvia asked such pointed questions. But Fanny's eyes were closed and her face slack. She had fallen asleep.

The priest also looked at Fanny, lowering his voice as he answered confidently. "There's nothing to worry about. The murderer has been caught. Any suggestion otherwise is miserably misguided."

Charlotte stepped into the conversation for the first time. "How so, Terence?"

The priest started, as if unused to hearing a woman address him by his Christian name. "I stood outside his cell when the man confessed."

"Karl spoke to you?" asked Sylvia. "He hardly ever spoke to me, even when I paid him his wages."

"He didn't speak in words but he...." The priest seemed to search for his words.

"Nodded?" asked Sylvia.

Boylan's dark eyebrows rose in agreement.

Charlotte placed her hands on her knees. "But he never really said he murdered her, did he?"

"The Commissioner asked him if he killed Nora and he offered no resistance." Terence answered Charlotte directly. "We all understood what he meant."

Charlotte flicked a stray crease from her lap. Fanny snored. Sylvia leaned back upon her cushions. "But Father Boylan, I thought only God could read our minds."

Boylan took a large breath and addressed Sylvia. "I came by to finish our earlier discussion, Miss Giddings but it looks like you are occupied this afternoon. We can continue another day."

Just as Terence Boylan put his hands on his hat, a sharp snore escaped from Fanny's open mouth.

Sylvia asked, "Charlotte, do you think you could take Fanny inside?"

"Of course," agreed Charlotte, already assisting Fanny to her feet. "I'm sure she'll be more comfortable there."

As the screen door slapped behind Fanny and Charlotte, Sylvia stoically gritted her teeth. Despite the throbbing in her ankle, the sunlight that threatened to mar her flawless complexion, and her vexing need to visit the outhouse, Sylvia was not going to let Terence Boylan leave her front gallery until she won some information from him.

"YOU ONLY PRETENDED TO fall asleep out there, didn't you?" Charlotte whispered as she and Fanny walked down the hallway. "But why?"

"The good Father seemed a little overwhelmed by the three of us. But if he's alone with Sylvia, she can work her charm." As they approached the infirmary, Fanny nodded at the ledge above the door. "Olive left a key up there."

Charlotte collected the key and unlocked the infirmary door. Fanny went directly to the jar on Olive's desk. "Olive said I needed to apply this ointment while she was gone." Fanny looked down at the top of her blistered hands. "But my hands are too stiff. Could you help me?"

In short order, Charlotte opened the jar, unwrapped the bandages, and began to delicately apply the ointment to Fanny's reddened hands. She looked carefully at Fanny's face—which exhibited the scarlet blotches of a woman caught in the sun without her parasol—and applied the ointment thinly across

Fanny's features. Once Charlotte seemed satisfied with her applications, she closed the jar.

"I know Sylvia told you about last night. About following deVille and the fire he started. But I didn't tell her everything. And I didn't tell the police the photographer's name." Fanny sat back gingerly. "Was I wrong? Something tells me that we should keep deVille's name a secret; perhaps until we learn why he was photographing those poor people?"

"As long as you're sure he started the fire accidentally and no one was badly hurt, I see no reason to share his name. Knowing his secret could be useful to you later."

Fanny relaxed against the chair. She had not told Sylvia or Olive about the door being held against her— she wasn't even sure if the blind men knew that someone had tried to deliberately trap them in a fiery room—and she wondered if she should tell Charlotte now. She wanted to, for she knew that the older woman would comfort and counsel her, but she did not want to alarm Charlotte. Fanny then asked Charlotte, "What did you find out about deVille?"

Charlotte ran her long finger over the top of the ointment jar. "He's one of many middle sons of an old Creole family, although most of the family has died out. Your photographer has jumped from job to job and worked as an auctioneer, insurance salesman, lottery promoter, and finally, as a photographer. All of his businesses failed after a few years and his debt built up. If an uncle had not left him a small bequest, deVille's debtors might have run him out of town. He's failed at everything he's tried. And I suppose that he'll fail at photography soon enough."

"Especially if he keeps blowing up his equipment and starting fires." Fanny smiled.

"In addition to taking photographs, he also performs magic lantern shows. Many of these shows are for exclusively male audiences." Charlotte looked at Fanny, as though wondering if the younger woman had understood her. Fanny did. And thought of the photograph of Nora in her bureau bottom drawer. Evidently satisfied with the disapproving look on Fanny's face, Charlotte continued, "I'm told he does a brisk business with his shows but still, he has many unpaid creditors. So, if Nora's death would have put money into deVille's pocket, he certainly would have a motive to kill her."

"Money is a powerful motivator, isn't it? If Nora had money and if deVille got it from her. But I visited his studio after Nora's death and everything was decidedly shabby. He must have made a lot of money last night, though."

"What was it like, his Ripper photograph?"

"It showed a man with a big knife. If anyone wanted to believe it was Jack the Ripper, I'm sure they would." Fanny squirmed, trying to adjust her sore body to Olive's unforgiving chair. "But I'm more curious about the photographs deVille took last night. It almost seemed as if he was photographing places rather than people."

"You'll be more comfortable over there." Charlotte offered her arm to Fanny and walked her over to a padded chair.

Fanny settled into the chair and allowed Charlotte to put her feet on an ottoman. But still she was perplexed about deVille's Ripper photograph. Why did people like to scare themselves? Why was it so satisfying to believe that Jack the Ripper was prowling just outside your door? Even her most sensible students reveled in terrible sensations. Fanny would much rather face a real problem than something imagined. And remembering that she had many real problems before her, she asked, "What did you find out about Lester Adams?"

"That man is a mystery, I'm sorry to say. I just don't know anyone who consorts with Yankees like him."

"What about his uncle?"

"John Remington?" The name lilted from Charlotte's lips like the song of a contented canary. "If the man were Catholic, he'd be a Saint. Through his quarantine efforts, he managed to stop last year's early outbreak of yellow fever almost single-handedly."

"You sound just like Olive."

"Olive's got a good head on her shoulders. If she senses that Remington is innocent, I'd listen to her."

"But his name was in the Sergeant's notebook. The police must have some reason to suspect him." Fanny yawned, a yawn so deep that she could not even cover her mouth. "What about the Boylans?"

"I heard at least three times this week that Terence does not want his brother to join the priesthood and that their brotherly relationship is strained because of it. You won't see them together in the same room."

Fanny rested her head upon the soft chair. "Do the Boylan brothers need money?"

"Certainly not."

"But what motives could they have to kill Nora? Why would Crenshaw suspect them?"

"Only he knows that. He's known these boys most of his life and would probably know any weaknesses of character."

"I hadn't thought of that." Fanny fell deeper into the chair. The temptation to close her eyes was great but she fought to keep them open. And then she couldn't fight any longer.

Charlotte watched as Fanny succumbed to sleep. The older woman removed a thin blanket from a shelf and draped it lightly over Fanny's shoulders. "No one can think of everything, child. But I'm sure you'll work it all out eventually."

ONCE THE SCREEN door slapped behind Charlotte and Fanny, Sylvia wasted no time with Father Boylan. "Since the last time we spoke, I've been thinking much about the murder at Conner's Court. Do you think Nora Keegan was murdered because she was a prostitute?"

"Any woman who falls so far from grace should expect to be carried down to the sewers of hell."

"But no woman deserves to be murdered."

"A woman who sells her body in prostitution doesn't respect the life God gave her and cannot expect anyone else to respect her life."

"But Nora was only a child; just seventeen. Surely you can't hold her responsible. When a child goes down the wrong road, surely an adult is responsible."

Boylan's face flushed red with unexpected anger. "Don't talk to me about women like Rose O'Sullivan." The landlady's name almost spat from his mouth. "She's the Devil incarnate."

"You know her?" Sylvia's eyes widened. She had not expected him to tell her that.

"To my misfortune. She worked for my mother as a laundress until one day I caught her selling our linens. I put her out on the street where she belonged. But did she come back begging for her position like a good woman would do? No, Miss Giddings, she did not. She hightailed it to the shady part of town and went to live with a friend of hers who ran an evil house. And she has been corrupting girls ever since." The priest shook his head eagerly, as though he was going to expound upon something very dear to his heart. "You do know—they must teach this in the Episcopal faith—that the path to heaven is extremely narrow and that women must work very hard to stay on that path."

Sylvia listened calmly as the priest expounded upon the Good Woman—who followed the dictates of the Church—and the Bad Woman—who followed only her desires. Throughout her life, Sylvia had heard—and discarded—this Good Woman/Bad Woman litany, but she had to admit that Terence Boylan was preaching forcefully and fluidly. If he was declaiming about any other subject, she might be swayed to his beliefs.

But Terence's words turned increasingly bitter as he warmed to the topic of Bad Women. "Women who refuse to marry. Women who are disobedient to the Church." Boylan took a long breath, more for emphasis, Sylvia was sure, than for sustenance. "Women who choose alcohol, tobacco, and education above their duty to God and their husbands."

Sylvia's initial sense of admiration crumbled. Boylan was now broaching dangerous territory. It might be just a minute or so until he said—no, he'd just said it. He'd said it *twice*.

"Fires of Hell," chanted Terence Boylan. "God has no choice but to dispatch these Bad Women to the Fires of Hell."

Even with the sun grazing the gallery, Sylvia shivered suddenly. She reached for her glass of lemonade and took a long sip, as though the cold liquid could protect her from the heat of Boylan's fiery furnace. "What you're saying all seems so *final*." Sylvia took another long sip of lemonade and placed the glass on her table. "I know, of course, that we are all sinners but I've never heard the argument of a woman's virtues and faults explained so forcefully. I thought I was a Good Woman but according to your definition, now I'm not so sure. Tell me, Father Boylan, which am I?"

Boylan was silent, as though realizing he had not only insulted his hostess but a member of a prominent New Orleans family. Bereft of his pulpit vigor, he said, "There is but one reward for the sinner. Redemption. A reward that all women must pray to receive."

"There's no reward in heaven for me?" Sylvia asked eagerly. "Because I left my father's home or because I opened a school that teaches girls to learn new skills and be independent? Or is it because I'm a spinster? Or am I guilty by association because my sister has entered a man's profession?"

"There are only two kinds of women," Boylan said, his voice rising with finality, "and a woman must make a choice."

"Is there no ground in-between?"

"Is there an acceptable middle ground between God and Satan? No, Miss Giddings, there is not. And if you believe there is, you are only fooling yourself. And God does not reward fools." Terence closed his lips tightly, as though he realized he had spoken too long. He stood up and fitted his hat upon his head. "I don't wish to overstay my visit, Miss Giddings. Good day to you."

As Sylvia watched Terence walk down the path, she realized that he did not offer his hand in parting nor did he wish her a speedy recovery. Although Sylvia deliberately antagonized the priest to shake information from him, she realized now that—for very possibly the first time in her life—she had not been able to charm a man back into friendship. In fact, Sylvia had probably made a serious enemy. But at least she had the enemy's information, information that Fanny, Olive, and Charlotte would be eager to hear. Sylvia had *some* reward for alienating Terence Boylan.

But first things first. Sylvia clutched the delicate silver bell and rang it for all it was worth. If she couldn't get to the outhouse in the next minute, she would burst.

25.

THE MAIN CORRIDOR OF CHARITY hospital was strangely quiet. There were no crazed shouts for *Doctor*, no moans from patient beds, and to Olive's surprise, no nuns scurrying from room to room.

As she turned the hallway corner to Remington's office Olive noticed two men huddled over a clutch of papers. Detective Crenshaw and Sergeant Flynn. Olive stifled a yawn. She had slept little last night, her mind dominated by visions of Lester Adams.

Olive found Remington in his examination room. He looked up, shaking his hands over a basin of blood-tinged water. His sleeves were gartered to above his elbows, but he did not wear a surgical apron. He hastily pulled an already-bloodied sheet over the corpse of a potbellied man.

Underneath a gray hospital sheet, a body lay on Remington's second examination table. As the bright light of the ceiling lamp bore down on the blanket, Olive could tell from the corpse's curves and lumps that it was a woman's body. Olive closed the door behind her. She reached forward to remove the blanket from the woman's head. Was it the unfortunate girl from last night? But before Olive could reach the blanket, the door opened and shut behind her. Crenshaw and Flynn stood beside her.

Remington grabbed a cloth from a shelf and began to dry his hands. He rubbed the cloth up to his elbows, making sure everything was wiped from his arms. He spoke to Olive. "A woman was found dead in the Channel last night."

Olive inhaled sharply. She would see Lester Adams burn in hell.

"An older woman," Remington emphasized, as if he were reading Olive's mind. "She was found in an alley off Justin and First streets."

"That's two blocks away from Wisdom Hall. When did this happen?"

Daniel Crenshaw folded his arms. "She was found only an hour ago. The newspaper reporters have been haunting the Channel and Charity this weekend. You can understand that we're trying to keep this as quiet as possible right now."

Olive's hand returned to the blanket in front of her. "I want to see her."

"Any objections, Daniel?"

"Fine with me."

Remington lifted the blanket over the corpse's head and settled it just below the chin. It was not the girl abducted by Lester Adams last night but an older woman, as Remington had said. Olive tugged at the sheet, exposing the woman's neck and upper shoulders. Then she pulled off the entire sheet, rolling it into a ball, which she hugged against her chest.

Sergeant Flynn's feet stamped on the floor like a horse shying with fear.

Detective Crenshaw asked, "Do you know her?"

Olive wasn't sure. The naked corpse looked like many of the middle-aged females who came to her infirmary: Beaten. Bruised. Broken. But her skin was intact. No sign of ripping—or strangulation—here. No one could even claim that Jack the Ripper had killed her.

"She had an empty bottle of beer in her pocket," offered the detective.

Olive pulled back the woman's lips and looked into her mouth. The two front teeth were missing; the others were chipped and darkened.

Remington lifted the corpse's right hand and inspected her forearm. He found a long scar, running from the top of the elbow to the bottom of the shoulder. He ran his finger along the very tiny, careful stitches, examining them as though he were appraising the work of a fine sculptor. "This is your work, isn't it Dr. Giddings?"

"Yes," Olive said as she put her hand under the woman's own. "I remember stitching this. She said it was an accident at the brewery but more likely it was a fight. She had an eye beginning to blacken and blood under her nails."

"Did she say which brewery?" asked the detective.

"No but the woman who carried her in gave her name as Carrie Reilly. 'Mrs.' Reilly, she was careful to say. She never came back to have the stitches removed."

Sergeant Flynn shuffled his feet again. He leaned toward the detective but spoke loudly enough for everyone to hear. "This could be Rusty Reilly's wife, sir. It does look something like her and chances are he probably hasn't missed her yet."

"Well, I know where we're going. Doctors." The plural salutation rolled off of Crenshaw's tongue easily. "I thank you for your information. Oh, and John, Leo McCready should be here within the hour. He shouldn't need too much of your time."

As soon as Crenshaw and Flynn left the room, Olive said, "Before you do anything else, I must know about that girl and your nephew."

"Of course." Remington pulled the sheet over the dead woman. "If you'll just give me a few minutes more, you'll have your answer." Remington charged into his office, pulled his suit coat from the back of his chair, and jammed his arms into the sleeves.

"We're leaving the hospital?"

"Just a short walk." Remington led Olive into the main hospital corridor, down the back hallway, through a door to the outside, and into one of the hospital's pocket gardens. Olive followed as Remington walked along a nearby street inhabited by austere wooden houses.

He stopped at the last house on the block. It was a lifeless wooden building with peeling paint, notable only for its elaborate wrought iron fencing. Olive followed him up the stairs to the narrow gallery. He knocked sharply at the front door. A severely dressed woman answered immediately. Remington was expected.

As she followed Remington through a hallway, Olive realized that everything about the house—from the unpainted walls and uncarpeted floors to the drab draperies and threadbare furniture—was colorless and dry. There was none of the texture and pattern so enjoyed by Sylvia at Wisdom Hall; no embellishment or decoration, no fragrance of jasmine or coffee to delight the senses. Even the windows were heavily draped and shuttered from the sunlight.

Remington took the stairs of the central staircase two at a time. Olive struggled to keep up. *He knows just where he's going.* Remington opened and entered through the first door at the top of the stairs. Olive followed behind him. It was a small room, shaded, dark, and close. Against the far wall was a cot, and ensnared within the coarse muslin bed sheets, was a pale face.

Olive went to the girl and drew her hand from beneath the sheet. "She's alive, at least." Olive pressed her fingers against the wrist. She looked at the cluster of half-filled pharmaceutical bottles on the table next to the cot but did not recognize any of the medicines. "But she's drugged."

"She is not." Lester Adam's sharp nasal accent assaulted Olive. She had not even known he was in the room and now he stood next to the closed window, in a pose that clearly stated he was the doctor in charge. "She's got an alcoholic hangover. If you'd smelled the gin on her breath last night—"

"A hangover from chloroform!" Olive glared at Adams, her mouth rigid with anger. "You kidnapped this girl last night! I saw you do it!"

Adams shrugged. "Sometimes it's necessary to battle evil with vigorous force. In cases like this, the means justifies the end."

Remington stepped between Olive and his nephew. "She's not dead and she'll be fine. I've looked at her myself."

"Yes," said Adams. "You can go about your own business now."

"I'm not leaving," Olive snapped. "And I'm not sure that I still don't want to talk to the police." Olive put her hand up to the girl's face, which had been scrubbed clean. Instead of rouge there were blister marks around her mouth and nose; confirmation that whatever Adams had placed over the girl's face last night contained a powerful dose of chloroform. Olive thought of Sylvia's own attempt to talk to the girl last night and wished now that she had not stopped her. Perhaps Sylvia should have intervened; perhaps the girl would not be in Lester Adams' control now. "What is this place?"

Remington folded his arms tightly and nodded at his nephew to speak.

"This is the Adams' Home of Refuge and Redemption, where we rescue girls from the horrors of prostitution."

"*We* rescue girls? Who else is involved in this?"

"Just one other man in the entire city of New Orleans is strong and moral enough to stand up to these women and to separate himself from the men who would destroy them."

"Who is he?" demanded Olive.

"His name will remain secret. It protects him from retribution from the men and women who run prostitution in this city."

Remington stepped toward his nephew, his whole body arched with anger. "His name, Lester."

Adams stepped away from his uncle until his body was against the wall. He almost seemed ready to answer honestly, but then he looked toward the bed. He seemed to gain strength from the girl's frailty. "Never."

Olive stood back from the bed and looked to Remington.

"No," he said, "I didn't know about any of this until after I left you last night." He nodded about the room, as if to include the entire house. "He told me he was just trying to persuade women to stop prostituting themselves. That seemed harmless enough."

Olive knew that there were many houses of refuge for girls and women throughout the country but had heard only about those hosted by older women or church groups. Never had she heard of a house of refuge run by a man or heard of a man who was so vigorous in his desire to rescue women from prostitution that he would stun them with chloroform. "How many women have you brought here?"

"Almost forty." Adams was quick to answer. "Almost forty women have been saved from a life of degradation. Almost forty women have been reunited with their families. They have turned away from their evil natures and been given a chance to redeem themselves by living chaste lives. These women crave sensation—physical, visual, emotional sensation—and once they are deprived of it, they are eager to cast aside their sins. I'm sure even a woman like you," Adams' nose tilted slightly, "can understand why we must fight for these children. Girls caught in prostitution are endangered every minute of the day. Not only from disease and abuse but from—"

"Murder?" interrupted Olive. Then she turned to Remington. "Nora Keegan was one of our students. She was walking home from a class at Wisdom Hall when she was murdered last week. Did you try to kidnap her, too?"

Remington looked truly alarmed and stepped toward his nephew, as if ready to nail him to the wall. "Lester, if there is anything you haven't told me—"

"It's all right, Uncle. I have nothing to hide. Yes, I saw her in the Channel many times."

"Just tell me if you—"

"And that night I saw her waiting on the corner, flirting with every man who passed by. I did try to redeem her. At first, she ignored me, like many of them do. They think I'm a bit mad. But then she yelled at me to go away. She even spat at me."

"Women do wait on corners," Olive spoke from behind clenched teeth, "that doesn't mean they are prostitutes."

"No good woman would wait at that spot at that hour. Even you should know that. Conner's Court is a well-known meeting place for prostitutes and men."

"You argued with her?" Remington probed.

"I discussed the possibilities of a new life with her."

"And you expect us to believe that you just left her there?" Remington looked at the girl in the bed. "After seeing all of this?"

"I had to report to work." Lester's chin lifted slightly and he managed to look offended that his professional integrity had been challenged. "And besides, murder defeats the purpose of Redemption. Even you could see that." Lester looked first at Olive and then at his uncle. "You can't really believe I killed that woman, Uncle. I can't be a suspect. I'm a witness."

"You saw Karl kill Nora?" asked Olive. "The police arrested Karl because of you?"

"I should certainly hope so." Adams smiled, a knowing, confident grimace that began to turn Olive's stomach. "I certainly hope so."

"WHAT WILL YOU do with this information?" Remington asked Olive as they reached Charity Hospital. "Will you go to the police?"

Olive considered the last few minutes. As Remington had attempted to ease her from Adam's house, Olive had demanded to bring the girl to the Wisdom Hall infirmary. But to her disgust, Adams provided a letter written by a man from Vicksburg, a letter that begged Adams to search New Orleans for his runaway daughter and gave Adams permission to take all measures to secure her rescue. Included with the letter was a photograph—a *carte de visite* of a father, mother, and four girls—one of whom clearly slept in the small cot against the wall. With this evidence of support from the girl's father, Olive knew that she could not take the girl from Adams.

"No," she said softly.

Remington seemed to breathe a great sigh of relief. "I must get back to the hospital. Leo McCready is probably already waiting for me."

"And who is Leo McCready?" asked Olive, relieved to talk of someone other than Lester Adams.

"He's the police photographer."

Olive put her hand on Remington's coat jacket. He looked down at it, as if she had challenged him, but she did not retract her hand. Instead, she gripped harder. "Did the police take photographs of Nora Keegan before your examination?"

"Yes."

"Do you have them at Charity?"

"Yes, of course."

Olive removed her hand from Remington's sleeve and put it to her chest. For some reason, her heart was beating wildly. "May I—"

"Yes, of course."

26.

FANNY FELL INTO A DEEP SLEEP AFTER cousin Charlotte departed. She awoke at four in the afternoon, drifted into Sylvia's office, and promptly fell asleep. She awoke four hours later, hearing Aunt Esther call her name.

"It's that detective policeman, Miss Fanny. He's at the door." Aunt Esther wiped her flour-covered hands on the bottom of her apron. "And Mr. Decatur, he was back again to see you."

Fanny met the detective at the front door and, at his request, joined him on the gallery. She was surprised at how much she delighted in the cool night air.

The detective pulled his cigar from his mouth. "You weren't doing anything you shouldn't be doing last night, were you?"

Fanny recoiled with surprise. In her still-sleepy state, she hadn't expected confrontation. She inhaled deeply and set her mind to working. "Something like?"

"Trying to play detective?"

"Why would—"

"You were out in the Channel on a night when every sane woman was hiding behind locked doors, scared to death that the Ripper was coming for her. Nora Keegan was a student of yours—I've known that from the beginning—and it's been plain that you don't believe Karl Schultz killed her. Flynn even told me that you presented some type of alibi to the Under Commissioner. You know what I think, Miss Newcomb? I think you were hoping to catch the Ripper last night."

"Of course I want to know who killed Nora." Fanny hoped her answer would satisfy the detective. "And even though Karl confessed, I'm sure he's not guilty. Lawrence Decatur—and my father, if he were still alive—could tell you that there are many reasons innocent men confess to murder." Fanny took a breath of fresh air before speaking. "They could be threatened or blackmailed or even beaten into a confession. Confession is not necessarily a measure of a man's guilt."

Crenshaw leaned back on the gallery rail, considering his cigar. Then he considered Fanny. "No one else may have told you this, Miss Newcomb, but it is my duty to do so. If you continue to search into Nora Keegan's murder, your own life may be in danger." He waited for a few seconds and then stepped down the gallery steps onto the gravel path leading to Annunciation Street.

Fanny watched the detective's slow stroll to the street. His warning sent a shivering chill through her burned body.

"Wait!" Fanny called out. The detective walked back to where Fanny stood. "I've been thinking about the fire all day and I may have remembered something." Fanny paused, just as the detective had done. Should she really tell him? Yes, she would. Last night she had learned she could be physically brave but never would she allow herself to be stupid. There was no need to sacrifice her own safety to find Nora's murderer. "Yes, I believe the photographer introduced himself to someone on the street," Fanny lied quickly. "And he was the same photographer who advertised the Ripper photograph. Pierre deVille."

LESS THAN A half an hour after Crenshaw's departure, Fanny paced the short distance between the front and back walls of the infirmary, frantically trying to understand exactly what the detective meant. She skirted around Olive, who sat slumped in her desk chair.

"Crenshaw said I'd be in danger but he didn't say from whom. But if I'm in danger for looking into Nora's murder, doesn't that mean that Karl can't be guilty? If he murdered Nora and he's in jail, he's no threat to me. So Crenshaw must mean that Karl is not the murderer and that the real murderer is still roaming at will. That's obvious. We must be getting close to the real murderer or else Crenshaw would not warn me off. But if he's warning me off, he must know who the real murderer is. So why doesn't he arrest him?"

As her feet crisscrossed the infirmary floor, Fanny stumbled slightly and steadied herself on the edge of Olive's desk. Olive didn't open her eyes.

Damnation! Just when Fanny needed Olive's keen wisdom, she was entirely befuddled, as though her body had been bullied into fatigue. Fanny knew she should encourage Olive to go to sleep but after sleeping all day herself, she wanted to talk. "Would you like a cup of coffee, Olive? It would help you stay awake."

Olive laid her arms on the table and sank into their soft cradle, moaning, "Uh, huh."

Fanny pulled up a chair and sat down next to her, determined that Olive should listen. "Of course, Crenshaw knows who the most likely suspects are. Their names are in his Sergeant's notebook. If only I could see Flynn's notebook again!"

Olive's body jerked up in her chair, as if a puppeteer were manipulating her. Her eyes charged with sudden recognition. "The book." She looked directly at Fanny. "I should have looked at his book."

"Sergeant Flynn's book?"

"Remington's book. The Death Register." Olive slapped her hands on the table. "I was there this afternoon. I should have looked at it but I forgot." Olive looked searchingly at Fanny, as though she was apologizing. "Because he distracted me." As if the puppeteer had released her strings, Olive slumped down onto her desk.

Fanny put her hand on Olive's shoulder, finally recognizing that Olive could offer no solace tonight. "It's all right, Olive. I'm sure you can look at that register book tomorrow."

SYLVIA TENSED IN her bedroom rocking chair, waiting for Olive to come to bed. She had not stopped thinking about her conversation with Terence Boylan and could hear him roundly declaiming about the evils of Bad Women. Even when she fell asleep earlier in the evening, her dreams had lingered on the priest and his words. And although his views angered her, he had made one very good suggestion this afternoon and Sylvia was almost convinced to take it. But she wanted Olive's agreement first.

Sylvia heard Olive's feet shuffling across the floor into her bedroom. Gingerly, Sylvia extracted herself from her chair and limped out to Olive's door. She entered without waiting for a reply. Olive was face-down on her bed, one shoe on and one shoe half off.

"Olive Giddings! What a mess you are!" Although Olive Giddings might be a highly-educated doctor, she was still just Sylvia's youngest sister. And Sylvia was keenly aware of her sibling responsibility. Sylvia rolled her sister over onto her back, then reached beneath Olive's pillow for her nightgown. "Let's get you in this."

Sylvia removed Olive's shoes and stockings. Without prompting, Olive unbuttoned and removed her jacket and bodice. "Uh, huh."

Sylvia rolled Olive on her side and unhooked her skirt. "Father Boylan came by today." Sylvia helped Olive shimmy out of her skirt and petticoats.

Olive began to pluck at her chemise. "Uh, huh."

"He said something about rewards. About posting a reward in order to find Nora's murderer. What do you think?" Sylvia lifted Olive's arms and slid off the chemise. She put Olive's head and hands into the proper holes of her nightdress and watched as her sister settled the gown about her.

Olive slid down on her bed, a faint mumble drifting from her dry lips. "Uh, huh."

Sylvia maneuvered Olive between the sheets and placed her head squarely on the pillow. "You think we should offer a reward, too?" Sylvia mused for only a second. Certainly, they should. People always offered rewards to find their runaway dogs or lost parakeets. Why not offer a reward to get information about who really killed Nora?

Sylvia brushed her lips against Olive's cheeks and whispered, "We'll need to offer a goodly amount. I could take a little from the school and the infirmary budget and then I could dip into Aunt Esther's household funds. That should do it."

As she closed the door, Sylvia was very glad that Olive agreed with her. A large reward posted in the newspaper would be just the thing to insure real information about Nora's killer.

OLIVE HALTED ON the staircase, tightening her robe about her. There it was again, that noise. Rats, probably, or squirrels invading the kitchen. Sylvia had heard it first—a squeaking sound, like a magnolia branch against a dry window—and had stumbled to Olive's room, demanding that Olive find out the source of the noise. After awakening—and really, she did not even know how she got into her nightdress—she agreed to Sylvia's directive. She had been caught off guard, however, by the pistol that Sylvia thrust into her hand.

There it was again. Coming from the dining room. No, the hallway. No, the classroom. Someone was moving things around in the classroom.

The pistol weighed heavily in Olive's hand. She knew Thomas and Esther were asleep in the carriage house. They might be able to hear screams and would certainly hear a gunshot. Suddenly, a woman's muffled voice cursed from behind the door. "*Damnation!*"

Olive pushed open the door with the tip of the pistol. "Fanny?"

By the light of a trio of oil lamps, she saw Fanny with her head engulfed in one of the deep wall cupboards. The typewriting tables, the chairs, even the floor and rugs, were littered with books and papers. Olive dropped the pistol to her side. "What are you doing in here?"

Fanny clawed at the books and papers in the cupboard like a woman possessed. She stepped back, coughing at the dust that pursued her. "I'm looking for Nora's ledgerbook."

"At four o'clock in the morning?" Olive shook her head sleepily. The way Fanny was moving things about, it was unlikely she would find anything.

"I didn't mean to wake you." As if seized by sudden inspiration, Fanny shoveled deeper into the shelves of her bookcase. "What you said last night—about Remington's book—got me thinking about my accounting students' ledgerbooks. Nora's ledgerbook is here, somewhere. I've got to find it."

"But didn't you say that you checked Nora's schoolwork already?"

"Yes, I did. But I didn't think of her ledgerbook until tonight."

"Don't students take them home too?"

"No. They use them in class and I grade them during the week. Now that I've thought of her ledgerbook, I can't find it. I can't find any of the ledgers. I'm never letting Aunt Esther clean my school room again."

"Do you want some help?" asked Olive, wondering where she could put the pistol so that it would be safely out of Fanny's furious search.

Fanny waved her head absently toward the door. "No, no, just go back to bed."

27.

OLIVE's MORNING TOILETTE was efficiently simple. She brushed her short curly hair back from her face, bathed her face in warm water, and scrubbed powder across her teeth.

But today, her hair would not stay in place and she clipped at her curls with her scissors, unusually pleased as the snippets of black hair floated to her bodice. She only wished she could use her scissors on Lester Adams. Wished she could snip away at his pompous self-righteousness. As she continued snipping—her basin now speckled with black hair—she might even take her scissors to John Remington. He'd had the photographs showing Nora's body slashed to shreds and he had not told her. How could he treat her like that?

Fanny appeared at Olive's door clutching a large book against her chest. "I may have discovered *why* Nora was murdered."

Olive paused mid-snip. Fanny was breathing heavily and her face was flushed. No, it glowed with success. Olive caught Fanny's enthusiasm immediately and returned the scissors to her pocket. She flapped a towel at the short hairs cluttering her face and chest.

"Time to wake up Sylvia."

FANNY STOOD AT the foot of the delicately canopied bed, slightly awed by Sylvia's elegant bedroom. The blue and white striped wallpaper was punctuated by pink roses and ribbons of gold; the curtains were made from a cotton much finer than any dress that Fanny had ever worn; and wisps of fragrant early honeysuckle glowed from a cut glass vase on the writing desk. And was that a songbird at the window?

Fanny brought herself down to business. "At the beginning of the session I provided my students with a ledgerbook for general ledger accounting."

Sylvia narrowed her eyes at Fanny's soft shape. "Did you bring coffee with you?"

Olive parted the window curtains and raised the blind. As the sun filtered sharply through the bedroom, she settled in her sister's rocking chair. "Pay attention, Sylvia. The sooner you hear Fanny out, the sooner we all get our coffee."

"Each week during class," said Fanny, "my students looked at the financial transactions of a particular business. Like an insurance agency or a cotton broker. We discussed the money going in and out of the business and the students recorded it in their ledgers and balanced their books. It tests them on how they understand debits and credits and how well they can add and subtract under pressure. When class is finished, they leave their ledgerbooks with me so that I can check their work before the next class. Last night, after I found Nora's ledgerbook, I checked her class examples. They were all as I remembered them. But I also found that she hadn't cut all the tops of the pages open yet."

Fanny opened the ledgerbook to the uncut pages and removed three large sheets of paper. "Slipped inside some of the uncut pages, I found other pieces of paper. They looked just like the pages of the general ledger, with columns for debits and credits."

"You're sure these loose pages belong to Nora?" asked Olive.

"Yes." Fanny placed the loose pages against the pages in the book, showing that the handwriting was the same. "The last entry was written the day Nora died. Maybe even hours before she was murdered."

"You think she wrote it here?" asked Sylvia.

"She could have written it during the class break," answered Fanny, "or, she might have kept the pages at Mrs. O's, finished the last entry before she came to class, and hid it in her ledgerbook that night. I'm convinced that this loose ledger might have something to do with why she was murdered."

"Why?"

"Because the final balance is $2,879.63."

Olive stopped rocking. "That's a lot of money."

"Yes, it is," replied Fanny. "And it looks like Nora made it all in a few months. These pages must have been important to her. Otherwise why would she hide them? There must be some connection between these numbers and Nora's murder. I think Nora was murdered because of this money. Charlotte and I even discussed it yesterday—that money is a powerful motive for murder."

"But how did she get it all?" asked Olive.

"I thought it was obvious. This must be a record of her..." Sylvia struggled for the correct word for a man who met with prostitutes. "Customers?"

"I don't think so," said Olive. "From what I've heard—"

"Just what have you heard?" Sylvia's voice shrilled, the older sister concerned about the younger sister's virtue. "And how did you hear it?"

"You know that my services are available to anyone who calls on me. And," Olive added, before her sister could protest, "I have attended women in houses of prostitution. I've been told things about their kind of business, including what they are paid."

Olive ran her finger along one column. "These credits seem much higher than the payments I was told about." Olive tried to look at the pages on Fanny's lap but Fanny folded them toward herself protectively.

"I'm not letting these pages out of my sight until I know what that connection is."

Sylvia tied the belt of her wrapper and looked toward her door. "That's fine with me, as long as I get my coffee in the next five minutes."

But Olive blocked Sylvia's path. "Before we go down for breakfast, I want to tell you what I found out about Lester Adams yesterday."

After Olive finished her report, Fanny said, "It seems a suitable alibi. But can any man be sincere about rescuing women?"

"Remington assures me that his nephew has no ulterior motives."

"I believe him," said Sylvia.

Fanny and Olive waited, unsure if Sylvia was being sarcastic or sincere.

"I believe that somewhere in this world a man is honestly trying to rescue women from prostitution," Sylvia stated. "I can't say that I believe Adams is that man but he could be. After all, Olive and I wanted to save that girl on Saturday night."

Fanny's eyes grew wistful. "I would have saved Nora, if I could have. If I had kno—"

"Isn't that what we are doing here? Isn't that why we are principal, teacher, doctor?" Sylvia's voice rose in sudden passion, like a mother bear awakening from hibernation to protect her cubs. "Is it right for us to rescue women because we are women and wrong for Adams to do so just because he's a man?"

Olive was too tired to debate with her sister. Instead she offered her hand and said, "Come along, Sylvia. Let me get you a cup of coffee. It might calm you down."

AS SYLVIA HOBBLED with her cane toward the dining room, Olive pulled Fanny aside at the bottom of the great stairs. "I didn't report everything about what happened last night."

"Tell me," said Fanny. "I want to know."

"Remington showed me photographs of Nora," she whispered.

"Did you get the name of the photographer? Was it deVille?"

"It wasn't. John said he'd never even heard of Pierre deVille." Olive took hold of Fanny's elbows, forcing her to look straight at her. "Listen to me. These photographs were taken just before John conducted his post-mortem examination. It was clear that Nora's neck had been nearly severed at the base with a knife. Much of her body had been slashed through, probably with the same knife."

Despite Olive's support, Fanny leaned back until she hit the round base of the sturdy newel post. "But you said Nora was strangled."

"She was. And I'd swear to it."

"But—"

"Hear me out: Nora was strangled in Conner's Court, brought to Charity, examined after her name was entered into the Death Register, and then slashed. And then John examined her." Olive steadied her gaze at Fanny. "That must be what happened."

"But—"

"And Nora wasn't just slashed; she was stabbed. And the stabs were deep. Remington showed me the report he released to the police. The one the newspapers used for their articles. Some of the stab wounds dug three inches into her body. It was worse than the wounds of any of the Ripper's victims."

"But her face—"

"Was untouched," responded Olive calmly. "He wanted her face to be seen. He wanted people to know who she was."

The ledgerbook drifted from Fanny's arms, as she began to sink down to the bottom step of the stairs. "He really hated her, didn't he?"

Olive put her hands under both of Fanny's elbows, forcing her to her feet. "He certainly hates *someone*."

Fanny took a deep breath, "Which means he'll keep hating and killing and ripping and stabbing—"

"Until someone—"

"Until *we*," Fanny stood tall and took another deep breath. "Until *we* stop him."

FANNY HAD NO taste for breakfast and took a large cup of coffee into the classroom. She looked up and down the columns of Nora's loose ledger pages but could not crack its secrets. Clearly, she needed help from someone, someone familiar with prostitution.

Mrs. O'Sullivan? No. She might be hiding something herself. Cousin Charlotte? Perhaps.

But as Fanny sat with the numbers and initials almost swimming before her tired eyes, she remembered one other person who might help her: Millie the strawberry-blond girl who had questioned Fanny outside Mrs. O'Sullivan's house.

Fanny quickly penned a note and gave it to Liam to deliver. Almost four hours later, in an ink-spotted handwriting that could benefit from Sylvia's penmanship class, Fanny received her reply.

Yes. Millie would meet Fanny at three o'clock today in the Ladies Salon of the Cafe de Bonne Chance on Canal Street.

28.

BUT BY FOUR O'CLOCK Millie had not arrived at the Café and the tomato, mint, and mayonnaise sandwiches that Fanny had ordered an hour earlier had wilted on the plate. Fanny—boiling in the piercing sunlight of the café's windows—vowed that she would wait only five minutes more.

Not that Fanny had wasted the last hour. She'd occupied her time trying to decipher Nora's journal. Whatever business Nora had been chronicling had earned close to three thousand dollars. The only conclusion Fanny could reach from the numbers, initials, and balance amount was that Nora would have made a fine accountant.

Just as Fanny gave her coins to the waitress, the bell above the front entrance tinkled sweetly. Fanny looked up hopefully for Millie, but saw instead three dark-haired and fashionably bustled women, four young girls with tight braids, and a thin woman in servant's attire. The café manager, a short stout man in a black suit, was quickly at their side. He bowed, welcomed them in French, and escorted the group to the café's largest table.

Fanny watched as the family—for the resemblance between the sharp-nosed and double-chinned Creole matriarch, daughters, and granddaughters was clear—settled at their table. The manager ensured that everyone was seated properly and presented each lady with a menu.

The café bell sounded again and Fanny saw Millie and another girl teetering at the threshold. Both girls wore bright plaid outfits and sported small, befeathered straw hats atop their brassy red hair. Both girls seemed relieved to see Fanny, but they flinched at the sight of the cozy group of women whispering to each other in French.

It was suddenly clear to Fanny that she'd made a mistake. Millie did not belong at the Café de Bonne Chance. Her loud dress and hair color marked Millie as an actress or dancer. Or worse, the prostitute that she was. But Fanny could not let Millie and her friend leave; she had to get Millie to talk.

Fanny rushed to meet the girls at the door, arriving just before the manager. She placed her hand firmly under Millie's elbow, breathed deeply to her full height, and looked down her nose at him.

"We'll need three glasses of lemonade." Fanny assumed Sylvia's most authoritative tone. "And fresh sandwiches." Fanny kept her hand under Millie's elbow, Millie grabbed the other girl's hand, and Fanny walked the girls to the table.

Millie pushed her companion—a wiry girl who stumbled twice before reaching the table—into her seat. "This is Deirdre." Millie took a seat against the wall where she could look directly at the still-whispering women.

A waitress shoved a tray of lemonade-filled glasses toward Fanny. Millie claimed a glass quickly and dumped a large spoonful of sugar into it. She beat the sugar stiffly as she looked around the room at the clusters of white-clothed tables, carefully avoiding the occupants of the table near-by. "You invited me here to ask questions, didn't you? Well, ask me."

"All right," Fanny lowered her voice and leaned toward Millie. "How much money was Nora paid each week?"

"How would I know?" Millie replied in her normal voice.

Deirdre counted out four of the wilted sandwiches and stacked them on her plate. "Mrs. O told me I'm going to have lots and lots of money some day. She's going to make sure a rich man marries me."

Fanny wanted to ask the girls if they had ever known a girl from Mrs. O's to marry a rich man, but bit her tongue.

Millie nodded toward the café entrance. "Deirdre, go look out the window for a minute, will you?"

"But...."

Millie nodded encouragingly at the girl and Deirdre stepped away from the table and stumbled into a chair at the next table.

From the corner of her eye Fanny could see the matriarch glaring at her. But Fanny focused only on Deirdre. "That child needs spectacles."

"She's got 'em but Mrs. O hid 'em away. Said they made her look like a spinster."

Fanny fumed, as she did every time spinsters were unfairly characterized. Not every spinster wore spectacles. But now was not the time to argue. Instead, Fanny recognized that Millie had maneuvered to be alone with her. Was Millie ready to talk plainly? Or was Deirdre the plain talker and Millie the secret keeper?

"When do you get paid?" Fanny returned to her low voice.

"Monday mornings." Millie slurped from her glass, her voice equally low this time. "Makes sure the girls stay through the weekend. You leave before Monday morning, you get nothing for your week."

"Where do you keep your money?"

"Mrs. O keeps it for us, of course. No bank would let one of us inside. No matter how much money we had." Millie plunged her long spoon back into the sugar bowl.

"People will do lots of things for money." As Fanny watched Millie fair face carefully, she realized the supreme irony of her statement. Millie was a prostitute. She was one of those people. Fanny swallowed hard before saying, "Murder is one of those things. If Nora had lots of money, she might have been killed for it. What do you think?"

Millie spilled her spoonful of sugar on the table and stared at it. Clearly, she was thinking something. If Fanny could only—

But just then Deirdre approached the table and tripped on the carpet. She grabbed at a chair and caught herself before falling.

"Blind as a bat and two left feet to boot." Millie pulled at Deirdre's hair until the girl sat down next to her.

"Millie," asked Deirdre. "Have you asked her yet? You said she could help. Nora always said she—"

"I can help you." Fanny glanced to her side, where the manager was reseating everyone at the other table so that the young girls could no longer look upon Millie and Deirdre. "What do you need?"

"We want to know about Karl," replied Deirdre. "What's going to happen to him?"

"I don't know. I've tried to talk to Karl, but he won't talk to me. He won't talk to anyone," Fanny replied. "But you could tell me something that might help him. Can you tell me how Karl and Nora knew each other?"

"That's easy," said Deirdre. "He did carpentry for Mrs. O."

"They both worked at Mrs. O's?" Fanny almost laughed, the explanation was so ordinary. She knew that Sylvia would also be pleased that Nora and Karl did not meet at Wisdom Hall. Fanny looked over at the other table, where for the first time everyone seemed busy with their food and too busy to listen to Millie or Deirdre. "Did Karl work for Mrs. O for long?"

"Weeks. And then Karl was gone and Nora was gone."

"But he didn't murder her," Fanny lowered her voice. "I know that for certain."

"I know that too," said Deirdre. "They were friends."

"What kind of friends?"

"They talked to each other. He was helping her—"

"They talked," said Millie. "That was that."

"I think that Karl was encouraged to confess to Nora's murder, even though he didn't do it. Whoever encouraged Karl to confess might have murdered Nora." Fanny paused, hearing her father's logical thoughts flowing from her lips. The real murderer had the most to gain from Karl's confession and should work the hardest of any man to secure it.

"I don't know what's going to happen to Karl, but I promise to tell you once I find out." Fanny burrowed into her purse. "Now it's your turn to tell me something."

"Mother of God, you're persistent!" Millie's voice rose in frustration. "All right! A hard working girl at Mrs. O's can make a hundred dollars a week. Minus her room and board."

The ladies at the other table turned toward Millie *en masse* and scowled. The matriarch signaled to the café manager. Fanny knew the girls would be forced from the café, yet she still pulled a cloth-covered object from her purse. "That's not what I meant. I wanted to ask you about something I have."

But Millie jumped up and yanked Deirdre to her feet. "We got to go!"

Before Fanny could protest, Millie and Deirdre charged toward the café entrance. Within seconds, the manager strode after them with a righteous indignation.

The girls were out the door before Fanny could press her coins into the waitress's hands.

"Wait! Please!"

Fanny caught up with the girls on Canal Street where Deirdre had stumbled on the banquette. Fanny helped Deirdre to her feet and drew the girls to her side. She pulled back the cloth to reveal the photograph of Nora naked. "Do you have any idea who made this photograph?"

Deirdre raised the image level to her chin and smiled. "That's Nora! The Professor took that picture!"

"Professor deVille?" asked Fanny.

Millie stepped between Deirdre and Fanny. "No more questions."

"But Nora—"

"Nora's dead." Millie grabbed the image from Deirdre's hand and pushed it against Fanny's chest. "And we're alive. And we'd like to stay that way." Millie quickly anchored her elbow with Deirdre's and turned away from Fanny. "So leave us be."

"REWARD OFFERED." Sylvia pulled her pen from the paper, admiring the large capital letters. She would have the advertisement printed in very large type so that no one could ignore it. She would also have broadsides printed and posted on every other telegraph pole so that even the illiterate would ask about it.

Quickly, she wrote the rest of her advertisement. *"For accurate and intimate information regarding the heinous murder of Nora Keegan in Conner's Court on Friday, April 26. If you have such information, promptly notify the Editor of this newspaper."*

After blotting off the excess ink, Sylvia took out another piece of paper and wrote *"LATEST FRENCH FASHIONS!* Gowns, Hats, and Frivolities displayed for Wisdom Hall students. Mrs. Charlotte Blanchard Decatur Sutter—a recent inhabitant of Paris—will display and discuss the latest fashions enjoyed by French women. Wednesday May 8, 7p.m. Wisdom Hall Settlement House, corner of Annunciation and Josephine."

Finally, Sylvia penned a short letter to Eliza Nicholson, Editor, *The Daily Picayune*, requesting that both advertisements appear in tomorrow's early morning edition. Of course, Sylvia's personal sponsorship of the reward should be told to no one.

As she looked once more at the Reward, Sylvia considered adding, "All information will remain entirely confidential." But she could not guarantee that and indeed she wanted information she could share with the police. The sooner the police took investigating Nora's murder seriously, the sooner Fanny would return her attention back to her students, and the sooner Sylvia could concentrate on Wisdom Hall entirely.

OLIVE DID NOT close the Infirmary until eleven o'clock. Throughout the day she had patched, sewn up, and lectured patients, steadily listening to their fears, rumors, and tall stories about the Irish Channel Ripper. With every patient, she had subtly probed for information about Lester Adams. *Have you seen the Charity Hospital ambulance waiting on your street? What about a man who scratches his head a lot? Are there any girls or women missing from the houses on your block?*

Lester Adams haunted her thoughts. He had seemed sincere enough in his wish to rescue prostitutes but was he really telling the truth? And did he have anything to do with Nora's murder?

Olive heard the infirmary's inner door open. And then the familiar tap of Sylvia's cane.

Sylvia wobbled to the chair next to Olive's desk and sat down. "You wanted to check my ankle today."

Olive moved her desk lamp closer to the desk's edge so that the light fell on Sylvia's skirt. Olive set a stool directly in front of her sister, removed her boot, and examined Sylvia's foot and ankle. "The swelling is coming down. If you continue being this careful, you'll be out recruiting new students by this weekend."

"Unless our students return this week, we may not have a school anymore."

Olive moved the lamp back into its proper place and went to her medical cabinet. She removed Sylvia's bottle of laudanum and poured the liquid into a small tumbler. "Tell me Sylvia, are you still glad you opened Wisdom Hall?"

"What kind of question is that? The people of the Channel need us, even though they may not know it. We are the only hope they have to work for a better life."

Olive had expected her sister to say as much and added, "Once these Ripper letters stop, your classes will be filled with students."

"What if the letters stop but we haven't identified Nora's real murderer by then? Until he's caught, the women of the Channel *are* in danger. In a perverse way, it's just as well that someone calling himself the Ripper is scaring them into staying inside their houses. Because there is a real murderer loose."

"There is one thing that has worried me from the beginning and I can't get past it." Olive paused, wondering how Sylvia would react to medical information. As long as she didn't mention blood, Sylvia *might* listen to her. But for good measure, Olive gave Sylvia her laudanum and watched as she drank it down.

Olive continued, "On the Sunday morning after Nora's murder, I read Nora's entry in Charity's Death Register. There was no mention of any wounds to the throat and no mention of any type of slashing of Nora's body in the Register. But John Remington showed me some photographs yesterday, photographs showing Nora's body before he began his examination. It was clear that Nora's throat had been cut."

"There were photographs?"

Olive leaned toward her sister, her voice almost a whisper, "Sylvia, what if I missed something?"

"But you were with her just after she died. If she had been cu—"

"It was very dark, Sylvia. What if I did miss something?"

"Why don't you look at the Register again? In fact, why didn't you ask Remington to show it to you?" Sylvia held out her tumbler—was she asking for another dose?—before answering for her sister, "I know why. Because the Register might prove Remington lied to you and you can't face that."

Olive took the tumbler and wiped it clean with her apron. Sylvia sighed. "Just where does Remington keep the Register?"

"It's usually in the examination room next to his office. But I can't go back there again."

"Under lock and key?"

"Why, Sylvia? What are you thinking?"

Sylvia reached for her cane before replying, "I'm thinking that Fanny is the solution to your problem."

29.

YOU WANT ME TO STEAL THE CHARITY Hospital Death Register?" Fanny's grip on the morning coffeepot wavered slightly.

"We will return it; just like Liam returned Sergeant Flynn's notebook." Sylvia carefully removed the lid from the biscuit platter and took her time selecting a small golden biscuit. "You can do it, can't you? I mean, you stole a photograph from Nora's room, didn't you?"

"You saw me?" Fanny had never been confronted about her stealing before. "I only took that photograph of Nora because I was feeling sentimental and wanted a memento. It's wrong to steal."

Sylvia pulled her biscuit apart in one quick twist and inhaled the fragrant steam. "You don't have to be a schoolmarm just now Fanny. We all know that stealing is wrong. But we also know that it can be very useful."

"Stealing is not a parlor game, Sylvia." Fanny looked to Olive for support but Olive's head was behind the morning newspaper, like a soldier hiding behind a shield. "Won't Remington just give the Register to you?"

"I can't ask him for it now," Olive said. "Not after my confrontation with Lester Adams."

"Then why can't you steal it yourself?"

"Because she wouldn't be any good at it," answered Sylvia.

Fanny reached for the milk pitcher and watched as the hot liquid swirled into her coffee. "I'll have to think about it."

Sylvia pushed the sugar bowl toward Fanny. "Olive needs it now."

Fanny dug her spoon into the sugar, remembering how much sugar Millie had emptied into her tea yesterday.

"No, I mean I'll have to think about how to steal it. In the past, I only took things from places I was familiar with. It was easy and that's why I never got caught." It soothed her to believe that Sylvia caught her in the act only because Fanny had been unfamiliar with Nora's room. "I knew the people and their daily routines."

"That wouldn't be a problem," replied Olive with sudden enthusiasm. "Remington's schedule is always posted outside his door."

"Do I have to steal that too?" asked Fanny.

"Not necessarily. Thomas is very friendly with some of the porters. He can get it from them."

"But if Thomas or the porters can get Remington's schedule, why can't they steal the register?"

"Because it's one thing for a white woman to have a stolen book in her possession. It's another thing entirely for a colored man. He'd be jailed immediately. Or worse."

"There's one more thing I need to know." Fanny sipped from her cup. The heavy coffee lingered on her tongue. "How will you save *me* if I get caught stealing?"

ADMISSION TO CHARITY HOSPITAL gave Fanny entry to all of the wards and she went directly to the Men's General Ward on the third floor. Olive had checked on the blind beggars on Sunday and had reported to Fanny that they were all recovering and due for discharge. Was it possible any of them were still here? And would they have any useful information about the midnight photographer?

The ward was a long narrow room with beds positioned against the walls. Tall windows ran between each bed, each window open to the fresh spring air. A large table, covered with piles of folded cotton and linen, bottles, bowls and ropes, was centered in the room. A lone nun commanded the ward, smoothing the bed sheets of the patient third from the front. From the tidy appearance of the first two beds, it was clear that the nun was going methodically down the line of beds attending to each patient.

Fanny gazed over the lengths of beds, trying not to stare at the men who lay in them. It only took a glance at their faces and postures to know their stories: disease, destitution, overdrink. The same stories heard throughout the Irish Channel. At the end of the long row of beds, Fanny saw a man wearing a pair of blackened spectacles. She approached the blind man deliberately, her boots beating a tattoo on the floors. Within two steps from his bed, he jerked his head toward her, his mouth puckered as he called out, "Who is it?"

His voice was parched and low; the same voice that Fanny had heard Saturday night in the blind beggar's room. It was the exhausted voice of someone continually having to fend and fight for himself; the voice of someone who had challenged the photographer on Saturday and then had his lodging burned down around him.

"Whoever you are, go away." The man grasped at something near his hand.

Fanny realized he was grabbing for a tin cup, almost charred black, but with a new white rag handle. Fanny was sure that this cup had survived the fire and wondered if he thought to use it as a weapon against her. But no, he held it more as a comfort, as a talisman.

As Fanny moved toward him, the man recoiled into his thin pillow, clutching the tin cup with both hands. When the cup slipped from his hand and rolled onto the bed sheets, he pounded on the top of the bed with both hands, looking for it.

Fanny put out her hand to collect the cup for him and his hand landed on hers. She began to withdraw her hand but he clutched at it. Then he grabbed it with both hands. Fanny winced at the pain from the grip of his hand on her injured one but did not pull away. The man's fingers eased slowly into Fanny's fingers, as though he was feeling his way into a familiar glove.

"It's you, isn't it? The lady in the fire."

Fanny swallowed hard, a lump of pain holding fast in the bottom of her throat. The pressure of his grasp frayed against her burned fingers. She bit her lip, not wanting to indulge her own pain in a room of men who had suffered far worse then she.

"Yes, sir," Fanny answered softly. With her free hand, she unwound the man's fingers from her own. She put her fingertips lightly on the top of his hand and stared at the ragged Confederate Army cap on his head. Although she already knew the answer, she asked, "You were in the war, sir?"

"Yes, I was, miss."

"Is that how you lost your sight?"

"Yes."

Neither Fanny nor the blind man spoke for a while. Then she asked, "Did anyone tell you what happened Saturday night?"

"Yes, miss. They said that a man was using a camera and he started a fire. And that he ran away and you saved us. I want to thank you for that, Miss."

"It was my honor to help a soldier of the South, sir." Fanny folded her lips together, mindful that she was attempting to charm the man into talking to her. And to her surprise he was responding to her. Fanny *was* honored to help an invalided Confederate veteran, and her father would have been proud of her, but she was disgusted with herself for attempting to ply the man. Still, she continued. "Did you know the photographer, sir?"

"No, Miss."

"Did he speak to you? Could you tell where he was from?"

"He was Irish, wasn't he?" The man answered in a swaggering Irish accent that surprised Fanny. He smiled at his jest and then returned to his own voice. "But I think he was putting on. He wasn't a Johnny off the boat. He'd been here a couple of years."

Fanny laughed sincerely at the blind man's joke. She had not heard the photographer speak and was surprised to learn that his accent was Irish. Pierre deVille did not have a marked French accent, but she did not think him the type to affect an accent. And again, why should he have? But, Fanny wondered...was it possible that the women had not followed deVille Saturday night?

"The nurse says I'm released in a day," the blind man offered. "All of the others have already gone. Been sent to the Blind home."

"Is that where you'll go, too?"

"I'd rather die than live in that place again. It's like a prison and I've already been in prison."

"Perhaps instead of going to the Blind home, you could return to where you lived before the fire."

The man's head shook so absolutely that his black glasses began to run down his swollen nose. "Not with the Ripper loose."

"Where did you live?"

"Conner's Court."

Fanny suppressed her surprise. "Were you there the night of the murder? Did you hear anything?"

The blind man attempted to shake his hand from Fanny's but held fast. He asked, "You don't have police with you, do you? I been asked all of this before."

Fanny stood as closely to him as she could. "I'm alone, I promise. But I'd like to know what you know about that night." It was wrong to play on the blind man's gratitude, but she had no choice. "It would be a great favor to me."

"Where's Sister?"

Fanny looked behind her and saw the nun two beds away assisting a man twice her size into a chair. "She can't hear us but there isn't much time before she can."

He ran the tip of his tongue across his bottom lip. "Can you pour me a glass of water?"

Fanny looked around and saw a covered jar on the table in the center of the room. She sniffed the liquid first and then poured the water into a small clean cup. The man drank, licked his wet lips, and took a deep breath. But before he could speak, Fanny asked, "Did you hear the photographer that night? He said he took a photograph of the murderer," and then, "There's an ambulance doctor who follows prostitutes about."

"That man. He's in the Channel almost every night, somewhere or other. I can hear him watching and then later, when he takes them away. He was there that night, with the girl."

"The girl who was killed?" Fanny knew it was possible that someone witnessed Nora's murder but once Karl has been arrested, the newspapers had not been interested in witnesses. And once Fanny decoded Sergeant Flynn's list of suspects, she had not thought of seeking out other suspects or witnesses. Of course, a large reward—posted in the appropriate places—might yield information about what happened in Conner's Court before Nora was murdered. Even the police offered rewards, when bullying did not work. Fanny's father had always doubted the virtues of offering a reward, believing that only dishonest people with dishonest information answered reward offers. But she knew, she would swear in court, that the blind man was honest. "You talked to her?"

"No but my brother...he was with me." Once more he took her hand, as if he needed to make sure she understood everything he said. "He's not blind; only wears the sign sometimes. Please don't turn him in...I know he does wrong, begging when he's not blind, but he's not well either and he's got no work." When Fanny assured him his brother's secret was safe, the blind man continued. "My brother swears he saw the girl before she was murdered. With that ambulance man."

From behind her, Fanny heard the nun's wooden beads clacking against each other. It would be only a minute before the nun was at the blind man's bed. Fanny leaned over until she was inches from the blind man's face. "What did he see?"

"An argument," he answered readily, "between the girl and the man."

Fanny's breath was short. "Did he hurt her?"

"He was going to. He was going to drive her away." He grabbed at Fanny's fingers. "But another man stopped him."

"And then?"

"Both men went away together."

"The girl?"

"She kept waiting."

"She was alive? Unharmed?"

"She was when we passed out of the court but then the alarm went out just a few minutes later."

The nun's headdress careened against Fanny's tense shoulders. The nun looked at Fanny and motioned toward the door with her eyes.

Fanny was so deep in thought that she did not move. She assumed the fire was deliberately set and was sure the doorknob had been held shut. Since escaping from the fire, she had wondered who were the photographer's intended victims: the blind men or herself. But Fanny had to be sure.

She watched as the nun answered the cries of a boy across the aisle before asking "Did the men see you that night? Did they know you were there?"

"No one ever knows we're there, Miss," he replied quickly, as if sensing the nun's return. "We're not just blind; we're invisible too."

ALTHOUGH FANNY LEFT the blind man's side to seek out John Remington's office, her thoughts remained with him. His information suggested that he was the target of the midnight photographer's fire, which meant that deVille was the second man in Conner's Court.

As she turned toward the offices on the first floor, she ran full-force into a slouching, shuffling man. She dropped her parasol, of course, and slowly, as though it cost him great physical effort, the man bent down to pick it up. His head was a rash of red blotches and scales. This *must* be Dr. Lester Adams.

This was the man who had demeaned Olive and chloroformed and kidnapped women. The man who might be forcing girls to remove their clothes and pose naked. The man who may have murdered Nora. As he rose up, Fanny's parasol in his hand, she realized that he was also a man who had been crying. Tears pooled in his eyes and his cheeks were flushed. Fanny had been ready to hate the man; to take her parasol and pound him over the head. But instead, she fought back a sympathetic tear of her own. For although Fanny had never met Adams before, she recognized his sorrow. She had seen that expression on Olive's face: the look of a dedicated healer who failed to save a patient.

Adams handed the parasol back to Fanny mutely, wiped his white sleeve across his eyes, and shuffled past her. She watched as he reached a doorway. He paused at the door, straightened himself up, and entered. Fanny followed after him. The door was not entirely closed and Fanny edged it open slowly until she could see Adams standing at a bedside, assisting two nuns as they bound a body in white sheets.

A child had just died. A very small child, from the shape of the shroud. Adams and the nuns finished binding the body and then gently laid it on a table with rollers. Then, from the bedding, one of the nuns pulled an old rag doll. At the sight of the doll, Adams burst into tears and the nuns cried along side him. As their tears dried, they talked, but so softly that Fanny could not hear. One of the nuns took both of Adams' hands in hers, held them briefly and then let them go. The other nun put one arm around the doctor and walked him to one of the windows that overlooked the gardens.

As a nun began to wheel the table toward the doorway, Fanny backed up. She left Charity Hospital soon after, without identifying the exact location of John Remington's office.

BACK AT WISDOM Hall, Fanny climbed the spiral staircase to the unfinished rooftop. Sylvia and Olive were up there already, standing at the only safe spot— the railed platform that rimmed the front elevation. Fanny looked at the sisters, amazed that Sylvia and her cane had negotiated the slippery tarpaulin that covered the thin framing. One misstep from the stairs to the railing and she would have fallen through. But Thomas and Liam were up on the roof and must have assisted the sisters. Or even carried Sylvia and her cane to the spot.

Still, if Sylvia and Olive could reach the railed platform, Fanny could too. She inspected the framing and tarpaulin to ensure that they were bone dry. Then she made her move. Slowly. Carefully.

As Fanny approached, she realized that Sylvia was smoking a cigarette while Liam stood next to her with a saucer. "The tarpaulin's leaking again," Sylvia greeted Fanny's slow shuffle. "And it's going to rain all week."

Fanny reached the perch, stood next to Olive, and saw the Irish Channel in all of its desperation. Wooden houses jammed up against each other, each building leaning against the other for support. No trees, outhouses, or cisterns, but dozens of broken windows, rotten stairs, and missing railings. And like Wisdom Hall, many buildings had missing roof timbers. Through one such gaping hole, Fanny could see a man in the attic of a building, walking about in his red union suit.

Fanny knew that these buildings had been hastily constructed for laborers in the early days of the American settlement and were annually flooded by the drenching New Orleans rains and overflowing river. She'd had heard stories about life in these rotting shanties: an entire family of nine might live, work, sleep, and eat together in one small room. Beds were shared between strangers and there was no privacy for anyone.

And this was where the students of Wisdom Hall lived. Fanny could well imagine why these girls might give in to the enticement of getting paid to have their photographs taken by men like Pierre deVille. Even if they had to remove their clothing to do so.

"There's no ventilation between the buildings." Olive seemed to sense Fanny's thoughts. "The fever usually starts down by the docks but it spreads quickest in the Channel. If the fever starts again this summer, we'll never be able to stop it."

A cooling breeze ruffled about the rooftop and smoke from Sylvia's cigarette curled above her head. Sylvia said a few quiet words to Liam, and Fanny watched as the boy and Thomas stepped delicately across the rooftop and down the stairs to the third floor.

Fanny was glad to be alone with Sylvia and Olive and quickly shared her strange observance of Lester Adams. "If both of you hadn't painted Adams as a thorough villain, I would have thought him a very fine physician. If you had just seen how the nuns respected him. And he respected them as well."

Olive crossed her arms, as though she could not believe any of Fanny's report. "Not every doctor who works at Charity wins the respect of the Daughters of Charity. And I have great admiration for their nursing and administrative skills." Still, she shook her head. "As for the respect being mutual, maybe Adams only hates prostitutes and spinsters."

"Well, there's nothing I can do about that," Sylvia inhaled sharply. "I was born a spinster and a spinster I'll die."

"You're no spinster, Sylvia," replied her sister. "You've been married to Good Works your entire life."

"I wouldn't marry anyway, after the accident," Sylvia snubbed her cigarette on the saucer. "I wouldn't even consider it."

Fanny had always wondered about Sylvia's fiancé and leaned forward gingerly. According to the newspapers, the fiancé had not even been injured in the carriage accident that maimed Sylvia's right leg and kept her invalided. Had Sylvia broken with him, or had he broken with her?

But Olive spoke up with sudden gusto, "Sylvia taught her dolls to speak French and English. Then she read them everything Dickens ever wrote. And then she gave them all jobs."

"You splashed all of my dolls with red paint," returned her sister. "Tied them up with cotton and put them into father's infirmary for treatment. You've been married to Medicine your entire life."

Just a few minutes earlier, Fanny had hoped Sylvia would offer her a cigarette. Now she realized that the sisters were offering her something more. Not friendship exactly, but certainly a friendly moment.

"Father is Olive's problem, of course," Sylvia pierced Fanny's reverie. "She fell in love with him at a very young age. No man can hold a candle to him."

"Father *is* perfection," Olive agreed readily. "The best surgeon in the south. Perhaps in the country."

"I heard that John Remington is also a fine surgeon," Sylvia smiled. "But as hard as he works at Charity, any woman who wants him will have to do the proposing."

As Olive's cheeks reddened, Sylvia turned casually to Fanny. "What about you? Surely you've had one proposal of marriage."

Surprised by Olive's embarrassment, Fanny answered absently, "Yes, I have."

"Really? Who?"

Fanny swallowed hard and pressed her lips together. But how could she not tell Olive and Sylvia now? How could she bait them and then refuse to answer? She answered in a voice that seemed unlike her own. "It was Lawrence."

"Lawrence Decatur?" asked Sylvia. "Your father's law partner proposed to you?"

"Yes. I mean, no. I mean, he didn't propose marriage. He offered to marry me. There's a difference."

"When did this happen?" asked Olive.

"Just after father died."

"Is that why you were so eager to teach at Wisdom Hall?" said Sylvia. "Because you were running away from Lawrence Decatur?"

"I was not running away, but—"

"But what?" demanded Sylvia. "What, Fanny?"

"He said I couldn't work once we were married," Fanny responded quietly. "He said I had to leave the law behind."

"That sounds just like Lawrence."

"But I thought you didn't know him."

"I certainly know *of* him," Sylvia ground her cane into the boards and called out for Liam. The boy popped his head up from the third floor and Thomas emerged behind him. "His uncle James was Charlotte's second husband."

"I didn't know that."

"That's not surprising. Lawrence thought his uncle was much too good for Charlotte. He refused to even acknowledge her after James died." Once Liam and Thomas were by her side Sylvia said, "Good for you Fanny, for refusing Lawrence Decatur. If he can treat Cousin Charlotte like a pariah, there's no telling what kind of husband he would have made."

Fanny watched silently as the boy, man, and doctor navigated Sylvia across the rooftop and down the spiral stairs. Despite the treacherous terrain, they made short work of getting Sylvia down to the third floor.

"I never actually refused Lawrence's offer," Fanny said quietly, sure that no one could hear her now. "I just moved out of the Law Offices. It seemed like the right thing to do. At the time, at least."

And despite his pigheaded views on women in law offices, Fanny suspected that Lawrence Decatur would make a very fine husband.

30.

FANNY LEFT WISDOM HALL A FEW HOURS later with Nora's photograph wrapped in a handkerchief and secured in her pocket. She needed to know anything she could about pornography and she wanted to know today. Lawrence would refuse to tell her, of course. Fanny briefly flirted with asking Daniel Crenshaw. She expected that the detective would answer her honestly, but did she have the courage to ask him?

No, she did not. And so she sought out the only other informed man she knew.

The newsroom of the *New Orleans Nightly Sensation* was on the third floor of a narrow cannon-pockmarked building located close to the offices of *The*

Daily Picayune. As Fanny pressed through the wooden door labeled *Sensation Editorial* she was met with a loose fog of smoke. She panicked briefly, the memories of the blind men's fire overcoming her. But within the smoke she caught the whiff of tobacco and relaxed. Through the light haze she could see randomly placed tables at which a bevy of men were seated and sleeping, their hat-covered heads cradled in their arms.

Only one man—sitting at the end of a long table by a shaded window, carefully scissoring up a newspaper—was not asleep. All of the smoke in the room generated from the thick cigar crunched between his lips. He looked up at Fanny, scowled, and returned to his scissors. Fanny realized that she had been holding her breath, as though she were going to be caught trespassing. From somewhere in the room, someone tapped a slow, sad, irregular cadence on a typewriter.

Fanny walked down the length of the narrow room, inspecting each of the sleeping men until she found Clarence Halloway. He was also asleep, a serene childlike snore lilting through his open mouth. He sat deeply in his wooden chair; hat slouched over his eyes, feet anchored on the top of his table.

"Mr. Halloway?"

The reporter pushed his hat onto his head and opened his eyes. At the sight of a woman's skirt, he pulled his feet off his desk but did not stand. He looked up at Fanny and then glared at the crew of men about him. Clutching his hat to his chest he said, "How in hell did you get in here?"

He jumped from his chair and grabbed his jacket from the back of his seat. He put his hand on Fanny's lower back and pushed her out of the newsroom and the building before he said, "This is no place for a lady like you, Miss Newcomb."

Fanny breathed easier out on the street. "I need some assistance from you, Mr. Halloway."

The reporter put his arms through the jacket sleeves. "I thought it was the other way around. You owe me or don't you remember?"

Fanny did remember. The reporter had already provided information about Karl's confession and they were beholden to him. But she could not let one obligation stop her from assuming another. "If you help me now, I'll be doubly in your debt."

Halloway nodded toward a storefront and the open front door. The scent of roasting beef floated through to the street. Despite the clatter of horse carts and the cry of the corner newsboy, Fanny thought she heard Halloway's stomach groan with hunger. He wanted to eat. He *needed* to eat. But Fanny needed to speak to the reporter privately.

"Can we keep walking? Please?"

Halloway grumbled loudly and then veered toward Canal Street, where, as it happened, a carter was selling fried catfish and hushpuppies. He purchased his food and then slid both fish and hushpuppy into his mouth. As he chewed, Fanny steered Halloway down toward the river. The landings would be filled with roustabouts and sailors; their clamor would give Fanny the privacy she wanted. She unwrapped the photograph and held it closely to her chest. When Halloway finished eating, he wiped his hands on his trousers. Fanny handed Nora's photograph to him.

"Jeee-sus!" The reporter pushed the photograph back at Fanny. "What are you doing with something like this?"

"Then it's not a figure study? Not something an artist would use to learn how to draw or sculpt the female figure?"

"No, Miss Newcomb," coughed the reporter. "It is not."

"It's pornography, isn't it?"

The reporter did not respond. Actually, he turned green. Fanny hoped it was from the catfish and not because she had embarrassed him. She sought to reassure him that they could speak truthfully to each other. "Please, Mr. Halloway. I can take an honest answer."

Halloway's hand reached to his back pants pocket, as though he were expecting something to be there. A notebook perhaps? But his hand returned empty. He swore softly before asking, "Who is this?"

"It's Nora Keegan."

Then Halloway's hand reached into his jacket, drew out an oblong tin and removed a cigarette. "Prostitutes often take such pictures. So that explains that."

"Not to me, Mr. Halloway. I need to know about the pornography business in New Orleans and I'd like to hear it from you." And indeed, she would. She had no connection with him and despite the sensational manner in which he wrote for the newspaper, she knew he could be objective.

Something in Fanny's speech must have convinced the reporter. "It's a huge business. Especially in a town like this with men coming in and out. Sailors. Gamblers. Yankees. There's always someone wanting to buy a dirty picture. Lots of money to be made at it."

Fanny stared at Nora's face. So regal. Assured. Commanding. "What about the girls?"

"There's hardly any money in it for them. The smarter girls get copies to sell on their own but most girls get nothing. That's not the worse of it." The reporter's words rolled on as though he was writing his newspaper column. "Sometimes girls are dragged in from the street to pose. Good girls who would never do anything like this are blackmailed into remaining quiet. Those girls have to be drugged before they sit in front of the camera."

"Drugged? With what?"

"Alcohol. Whisky. I've heard chloroform's used sometimes."

Olive had said that Lester Adams used chloroform to stun the girl he kidnapped. Was it possible that he kidnapped girls in order to photograph them naked? Or that his rescue mission was only a way to hide his pornographic photography?

As they walked along the waterfront Fanny asked, "How many pornographers are there in New Orleans?"

"There's no telling. At least a dozen, I'd guess. And besides that, all sorts of men know how to use a camera. Anyone who does can make dirty pictures."

"Pierre deVille's a pornographer, isn't he?"

"My experience doesn't go that far." Halloway took the cigarette he had been holding between his fingers and gingerly tucked it back into his coat pocket. "And yours shouldn't either."

Halloway sounded just like Lawrence. Fanny responded in kind, "It's unladylike, is that what you mean?"

Then, just like Lawrence would, Halloway pulled Fanny toward him until she was inches from his face. He lowered his voice and said, "I mean it's dangerous, Miss Newcomb. You know how things work here. There's lots of things that get done under the table, so to speak. And you just got to leave those things alone."

Fanny pulled away from the reporter. "Murder should never be left alone. If you'd known Nora, you'd want to know who murdered her too." She would not let him deter her. "Where do pornographers sell their pictures?"

The reporter shook his head, as though he could not believe he was going to answer. But he did. "Saloons. Clubs. Magic lantern shows. Whorehouses. I don't know as much about this business as you think I do. But I wouldn't think there's any reason for a pornographer to murder his bread and butter, if that's what you're thinking. The only people pornographers want to kill are each other."

"But you said there was lots of business, lots of money."

"Starts out as lots of money until the police take their cut of it. A large cut. And there's talk now that the

Italians in the quarter are involved. And the talk is they're just as good as the police at making people pay for protection."

The reporter brightened suddenly, as though he had just thought of something. He veered toward Fanny and said, "I like you, Miss Newcomb. I really do. You're a lot like me—sticking your nose into other people's business, going where you don't belong—but all you've got is a dirty picture of a dead girl. So what? Just because you think Karl Schultz didn't kill her, you think a pornographer did?"

"I know other things, too. This dirty picture"—even the words tasted unclean on Fanny's lips— "is just one more piece of evidence."

"Evidence that no one will listen to. And if you think that Pierre deVille has the nerve to kill—"

"I'm not looking for a man with nerve, Mr. Halloway. I'm looking for a coward. Only a coward would have murdered Nora."

The reporter stood in silence as if he'd been physically rebuked and Fanny knew he would tell her no more. But before she could go more than a few steps, the reporter called after her.

"Not so fast."

Had Halloway thought of something else? Fanny returned to stand next to him, ready to hear what else he had to tell her. But all he said was, "You still owe me from before. And for today. Be ready when I come to collect."

FANNY CONSIDERED Halloway's information throughout the evening: Yankees. Chloroform. Pierre deVille. Italians. What did they all mean?

She also considered that she now *owed* the reporter. But how could she repay Halloway? What would satisfy him? Fanny hated being in Halloway's debt, but she needed his intimate knowledge of the New

Orleans underworld. There was no other way to understand what happened to Nora.

As she prepared for sleep, Fanny returned Nora's photograph to her bottom bureau drawer. After a few seconds she moved aside a length of golden silk that her father had bought her long ago and retrieved an unsealed envelope. She pulled out the contents: a check drawn on the bank account of Lawrence Decatur. The check was made out to Fanny Newcomb. The amount was blank. Lawrence had given her this check in September on the day he asked her to marry him.

Fanny loved Lawrence Decatur. She always had and imagined that she always would. She would have accepted his proposal of marriage, if it had come with even a little professional encouragement. Instead, Lawrence had insisted that *his wife* give up all of her legal work: give up thinking about juries and judges; about snooping and eavesdropping; about justice and fairness.

But it wasn't just and it wasn't fair to ask Fanny to be less than the woman than she was; to be less than the woman that her father and *Lawrence himself* had encouraged her to be.

Fanny tried to see the check as payment for those busy months after her father's death when she had settled his legal affairs, transferred his clients to other attorneys, and even wrote up the closing statements that Lawrence would make on his behalf. But Lawrence was adamant: the check was for Fanny to purchase her trousseau; to purchase all of the items she would need for her new life as Mrs. Lawrence Decatur.

Fanny had flung the check at Lawrence that September night and had been surprised to find it inside her suitcase when she unpacked at her first boarding house. Despite her many financial hardships after leaving Lawrence and the law office, Fanny had never thought to cash the check. Until tonight.

This check could quickly settle her debt to Clarence Halloway. But, Fanny realized just as quickly, the check could open the doors to other information about Nora that she desperately needed.

As she held the check within her fingers, weighing the reasons and costs for spending it, Fanny finally understood why she kept the check hidden. For Fanny Newcomb, exchanging her spinsterhood for mere money—and a life that did not include lawyering or investigating or employing her intelligence—was much too much like prostitution.

31.

EARLY WEDNESDAY MORNING OLIVE swept the broom across the floor of the infirmary gallery, blowing a trail of dirt and dead flies out into the yard. "If you can't steal the Register tell me now."

Fanny peered over the top of the folded newspaper. "Oh, I can steal it. And by lunchtime. But have you decided how to return it?"

"No, I haven't."

"Olive, I can—"

"No, I'll do it. I have to speak to him directly." Olive pulled a rolled piece of paper out of her pocket. "I've written out Remington's schedule for you so you'll know exactly when he'll be out of his office. I've drawn a map of his office and examination room on the back and marked where the Register should be."

"In his examination room on the shelf under the window or in the middle drawer on the right side of his desk." Fanny opened up the newspaper, turned the page, and folded the paper once more in half.

"Unless someone is actually using it. In that event...." Olive glanced over at Fanny, whose finger tapped the center of the newspaper page, as if she was deep in concentration. "Fanny, are you listening to me?"

"There's an illustration in the *Picayune*," Fanny answered. "It's a woodcut of one of the photographs Pierre deVille took in the Channel on Saturday night."

"Are you sure?"

"Sure about what?" Sylvia limped onto the gallery, her eyes fixed on the newspaper clutched in Fanny's hands.

Fanny rustled the newspaper toward Sylvia. "Come look at this. It's the photographs from Saturday night."

Sylvia sat down on the bench next to Fanny. Olive, still holding the broom, sat on the other side of Fanny. Although a large headline blazoned above the typeset, the women's attention was drawn to the illustrations. The first showed a woman tumbled on a heap of trash against an outdoor wall of a saloon. From the hard angle of her body against the refuse and the bottle that waited on the ground just beyond her fingertips, it was clear that she had fallen drunk into the debris. In the next image, three little boys also slept, but this time upon the hard gravel road, against the wall of well-tended brick. Dressed in dirty, too-small clothing, their exposed limbs were still plump with baby fat; the boys could be no more than four years old. Fanny's heart ached at the sight of their chubby cheeks, which reminded her of cherubs painted on a chapel wall. "He must have taken these pictures before we caught up with him."

Sylvia shook her head. "It's just as real, isn't it, seeing the image in the newspaper? Just as real as when we were there. It makes me want to open a thousand settlement houses, get these poor people a decent place to live. It makes me want to put a torch to the Channel, to burn down all of those crumbling buildings, and put up new ones in their place."

"You almost had your wish," replied her sister. "The whole Channel could have gone up in flames Saturday night."

Olive nodded to the last illustration but Fanny's eyes were already fixed on the image of the row of men slumped against each other like fallen dominoes. The label on the enamel signs they wore around their necks glistened: BLIND. Although they all appeared to slumber, one man stared straight toward the place where the photographer would have stood and, from under the visor of his shabby cap, his eyes sparked like a wild man.

"'*Shame in the Irish Channel*,'" read Sylvia.

> One in a series of articles exposing the Catholic Diocese of New Orleans for their well-known disregard of the people forced to rent its properties. Unnatural desires in the family! Disease! Insanity! Even murder can all be laid at the feet of the Catholic Church.
>
> Owners of the lion's share of property in the section of New Orleans known as the Irish Channel, the Catholic Church has allowed their buildings to deteriorate while double and triple charging renters. Buildings constructed for single families are now home to eight and ten families. Entire families live in a single room, sharing common sleeping, eating, and washing areas. The very fetid walls almost force people out into the street. Most of the buildings were constructed long before the late War of Northern Aggression and are ravaged throughout the year by low tides and floodwaters. The wood is rotting and people fall through stairs and floors every day. Every inch of these houses is infested with vermin. As the season of yellow fever approaches, the slum housing will only contribute to this summer's inevitable epidemic.
>
> The primary villain of this barbaric travesty is Father Terence Boylan of St. Alphonsus Parish. Although a native son of New Orleans, Boylan has allowed the buildings given to his care to rot like the

> foulest devils in hell. Boylan's entire faults will be detailed in the next article in this series.

Fanny searched the next page, which was lined with advertisements. "No author. And deVille's taken no credit for the photographs either. In fact, his name isn't even mentioned. That's a surprise, since he's been so eager for publicity."

Sylvia looked up at Fanny and Olive. "Even though deVille caused so much trouble with his magnesium flash, I say hooray for the photographs. And hooray for this article. The whole town has known for years that the Catholic Church squeezes out every bit of rent money they can and still does nothing to improve the buildings. Whoever wrote this article is only telling the truth and it's time that someone exposed those horrible conditions. I was thinking about doing it myself. Someday."

"You were thinking about insulting the Archbishop of New Orleans and accusing him of abusing his parishioners?" Olive asked.

"Of course not. I would have shown the information to the Archbishop first and given him the opportunity to make changes. If he refused, *then* I would have printed it in the newspaper."

Fanny tapped her finger just under the headline. "It shouldn't be too difficult to find out who wrote this article."

"Eliza could tell us," replied Olive.

"Then one of you must find out and today if possible," said Fanny. "I'd go myself but I've got a book to steal."

AS SHE RODE the multiple streetcars to Charity Hospital, Fanny reviewed Olive's drawing of Remington's office. Once she understood the locations of Remington's desk, doors, and windows, Fanny finalized her plan: she would be swift; she would be quiet; and she would not leave until she had the information she came for.

Fortunately for Olive, Fanny had much more experience stealing than she would admit. Lawrence had often put Fanny to good work and had never called it stealing. As a talented card magician, Lawrence preferred the term *borrowing*, although Fanny often thought of it as *justice*. Under Lawrence's tutelage, Fanny learned how to listen to the tumblers of a wall safe, use a wire to open a lock, and even pick a pocket. She became so adept that she had imagined herself a female Artful Dodger. Fanny's father had been appalled at Fanny's stealing—after all, *Thou Shalt Not Steal* was the seventh commandment—but she had continued to practice her particular justice whenever it was warranted.

As Fanny left the final streetcar, she deposited the plans in her small, covered market basket and inspected the watch brooch that Olive had given her. Yes, by the time she paid her admission to enter Charity Hospital, Dr. John Remington would be out of his office.

Once inside the hospital, Fanny walked the central corridor and turned into the hallway of doctors' offices. As Chief of Surgery, John Remington's suite of offices was the first in the wing. Fanny stopped at his door, as if to read the nameplate that adorned it. She put her hand on the knob, turned, and pushed through. She locked the door behind her, her hand lingering on the doorknob. A frisson of fear sizzled through her. She was locked inside a room she should not be in. Yet, she knew that there were two other doors out of Remington's office; one led into the examination room and the other led to his consulting room. Both of those rooms had exits directly into the main hallway.

As she crossed the room to Remington's desk, Fanny's fear was replaced by an unexpected sense of disappointment. Getting into Remington's office had been too easy. She had been looking forward to the challenge of a locked door or a hallway full of nosy nuns or a guard patrolling the corridor. She would have to content herself with the challenge of finding the Death Register. For a wild second, she hoped that the book was hidden in a wall safe. Now that would have been a challenge worthy of her skills.

In truth, Fanny enjoyed the prowl, craved the hunt for the object, and to her disappointment, the Death Register was in the middle drawer of Remington's desk. Fanny inspected the label on the front cover: *Charity Hospital, Records beginning February 11, 1889.* She paged through the book, until she found the entry for Nora's body and the description of her cause of death. Fanny sobered instantly; her sense of adventure evaporated. She marked the page with a hairpin, closed the book, and covered it with the muslin in her basket.

Fanny expected that the photographs of Nora's slashed body would be with the post-mortem notes but they were not. She wanted to see them; needed to witness the full extent of her student's indignities; wondered if something in the photographs might offer information that Olive had not seen. Fanny looked at the watch brooch; Remington should be away for another half-hour. Fanny gave herself twenty minutes to locate Nora's photographs.

Olive had told her that the photographs had been in a brown paper envelope and Fanny began her search at Remington's desk. Almost every drawer held the scent of his pipe tobacco, a fruity, fragrant blend that pleased Fanny. His clothes smelled of the tobacco, as she recalled, and Fanny wondered if Olive had fallen prey to Remington's aroma as much as his expertise— for Olive had certainly turned a blind eye towards Remington's motive to murder Nora. As Fanny prowled through his desk, she almost had to agree that it was unlikely someone so renowned for saving lives could have deliberately taken one. But still, as Fanny's father had told her, the appearance of a man can be deceptive.

This could be the murderer's office, Fanny reminded herself. Or the office of the murderer's uncle.

There were many envelopes in Remington's desk and Fanny opened each one. None of them held any photographs. She finished with Remington's desk and approached the glass-fronted cases on the near wall. One entire case was stacked with envelopes. Fanny riffled through them quickly; their contents all disappointed her.

The clock atop the case chimed the hour. Fanny checked her watch brooch: five minutes before the hour. She had stayed too long. Remington would return within minutes. Confident that she had left everything as she found it, she tilted her ear against the corridor door and listened. There were no sounds from the hallway, not even the swish of the nuns' stiff skirts. Fanny left Remington's office with the Register in her basket, certain that no one was any the wiser. Except Fanny Newcomb.

OLIVE SURPRISED FANNY a block away from Charity. "Did you get it?"

"Olive, what are you doing here?"

"I couldn't wait." Olive grabbed Fanny by the elbow. "Did you get it?"

"Of course I did," Fanny pulled away from Olive before retrieving the book from her basket. "It's all in there. Exactly as you said."

Olive scrambled to open the register. She ran her ringers along the pages until she read, "*Red marks around throat.... Death resulted from strangulation.*"

"You were right," said Fanny.

"Yes, I was." Olive fingers sifted through the rest of the book.

"And now that you have proof, you need to—"

"I need to think," Olive closed the book and held it firmly in her hands. "John Remington is my friend and

I don't take his friendship lightly. I need a night to think this all through."

AFTER OLIVE TOOK off with the register, Fanny continued along Tulane Avenue. She easily identified Adams' House of Refuge and Redemption by its ornate wrought iron fencing and curtained windows. There was a streetcar stop across from the house and Fanny waited by it. She unfurled her parasol, confident that it would obscure her face should anyone be watching her as she watched the Refuge.

Her instincts told her to distrust everything about Adams and his motives in kidnapping women. Fanny imagined that only powerful forces could draw a woman into prostituting herself and found it hard to believe that Adams could be successful in convincing women to change.

Fanny wondered if Nora had ever been dragged back to this house; if Adams had captured Nora and if he had, how she had gotten away. Perhaps Nora had escaped and he was so shamed by his failure that he had strangled her. Or perhaps Lester Adams—in some type of redemptive fever—had snapped. And instead of rescuing Nora, he had killed her.

Could Fanny get into Adams' house? Could she pretend to be a prostitute and get Adams to chloroform and kidnap her and haul her into his Refuge? Although Fanny and Adams had met briefly yesterday, if Fanny loosened her hair, gargled whiskey, bought clothes from the ragman, wasn't it possible she could convince Adams she was an unfortunate? She'd read in the London newspapers about police officers dressing as prostitutes, waiting to be approached by Jack the Ripper. The *London Illustrated Police Gazette* had even sketched a stubble-faced man crouching in a tattered shawl and skirt. The police ruse had not worked but couldn't Fanny make Adams believe she needed redeeming?

And if she did, what might she find inside his refuge? Could there be something inside that linked Adams to Nora? Perhaps a list of the women he kidnapped and redeemed?

As Fanny mulled this thought, she realized that a man had opened and closed the iron fence enveloping the barren grounds of the house. As he jogged up the steps to the front door, Fanny thought she recognized him immediately. And how could she not? On Sunday afternoon, she had admired Terence Boylan's square shoulders and glossy black suit. Now he was knocking on the door of Adams' Refuge. Fanny tried to remember: had either Olive or Sylvia found any connection between Terence Boylan and Lester Adams?

Olive had mentioned that Adams had a partner in his work. An excited tingle ran up Fanny's spine. Could Father Boylan be that partner? From Sylvia's recounting of her conversation with Boylan, he clearly hated Bad Women.

As Fanny focused on Terence Boylan waiting at the front door, a streetcar reached the stop, completely obscuring Fanny's view. One passenger, laden with boxes and canvas bags, almost fell from the car onto Fanny. He straightened himself and Fanny was face to face with Pierre deVille, inches away from his inky-black moustache and badly shaped toupee; inches away from the stench of bay rum infused into his clothing. This was the man who started the fire in the blind men's room and disappeared without helping them; the man who may have held the door against Fanny; the man who might have *killed* Fanny. The excited tingle that had propelled Fanny earlier evolved into a frisson of fear. She backed away from him.

Hitching his tripod and camera higher, deVille crossed Tulane Avenue, dropping and retrieving one article of his equipment every few steps. As he jumbled across the street, his toupee took on a life of its own, scampering across his scalp and gliding recklessly over his bald head.

The photographer stopped at the elaborate fence, juggled his equipment against the fence, unlocked the gate, and with great effort, navigated his way up to the front door. As the man still waiting at the front door turned to look at the clattering photographer, Fanny realized that she had been wrong earlier. The broad black-clothed shoulders she had watched walk up the steps did not belong to Terence Boylan. They belonged to his brother, Gabriel.

32.

FANNY SAT AT THE STREETCAR STOP FOR another quarter hour. She had to see if anyone else entered or left Adams' Refuge. She searched her memory of last Saturday night and could not remember the scent of the photographer's ever-present bay rum, which led her to an almost impossible premise.

Perhaps deVille wasn't the photographer in the Channel on Saturday night. Or perhaps there were two photographers in the Channel that night. Had deVille's publicly announced decision to photograph the Ripper inspired another photographer? One who was less agile with magnesium powder?

As the streetcar ambled up to the stop, Fanny forced herself to return to Wisdom Hall. She sat at the back of the car and looked out the window, as if she would find answers among the warehouses, carts, and shop signs along Annunciation Street. As her gaze returned to the inside of the streetcar, she realized that Daniel Crenshaw and his sergeant rode in the front of the car.

The car stopped in front of Wisdom Hall and Fanny watched as Crenshaw and Flynn exited through the front and walked up the Hall's front steps. Flynn knocked at Wisdom Hall's front door. Aunt Esther answered, allowing Flynn and Crenshaw inside. Fanny could see the dogs clustering around Crenshaw and the police entering Sylvia's office.

Fanny went to the infirmary and then through the back corridors that led into the central hallway of Wisdom Hall. Daniel Crenshaw's voice trumpeted from inside Sylvia's study. "An incredibly stupid thing, Miss Giddings. That's what it was."

In the silence that followed, Fanny slid into the room and stood behind Sylvia, who sat at her desk. Crenshaw, a yard away from the edge of Sylvia's desk, met Fanny's entrance coolly, but Flynn could not hide his surprise. Sylvia, as though buoyed by Fanny's presence, attempted to answer the detective. "But—"

"Incredibly stupid thing to post a murder reward," repeated the detective. Cain and Abel looked up at him.

Sylvia shifted uneasily in her chair but did not yield her point. "I still don't understand how you found out that I posted the reward. It clearly says to talk to the Editor of the newspaper. It did not mention my name."

"What reward?" asked Fanny.

Flynn reached into his tunic and pulled out a folded newspaper page. He handed it to Crenshaw, who unfolded it, and placed it carefully on the top of Sylvia's desk. It took Fanny only a few moments of looking up and down the columns before she found the double-bordered box.

"Reward" she read aloud. "For accurate and intimate information regarding the heinous murder of Nora Keegan." Fanny had considered the benefits of posting a reward only a few hours earlier, and now Sylvia had actually posted one. Was it really possible that the reward could get Fanny the information she wanted? Despite the tension between Sylvia and the detective, Fanny felt a surge of optimism. Until the detective spoke.

"I found out," Crenshaw looked at Sylvia as though he was explaining to a child, "because I went down to the *Picayune's* office and asked the editor."

"And Eliza told you?" Sylvia's mouth hung open in surprise. "I can't believe she would do that."

"As it happens, she did not. But when she left her office, her assistant was all too happy to tell me. Douglas Shaunasey, you may know him?" Crenshaw paused, as if allowing the betrayal to take full effect. "And I'm here to tell you plain Miss Giddings, if Shaunasey told me, he's likely to tell other people...even though I warned him against it. By posting this reward you've put yourself into danger. I've pulled the advertisement from the newspaper and told Mrs. Nicholson to deliver any information she receives directly to me."

"You had no right to do that!" protested Sylvia. "I'm trying to find useful information about Nora's murderer."

"It's the murderer I'm concerned about."

"But you have already caught Nora's murderer," Fanny spoke directly to Crenshaw. "Or so you have been saying. Are you telling us now that you know Karl is not Nora's murderer?"

The muscles tensed in Crenshaw's jaw. His gaze met Fanny's and then shifted to Flynn, "Sergeant, wait outside for me."

But a full minute after the screened door slammed after Flynn, Crenshaw had not spoken. Fanny, her sights still fixed on the detective, crossed her arms. "Well?"

Crenshaw's mouth twisted painfully. "There might be certain aspects about Karl Schultz's arrest that don't ring true."

"Such as?" Fanny and Sylvia asked in one voice.

"The knife found at Schultz's lodgings did not belong to him. When the blood was washed off the knife, a mark was found inscribed on the handle. In fact, the knife belonged to a cobbler who had a workshop a few streets away from Schultz's lodgings. He—"

"The cobbler?" asked Fanny.

"Yes," replied Crenshaw. "He remembers using that particular knife the morning *after* the girl was murdered. He said that it went missing after his midday break on Saturday. After the police questioned him at his shop."

"What are the police doing about this?" asked Sylvia. "Why hasn't Karl been released?"

When Sylvia paused to breathe, Fanny asked the question that was foremost in her mind. "What are you doing to find Nora's real murderer?"

Crenshaw sat down, choosing the sturdiest of Sylvia's delicate chairs. He put his hands on his thighs and looked directly at both of them. "It would appear that there was some tampering with evidence. While I have explained and discussed this with the Under Commissioner of Police, he has not agreed with me. All that concerns you is that it is *possible* that Schultz is not the murderer. Which means that the murderer might be glancing at the *Picayune* and might want to find out who is seeking information about him."

Sylvia's hands gripped the arms of her chair. "You're suggesting he might seek us out here and do us some harm?"

"If someone was trying to find information about me, I'd nip it in the bud." Crenshaw sat back gingerly in the chair, as if waiting for Sylvia to understand the gravity of her actions.

"Even if the persons trying to find out information were just a couple of spinsters?" asked Fanny.

Before he could reply, Sylvia spoke harshly to the detective, as though she could not concede she had made a mistake. "But the police offer plenty of rewards."

Crenshaw stood up. "That's because the police are the police and no harm will come to them. But you...you don't know what you might have let yourself open to. Some people are just plum crazy and will say and do anything. You've opened yourself up not only to the real murderer—and his accomplices, if he had any—but also to any man jack loony enough to find out where you live. And although I've warned him against it, Shaunasey could easily spill the secret of your address. I'm hoping a word to the wise will be sufficient, Miss Giddings." He looked at Sylvia as sternly as a schoolmaster. "The last thing the Channel needs is another murder."

Sylvia paled and Fanny knew that she finally understood the gravity of the situation. Crenshaw nodded to the newspaper on Sylvia's table, which was folded open to the page of Irish Channel photographs. "I do have some information on your Saturday night photographer. It appears that—"

"It wasn't Pierre deVille," Fanny completed the sentence. The detective's jaw dropped slightly and his eyes tightened. Fanny took an extravagant breath, pleased at her deduction.

Crenshaw's gaze hardened. "That's right. After he closed up shop at the St. Charles, deVille ran a magic lantern show at a private residence." The detective's words were flat and ordered. "Since you know so much about it all, if it wasn't deVille, who was it?"

"That I don't know," Fanny replied. "And I only realized today that it wasn't deVille Saturday night. When you and I spoke before, I really thought it was him."

Sylvia ran her finger along the edge of the folded newspaper and stopped at the pictures of the dilapidated buildings. "When you were at the *Picayune* today, inquiring about my reward, did you also find out who the photographer was for these pictures? Or even the author of the accompanying piece?"

"No, Miss Giddings, I did not."

"Mr. Shaunasey didn't tell you *that*?"

"He did not know and I'll guarantee that. He said that the photographs and the editorial had been anonymously submitted and that the editor had been all too glad to publish them. Seems that Mrs. Nicholson's had her own disagreement with the Catholic Church as landlord."

As Fanny and Sylvia exchanged glances, the detective asked, "Is there anything that you haven't told me? Anything you've forgotten to tell me?" When it became clear the women would not answer him, he said, "Well, then. I hope you're going to stay out of police business now."

FANNY FOLLOWED THE detective into the hallway. Crenshaw turned to Fanny as if he was expecting something from her. She debated: perhaps it *was* time to tell him what she knew about the men who may have killed Nora. But really, she had no heart for it. Although she had taken up this investigation because of her affection for Nora, Fanny had enjoyed the intellectual stimulation of the manhunt. She did not want *that* to stop.

Could Fanny really trust this detective? If she told him what she knew, would he get Karl released? Would he make sure that the citizens of New Orleans understood that the real murderer at large was not Jack the Ripper? And how much should she tell him?

The detective stared at her. Their eyes caught and held. She would be sorry to surrender that mental satisfaction but, of course, Fanny could not allow her enthusiasm to endanger Olive or Sylvia or their servants or the girls who attended class at Wisdom Hall. Fanny put her hand on the parlor door. Daniel Crenshaw dusted his hat against his thigh and followed her inside.

AT DINNERTIME, FANNY was pleased to see Cousin Charlotte seated across from her. The older woman was covered from shoulder to waist in thick linen napkins, a reminder that Sylvia was using the *LATEST FRENCH FASHIONS!* to lure students back to Wisdom Hall tonight.

At the head of the table, Sylvia was dressed in an evening gown of azure silk that included—Fanny suspected from the way that Sylvia was launched forward in her chair—her largest bustle. Fanny had never seen Sylvia's décolleté before, nor the sparkling jewels hanging from her ears, and it was hard not to admire the Principal of Wisdom Hall.

Fanny looked down at her own dark cotton dress and then at Olive, who wore her daily uniform, *sans* doctor's smock. At least Fanny had brushed and twisted her golden hair into a tidy bun and washed her neck and sewn a missing button onto her bodice tonight. Fanny might not sparkle like Charlotte and Sylvia, but she had made an effort.

As Fanny removed her napkin from its ring, it was clear that Sylvia had just told Olive and Charlotte about posting the reward and Detective Crenshaw's stern warning.

As if anticipating criticism, Sylvia said, "Terence Boylan talked about a reward when he was here on Sunday. It seemed like a very good idea. And if it wasn't, why didn't Eliza stop me? She must have thought it was a good idea."

"Eliza probably thought she couldn't stop you," replied Charlotte. "She knows how you are when you are settled on an idea." Charlotte had spoken kindly but Sylvia sat back in her chair, as though she had been rebuked.

Fanny considered: should she tell the women about her private conversation with Crenshaw? No, she would not. Although she had thought to tell him everything, she had only told him about Nora's ledgerbook and the monies she had made. And she had suggested he ask his aunt about that money.

As Sylvia's silence continued, Fanny described her conversation yesterday with the blind man and then how she saw Pierre deVille and Gabriel Boylan enter Lester Adams' house. After she described how she had realized that deVille had not been photographing in the Channel Saturday night, Fanny said, "I've been thinking, Sylvia. Don't you think we should have a photograph of our first graduation class?"

"You're suggesting that I hire deVille to photograph our girls?"

"Now that I know that he didn't start the fire, it would be safe to let him load his magnesium tray."

"But he's a pornographer," Sylvia spoke the word uneasily and then took a sip of wine as if to wash the word from her mouth. "And he could still be Nora's murderer. He's hardly safe and I don't want him at Wisdom Hall."

Cousin Charlotte eyed Fanny keenly, as if she was trying to read her mind, and then said to her niece, "You will want a photograph though."

"I'm sure now that Nora was strangled," Olive blurted out. "Now that I've seen Charity's Death Register again."

Charlotte looked from Olive to Sylvia and put down her knife and fork. "I'm sure you can explain this all to me."

Fanny leapt into the conversation, desperate to keep her thievery a secret from Charlotte. Fanny explained Olive's discovery about the discrepancy between the entry in Charity's Death Register (stating that Nora was strangled to death) and Remington's post-mortem report (identifying that Nora was slashed to death).

"Now we know that Lester Adams butchered Nora," said Olive. "He was the only one with opportunity and motive."

"I can understand his opportunity," Charlotte moved her chair back from the table and began to remove her layers of linen. Fanny watched with interest as Charlotte slowly revealed her *LATEST FRENCH FASHION*, a peach silk evening gown that glistened with pale green trim. Charlotte removed the final napkin and collected her gloves, which must have lain on her lap. As the older woman fitted the first glove over her fingers she asked, "But what was his motive?"

"I don't know yet," Olive replied.

Sylvia leaned forward, trying to assert as much sisterly control as she could. "Take the Register to Daniel Crenshaw so that he can confront Adams."

"I'm not going to the police for assistance," Olive declared. "I'm confronting Adams myself."

"You mustn't," said Sylvia. "There's no telling how he'll react. You must alert the police."

"I can't have the police there. They'd only get in the way. They might even protect him."

"But...." To Fanny's surprise, Sylvia looked to Charlotte as though the older woman might be able to sway Olive from acting rashly. But Charlotte was mute.

"Don't worry, Sylvia." Olive stood up and addressed the women at the table. "I'm not walking into any danger. John Remington will be with me."

TO FANNY'S RELIEF, all of her students (and Sylvia's too) showed up for Cousin Charlotte's talk. Despite their long workday, it was obvious that many of the girls primped for the occasion: Colleen's hat boasted a new red ribbon; Meggie's dark locks were oiled into obedience; and Siobhan's long neck reeked of lilac soap. Some students had even brought their girlfriends and female relatives. (All of the students brought male relatives to escort them home, and these feisty champions sat smoking on the front gallery.)

Fanny—who ignored all mentions of fashion in the newspapers—was amazed that Sylvia's advertisement was so successful. And Cousin Charlotte was more than equal to the occasion, not only parading her elegant silk gown and demi-bustle to the oohs and ahhs of the assembly, but also allowing her bonnet, gloves, and a pair of embroidered stockings to be passed amongst the assembly.

Eventually, Charlotte's show of fashion segued into an address about Education. Finding Employment. Keeping Employment. And—to Fanny's surprise—Destiny.

"Your real job," Charlotte stood behind the podium Sylvia had erected, "is to find your calling in life. Are you called to be a teacher—like Sylvia Giddings? Or perhaps a doctor—like Olive Giddings?"

Fanny tensed slightly, wondering if Charlotte would mention Fanny's calling. It wasn't teaching—Fanny was sure of that—and she wondered if Charlotte could tell Fanny what she should do with her life. Or if what she should do is marry Lawrence.

"And how do you find out what your calling is?" Charlotte leaned toward the assembly. "You must open yourself to hear that voice inside of you that tells you exactly what you should do. And sometimes you must close yourself off from the people who would tell you that you can have no calling. Or that women have only one calling—as wife and mother.

"You may think my advice is hopelessly romantic. But I believe that it is entirely realistic. You can do anything, as long as you work hard. You must put your mind and your soul and all of your energy into it. Your graduation from these classes at Wisdom Hall on Saturday is the beginning of a new adventure."

As Charlotte's words rang through the parlor, she looked directly at Fanny. Was Charlotte deliberately encouraging Fanny to continue seeking Nora's murderer?

Fanny was so caught in Charlotte's words, she had not realized that Olive stood next to her. As the students began to applaud, Fanny pulled Olive out onto the front gallery. "Charlotte has some very progressive thoughts."

"She's always been ahead of her time," replied Olive. "You should hear what she did when the Yankees occupied the city during the war. She's only told a few of us, but I think she'd tell you."

"Olive," Fanny paused before continuing, "Do you remember telling me about the man who murdered the doctor's wife in Germany? The murderer you discovered?"

"Of course."

"How did you discover he was guilty?"

"Scientifically, of course. He found me in the lab as I was analyzing the poison and realized what I was doing. He admitted his role in the murder, although there was nothing of the confession about it. He was proud to have fooled the police and his professor. And he showed no remorse about the professor's wife." Olive jammed her hands in her pockets. "I was lucky to get away from him."

"He attacked you?"

"With my own scalpel. I tried to run from him but he cornered me. I knew he would kill me to keep his secret."

"What did you do?"

"I lied to him," said Olive matter-of-factly. "I told him that I'd completed my work earlier and had sent for the police and that they would be there immediately. He must have believed me, because he turned and ran. As it happened, the police were waiting at his lodging to question him and he confessed directly to them."

Fanny stood silently until Olive said, "What are you thinking, Fanny? I can tell you've thought of something."

"I was thinking that you're incredibly brave, Olive Giddings. And that I'm glad to know you." Fanny surprised herself by linking her arm in Olive's and was rewarded when Olive did not pull away. "Your quick thinking saved your life. I'm not sure I could react so quickly."

Without warning, Liam bounded through the door way and onto the gallery. He charged toward Olive, "Miss Sylvia says come right now, Dr. Olive!"

Olive held on to Fanny for the briefest moment. "But you saved those blind beggars from the fire. I'm not sure I could have done *that*." As Liam pulled Olive toward the door, the doctor said softly, "And I'm glad to know you too."

33.

FANNY REMAINED ALONE ON THE FRONT gallery, watching as a solitary girl stumbled under the heavy shadow of the magnolia trees. A stray glint of lamplight caught the glow of her unnaturally colored strawberry blond hair and the thick glass of her spectacles.

"Deirdre." The name slipped once from Fanny's lips and as she saw the girl hesitate, Fanny called her name loudly enough for the girl to hear. But instead of meeting Fanny on the gallery, the girl turned and walked away. No, she ran away, back to the street.

Fanny followed after her, but the girl was gone. No, there she was, just inside the front door of a streetcar going uptown, her harsh hair color caught once more by the streetcar driver's lantern. Fanny ran after the car and grabbed the bar of the back door. Since the mules had not gained much speed after their stop, she was able to lift herself aboard the car.

Deirdre sat in the last seat and Fanny sat down beside her, boxing her in. The front of the car was full of men smoking cigarettes and laughing with the driver. Since the driver could not see them tucked away in the back, Fanny realized that she and Deirdre would be able to ride without paying. Clever girl, Deirdre.

Fanny was shocked at the thickness of the girl's spectacles. It was almost unfair, to catch an almost-blind girl so easily. But Fanny, huffing slightly from the chase, didn't care. She would use any advantage she could. She gathered her breath before asking, "Were you looking for me?"

Deirdre answered readily, as though she was used to being chased and caught, confronted and questioned. "How much money is that reward?"

Fanny could smell the warmth of alcohol drifting from Deirdre's breath. Was the girl plied with spirits at Mrs. O'Sullivan's? Did it make her docile and attractive? Or had she sought it out herself, to find the courage to travel through town and talk to Fanny?

"All the girls said you were offering a reward. Said they saw it in the newspaper."

Fanny leaned toward the girl. "Do you know something about the man who killed Nora?"

Deirdre twisted her lips, refusing to speak. She pushed her spectacles up her nose and Fanny saw that one lens was badly chipped on the side, as though someone had stepped on it. Fanny asked, "Would you know something, if there was a reward?"

"I might."

Fanny wanted to help—no, she wanted to *save* Deirdre, like she couldn't save Nora. But how could she? As she thought this through, Fanny felt an unnerving sensation of being watched. She peered up and down the car, meeting the stare of a thin man outfitted in a garishly checkered suit. He wore spectacles almost as thick as Deirdre's but his were fogged. Still he stared at Fanny until she felt revealed to him. Then she realized that without a shawl or bonnet she *was* revealed.

Fanny saw a way to get Deirdre back to Wisdom Hall and away from Mrs. O'Sullivan's. "I don't have any reward money but if you return with me, I'll repay you for the streetcar uptown. And perhaps we could talk. You could sleep in the infirmary. It's very clean and doesn't smell bad at all. I can stay there with you, if you're scared. And tomorrow we can talk things through."

"I *need* the reward money." Although Deirdre's voice turned mean and certain, a tear escaped the shield of her spectacles and ran toward the corner of her mouth. "Soon."

Fanny took Deirdre's hand in hers and was surprised to find it hot and wet. She pressed Deirdre's fingers firmly and the girl looked at her. But Fanny could not read her emotions. "Tell me what you know. I'll find a way to help you."

Although it was clear from the pained expression on her face that she was thinking deeply of something, the girl did not answer. All too soon the car approached Canal Street and the turnaround. As the car lumbered down the street, the mules pulled up short. Deirdre skirted around Fanny and dashed from the car, almost falling down the steps. Fanny followed her out, surprised at the girl's speed. But unencumbered by hat, parasol, and purse, Fanny ran fast, too. Still she was unable to catch up with Deirdre.

As Deirdre neared Basin Street and Mrs. O'Sullivan's house, she tore off her spectacles and jammed them into the waistband of her skirt. With arms out in front of her, she gained hold of the side of the building and walked toward the back door until she was swallowed by the darkness between the whorehouses.

Fanny halted in the darkness, suddenly aware of the jaunty piano music that glided from the long open windows. She watched as a carriage stopped in front of the house and a group of men stagger up the front stairs. As much as she wanted to pursue Deirdre, Fanny couldn't propel herself to approach a house of prostitution at night time. She walked across Canal

Street, ready to avoid another fare by slipping into the back of the next streetcar.

A knot of men parted in front of a telegraph pole, displaying the broadside that they had been reading. The pole was within the arc of a strong pool of electrical light and even from afar, Fanny could make out the first word of the note: "Whores!" The letters were large and bold, luring people to read it. Fanny's heart sank, knowing it must be another missive from the Irish Channel Ripper; another brutal letter threatening women with disembowelment, mutilation, and death. When the men moved aside, Fanny went to the notice and read it.

> **Whores! Scarlet and Fallen Women! New Orleans' finest young ladies captured for your enjoyment and bound into white slavery! Learn about their Shameful Secret Lives! Vividly portrayed in illuminated photographs.**
>
> **Presented by 'M. deV', Well-Admired Master of the Magic Lantern. At midnight, tonight only, back of O'Reilly's saloon. The corner of Front and Gravier. Twenty-Five Cents Admission.**

Fanny recoiled. Just this evening she had thought to have Pierre deVille photograph the class of graduating girls and she cursed herself for her innocence. No, her stupidity.

She tore the broadside from the pole, intending to shred it to bits. As she stared at the words, she decided to walk up and down Canal Street tearing down every broadside she found. Then her anger subsided and her reasoning returned. She would tell deVille exactly what she thought of him. Tonight.

But when Fanny reached O'Reilly's Saloon, it was Lester Adams, not Pierre deVille who was taking money at the saloon's back door. Adams was wearing a red carnation in his lapel. But if his goal was to redeem women from prostitution, why would he sell tickets to see women's naked bodies? Was his concern for redeeming prostitutes just a sham?

If this magic lantern show had anything to do with Lester Adams, Olive would want to know about it. But there was no time for Fanny to return to Wisdom Hall to collect Olive. Fanny was sure there was some piece of information to be gained at the magic lantern show and she was determined to find it. First, she would have to gain entry. For that, she would need twenty-five cents. And a male escort.

LAWRENCE SLAMMED THE large book in front of him, splattering dust across his cluttered desk and launching the magic lantern broadside into the air. "Good Lord Fanny, what kind of crazy idea do you have in your head now?"

Fanny jerked away from Lawrence's desk, as much from the cloud of dust as from Lawrence's critical tone. The broadside floated toward her and she trapped it between her hands. She watched as the thick dust settled over Lawrence's fine white suit and then she joined him on his side of the desk. She reached into his top drawer, retrieved one of his enormous white kerchiefs, and began to wave at the floating dust attacking her.

"I thought I explained it very well. One of the men who may have murdered Nora is running a magic lantern show tonight. And there's another man taking tickets; he's also suspected of murdering Nora and he's been kidnapping women off the streets of the Irish Channel. I want to see the show but I'm sure they won't let me in." She looked up at the grandfather clock that was directly across Lawrence's desk. "I need you to escort me. And pay my admission."

Lawrence took the kerchief from Fanny. He stared at her so forcefully that she backed away and into the chair opposite his. "I suppose I should be grateful that you came to me at all."

"I know that I can always count on you," Fanny replied sweetly, beginning to realize that despite the urgency of her request, she still relished tussling with Lawrence. It was almost like working with him again and how—

But Fanny's thoughts were cut short by the clock striking the hour. She stood up. She could not let Lawrence dissuade her; she must charge forward for Nora. "There's no time to waste talking. They might already have started."

Lawrence Decatur stood up also, flattening both hands on his desk. "You told me you had stopped all of your investigating."

"I told you I wouldn't get in trouble and I haven't. But I can't stop now. Daniel Crenshaw has admitted that Karl is innocent. That means the murderer is still out there. And one of these men must be the murderer."

"That show is no place for a lady."

"But one of the men going inside had a woman with him."

"Any man who takes a woman into a show like that wants only one thing." Lawrence stopped himself before he said more.

Damnation! Fanny's father had encouraged her to understand the many shades of New Orleans life but had, of course, shielded her from unmaidenly vulgarities. Fanny knew that Lawrence had committed himself to doing the same. But still, Fanny had a job to do tonight.

"Have you no regard for your reputation?" Lawrence took a calming, calculating breath. "And it will look bad for me also, Fanny. Can't you spare a thought for my reputation?"

Fanny smiled; she had him now. "You've broken every social law in the book and probably some laws that I haven't heard of. Nothing tarnishes you."

"Dammit, Fanny, sometimes I think you like tormenting me. No and I mean no. That show is absolutely no place for a lady."

Fanny looked once more at the clock, hoping deVille and Adams were running late. Even so, she had only one option remaining. "I'm willing to compromise with you."

"There is no compromise that would make me—"

Fanny joined Lawrence once more at his side of the desk. Although she was tall, Lawrence was taller by a few inches, and standing this close to him always made Fanny feel capable and confident. She put her fingertips on his hand, and as she traced the bottom of his ring finger she whispered up to him, "Yes *Uncle*, I think there is."

BY THE TIME Lawrence and Fanny arrived at Reilly's saloon, a different man was taking money at the door. Fanny dug her head into the crook of Lawrence's neck as they entered the room, which reeked of spilled beer and damp sawdust. She had been given a tour of a saloon owned by the parents of one of her students and this room was just as she expected it: small and built for storage, with boxes of empty bottles stacked against the walls and sawdust strewn on the floor. An odd assortment of chairs was positioned in the room. On one chair sat Gabriel Boylan, his eyes closed, his hands folded gracefully on his lap, as if he were praying.

Would Gabriel Boylan recognize Fanny or Lawrence? She did not care for her reputation's sake but if he was the murderer...if he was alert to Sylvia's reward...it was possible he knew that the women of Wisdom Hall suspected him. That was a danger Fanny was not willing to take. She continued to cuddle close to Lawrence, finding sudden comfort from the sour odors of the tattered hunting jacket he had changed into.

Between the chairs ran a throughway, which allowed room for the magic lantern. Perched on a tall pedestal, the lantern pointed toward a large white sheet stretched and nailed across the wall. But where was the magician? Where was Pierre deVille? Fanny uncurled her head slightly and looked around but could not see the magician. Instead, she watched as Boylan opened his eyes and went straight to the magic lantern. He pulled a cloth from his vest pocket and began polishing the slides. Fanny was not surprised to see a red carnation pinned to his jacket. She was about to share her discovery with Lawrence—who had held her in a vise grip since they approached the saloon—but his steely alertness stopped her.

Lawrence led Fanny to seats on the end of the last row. As they sat, he glared at the doorway, as if measuring their distance from it. Fanny was glad that he did. Despite her determination to cast herself into this audience, she was uneasy. No Canal Street bankers or lawyers were in this crowd. No forthright insurance or cotton brokers. No church deacons or vestrymen. This was a crowd of roughs, reminiscent of the mob that had almost rioted outside the Parish Prison. These men labored on the docks and, from the snippets of Italian and Spanish she heard, Fanny imagined that some of the men taking long gulps from jars were sailors from other countries. There were women in the audience, just as Fanny had told Lawrence earlier and two of them had begun to yell at each other—insults that Fanny had never heard before—while a giant of a man sitting between them laughed.

Lawrence could not stop glaring at anyone who looked Fanny's way. "I don't like this one bit."

"Please, Lawrence. Just for a few minutes."

"There's nothing to learn here."

Fanny had spoken bravely in Lawrence's office but now she was not so sure. There *had* to be some connection between Nora and deVille and now to Adams and Gabriel Boylan. But what was it? Had Boylan, not Adams, kidnapped Nora? Had Adams forced Nora to pose for deVille? Was it possible that Adams forced all of the girls he kidnapped to pose for deVille? And where was deVille? Perhaps all three men worked together: perhaps Boylan enticed girls to Adams' refuge, where deVille made them pose nude before the camera. Fanny squirmed in her chair.

The argument between the women in the front escalated into a fight, as they clawed at each other like rabid cats. Decatur launched from his chair like a firecracker, yanking Fanny's arm. "I'm taking you out of here."

But before he could shake Fanny from her chair, the giant sitting between the women slapped both women hard on their heads and shoved them into their seats. The gaslights dimmed. Silence spread amongst the audience. Fanny tugged at Lawrence's jacket and pulled him back into his seat. He was right. They should go now. But something stronger than her own self-preservation held her in the chair.

A foggy light appeared on the white sheet and by it Fanny could see that Gabriel Boylan was commanding the magic lantern. An image began to focus within the circle of light and the audience crowded toward the center of the chairs. Men huddled against the back of Fanny and Lawrence's chairs, trying to see. An almost animal growl arose from the back of Lawrence's throat. The men hustled sideways, away from Lawrence and Fanny.

The image on the white sheet focused on a glossy-haired, dark-eyed girl as young as Nora and wearing absolutely no clothing. She leaned against a fluted marble column but Fanny knew instantly that this was no figure study for sculpture, no pose of the innocent nymph or muse. This girl was touching her body in intimate areas, one hand cupping her full breast, the other caressing her belly. Fanny's stomach churned.

Nora had been naked but her image had been noble. Put a sword in Nora's hand and she could have conquered the world.

Adams' Yankee voice pierced the low murmurs of the audience. "All over New Orleans, women are enslaved. Whorehouses exist on every street in New Orleans and women ply their wares on every street corner."

Fanny doubted that anyone in the audience listened to Adam's exposition, so intent were they upon the image of the girl's naked body. Fanny was barely listening to Adams herself, so caught up was she with her thoughts of Nora.

Adams continued, "Even with a monster on the loose, women are still going about exposing their flesh and selling themselves. And it's all because of you. You weak men."

Gabriel Boylan changed the magic lantern slide and a hand-tinted image of a naked fair-haired girl appeared. Fanny gasped. It was Deirdre. Or was it? The image was gone—Gabriel Boylan was changing the magic lantern slides at a rapid rate. Every image showed a different girl: unclothed, partially clothed, and oblivious to the camera.

Fanny was ashamed that she had forced Lawrence to join her. It was one thing to ask someone like Clarence Halloway about the business of pornography but another thing to subject her oldest friend to viewing it. Fanny had seen enough and would not force Lawrence to endure anymore.

Just as Fanny pressed Lawrence's arm to tell him they should leave, the image changed again. This time the girl was not naked but was dressed in the work clothes of a wash girl. As Fanny looked closer she realized that it was one of the girls already seen naked. But she was entirely changed. Not only by her domestic dress and apron but by the washboard and bucket and the piousness of her face. At the bottom of the slide was an inscription: *Hard Work Will Wash Away Dirt And Sin.*

"*Hard Work Will Wash Away Dirt And Sin,*" Adams exclaimed to the crowd, as though anticipating much of the audience could not read. "Redeemed from a life of sin!"

In one voice, the audience began to hiss. Throughout the room people shouted their displeasure, "Give us the show!"

"We've been tricked!"

"We didn't come here for no damn lecture!"

A green bottle flew at the sheet, which rippled slightly, distorting the girl's image.

Adams' thin voice could still be heard over the noise, like a sharp whistle used to call dogs. "Over a week ago, a woman was killed in the dark streets of the Irish Channel. Brutally slashed to death. Her blood still marks the spots where she was ripped to pieces. Yes, there's a man in jail for her murder but I tell you plainly, gentlemen," Adams sneered his last word, "the real murderer may be in this room this very minute."

Fanny clutched Lawrence's arm. What was Adams up to?

Adams took a notebook from his pants pocket and waved it at the men. "I've got your names right here! I've been following you as you hunt these girls." Adams seemed almost possessed and Fanny didn't know which scared her most: red-faced Lester Adams, about to succumb to an apoplectic fit or the giant in the front row, who had risen to his full height.

"Is it you? Is it you?" Adams' voice rose to a whiny pitch as he pointed to people throughout the room, finally resting on someone in the front row. "Is it you?"

A high, hysterical female sob escaped from the first row. "No, it ain't me, mister."

"I say it is. It is all of you. All of you who chase after...." Adams faltered and staggered slightly, put his hands on his chest as though physically attacked. Gabriel Boylan stepped forward and put his hand confidently on Adams' back. He whispered something to Adams and then turned to the crowd. But before he could speak, the giant from the front row lurched forward and rammed into him. Boylan fell back and landed upon Adams, who pushed him away and into the fists of the giant.

Lawrence clutched Fanny to him and they rose from their seats as one. One of the sailors tugged at Fanny's skirt, pulling her toward him. Lawrence went after him, attempting to shield Fanny as he aimed his knuckles at the man's jaw. Fanny backed up, tumbling into one of towers of empty bottles that lined the walls. When she looked up, Lawrence had disappeared into the dusty fray. Fanny stepped forward to find him and then stepped back, this time avoiding the glass wall. She had never witnessed a full-blown fistfight before and the brutal sounds of the men hitting each other made her stomach heave. She was going to be sick; she needed to get outside.

With the dust kicking up about her, Fanny edged toward the door. She saw the light sconce on the wall and wondered: if she cut off all of the gaslight, if no one could see, maybe they would stop fighting. Before she could put her hand on the key, a man flew at her, forcing her away from the gas and directly behind Gabriel Boylan. Fanny watched as he took up a classic boxing stance, almost humorous in its formality. But his fist shot out quickly and cleanly. He dispatched three men into lumps on the floor.

Fanny's eyes lit on the magic lantern and the box of slides on the chair next to it. Although men and women were tearing at each other around the room, the lantern and slides were undisturbed. She had to get those slides. She had to see the faces on those girls, had to know if Nora or Deirdre was among them.

Fanny inched forward to the center of the room, skirting the men and women beating at each other. Just as she neared the lantern she was pushed and fell into it. The lantern fell onto the floor and cracked into pieces. Fanny was transfixed, expecting oil to leak onto the sawdust, expecting the lighted wick to ignite the floor into a fire, expecting the smoke. She saw the burning wick among the wreckage of the lantern and stomped on it with both of her feet, grinding it into the floor.

The box of slides was still safe on the chair and a broken slide lay on the floor next to it. She bent down to retrieve it and as she came up, she was face-to-face with a tangled-haired, toothless woman. The woman pushed up her long sleeves, displaying her muscled forearms. Fanny's body swayed with fear. Could she fight this woman? And if she tried, could she win the fight?

But Lawrence appeared at her side, catching Fanny and the box of slides in his arms. The woman backed away. Lawrence turned, sighted the door, and whisked Fanny out of the saloon.

34.

IT WAS ALMOST TWO O'CLOCK WHEN Lawrence returned Fanny to Wisdom Hall. His temper had exploded once they reached the safety of the law office and he continued to rail at her as they rode through the Irish Channel. But as they neared Wisdom Hall he froze into silence, his anger spent.

Fanny was alarmed to see that the two front rooms of Wisdom Hall were ablaze with light. Something had happened. Had Daniel Crenshaw been correct? Had Nora's murderer accosted Sylvia? As Lawrence stopped the carriage, Fanny clutched the battered box of magic lantern slides to her chest and ran toward Wisdom Hall. Lawrence ran after her.

Sylvia burst through the screened door and onto the gallery, Charlotte at her side. Olive, Thomas,

Liam—and was that Daniel Crenshaw?—followed on Sylvia's heels.

"Fanny!" Sylvia's voice cracked slightly. "Where have you been? We were worried to death about you."

Lawrence came up behind Fanny, put his arm around her waist and walked her to the bottom of the steps. He surveyed the group on the gallery, his eyes settling on Detective Daniel Crenshaw. "We've just been out for a ride." As Crenshaw surveyed Decatur's dusty jacket and cut lip, Lawrence was forced to elaborate. "We took a spill. Damned horse shied at a stray dog."

"If everything's all right, I'll be going then." Daniel Crenshaw looked at the box in Fanny's arms. "Miss Giddings. Doctor." The detective spoke as though he knew he was being lied to and wanted his time wasted no further. "Miss Newcomb. Lawrence."

Charlotte said, "Detective, I would be glad for an escort home." As she descended the stairs, she stopped to stroke Fanny's cheek with the back of her hand.

A few minutes later, Lawrence joined the women in Sylvia's office. He sat stiffly as Fanny—her hands folded over the box of lantern slides on her lap—explained the events of the evening. A quarter of an hour later, Lawrence said goodnight to the sisters.

Fanny walked Lawrence to his carriage, both of their steps slowed by a strange brewing of fatigue and fascination. As he bent to kiss her good night, Fanny boldly asked Lawrence for one more favor. And why not? After what Fanny had negotiated tonight, she had nothing to lose by asking.

FANNY'S SLEEP WAS haunted by images of naked girls. And Lawrence Decatur tumbling amongst them.

She tossed on her narrow bed throughout the night and awoke Thursday morning tired and dissatisfied. From deep under her cotton sheets, she looked at the top of her bureau and at the pair of images that had defined her life: the small daguerreotype of her mother and the formal portrait of Fanny, her father, and Lawrence taken at the Cotton Exposition. Fanny rolled out of the bed and opened the bureau's bottom drawer. She lifted up her folded nightdresses and brought out the photograph of Nora, the naked Nora, the exposed Nora, the strangely confident Nora.

Fanny brought out the glass slides she had rescued last night. Three slides of naked girls and many more of girls in working costumes. None of them were Deirdre or Millie. Or Nora. *These photographs have some information about Nora's murder,* Fanny whispered to her father's photo. *But what is it?*

She pulled out Nora's ledgerbook from the armoire shelf. From the seat of her desk chair she retrieved the clipped advertisements, Ripper broadsides, and newspaper reportings. From her apron pocket, she took the newspaper article about the slums of St. Alphonsus. If she could make no sense of thoughts, perhaps she could make sense of things. She placed each item carefully on her desk, next to the pile of newspapers from which she had cut all of the articles that seemed to apply to Nora's murderer. The desk was too small so she moved everything to her bed.

She arranged the items in the order received and stared at them. Then she rearranged the items in the order of the places they were found and stared at them. Next, she arranged them in order of who the things belonged to or who they might belong to and why. Overwhelmed by their silence, Fanny tossed all of the papers on the floor. And stared at them.

She ran her finger along the frame of the Cotton Exposition image. It was her favorite photograph of her father, for he stood tall, proud, and sensible. He exhibited none of the religious fanaticism of his last years, those tortured years, when his light blue eyes pulsed too brightly, his white hair stood out wildly. But even in those years, when he applied himself, his mind was keen and his instinct accurate.

"You would have the answer by now, wouldn't you?" Fanny addressed the image. "Where did I go wrong? What did I miss?"

As though her father had answered her invocation, Fanny *did* remember something else. She hurried downstairs to Sylvia's parlor, went to the bookcase, and snatched both copies of *The Lives of our Lady Saints and Martyrs* from the bookshelf.

She brought the books to Sylvia's parlor table and examined the flyleaves for inscriptions and dedications. Thumbing through each page, she sought messages written on pieces of notepaper, writings in the margins, or underlined words. She read the tables of contents and looked at each colored image. She paused at the colorful and gilt-edged illustrations, jarred at how much these veiled saints differed from the images of the naked girls upstairs. Finally, she took each book by the cover and opened it up and shook it, waiting for something to fall out.

Fanny did not hear Sylvia enter the room until she said, "Did you really think you'd find something in those books?"

Fanny responded without looking up. "Didn't the Boylans bring you more than one book? Where are the others?"

Sylvia brought out four pamphlets from her top desk drawer. As Sylvia watched, Fanny shook, thumbed, and inspected each of the books thoroughly. Disappointed, she held the pamphlets out to Sylvia.

"No inscriptions, no telling bookmarkers, no coded pages?" asked Sylvia coyly.

"Not even a saint named Nora."

"How about Gabriel or Terence?"

"It's a book about women saints, Sylvia, or haven't you read it?"

"I looked it over when Gabriel first brought it over. But there were only two differing stories: a woman was good to begin with, became better and became a saint.

Or a woman was very evil, was rescued, became good, became better and then became a saint."

Fanny leaned back in her chair, exhausted from her failed expectations. "So, you're not going to pursue Catholicism?"

"Of course not."

"Then you should take these books back to the Boylans." Fanny pushed the pamphlets toward Sylvia. "And while you're at St. Alphonsus, you can ask Terence Boylan what he knows about Redeemers."

"I've asked Terence Boylan enough questions, thank you. And what's more, I think he's innocent of Nora's murder. From everything I've seen, he's dedicated his ministry to helping the poor of the Irish Channel. And even though his views on the status and rights of women are rather...*catholic*...it's not motive for murder. If it were, almost every man in the city could be suspect."

"That wasn't what the midnight photographer thought. Reading his article made you believe that Boylan was the Devil himself."

"It's a shame that he had to be embarrassed so badly in the newspaper with the photos. And his bro-"

"I know what you think: Gabriel Boylan is dedicated to educating the young boys of the Irish Channel. You've already elevated both Boylans to the sainthood."

"I do admire them." Sylvia's voice was suddenly fierce. "They were born with silver spoons in their mouths but th—"

"I *know*, Sylvia. 'Dedicated their lives to Redeeming Sinners and Rescuing the Downtrodden.' In one way or another. But what about Pierre deVille and Lester Adams? Are they innocent too?"

"Of course not. They are both despicable. But you haven't found anything to prove they murdered Nora. Nor does it seem likely you will." Sylvia pulled a chair from the parlor table and sat down opposite Fanny. "Fanny, it's time. We've reached a dead end."

Now Fanny understood why Sylvia had been protesting each man's innocence. "I can't stop. I won't. We've done everything correctly. Just think of how much we've found out already about these men, Sylvia. And we've found motives for murder for each of them."

"Fanny, we must stop."

"But we know Karl is innocent. If we don't find Nora's mur—"

"Fanny, that is a job for the police. We haven't proved that we can find the murderer any better than they can. And we have worn ourselves down in the process."

"I like wearing myself down. I've enjoyed every minute of asking questions and watching people and understanding what they do and say and finding answers."

"Yes, I know you enjoyed yourself but...." Sylvia put her hand over Fanny's. "You didn't enjoy that magic lantern show last night. I know you didn't. Your face was green when you got home and I heard you getting sick in your room. And Lawrence looked like he could have strangled you."

Fanny folded her arms about herself. "You're right about the magic lantern show. I felt filthy. But even so, I knew that I was there for the right purpose. All of this has to get us somewhere, Sylvia, in time."

"There is no more time left. We've got to move on. We have graduation on Saturday and after that, a new session for school. We need to start fresh and focus our work on our living students. On Monday morning, we will meet with Detective Crenshaw and give him all the information we have."

Fanny's protest was halted by Aunt Esther, who stood at the parlor door.

"Miss Fanny, a boy dropped off a message for you."

Fanny snatched the envelope from Aunt Esther's hands. She tore open the fold and read the note. "We're in luck. Karl has agreed to see us this afternoon. Lawrence says we're to meet him at the Parish Prison."

"When?" asked Sylvia.

"Now."

"Lawrence arranged this? But things seemed so strained between you last night. How did you get him to agree?"

Fanny rolled the note into a tight straw. And clutched it with all of her might. Fanny knew that she could put all of the pieces together into a completed puzzle. Eventually. She could identify Nora's murderer. She could free Karl from prison. She could free New Orleans from the horrendous fear of the Irish Channel Ripper.

She looked down to see the rolled note beating a furious tattoo against her other hand. "All I ever wanted was justice for Nora."

"Fanny?" Sylvia put her hand over Fanny's hand once more. "What exactly did you say to Lawrence last night?"

"The only words he wanted to hear," replied Fanny, almost apologetically. "I told him that I'd marry him."

35.

LAWRENCE WAITED FOR FANNY AND Sylvia in front of the prison. As he escorted them through the gates, Fanny saw Daniel Crenshaw leaning against a wall, watching their arrival. Lawrence led the women into a small, windowless room. It had a regular wooden door so Fanny knew it was not a cell but it was so small and airless that Fanny felt imprisoned. Within minutes the door opened and Karl was brought inside, seated, and shackled to the table. Two beefy guards positioned themselves directly behind him. Lawrence coughed gruffly and the guards left the room.

"Be quick about this," he told Fanny.

Karl's head hung low upon his chest and Fanny could not tell if his eyes were open or closed. Beneath the table, Sylvia clutched Fanny's hand. Fanny hardly flinched as Sylvia's pressure bruised her burned fingers.

Surprised by Fanny's silence, Lawrence addressed Karl. "These fine women are the only ones in the world who care if you live or die." Lawrence peered at Karl. Sylvia had said Karl spoke and wrote English, but did the poor man really understand anything? Lawrence had no choice but to continue in English. "Now, there are many reasons why a man would confess to a murder he didn't commit. He might be protecting someone. Someone who's guilty or someone who's innocent. He might have been blackmailed or intimidated into confessing. He might just like the notoriety; like being famous, even if it's for something evil. Or he may have lived his entire life without hope and think that he has no chance of being heard. He might be a well-known rascal and liar and think that no one will believe him."

Lawrence did not move a muscle. but Fanny knew he was carefully studying Karl. "Which one is it, son, with you?"

Sylvia clenched Fanny's hand so sharply that one of her scabs shifted from its wound. Fanny removed her hand from Sylvia and pulled a wad of paper from her large pocket. She unfolded it slowly, wishing that she had talked to Karl more when he worked at Wisdom Hall; wishing that she knew how to find out what he *must* know about Nora.

"These are pages from a ledgerbook that Nora kept hidden at Wisdom Hall. It shows that she had a lot of money. Almost three thousand dollars." Fanny paused, expecting to see some reaction from Karl. "It's possible that whoever killed her may have stolen this money. I know you knew Nora. I know that you didn't kill her, because I know you were at Wisdom Hall when she was killed. We know there are a few men who had motives to kill Nora and this money may have been a motive for at least one of them. Did she ever tell you about this money? Do you know why she kept her ledger hidden at the Hall? Did you talk to her the night she was murdered?"

When Karl said nothing, Fanny turned to Lawrence. "You said he'd speak to us."

"He never agreed to talk to you, but Daniel thought he might, if he saw you. Who knows? He might not have understood a word that we've said."

"But he knows he's going to hang. There's got to be a reason he won't talk." Fanny looked at Lawrence for confirmation and when she saw it in his eyes, she said to Karl, "You're protecting someone aren't you? But who? I know you don't have a wife or sweetheart."

Sylvia clutched Fanny's hand once more and Fanny winced in pain. Then Sylvia blurted out to Karl, "Olive and I went to your rooming house. We saw your bed in that room and the photograph you had under your mattress. We heard how you sent money back every week to your parents."

Karl's head jerked up and he glared at Sylvia as if she had slapped him across the face. Sylvia did not flinch. But Fanny was frightened by what she saw: the man did not want to be cleared of Nora's murder.

"You can't send your parents money if you're in jail," said Fanny, "but someone else could. If you agreed to confess. But the person who blackmailed you into confessing, who is sending money to your parents, might be the murderer. Had you thought of that?" Who would Karl trust to send his parents money every week? Someone with money, of course. Someone whose word was trustworthy. "Terence Boylan offered to take care of your parents if you confessed, didn't he?"

"Stop right now Fanny," Lawrence growled, like one dog warning another dog away from its bone. "Terence wasn't the only person to visit Karl."

Fanny scowled back at Lawrence, but she could not stop. She was so close, she had come so far. The answers to Nora's murder were in this room. "Terence Boylan killed Nora, didn't he?"

Suddenly, Karl's eyes locked on Fanny's. Through his terror, through his exhaustion, through the dirt and hair that clouded his face, she thought she saw him answer her. Karl's jaw dropped down and his lips drew together but only a grunt escaped his mouth. Lawrence took his flask from his inner pocket and put it close to Karl's mouth. Karl sucked at the whiskey, bending his head back, as though he was a child trying to get all the rainwater from a daffodil cup. One word fell from his between his lips. "No."

Then Karl turned his head away, his shoulders slumping toward the table.

Lawrence capped the flask and shoved it back into his jacket. "At least we know he can talk. But Fanny, that's enough." Lawrence banged on the door into the hallway. It was unlocked quickly and Daniel Crenshaw and Sergeant Flynn entered. The detective looked from Lawrence to Sylvia to Fanny to Karl and called for the guards to take Karl away.

Sylvia watched as Karl was shuffled from the room and then stood up. "I'm going home."

Lawrence escorted Sylvia from the room and Crenshaw joined Fanny at the table. As the detective scribbled in his notebook, Fanny thought through the last few minutes. Who was sending money to Karl's parents? Not deVille; he had no money to spare. And how much money did Adams have after purchasing and outfitting his Refuge? Fanny still thought Terence Boylan was the most likely. He came from a very wealthy family, although as a priest, had he taken a vow of poverty? But his brother—as yet, unbound by any vow—certainly had access to money. Last night Fanny had discovered that Gabriel Boylan was associated with Lester Adams. If it was Gabriel, who was the seminarian attempting to protect? Adams, his brother or himself?

Crenshaw looked up at Fanny and Flynn every few minutes, until finally Crenshaw looked solidly at Flynn and nodded toward the door. Once Flynn was gone, Crenshaw said, "Lawrence told me about last night. About the magic lantern show."

When Fanny did not respond, Crenshaw added, "He's worried about you, Lawrence is, because you know a lot more about this business than you should."

Fanny wondered at the relationship between Lawrence and this detective. They were not social equals: Lawrence was the son of a well-known New Orleans family; Crenshaw was working-class Irish. Fanny assumed they had met in the legal arena but whatever their history, they seemed to trust each other. And neither seemed to trust Fanny to take care of herself.

"And if I tell you everything, he thinks that both of you can keep me safe? You know what I think? I think— no I'm sure—that if I tell you everything I know, I'll be cut out."

"You mean that I'll find Nora's murderer without you?" His voice took on a schoolmaster's tone, as if he was about to lecture her. He didn't need to; Fanny knew she was being selfish. She knew that she wanted the intellectual triumph of identifying Nora's killer and knew, at the same time, that it didn't matter who caught the murderer as long as he was caught.

"It's that important to you, is it? Being right, being the first, being the best?"

"It never was before," Fanny answered honestly, "but about this, yes. Yes, it is."

From across the table, the detective stared at her. She wondered what he thought about her. Selfish? Headstrong? Arrogant? She knew what she hoped he thought: Intelligent. Analytical. Persistent.

The detective closed his notebook. "Perhaps we can have a truce. I'll share information with you if you share information with me." The detective nodded to the ledger papers Fanny held in her hand. "I have an answer to all that."

"You do?

"I went to Mrs. O' Sullivan, just as you suggested, and asked her for Nora's money."

"But she didn't."

"But she did."

Irritated by the detective's success, Fanny still doubted that Mrs. O'Sullivan had handed over all of Nora's of money. "How much did your dear Aunt give you?"

Crenshaw stared at Fanny as though surprised she knew his relation to Nora's landlady. Then he opened his notebook and flipped to a well-penciled page, "Twenty-eight hundred dollars. And seventy-nine cents"

"What did Mrs. O'Sullivan say when you asked about it?"

"She was grateful. 'A terrible burden, not knowing who this money should go to.'"

"And you believed her?"

"As you said, she's my dear Aunt." The detective closed his notebook firmly. "Now it's your turn to talk."

Fanny considered for a moment before replying. "Nora *was* strangled to death. Her body was ripped after she was murdered." Fanny was pleased to see the detective's disbelief. She had told him something he had not known.

"And would you happen to know who was responsible for ripping her up?"

"Yes," Fanny felt a distinct triumph as she looked into the detective's eyes. Fanny knew much more than Crenshaw knew and she wanted to savor the moment. "Lester Adams, John Remington's nephew."

"I know who he is."

"Olive knew it all along; she was the first doctor on the sce—"

"And why didn't she come forward with this information earlier?"

"She told the Under Commissioner." Fanny flared, her moment of triumph deflating suddenly. "Two days after you arrested Karl we went to his office and told him everything. Olive's going to talk to Adams about this today."

His eyes riveted on Fanny, the detective stuck his notebook inside his coat. When he spoke, his tone was gentle and respectful, as if he knew what sharing her hard-won information cost Fanny's pride. "I suppose you're planning to meet Dr. Giddings when she speaks to Dr. Adams?"

Fanny tensed. She had made Crenshaw's job so easy. She had done his job *for* him and when the time came to identify Nora's murderer, Fanny would not be allowed to participate. She wanted justice for Nora and justice for Karl but Fanny realized that she wanted a certain justice for herself. She had sought and analyzed and listened and stolen. She had done what the police could not or would not do. Good Lord, she had even agreed to marry Lawrence.

The detective was about to speak when Lawrence entered the room. Lawrence watched the pair—their eyes locked; their postures stiffened—for a few seconds before calling Fanny's name.

It took Fanny a few seconds longer to turn to him. He put his hand on her shoulder and she followed him out into the corridor. A pair of guards walked past them and turned the corner before they were alone.

"Sorry to leave you for so long," Lawrence guided Fanny's arm through his. "I have just time enough to take you to lunch before I have to be in court. We have so much to discuss."

Fanny could not look up at Lawrence; not just yet. Despite her love for Lawrence, she was still surprised that she agreed to marry him last night. As he leaned closer to her now, she caught the scent of his citrus soap and wondered: would she want his tangy fragrance to accompany her for the rest of her life? He pressed his hand against the small of her back as if he was leading her to dance. Suddenly, Fanny was keen to honor her word. But would Lawrence want to marry her if—no, *once*—she solved Nora's murder? Would any man want to marry her after she proved how capable she was?

"I can't join you for lunch today," Fanny replied as Detective Crenshaw joined them in the corridor. "I must return to Wisdom Hall."

She spoke to the detective. "And I suppose you're going to Adams' House of Refuge right now, aren't you? To be with Olive when she confronts him?" Fanny bit her lip, as if she had not meant to say what she just had. Would Crenshaw take the bait?

Crenshaw tilted his head slightly, as though he had seen Fanny and Lawrence together for the first time. He shoved his hat on his head. "Yes, yes I will."

As Crenshaw bolted down the corridor Fanny repressed a small smile. While Crenshaw would meet only frustration seeking Olive and Adams at the House of Refuge, Fanny would find both doctors at Charity Hospital.

Fanny would never let Daniel Crenshaw—nor Lawrence, who had suddenly tightened his grasp on her arm—get the better of her.

36.

JOHN REMINGTON WAS NOT IN HIS Charity Hospital office but Lester Adams was. He sat at the large worktable with the contents of his doctor's bag before him. In his hands was a long, narrow knife. Perfect, Olive knew, for digging out bullets, but it could also be used to slice skin open. She shuddered. Had he used it to mutilate Nora?

Adams looked up and the path of red welts and bruises that ran across his face reminded Olive that he had been in a brawl last night. The knife twisted in his left hand. "Ah, Dr. Giddings. Protector of Prostitutes. What righteous indignation brings you to Charity Hospital today?"

Olive clutched at her doctor's bag, in which she had placed the Charity Death Register. Steps away from her sat the man who had certainly ripped Nora's body to pieces, perhaps murdered her. Olive pressed her back against the doorframe. She peered down the empty hallway. Where was Remington?

She was disgusted that Adams held the title of Doctor. He was a detestable man, with a cancer of evil and self-righteousness that needed to be revealed and punished. She could not wait for Remington to serve as her witness; she could not wait to wipe the smug self-satisfaction from Adams' scaly face. With clear certainty of her information, she was ready to confront him.

She removed the Death Register from her bag and shook it before his face. When his eyes bulged as they lighted on the book, she knew she had hit her target. She opened it to her marked place and began to read. "Red marks around throat. No outward signs of distress or other injuries. Death resulted from strangulation."

Adams' face turned pale; the welts were even harsher against his bloodless skin. He had taken out his handkerchief and dabbed at the flakes of skin on his flushed forehead. The knife teetered limply in his left hand until it fell to the table.

Olive pressed her advantage. "Nora's throat was cut wide open and her body was slashed and stabbed *after* she died. You brought her body to Charity and wrote these notes in the Register. And then...you mutilated her." Olive's breathing was sharp as she waited, their eyes locked in certain challenge. "Have you no shame?"

Adams picked up his knife and slid it into its sheath. As he pulled a new knife from his kit, he seemed to speak directly to it. "The only shame is seeing something wrong and doing nothing about it."

"But you—"

"Cut her throat straight through and ripped open her skin," Adams replied evenly. "Why should I deny it? By ripping her up, I saved the lives of countless girls and women. Thanks to me, they're off the streets, too afraid that they'll be the Ripper's next victim." Adams pointed the knife toward Olive, riveting her attention. "What you're doing at your little infirmary is nothing compared to what I'm doing. You merely wipe noses and pat heads. I'm rescuing women from the grasp of the Grim Reaper everyday."

"You're keeping them hostage. The women of the Irish Channel are too terrified to carry on with their honest work for fear that they'll be ripped to death."

"So now that you know about my good works, what will you do?"

The familiar voice of John Remington answered, "Nothing. Nothing at all."

Both Olive and Adams jerked their heads toward Remington, who stood at the corridor door.

"What?" Olive's question broke harshly from her throat. "But John, we mu—"

"Tell the police?" finished Adams. "No need for that. They already know. Or some of them at least. I've had to pay the police plenty, to allow me to conduct my rescues."

"And to stay quiet about Nora's death?" Olive addressed Remington, "The police must have seen her body after you took it away. They must have known all along that something was false; that her body was unbloodied."

"In New Orleans, the police see what they are paid to see and little else," replied Adams. "If I told them her throat was cut, they believed me."

Remington leaned wearily against the door surround. His voice was low but even. "I can't change what happened in the past but I can damn well change the future. I will not allow my hospital to be involved in your misdeeds. You will surrender your connection to

Charity immediately. If I see you near our ambulance at any time, if I ever see you talk to any of the doctors or staff here, if you ever approach me ag—"

"But Uncle...."

Olive moved toward Remington. "But John, the police must arrest him. Nora Keegan was grossly violated."

"That whore was *dead*. A corpse," interjected Adams. "And I found a good use for her sorry body."

"But why did you enter the correct information in the Death Register before you slashed her?" asked Remington.

Adams' features assumed a self-satisfied smirk. "I've been planning to do this for quite a while but I needed a prostitute. A dead prostitute. I couldn't be absolutely sure about this one. I would never allow a virtuous woman to be defiled. And so, I recorded my initial findings in the Death Register. And then the police brought me her belongings and I found that she had been carrying some photographs—the horrid, disgusting photographs that prostitutes sell to their men. I knew she was a prostitute. People were already screaming when I left Conner's Court that she'd been killed by Jack the Ripper. It was all too easy to assist that belief."

"Then you asked me to do her post-mortem examination. You used me to lie for you."

Olive recoiled at the anger in Remington's voice as he continued to berate his nephew. "You cared nothing about the work I've done here. The trust and respect I've built up."

"And I wrote to the newspapers." Adams' chest puffed out slightly. "Pretending I was the Ripper and ready for more blood."

Remington moved toward his nephew. "That was you?"

"It took only one letter. After that, other good men were glad to take up the message." Adams began forcing items into his bag.

Olive put her hand on Remington's forearm; his body was tense with anger. "You can't let him go, John. He could have strangled her in order to mutilate her. He could be Nora's murderer. We need to inform the police."

For the first time, Adams looked truly alarmed. "I'm no murderer. I'm a savior!" He grabbed his coat from the chair and strode past Remington and Olive to the door. "You should be thanking me. The whole city of New Orleans should be thanking me. I've saved the lives of more women in this city than either of you."

"He can't go!" Olive crossed over and flung herself against the door. Adams stood just a foot away from her, his face red with anger. "He's had a partner in his redemption work and I need to know who. Was Gabriel Boylan out with you the night Nora was murdered?"

Adams's reply was cut off by someone pounding on the door. Olive stepped way from the door, just as it opened. Gabriel Boylan barged through, breathing hard as though he'd been running but he was able to say, "There's a emergency at the Refuge. One of the girls. The nurse sent me to get you. She said you must come now." Boylan looked as though he was going to fall over, "Water?"

"Down that corridor, third door on the right," directed Remington. "On a table by the window."

Boylan's steps quickly plodded down the hallway.

Olive put her hand on Remington's arm and glared toward Adams. "John, you can't let him go back to those girls. Not after what we know now."

"You can't stop me," said Adams. "Those girls are my responsibility."

"Not anymore," replied his uncle. "You will come with us but Olive and I will see to any medical needs."

Just then Daniel Crenshaw appeared at the open door. Sergeant Flynn appeared behind him and from down the hallway, Olive could see Fanny.

Olive stepped forward. "Arrest this man, Detective Crenshaw. He mutilated Nora Keegan and he may have murdered her."

FANNY HAD TURNED the corner to Remington's office to see Daniel Crenshaw standing at the office door. How could the detective have gotten there before her?

From inside Remington's office, she heard Olive's voice, "All of the information you need is in this Death Register. Nora was strangled. He ripped up her body afterwards to scare women."

Fanny stepped closer to the office until she stood just to the side of Sergeant Flynn. Although Crenshaw's frame filled the doorway, she could see Lester Adams attempt to step past the detective.

"Out of my way," said Adams.

"Remington?" asked Crenshaw.

"Just as she said, Detective."

"There's no crime in anything I've done," said Adams. "And if you don't let me go now, there will be another dead woman on your hands."

"Oh, he can go all right," declared the detective.

Olive protested, "But—"

"You two go with him," the detective told Olive and Remington, "and Sergeant Flynn will escort you. When he's finished, Flynn will bring him back to police headquarters."

AS THE FOOTSTEPS of Flynn and the three doctors echoed down the hallway, Fanny and Crenshaw were alone in Remington's office. Crenshaw walked over to Remington's desk, as if he were long acquainted with the office, and sat in the doctor's chair. "I'm surprised to see you here, Miss Newcomb. I thought you were returning to Wisdom Hall. Or did Lawrence change your mind?"

Fanny stood tall. She was not embarrassed to have misdirected the detective, but was irked that somehow he had outthought her and was at Charity Hospital instead of Adams' Refuge.

Gabriel Boylan rushed into Remington's office. He stopped short, his eyebrows raised in alarm at seeing Fanny and Crenshaw. His eyes cast briefly about the room, as though making sure he was in the right place.

If Crenshaw was surprised to see Boylan he hid it well. The detective leaned back in the chair. "You've saved me a trip. I have some questions to ask you."

"But I—"

"We can go down to the precinct but I'm sure John Remington won't be needing his office just now."

Gabriel Boylan fell into the wing chair directly across from the seated detective. Crenshaw looked at Fanny and then nodded at the door. He was telling her to leave but was not going to. She was going to hear everything Gabriel Boylan had to say. Still, Fanny stepped toward the door. Poised directly at the detective, she reached back and closed the door firmly. The detective seemed to expect that she would stay in the room. But what of Gabriel Boylan? Fanny could only hope he believed she had closed the door behind her and did not hear her heart beating excitingly.

"There was a scuffle at O'Reilly's saloon last night," Crenshaw began. "The fight went out into the street and innocent people were hurt. Twenty people were arrested. But not you."

Fanny was alarmed to hear how the fistfight had escalated, but wondered why the detective was talking about last night. Why wasn't he asking Boylan about his visits to Karl in prison?

"It seems the problem began because someone promised a magic lantern show—shall we say for men only?—but delivered something that was more appropriate for a church social."

"You're usually much more direct, Daniel." Gabriel Boylan cross his legs casually. "I can only guess that you want to know my part in all of this. Although I don't see why it's any of your business. If the police would do their job in keeping prostitutes off of the street, my work wouldn't be necessary." Boylan continued, his manner as light as if he were being interviewed by the *Daily Picayune*. "The idea for the magic lantern show comes from one of our British brethren; a gentleman who specializes in saving children from the streets. He photographs them first in their initial shameful state and then in their new clothes and working habitat."

"I could see how the initial photographs could be obtained but how did you get the new ones?"

"Those women are from the Refuge. Lester had them photographed before they returned to their families."

Fanny strained forward, waiting for the detective to ask the photographer's name. But Crenshaw said, "And about this refuge...we've had complaints that women are being kidnapped." As if to make no doubts about the seriousness of the claim Crenshaw added, "White women."

Boylan replied, "Are you sure Miss Newcomb should be here when we discuss prostitutes, Daniel?"

"I'll take responsibility for what Miss Newcomb hears," growled Crenshaw. He caught Fanny's eyes and nodded toward a chair a few feet behind the one in which Gabriel Boylan sat. But Fanny walked around the chair and over to the desk. She sat down in a chair behind Crenshaw. As long as Boylan knew she was here, she might as well watch him as he spoke.

"We all must fight against our baser instincts," said the seminarian. "And when these women cannot do it for themselves, we fight for them. Sometimes that means force is involved."

Fanny could not hold back. "Did you help Nora Keegan fight against her baser instincts?"

"My relationship with Nora was unconventional."

The detective spoke before Fanny could. "What do you mean by that?"

"You don't know? I was one of her customers. Every Friday afternoon, I paid for an hour of her time." Boylan paused, as if enjoying the confusion that might be traveling through Fanny and Crenshaw's thoughts. "I paid to talk to her."

Crenshaw looked at Boylan doubtfully. "What did you talk about?"

"Would you like chapter and verse? Generally, most of our conversations were about the redemption of Mary Magdalene," he answered earnestly. "Nora wasn't like the other women at Mrs. O'Sullivan's. She was smart. She could have turned away from that life if she wanted. But she needed my help."

Fanny shivered. That was almost exactly what she thought about Nora. The girl could have gone far, with the right help.

"But you were unsuccessful," said Crenshaw. "In fact, you failed."

"Yes," Boylan admitted, "but I will not fail the next girl. Deirdre is not as smart as Nora but is more attentive. I'm sure that with a few more sessions, I'll be able to claim her." Boylan rose from the chair. "And now Daniel, Miss Newcomb."

Crenshaw allowed the seminarian to walk to the door before saying, "Just one more thing. I've come from the Parish Prison where I had a long talk with Karl Schultz. And although it took some doing, I found out that someone blackmailed him into confessing to Nora Keegan's murder. Now I'm wondering, Gabriel, if you would know who that someone was."

Fanny fumed as the detective took credit for the information she had found; Crenshaw was cheating her of her victory. But she swallowed her anger as she looked at Gabriel Boylan. From his confused expression, it was clear that he knew nothing about Karl's confession.

37.

SYLVIA AND OLIVE WERE SITTING AT THE dining table when Fanny returned, an unfolded piece of paper lying on the table between them. Fanny rushed toward the table, her eyes on the paper. "Is that a reply to your reward?"

"No," Sylvia bit her lip. "It's a letter from Jack the Ripper."

Fanny took a chair next to Sylvia, stunned to see her already pale complexion drained of all color. "You're not taking this seriously? You know that Nora was strangled."

"Yes, of course I know that there is no Irish Channel Ripper. But still," Sylvia eyed the paper as though it had been sent straight from Satan. "Someone is threatening to kill us Saturday night."

Even as Sylvia spoke, Fanny grabbed the paper and read: "W*hores—I'll cut you to pieces, just like I did the other one. You can't hide in your fancy houses. Look for me this weekend. You may not know me but I'll know you sure. Jack's the name.*" Fanny looked up at the sisters, "We've got to do something about it."

"*Look for me this weekend,*" Sylvia shuddered. "Saturday is our class Graduation. We'll have a hall full of students and families here. I hope."

Olive frowned as she looked up at Fanny. "Some lunatic is trying to scare us."

"But..." said Sylvia, "It's not like the others."

"Other Ripper letters?" asked Fanny.

Sylvia shook her head. "No. I've been getting hateful letters ever since I opened up Wisdom Hall. Letters telling me to stop teaching school; that my real job was to get married and have children; or to stop teaching the Irish to be better than they are."

"Sylvia, why didn't you tell me about this?" Olive put her hand on Sylvia's. "I had no idea."

"I wanted to shield you from it. And those letters never threatened us harm...never threatened to harm any of our students or patients."

Fanny said, "It's odd that we got this letter just after Sylvia posted her reward. It's almost as Crenshaw said, that someone found out the reward was posted from Wisdom Hall. There may be no reason at all for this letter beyond the desire to frighten us. But if this letter was written by someone who found out Sylvia posted the reward, that person has realized that we are interested in finding Nora's murderer. And I can think of at least two reasons someone might send us such a letter: to caution us that we are getting close and might be in danger. Or to scare us into stopping."

"You mean we should take this letter seriously?" asked Olive.

Fanny thought of Gabriel Boylan's paying to meet with Nora, trying to convince her to stop prostituting herself. "I'm taking everything seriously these days."

"I'll have Liam take this letter to Detective Crenshaw right now." Sylvia extended her hand toward Fanny, clearly expecting Fanny to give her the letter.

But Fanny pulled back. "Let me look at it, Sylvia. It won't hurt for Liam to take it later. Crenshaw probably won't even see it until tomorrow, if he sees it at all."

"Speaking of Detective Crenshaw." Olive nodded to Fanny and then motioned to her sister to sit back down. "What happened after I left you and him with Gabriel Boylan?"

Fanny explained Crenshaw's interview of Gabriel Boylan in short order and then listened as Olive detailed her confrontation with Adams. When Olive finished, Sylvia asked, "What happened when you went back to the Refuge?"

"There was no emergency. The nurse thought that one of the girls had broken her arm but it turned out she had not. When we realized that, Sergeant Flynn took Adams to the police precinct."

"How is Dr. Remington?" asked Sylvia.

"How do you think? He's furious. He went up to Adams' office and searched through his desk and papers."

"What did you find?" asked Fanny. "You did go up with him, didn't you?"

"Adams had been burning his papers; that's what we found. He also had a cabinet full of patent medicines 'guaranteed to restore a woman's good order'. I did find some photographs of women among his things. I've brought them with me, if you want to see them."

"If they're like the ones I saw last night..." began Fanny,

"They are."

"I do not want to see them. Or any more of them ever again."

FANNY REREAD THE Ripper letter but no fresh ideas came to her. She wondered what Daniel Crenshaw would think of the letter and then wondered what he was doing just now. He must be talking to Mrs. O'Sullivan about Gabriel Boylan's visits.

Fanny folded up the letter and stuffed it into the envelope. Daniel Crenshaw might be questioning Mrs. O'Sullivan and her girls right now, but Fanny would see Millie and Deirdre tomorrow. Before she could go to Mrs. O'Sullivan's Palace of Pleasure, she would need to get her hands on some money. Lots of money.

"THIS IS VERY queer." Millie tightened the sash around her silken wrapper and pushed the sleep from her bloated eyelids. As she faced Fanny in the entry of Mrs. O'Sullivan's house, a porter rushed through with a bucket of water. Millie refused to budge and the porter squeezed behind her. "It's just not right."

Only a few minutes earlier, Fanny had been glad that she did not have to negotiate with Mrs. O'Sullivan but now she was finding Millie very disagreeable. Fanny tilted her chin determinedly to let Millie know she would not accept her answer. "Mrs. O'Sullivan let Gabriel Boylan pay to talk to Nora. I don't see why I can't pay to talk to Deirdre." Fanny dug into her purse and retrieved a long envelope. She removed the piece of paper and displayed it to Millie. "This is a check drawn upon an account at the Planters and Merchants Bank on Canal Street." Fanny paused to let her words and the check take their effect on Millie. "This is a blank check, which I'm willing to make out to Mrs. O'Sullivan in order to speak to Deirdre. I will pay twice what Gabriel Boylan paid for Nora's time and I'll sign the check over when I've finished talking to Deirdre."

Millie gave Fanny a long glance, as if trying to determine exactly when Fanny had lost her senses. "What do you have to say to her?"

"That's between her and me."

"Let's see that check."

Fanny handed it over to Millie, who appeared to read it. "It's already made out to someone."

"It's made out to me," replied Fanny, silently confirming that Millie could not read, which might be useful information later. "And I'll sign it over to Mrs. O'Sullivan to cash. Or I'll sign it over to you, Millie."

As Millie stared at the blank check—perhaps calculating what it could buy for her—Fanny thought of what the check was supposed to buy. For this was the check that Lawrence had given Fanny when he had proposed marriage. This check was meant to purchase her wedding trousseau.

Millie handed the check back to Fanny. "Oh, all right. Let me see if she's awake yet."

IT TOOK A quarter of an hour for Fanny to get into Deirdre's bedroom and Fanny cursed every minute, anxious that Mrs. O'Sullivan would return soon.

At last, Millie brought Fanny upstairs to the very same room shown to Fanny and Sylvia as Nora's room. As Millie set down the cup of coffee she brought for Deirdre, Fanny looked around the room, wondering if it could still provide any clues about Nora. But no, it was impossible to see anything left of Nora. The once whitewashed walls had been painted a deep mauve and strips of flowered wallpaper had been pasted close to the ceiling. There was clutter everywhere, a disarray that Fanny had not thought possible. No, it certainly was possible. It reminded her of Lawrence's law office. Fanny opened the curtains a bit so that the bright sunlight hit the bed where Deirdre lay.

Deirdre had gone to bed wearing so many colored cosmetics that she looked like a doll whose face had been smashed on the floor. Clumps of hair rats fell from the top of her head. There was a large lump in the bed beside Deirdre that made Fanny uneasy. To Fanny's relief, as Millie arranged Deirdre against the headboard, it was clear that the lumps were pillows.

Millie lit a cigarette and exhaled an aromatic plume over Deirdre and Fanny's heads. "Well, talk."

"I want to talk to Deirdre alone."

"No. I'm staying."

But Fanny had not come so far to have Millie intimidate or speak for Deirdre. She asked Millie, "Did you stay with Nora when Gabriel Boylan talked to her?"

Once more, Millie blew a steady steam of smoke. "I did not but I'm staying this morning."

"*I* was there." Deirdre took a large sip from her cup of coffee. She blinked and narrowed her eyes, as though getting used to the small shaft of light from the open blind. "Every time he came."

As Fanny leaned forward, she forced herself not to wipe the rouge off of Deirdre's stained cheeks. "You were?"

"He came every Friday afternoon at four. And after he left, we'd go down for an early supper and have a good laugh. Then Nora would go to your class."

"What did he say to Nora that last afternoon?"

"Just what he did every week. Told her she was going to hell. "

"Is that all?"

Deirdre looked at Millie before she replied, "Just about."

"What do you mean? What else did he say?"

Millie pushed herself between Fanny and Deirdre. "That's enough. She doesn't get paid to answer questions, just to listen to you preach."

"I'm not going to preach to her."

"But...." Millie's forehead creased in confusion.

"I never said I was. I just want to find out if Gabriel killed Nora."

Millie laughed. "Him? That's a good one."

"Why?"

"He always minded his manners. Always *please* and *thank you* when he was about here. Always respecting his time limit, just like he punched a clock at the brewery."

"Brought us presents," piped Deirdre.

"Brought us books," corrected Millie. "Bibles and such."

"Flowers once." Deirdre looked at Millie. "Just like he was courting."

"Was it possible that Gabriel loved Nora? As a man loves a woman? Physically?" Fanny fully realized the irony: she was trying to delicately describe the sexual relation between men and women to two young girls who lived that relationship every day.

"Oh no," replied both girls.

"How do you know?"

"Like I said," replied Deirdre, "I was with them every Friday. All he talked about was how bad she was to prostitute herself. How evil she was and how she was going to hell."

"Did he ever get mad at her? Threaten her?"

"Only once," Deirdre looked at Millie before she continued, "And that was when Karl interrupted them."

"When was this? The night she was murdered?"

"No, when he was working here…months ago."

"What did Karl want?" asked Fanny.

"How do I know?" Deirdre replied. "Gabriel wouldn't let him talk. Boxed his ears."

Fanny remembered Gabriel's boxing stance at the Saloon. "They fought?"

"They tried but Mrs. O broke it up."

Millie took over, "And then Gabriel's time was over and he was out the door."

"Why would seeing Karl upset Gabriel?" Fanny directed her question to both girls, sure that one had the answer.

The girls looked at each other for a full minute before Millie replied evenly, "If we tell you anything more, it's got to be worth it."

"But I'm already paying you everything I have." Fanny thought about the unsigned check in her purse and how she was using poor Lawrence's money against his wishes. And as Deirdre rolled out of her bed in a delicate silk and lace negligee, Fanny wondered if she'd ever be offered a wedding trousseau again.

"No," replied Millie. "I mean you got to use what we show you to catch the bastard that killed our Nora."

38.

DEIRDRE PULLED HER BROKEN spectacles from her nightstand drawer and led Fanny and Millie up the back stairs. As Deirdre opened the attic door, a flood of light spread over the dark staircase. Millie backed down the stairs. "I'll watch out for you."

Deirdre led Fanny through a pathway of trunks, cases, and broken brass bedsteads, until they reached a shield of sunlight. An unusually large window—even

Fanny could tell that it was out of place in an attic and must have been recently installed into the wall—provided a steady block of light, which illuminated an elaborately scrolled red brocade chaise. Feather boas, stockings, lace garters, and a striped flowered hat were scattered across the chaise, as though a woman would soon return to claim them. A few feet back from the furniture was a box camera upon its tripod, the black focusing cloth hanging like an executioner's mask. A rectangular box, marked "glass slides" in block letters, sat at the base of the tripod.

As all of these items took their rightful place in Fanny's thoughts, she suddenly knew that not only had Nora been in front of the camera, she had been behind it as well, taking pornographic photographs. Then Fanny knew as well: Nora as a prostitute threatened no one. But as a pornographer...well, that was a man's occupation and many men would be threatened.

Motive. Fanny had finally found the motive for Nora's murder.

She staggered slightly with the weight of her discovery and grabbed the top of a chair. Then, to Fanny's surprise, to her amazement, she laughed. She let the laughter ripple long and freely, and laughed even harder as tears began to roll down her cheeks. And why not? Fanny had been brazen and bold and now she had her answer. She deserved her moment of satisfaction.

Every inch of her soul shattered with emotion as she looked around the room at the business of Nora's pornography. Her gaze rested finally on Deirdre, who seemed to shrink away in confusion and horror. Fanny bit her lip and swallowed her laughter. She wiped the tears from her face and reached out for the bedraggled girl by her side.

"Tell me everything Deirdre."

The girl seemed to inspect Fanny for a whole minute—*Was she crazy? Was she dangerous? Should I run?*—before whispering. "All I know is Nora took photos of us up here. Only Mrs. O knows everything."

Fanny sniffed. "But...."

Deirdre looked at Fanny as though she was an exceptionally stupid child. "That's why I brought you up here. To find out what it all means."

Fanny looked about the attic room, as if the floor and walls and ceiling could speak their history to her. Vain hopes but then, the large window did speak. The construction, the type of wood, the scoring about the surrounds, and the handle were just like the skylight planned for the rooftop of Wisdom Hall. One more piece of the puzzle was explained. "Karl put in this window, didn't he? And that's how he knew Nora?"

Fanny took the check from her pocket and handed it to Deirdre. If anything in this attic would explain why Nora was murdered or who murdered her, Fanny would find it.

Fanny stayed in the attic throughout the morning. She looked at everything: searching through drawers, riffling through baskets, tapping lightly on a brand-new Hammond typewriter machine, reading the labels of developing solutions, and almost cutting her fingers on the rough edges of the glass negatives.

Fanny wanted to create an inventory that would provide absolute information about Nora's studio. She wished she had the facility to remember everything she saw and touched and to remember every thought that came to her mind as she looked at every item. She wished she knew how to operate the big box camera so that she could have recorded everything in Nora's studio. Surely, there was at least one item, one detail, one piece of something that would tell her who killed Nora. Finally, as the sun was at its highest, Fanny looked through the first box of photographs.

"LUNCH." DEIRDRE's VOICE cut through the hot silence of the attic.

Almost unnerved by the interruption, Fanny dropped the photographs across the floor. Before she could reply, Mrs. O'Sullivan's voice called from below, "And just what are you doing up in my attic, Deirdre Moran? Nobody goes up there without my approval."

Deirdre was still. Fanny rose to her feet, hoping her voice would carry the authority she needed. "She's with me."

Huffing slightly and holding her hand upon her breast, Mrs. O'Sullivan entered the attic. She looked at Fanny, then Deirdre, then at the contents of Nora's studio spread out across the room.

As the light from the large window dusted over the chaise, Fanny said, "I know about Nora but I need to know about Karl." Then realizing she could get Deirdre into trouble, she quickly added, "I know he worked here—we found out that from his landlady."

Mrs. O'Sullivan nodded toward the window. "Karl's work."

"He and Nora were friends?"

"Not them. After the window was finished, he wanted nothing to do with us. He had no stomach for her business."

"But they saw each other afterwards. She took a photograph of him."

"She took lots of photographs. That's what she did, wasn't it?"

"But you said he killed her."

"In my business, it's not wise to disagree with the police. If they say Karl killed her...." Mrs. O'Sullivan's chest lurched, as if she was in sudden pain. She slumped on the chaise, feathers from the boa floating to the dusty floor, and dug herself into the chaise before saying, "Nora was a smart one. Walked right up to my door her first day in New Orleans. She knew a girl here and said she wanted to go into the business. I just laughed at her; I could tell that she knew nothing about our business here. But she knew she could make good money working for me and didn't flinch at what she had to do to make it."

Fanny gulped. She couldn't even begin to imagine what learning about prostitution might entail. How did one learn to be a slave?

"The poor girl left five sisters back in Ireland, did you know that? She was the oldest and came over here all by herself. She didn't want her sisters to follow her to America, didn't want them to see her in a whorehouse, or have them end up in one either. From the beginning, Nora was always looking for ways to make more money to send home. Wanted to keep her sisters safe in Ireland. I thought she might take over my job one day, but she wasn't willing to wait that long."

Fanny touched the black box camera gingerly, mindful that it was intricately connected to Nora's murder. "When did she turn to pornography?"

"When she found out how much money was to be made. Many a man can't afford to come to a fine house like mine, but they still have their wants. A photograph satisfies them for a while. Nora went with the other girls to the photographer's studio one day to have her picture taken."

"Pierre deVille?"

"Yes, him." Mrs. O'Sullivan frowned. "But the whole thing didn't sit right with her. She had to pay the photographer to take her photo, pay to get copies to sell to her gents, and then, even after that, she knew deVille would make copies for himself and sell her photo at as many places as he could around town. Nora was no man's fool and she wasn't going to let all of that money go to someone else, just because he had a camera and a few fancy backdrops. So she bought this camera, taught herself how to photograph, and convinced the other girls to sit for her. And she made money. Yes, she did. She made so much money that she had no use for men anymore. Nora thought just like a man. Just like you and me. So, just like deVille, she made more copies of the girls' photos and began selling them throughout the city. And Nora was expanding, going to do advertising brochures and books for me and my friends. She was going to do magic lantern shows, just like deVille." The landlady nodded to a stack of broadsides, with the photographer's name emblazoned upon them. "She was undercutting him and she was better at her craft. She made the women look better."

"But something went wrong, didn't it?"

"No one knew who was taking her photos. For a while. But deVille figured it out when my girls stopped coming to him. And nothing gets done in this city unless the police are paid off and Nora wouldn't do that. Of course, for the longest time the police didn't know what she was doing, Nora was that smart."

Or our police are that stupid, reflected Fanny.

"But then Nora was attacked one night returning from one of her errands. I told her she had to be more careful, pay a man to make her deliveries for her. She said she would the next week. But by the next week, she was dead."

"What happened after Nora died? Did deVille come around?"

"She sold him Nora's photos," replied Deirdre.

Both Mrs. O'Sullivan and Fanny jumped at the sound of Deirdre's voice. The landlady said, "That man was knocking down my door even before her body was delivered. He paid good money to be the only one to photograph her in her casket. He cleaned up on those pictures, I'm sure he did. Nora would have loved that, me charging deVille to take her last picture. And what good were those glass slides to me, anyway?"

"What about these?" Fanny pointed to a box of mounted photographs.

"I'm going to make them into an album. Everyone should have an album of their happy times; it makes the bad times so much easier to bear." Mrs. O'Sullivan paused, as if thinking about the bad times to come. Then she looked at Deirdre and said, "Get yourself washed up."

Deirdre put down the tray of food, and when the girl was gone Fanny asked, "Deirdre said that when

Gabriel left, she and Nora would go downstairs and have a good laugh at supper."

"She says a lot, that Deirdre. Some of it's true. We did have a good laugh after he left. Until that last night. That was when she told him that she was done with prostitution. He was very happy about it, to hear it from Deirdre."

"That's understandable."

"Until Nora told him that she hadn't been working herself for a while. And then he exploded. We could hear him down in the kitchen."

That was understandable too. Fanny could fully imagine Gabriel's anger if he thought he'd been made a fool of. "How did Gabriel come to meet with Nora every week?"

"He wanted a girl to talk to. I gave him Nora. He knew me from long ago." Mrs. O'Sullivan's voice eased off, as though she was deciding how much to tell Fanny. "But it was the other one that encouraged him to come here."

"Terence."

"No. That madman, Dr. Adams. He found his way here one night, entered my place with one of my regular customers—who was drunk at the time, should have told me something—and settled into my parlor. And when the place was full, he started ranting."

"At the girls?"

"No, at the men. For 'wickedly molesting' my girls. He said he kept a notebook that had their names in it. I had him thrown out. Told him never to come back here."

"And did he?"

"Not sneaking in as a customer again...but he was the one who brought Nora back here. He drove her body from Charity. Strutted about like a rooster while he was here."

Fanny tried to absorb it all. "When Gabriel first paid to talk to Nora. Was it before or after she had stop prostituting herself?"

"After, as it happens. That was the beauty of it. While he was earnestly preaching to her to change her ways, she had already done so and was making more money with her camera than she had with her body."

"You said he was very angry that night he found out. And that was the same night Nora was murdered."

"Mad as Hades at her news. But he never touched her. Never ever moved toward her. Or me. And I was the one who set him up with Nora."

"He just walked out?"

"Of course not. He damned us all to Hell and back, for a good quarter hour. *Then* he pointed at Deirdre and said he'd be back the next Friday at four. And she should be ready for him."

FANNY SETTLED INTO looking at Nora's photographs. After hours of viewing images of naked women, she had only one conclusion: if these photographs truly appealed to men, she wanted nothing more to do with the male gender.

As the sun began to settle, Fanny still had two stacks of photographs to review. Many of the photographs were taken on the very chaise lounge Fanny sat on. Others were taken in Mrs. O'Sullivan's parlor and some were taken outside, against the houses, under the trees. Fanny began shuffling through the images and moved so quickly that she almost did not discern the first change: the women were clothed. These were still the girls of Mrs. O'Sullivan's house but they were dressed. Entirely dressed, not even an ankle exposed. Their hair was tightly bound on their heads, their bonnets demure. These were photos that a girl away at school could send back to her loved ones. And then the girls were dressed in black and grouped together, around a small coffin holding a dead baby. It was similar to a photograph Fanny had seen in Pierre deVille's waiting room but where deVille's image had been coarse and intrusive, Nora's portrait was loving and sincere.

Once more the feminine images changed. These women were clothed but dressed in battered bonnets, old confederate uniform jackets, kerchiefs, and dirty shifts; their faces were smudged with grime. These were not Mrs. O'Sullivan's fancy girls; they were the hopeless women of the Irish Channel.

Then the scale of the photographs widened. Individual portraits of women yielded to scenes of people in the streets of the Irish Channel: women behind oyster carts; men leaning against saloon walls; boys huddled asleep upon each other. Fanny's heart raced. She had seen this photograph before, in *The Daily Picayune*. These were the images taken by the midnight photographer; taken on the night when he trapped Fanny and the blind men in the fire. But no, these were Nora's photographs, stored precisely in her studio. And although she was not sure what it meant, Fanny knew this was what she had been searching for among Nora's things.

There was only one more box to inspect and it contained only a small stack of unmounted photographs. Nora herself, dressed in the same clothes she wore to class at Wisdom Hall. Fanny saw a bulb with a tube running from it in Nora's hand and realized that Nora had photographed herself.

"You were a very clever girl, weren't you? Taking a man's business and making it your own. Turning a profit and keeping your sisters out of prostitution. Yes, you were clever." Fanny looked into the depth of Nora's brilliant brown eyes. "No wonder someone killed you."

FANNY WALKED DOWN the stairs a few minutes later, clutching a parcel of Nora's photographs to her chest. She was taking so many images with her that she could not hide them on her body and decided to brazenly carry them out.

On the ground floor, the double pocket doors to Mrs. O'Sullivan's parlor were wide open. A plush round ottoman covered with cushions was centered in the room, exactly where Nora's coffin had last rested. In the corner of the parlor, a colored man leaned over the keyboard of an upright piano, romancing a sad syncopation from the instrument. He turned his head at the sound of Fanny's footsteps and their eyes caught. They stared at each other for a few seconds, as if realizing that neither of them belonged in a house of prostitution. The man turned back to the piano. Fanny scurried down the front stairs to Basin Street, as the keys on the piano hammered out a happier melody.

On the walkway, a boy ran past Fanny and then stopped at a telegraph pole. He put down a large square box and pulled a piece of paper from a pouch slung about his shoulders. With a hammer and nail he pounded the paper into the telegraph pole. Then he picked up the box, ran to a thin magnolia tree and posted another paper.

Magic Lantern Show for Gentlemen. The best show in the Crescent City. Friday nights only. Three weeks running; must conclude this Friday night. Ten o'clock. Spanish Depot. Pierre deVille, Master of the Magic Lantern.

Fanny tore the broadside from the pole. She neared the magnolia—ready to tear off that broadside too—when she heard the clang of the streetcar bell and hurried toward Canal Street. She crossed the street just in time to reach the front of the car.

Halfway down the aisle, headed toward the rear of the car, she saw the boy with the box. Then she saw Pierre deVille, sitting on an aisle seat. On the window seat beside him was his box camera and tripod. The boy must be carrying deVille's glass slides. Fanny could only imagine that he had been at a house of prostitution this afternoon, photographing women. Fanny sat on the aisle directly next to deVille. Their shoulders would touch if the streetcar turned a corner.

Two men stood in the aisle, bargaining with deVille for copies of his photograph of Jack the Ripper. Fanny heard the boy remove something from his pouch and watched him hand it to deVille, who passed it to the men. They reached into their pockets, drew out coins, and handed them to deVille. Apparently satisfied, they sat in seats in front of deVille.

Fanny spread deVille's broadside on top of the parcel of Nora's photographs. She stared at the words, thinking of Nora and the pornographic images she carried with her. She turned to deVille. He too was looking at the paper spread beneath her hands and his eyes quivered, as though appalled that a lady should see his illicit advertisement. He looked up at Fanny; she could tell that he did not recognize her. And why should he? She was just a plain spinster. But at that moment, she possessed the information to tie a noose around Nora's murderer. Fanny addressed the photographer. "How could you give a magic lantern show and photograph Jack the Ripper at the same time?"

DeVille's forehead creased; his toupee slouched forward.

"If you were at Spanish Depot the Friday night Nora was murdered, you couldn't have been in the Channel photographing. You've been lying from the very start."

The photographer eyed the men seated in front of him. "My show was cancelled that night. I wasn't at Spanish Depot. I was in the Channel. I saw Jack the Ripper."

"That's what you say, but I'm sure I could find out for certain about that. And I will. I'll find a man who was there. Perhaps a policeman who was there, protecting you."

The car stopped and the boy with the black box got out of his seat and walked between Fanny and deVille. The photographer collected his camera and tripod and followed the boy. As deVille stepped down from the car, he leered at Fanny, as if committing her features to memory.

39.

WITH SYLVIA's PERMISSION, FANNY LED the sisters into Sylvia's office and carefully placed the pornographic photographs on the table. Fanny raised the gaslight so that every photograph was harshly illuminated.

Sylvia took a brief glance at the images and then leaned on her cane. "You think Nora was killed because of these?"

"She must have been," replied Fanny. "And it is not too hard to find a motive for each of our suspects to kill her, starting with Pierre deVille. Nora was his competition. She took his models away and cut into his business and took his profits."

Olive burrowed her hands in the pockets of her smock as she studied the images. "Every businessman has his competitors and they don't have to murder them."

"But Nora was a *woman* and she was better than he was. Do you know any businessman who would allow a woman to best him? The only problem is that deVille may not really be a suspect." Fanny brought out the broadside and explained her encounter with deVille. "There must be some way to confirm he was giving a show the same time Nora was murdered."

"Lester Adams called pornography *disgusting*," replied Olive. "Isn't it likely that someone who hates pornography would kill a pornographer?"

"What about the Boylans?" added Sylvia.

"Even if one of the Boylans had an appetite for all this," said Olive, "does that translate into a motive for murder? I still think Adams is—"

"We've had to accept from the beginning that either of the Boylans could have been a murderer," interrupted Fanny. "A priest or seminarian with a secret obsession might kill to keep it a secret. And Gabriel saw Nora every week"

"Knowing that Nora was a pornographer gives other people a motive for killing her," said Olive. "Any motive applied to the Boylans or Lester Adams or even Pierre deVille, would apply to many others as well. Perhaps some girls at Mrs. O'Sullivan's. Or Mrs. O'Sullivan herself."

"That's why the photographs of the Channel are so important. Nora took those photographs but the midnight photographer used them." Fanny cringed at the memory of the midnight photographer setting the blind beggars' room on fire and how the hot flames ran up her dress. "We need to question the midnight photographer."

"And just who would that be?"

"Since it wasn't deVille and it wasn't Adams, it must be Gabriel or Terence Boylan." Fanny surprised herself by how efficiently she settled on the Boylan brothers, but who else could it be? "It must be one of the Boylans. We'll need to question them tomorrow night. Before graduation."

"I'd like to be there and—" Olive turned to her sister, "—about tomorrow night, Sylvia. What did Detective Crenshaw say about your letter?"

"I didn't send it to him."

"Why not?"

"Someone is trying to scare me out of Wisdom Hall and I will not allow it," Sylvia replied sharply. "We'll be perfectly safe tomorrow night. We've got Thomas and the dogs, and I can ask Father to send Sam and Joe."

Olive and Fanny spoke in one voice, "But Syl—"

"Fanny." Sylvia folded her arms in a clear sign of dismissal. "Bundle up all of these photographs now and put them away somewhere. Or better yet, burn them."

FANNY ARRIVED AT Daniel Crenshaw's office early Saturday afternoon but the detective was not there. Nor would the Sergeant tell her where he was or when he would return.

Fanny fumed: just when she needed Crenshaw, he was gone.

She asked for pen and paper and sat at Crenshaw's desk as she wrote. She relished the feel of his sturdy wooden desk. It was so much like her father's desk; so much like Lawrence's. She gazed over the neatly stacked piles of papers and folders and wondered if Crenshaw knew how lucky he was to be employed as a real police detective.

When she finished writing, she folded Sylvia's Ripper letter and Pierre deVille's magic lantern broadside in with her own and handed it to the sergeant, who inserted the papers into his tunic.

"Give this to him as soon as he comes in," she told Flynn. "He will want to see it."

Fanny returned to Wisdom Hall unable to think of anything except the vicious letter to Sylvia. Someone was using the Ripper's legend to scare them from finding Nora's murderer. Had Lester Adams written the letter? After all, he had already tried to cause citywide panic by writing the first Ripper letter. And Olive had exposed him as a post-mortem ripper and gotten him arrested. Could he have posted the letter from jail? Or perhaps Gabriel Boylan had written the letter? Or his brother? And what about the midnight photographer? Who was he?

The streetcar shuddered as it approached Wisdom Hall. For tonight's ceremonies, Sylvia had moved all of the tables onto the front lawn and was decorating them with centerpieces of magnolia buds and branches. She was determined to make her students' graduation as different as possible from the waxworks social—and the horror of Karl's arrest—and despite the threat of rain, Sylvia had decided to set up the refreshments on the front lawn. Fanny knew that Sylvia also hoped that placing the refreshments so close to Annunciation Street would entice other neighbors to visit.

Fanny hopped from the back of the streetcar as it approached Wisdom Hall and started for the infirmary. If she was going to discover the identity of the midnight photographer, she would need Olive's help.

40.

A FEW HOURS LATER, LIAM RUSHED INTO the infirmary from the back garden. Terence Boylan ran up behind him, protectively holding a large wooden box.

At the doorway the priest stopped and gasped for air. "Where is she?"

As Boylan jolted into the infirmary behind Liam, Fanny emerged from the corner and closed and locked the infirmary door. "Not here."

The priest frowned at Liam and looked around the infirmary as though he might find the woman he sought. He shifted the last rites box gently in his grasp. His hair, coat, and pant legs were soaked and for the first time tonight, Fanny realized it was raining.

"No one's dying here." Fanny looked at the priest's wooden box. "And no one needs last rites."

The priest removed a cloth from his pants pocket and attempted to dry off the box. "But the boy sa—"

"Just what we told him what to say." Olive stepped in front of Liam, as if the priest was going to physically rebuke him. Although Olive had heard much about Terence Boylan, she had never met the man and didn't know what to expect from him. "He didn't lie to you. We did. We wanted to ask you a few questions and we thought this was the best way to get your undivided attention."

"Questions about what?" The priest pushed his wet hair away from his face and squared himself toward Fanny.

"Photography." Fanny unrolled her copy of the *Daily Picayune* article and shook the images and words at the priest, just like a teacher scolding an errant pupil. "You were photographing out in the Irish Channel Saturday night a week ago. You started the fire and wrote the article and submitted the photographs to the *Picayune*."

And you tried to kill me, she was tempted to say. *You held the doorknob shut when I tried to escape.* But she caught those words in her throat. There was other information she wanted from him first.

It was a great gamble. Fanny was not sure that Terence Boylan was the midnight photographer, but what did she have to lose? Even as she waited for the priest to respond, she restrained herself from saying *And you killed Nora Keegan.*

The color drained from the priest's flushed face. He grasped the box to his chest and slumped into the nearest chair.

"Yes." He stared at the images in Fanny's hand. "Yes, I took the photographs. I started the fire."

Fanny caught Olive's eye and then looked at Liam. As if reading Fanny's mind, Olive took Liam by the hand and walked him to the door leading to the hallway. Liam protested his dismissal loudly, but Fanny heard Olive firmly push the boy out of the infirmary and turn the lock.

"But I put it out," the priest said quickly. "I had no idea that it would restart. And I was very sorry to see that you had been injured."

Suddenly, Fanny knew more. "That's why you came to Wisdom Hall the day after the fire, wasn't it? To see if I was all right? Or did you come to see if I knew it was you that night?"

The priest sat up straighter. "I'm not ashamed of these photographs or the article. The only shame is that the Church hasn't been a better steward toward its own people."

"Then why did you photograph *in cognito*? And not sign your name to the article?"

"I had to be careful. The Archbishop already knows how I feel about the conditions here. But beautifying the church is more important to him than fixing broken staircases and mending roofs." The priest took a deep breath and continued, "We've got two churches across the street from each other because the Germans and Irish can't praise God together. We can afford two churches but we can't afford to clean up the houses our people inhabit. If the Archbishop knew I was the rabble-rouser, he would get me reassigned and then nothing would be done. All of my good work would be frustrated."

"I don't care about your Archbishop," replied Fanny. "All I care about is Nora Keegan and you've lied about what you know about her."

Boylan blanched at the mention of Nora's name.

"Nora's death helped you keep your secret," added Olive.

"I didn't kill her, if that's what you're suggesting." The priest looked around as if he was about to bolt, but Olive and Fanny moved closer to him. He lapsed into silence and then words rushed from his mouth rapidly. "And it wasn't Gabriel, either."

"But you and your brother *were* in Conner's Court the night Nora was killed and we need to know everything that happened that night." Fanny watched his face closely, wondering if he was collecting his thoughts or fabricating his lies. It would be only natural for him to take a moment to build a lie but from the clouds of pain that cross his face, Fanny thought what he would say would be the truth.

"It goes back long before Nora's death," said the priest. "Long before my appointment to St. Alphonsus, I was aware that the Channel houses were falling apart and that much of the parishioners' ills were caused by the miserable conditions in which they lived. It was more and more difficult for me to take up a special collection for new stained glass windows when I knew that many of the poor women sitting in my pews didn't have any glass at all in their windows."

The priest resettled the box on his lap. "What was worse, my own order had purchased and owned many of these houses, because they were planning to tear them down and build new quarters. But every year the plan to tear down the houses was postponed and every year these buildings fell into more decay. They were a constant cause of the illness and misery among the renters. And I was forced to collect rent from these poor parishioners."

The priest expression turned sorrowful and Fanny almost pitied him. Almost. "What about Nora?"

The priest put up his hand to forestall Fanny's questions. "When I was sent to Ireland last year, I spent a few weeks in London. I took a tour of the slums of Whitechapel, where I met John Thomson. He was photographing living conditions in the Whitechapel slums and going to publish the photographs in order to shame the landlords into improving the buildings. His idea appealed tremendously to me. I was determined to take photographs of my own in New Orleans and to use them to compel the Archbishop to change things."

"You knew how to photograph?" asked Olive.

"No." Terence looked at his hands, fixing his gaze along the long dark stain that discolored his index finger. "So I decided to employ a professional to take the photographs for me. I needed this all to be a secret, of course. Pierre deVille agreed to my terms and forced me to pay a hefty fee for his silence. But then I found out that he was not the person he represented himself to be."

Fanny leaned in toward the priest, her body just a few feet from his. "You found out that he was a pornographer?"

Terence looked up at Fanny. His face had almost the same degree of surprise as Clarence Halloway had, when Fanny first mentioned the word. "Of course, I couldn't do business with him anymore. And I refused to pay him anything."

"He couldn't have been happy about that," Olive spoke directly to Fanny.

"He threatened me. Said he would go straight to the Archbishop but I...I threatened him in turn. I know that many vices are tolerated in New Orleans but if a priest were to expose and condemn a photographer as a pornographer, that photographer would be finished in New Orleans."

"And then you got Nora to take your photographs?" Fanny backed away slightly before saying, "But she was a pornographer too."

"Yes, but once again, I didn't know that until after I engaged her and I thought that if I engaged her in honest wor—"

"That you could redeem her?" Fanny fought her disgust at the idea that Nora needed redeeming.

"Yes. When I saw what a good photographer she was, I offered to set her up in business, honest photographic business. I could tell she had talent and she had a good business sense. But she refused. We were meeting at Conner's Court that night. I wanted to show her what to photograph next. I was on my way to Conner's Court when duty called me away."

"Nora was killed waiting to meet with you?"

New emotions overtook the priest but Fanny could not read them. Was it guilt from failed responsibility? Or fear of discovery?

"If only I had met her," the priest said softly, "she might still be alive."

All three were silent until a soft rap at the hallway door interrupted. The door was unlocked from the outside and opened. Thomas looked at the trio briefly and then spoke to Olive. "Miss Sylvia says it's past time for you to be there."

The priest looked up hopefully at Fanny, as though he was going to be excused. But Olive was not finished with him. "How did you meet Nora?"

Terence Boylan hesitated. But information was fitting together so quickly that Fanny could not resist answering Olive directly. "It was his brother. He was already trying to redeem Nora and he introduced them."

"Did your brother tell you Nora was a prostitute?"

"No, I didn't know that until she was dead."

"But what makes you think that Karl killed Nora?"

"Lester keeps a list," replied the priest. "It has the names of the men he sees soliciting women. Karl Schultz's name was on his list for speaking to Nora."

Olive asked, "Who told you about Adams' list?"

"He did, a few months ago. That's how I met the man. He came to me at St. Alphonsus and said that his notebook listed men from my parish who were mingling with prostitutes. He wanted me to read the list to my congregation at Sunday Mass."

"Did you?"

"Of course not. I didn't even look inside it. Life is hard enough for the women of the parish without being publicly shamed by their husbands' sins." The priest looked up at Thomas, as if perhaps he would understand him. "After Nora died, Gabriel went to the police and showed them Karl's name on Adams' list."

"Karl was arrested for Nora's murder just because Gabriel showed the police a list with Karl's name on it?" asked Fanny. "The police believed him? Lester could have written any man's name in his notebook."

"The police found Karl's bloody knife. It was clear to anyone that the man killed and ripped her up."

"But it wasn't Karl's knife. It wasn't even a carpenter's knife."

"And it wasn't even found with his things," said Olive. "Just in the back of his boarding house where anyone could have dropped it."

Liam plunged through the infirmary door and yelled out to Olive. "Miss Sylvia's ready to start."

Boylan studied the door as if he was ready to escape through it but Fanny persisted. "During the fire—after you ran out of the room—did you come back?"

The priest shook his head.

"I know you shut the door when you left," said Fanny. "But did you hold it shut?"

"I didn't shut the door. I never saw the door. And I didn't hol—"

"Was anyone there when you left? Downstairs? Outside?"

"I wasn't looking about. I knew I had to get away from there as quickly as possible. I was only trying to get down those damned stairs."

Olive said, "We have to go now, Fanny. We promised Sylvia."

As Fanny followed Thomas and Liam through the door, Boylan pulled Fanny to his side. "You must remain quiet about the photographs. If the Archbishop finds out it was me, any chance of reforming the Channel will be lost."

Fanny looked back at Olive who was locking the door. "Your secrets are safe with us, Father Boylan. So far."

FANNY WAS AWARE that Terence Boylan followed as she and Olive plunged into the main room but lost him in the crowd. The entire double parlor was filled and people stood against the walls waiting to watch the graduation ceremony.

Fanny's students pressed about her. Colleen was the first to speak. "I've got everyone scrubbed and on their best behavior, Miss Fanny. Even the nasty rain won't dampen our spirits."

Fanny greeted each of her students, admiring Meggie's new red ribbon, noticing the tear in Molly's eye, realizing that she still could not tell Kelly, Kathy, and Bridget apart. Fanny brushed Cara's cheek. "You all look wonderful and you've worked so hard. I'm so proud of you."

Patsy stepped from behind her sister and said, "And all the family's come, as you can see."

Before Fanny could reply, a large flash of magnesium powder erupted through the room. Then a wave of thunder rolled overhead. Patsy grabbed her hand and screamed. Fanny winced, the memory of the fire at the blind beggar's rooms rising in her senses. A sudden panic gripped her: was Terence Boylan starting another fire? Then her eyes were drawn to the smoky magnesium tray at the front of the parlor. As the haze cleared, Fanny was astounded to see Pierre deVille behind a large camera.

"He's taking our class photograph tonight." Moira brushed down the large cowlick on the top of her head. "Said he'd take individual photographs of us if we came to his studio. Just like we were actresses and all."

"But we want our photograph taken together," protested Kelly, Kathy, or Bridget.

Then Moira nodded toward Clarence Halloway, who stood a few feet from deVille, pushing a piece of cake into his mouth. "And he's going to publish a drawing of our class photograph in the *Sensation*."

Fanny rushed toward Clarence Halloway as another crackle of thunder split through the skies. As the reporter lifted a glass of beer to his lips, Fanny scowled, "What's he doing here?"

Halloway swallowed and wiped the back of his hand across his lips. "I always like to bring a photographer when there's good story."

"But why? This is just a graduation."

"So you say. But if the Ripper shows tonight, I—"

"What?"

"'What?' 'Why?' You sound like a reporter, Miss Newcomb." Halloway slurped from the beer mug. "I brought deVille with me and I'll watch out for him." The reporter removed his notebook from his jacket. He pulled a pencil from his pocket and licked the tip with his tongue like it was a sugar stick. "You know Miss Newcomb, I've been thinking about that piece of information that you and the other ladies owe me."

"Tonight, Mr. Halloway? We're just about to start our graduation. Sylvia won't have time to talk to you until tomorrow."

"It's not Miss Sylvia I need. It's you. I saw you come in the room with Father Boylan and he looked disturbed. I've been thinking about the subject of our last conversion. You know...."

The reporter leaned toward Fanny as though he was going to whisper *pornography* in her ear, but Fanny preempted him. As she scanned the crowd for signs of Daniel Crenshaw, her eyes lighted on Lawrence. She was glad to see him, for she needed to tell him that she had given his check to Millie. She needed to warn him to have money in the bank. To her surprise, Lawrence hurried to her side and pulled her away from the reporter. "I've heard about the letter from Jack the Ripper."

Fanny tugged herself away from Lawrence's grasp. "How—"

"Dammit, Fanny, you're in danger here." Lawrence glared at a pair of boisterous girls who tripped into him. "I can't protect you as long as you remain here." And then, a threatening undercurrent tinged his concern, "If you don't stop all of this investigating immediately, I'll, I'll...."

Fanny flared back at him. "You'll what?"

Before Lawrence could answer her, Cousin Charlotte's voice cut through. "There you are dear."

Lawrence turned from Fanny and glared at Charlotte with a look that clearly suggested she leave. But the older woman would not depart. In fact, she came closer, saying, "Sylvia's ready to begin. She sent me to find you." As Charlotte kissed Fanny's cheek, Lawrence turned sharply on his heels and walked out of Wisdom Hall.

Fanny heard the screen door slam shut. Shouldn't she go make peace with Lawrence? He only wanted her to be safe and secure; exactly what she wanted for all of her students.

"Let him cool off for a while," said Charlotte. "If he's out there long enough the storm will catch him and a strong dousing might be good for him." She put her arm through Fanny's. "Now, why don't we go watch your students graduate?"

Charlotte and Fanny entered the parlor to find everyone seated and Sylvia standing at the front of the double parlor. All of Fanny's students were seated together and she joined them sitting at the end of the third row.

Tonight's program was as different from the night of the waxworks as possible: one inspiring speech, the distribution of certificates, and then refreshments on the front lawn. Sylvia had wanted Eliza Nicholson to speak to the students, but Charlotte had convinced her that the owner of the Crescent City Brewery would be a better choice. Not a better speaker, of course, but someone already popular and acceptable to the parents of the girls, many of whom already worked for the brewery. If the owner of largest brewery in town dispensed wisdom (and beer afterwards), his employees would attend the event.

Sylvia introduced the brewery owner and he took the podium to hearty applause. He began his speech in a high, trembling voice but he warmed quickly to his task and his voice steadied. As he began to drone, Fanny's thoughts veered toward Nora. She should be here. She should be receiving her certificate. She should be laughing. She should be living.

Siobhan took her hand. "Oh, Miss Newcomb, isn't it thrilling?"

As Siobhan pressed her hand, Fanny could actually feel the girl's thrill. She looked down the row of her students. Their faces were glowing with pride and accomplishment. Sylvia had been right to demand the students be left out of the investigation. Fanny's heart lightened slightly; tonight, was her students' night, and they deserved their limelight.

Still, as the brewery owner's speech ran on, Fanny could not help but consider Terence Boylan's story. If he was telling the truth, only two of the other suspects could have tried to kill her. From everything she knew about John Remington, she was certain he would never sacrifice anyone's life for his own. But she had no such confidence in Gabriel Boylan.

Fanny felt a hand on her shoulder. It was Olive, who nodded toward the hallway. Fanny followed Olive onto the front gallery and took a deep breath of air. "Rain's stopped. For now."

Olive looked at the lawn where Aunt Esther stood guard over the tables and said, "Across the street. Can you see them?"

Fanny saw nothing through the darkened night but a mule-drawn dray. As it ambled down the street, Fanny squinted enough to make out two men with red carnations in their lapels: Gabriel Boylan and Lester Adams. Fanny gasped, "Shouldn't Adams be in jail?"

Olive glared at the two figures. "He's been released. Remington rushed here from Charity to tell us."

"But what are they doing here?"

"I don't know but I've told Aunt Esther to keep a watch on them." Olive looked confidently at Esther. "Remington's washing up in the infirmary. He's found out something about Sylvia's Ripper letter and said he'd tell us everything when he's dry." For a minute more the women watched the two men. Olive shook her head. "I don't like this."

"It's not just them," added Fanny. "Pierre deVille is inside. And Terence Boylan might still be here."

A man and a woman hurried past Adams and into an alleyway. Adams took something from his pocket. A notebook? He scribbled something inside. A name?

Fanny could not help but remember the many notebooks involved in Nora's murder: Sergeant Flynn's notebook identified the suspects; Nora's own ledger identified her pornography business; and now the notebook that Adams held in his hand must hold some useful information.

Fanny grabbed Olive's arm and pulled the doctor toward her. "That's the notebook that got Karl arrested. I thought that whoever got Karl to confess might be Nora's murderer. But maybe I'm wrong. Maybe the murderer was the man who got Karl arrested. Gabriel Boylan."

"But Adams boasted to Remington and me that he had gotten Karl arrested," Olive leaned closer to Fanny "although I thought he was lying, trying to get on John's good side."

The screen door slammed behind them. Fanny and Olive looked back, expecting to see John Remington. But Clarence Halloway stood at the door, looking at the long table that held a barrel of beer. As he walked toward it, Fanny demanded, "Why didn't you tell me that Lester Adams turned Karl into the police?"

Halloway ambled toward the women. "Because I never heard anything like that. I heard it was 'evidence from an impeccable citizen of New Orleans' that nailed him." He surveyed the beer table again before asking, "Outhouse?"

Fanny nodded toward the back lawn. When the reporter was out of sight, she refocused her gaze on the men across the street. "Both Boylans knew about Adams' notebook," she said to herself as much as to Olive, "but Terence said he never read it."

"So Adams and the Boylan brothers are still equally suspect," replied Olive.

Then Adams handed the notebook to Gabriel Boylan and Fanny knew what she had to do.

"No, they're not." Fanny started down the walkway to Annunciation Street.

"Fanny!" Olive reached out. "Fanny! What are you doing?"

"I'm going to find Nora's murderer. You go get
Remington. And then go get your father's pistol."

41.

THROUGH THE DARK, FANNY SAW A streetcar
coming down Annunciation and *thought* she saw
Daniel Crenshaw's bowler-topped head lean out
the back door. If Fanny was going to find Nora's
murderer herself, it must be now.

She walked directly toward Adams and Boylan,
barely aware of the rain that sprinkled on her. She half
expected the men to evaporate before she reached them
but they did not.

The two men looked at her, waiting for her to
speak. She looked at them in turn: the scalp-scratching
Yankee ambulance doctor and the confident uptown
seminarian. Both men were hideous: Lester slashed
Nora's dead body; and Gabriel must have been the
villain who almost suffocated Fanny and the blind men.
Either man could have strangled Nora, but only one of
them could be called an impeccable citizen of New
Orleans.

Fanny glanced through the light rain toward the
streetcar before confronting them. "We're having
graduation ceremonies for our students tonight. Nora
Keegan should be graduating but one of you killed her.
And I can prove it."

She looked at Boylan. "You paid to talk to Nora
every week at Mrs. O'Sullivan's and tried to convince
her to stop prostituting herself. But you failed. Nora
had already abandoned prostitution for photography."

She turned to Adams. "And you saw her on the
streets of the Irish Channel and tried to redeem her.
You also failed."

Fanny had both men's full attention. Her only chance was now.

She returned to Adams. "You ripped up Nora's body after she died and then you wrote the newspaper claiming to be Jack the Ripper on a bloody rampage. You did everything you could to scare women off the streets. But why would you take your notebook to the police and tell them that Karl murdered Nora? Why would you work so hard to keep women from prostituting themselves and then identify the murderer and let women feel safe again? Why would you work against yourself? It would be more to your purpose if the murderer were never found, if women remained terrified. Someone else told the police about your notebook and made sure that Karl was arrested. And that man murdered Nora."

"That's impossible. Only Gabriel has seen inside my notebook. He was with me the entire time that ni... ni...." Adams stuttered and stopped.

"Was he?" asked Fanny. She held her breath and waited, unable to look away from the doctor. She had put a suggestion in Adams's mind and he had latched onto it.

Adams faced Gabriel Boylan, as if expecting him to correct Fanny. Under Adams's stern glare, Boylan's lips curled slightly. Adams clenched his fist and rammed it into Boylan's stomach. Boylan doubled over and stumbled back. The doctor ran forward and knocked both his fists into Boylan's stomach, pummeling his midsection until the seminarian was bent over. Then the doctor stepped back for air. Boylan balanced himself against a storefront with one hand and gasped for air.

As Boylan attempted to straighten, Adams launched back into him. But this time, John Remington emerged suddenly from the dark and tackled his nephew. Fanny looked around for the police, before realizing that Remington was alone in his fight.

Adams fought his uncle, almost as hard as he'd attacked Boylan. As Remington grabbed his nephew, Gabriel Boylan rushed into the middle of Annunciation Street. Daniel Crenshaw and a half dozen policemen flanked his path. Boylan turned to the other direction but another half dozen policemen blocked him. The seminarian took the only exit available and ran up the gravel walk leading into Wisdom Hall. When Aunt Esther stepped into his path, he smacked her to the ground.

Fanny tried to outrun the rain as she ran to help Aunt Esther to her feet. Fanny rushed into Wisdom Hall and saw Gabriel run up the grand staircase to the second floor. Fully expecting that Crenshaw was behind her, she followed after Gabriel. Crenshaw would subdue Gabriel with physical force; perhaps render him unconscious. But if Fanny could get Gabriel to speak, to confess, she could end this nightmare. When she reached the second floor landing, Gabriel Boylan was waiting for her. And so was his brother.

She wavered on the edge of the top stair of the second floor. Where was Daniel Crenshaw? He should be rushing up behind her right now. Was it possible he was still outside with Adams and Remington? Fanny grabbed the railing with one hand, her skirts with the other, and backed down the stairs. But Gabriel Boylan swooped down and tugged her into the second floor hallway. She landed between the brothers; Gabriel blocked her path downstairs.

"Murderer!" Fanny cried out.

"Are you out of your mind? Gabriel hasn't killed anyone." The priest protested harshly before turning to his brother for agreement. "Tell her about Lester. Tell her about Karl."

"I already know everything." Fanny gulped for air and wondered how she could get around Gabriel, who appeared to have gotten taller and broader than she remembered. *Damnation! When would the police arrive?*

"He gave Karl's name to the police and got him arrested for Nora's murder." Fanny turned to the priest. "But you convinced Karl to confess by making payments to his parents in Germany. Or was that blackmail?"

The priest clutched his last rites box to his chest. "I was in London when the Ripper was murdering those women. Everyone lived in terror. I knew it would be better for everyone if Karl confessed as quickly as possible."

Fanny narrowed her eyes. "I can prove Karl didn't kill Nora."

"But the police found his knife."

"Nora wasn't killed with a knife. She was strangled!"

"Strangled?" The box slipped from Terence's hands; then he caught it and he clutched it closer to his chest.

"I can prove that too. She was ripped up at Charity after she died. The bloody knife has nothing to do with Karl or Nora and the police know that now." Fanny took a deep breath, satisfied. All of the information collected over the last weeks—the last minutes—fit together. She had Nora's murderer in front of her.

"Gabriel convinced me Karl was guilty. I only offered to help Karl's parents because...."

Although she knew she should keep her eyes on Gabriel, Fanny watched the priest instead. She could almost read his mind, as his thoughts traveled from Lester to Gabriel to Karl. Finally, Terence said, "If it wasn't Karl, it was Lester."

"It was not," she replied. "Adams wanted to scare women. He had no reason to have anyone arrested or to have Karl confess. It defeated his scheme." She spoke directly to Gabriel. "But your scheme was already defeated. You tried to redeem Nora from prostituting herself but had already stopped. She made a fool of you."

"Yes, she did. She did indeed. But at least she proved you right, Terence." Gabriel acknowledged his brother with a grim curl of his lips. "You never believed I could redeem Nora. I knew from the start why you introduced me to Adams. You wanted to test me. See if I was worthy of the priesthood. See if I would give into physical temptation." Gabriel's smile shattered. "And I did. Just not the kind you expected. There was no love between Nora and me. She disgusted me from the beginning. Only her redemption tempted me. Kept me returning to her."

Fanny listened for sounds of police footsteps as she said, "And when she told you she had stopped prosti—"

"She lost her purpose. Her reason for being."

"You wanted her to stop and she did. But you couldn't redeem her because she redeemed herself. And that's why you mur—"

"Yes." Gabriel whispered. "I murdered her."

"And you almost murdered me!" Despite her fright, Fanny stamped toward Gabriel. "You must have followed your brother the night he took photographs. He started the fire, but you must have held the door shut!"

"*You* ruined Nora!" Gabriel roared back. "Every Friday after I left her she went to your classes! I paid her to listen to me but she only listened to you. Something she was only too pleased to tell me. I could have saved her, if you hadn't corrupted her!"

"No." Terence Boylan's voice was parched. The box dropped from his hold and he lurched at his brother. Gabriel slammed his flat hand directly into his brother's face. Terence reeled backwards a few steps before coming at his brother again. Gabriel punched Terence hard in the stomach and the priest dropped to his knees and rose, only to fall against the massive newel post. Fanny heard his head crack. She rushed toward him, but his brother wrenched her by the forearm and held her back. Fanny jabbed at Terence Boylan with her foot but he remained motionless.

The hard stamps of men's feet broke through the front door. Fanny shouted, only to have her voice muffled by the sudden strike of thunder. Gabriel dropped his hold on Fanny and ran up the stairs. Fanny hesitated for a second and then ran after him.

The third floor was illuminated only by the moon and sparks of lightning. Fanny glanced through the front windows. It was raining harder and men with quivering torches stood along Annunciation Street and down the path to Wisdom Hall. Soon, the rain would extinguish the torchlight entirely. She heard metal thudding against the wood floor and realized that Gabriel was searching Karl's toolboxes.

"I've already gone through his things." Fanny whispered, trying to keep her location hidden.

More tools thudded against the flooring before he spoke. "So you've seen his stacks of pornography. You've got them. You know he was no innocent. Nora employed him to deliver her photographs to saloons and whorehouses."

"You're wrong. Only one of Nora's photos was among Karl's tools. It was a portrait of Karl to send to his parents in Germany."

Gabriel upended the last toolbox. A shaft of lightening blazed through the window and Gabriel looked directly at Fanny. He kept his eyes on her as he selected a long, thin knife from the rubble on the floor and stuck it into his belt. Gabriel flinched and Fanny understood immediately: *The police were trudging up the stairs.*

Gabriel lunged at Fanny and clutched her waist brutally. "If we can't go down, we'll go up."

She clawed at him blindly and heard her sleeves rip from her bodice. She tried to yell out, but he held her so tightly that she had no voice. He pushed her up the circular stairs in front of him. She stumbled over her skirts, but he prodded her until they both reached the rooftop. A pounding rain beat down upon the tarpaulin that covered the wooden roof framing. Fanny blinked back the rain from her face. As raindrops pelted her mouth, she could not even scream for help. Gabriel pushed her forward. Fanny stood her ground. Very few parts of the roof would support the weight of two people.

Gabriel slapped her. "Which way?"

Fanny's indecision might be her savior. If she could maneuver him to one of the weak spots on the roof, if together they were both heavy enough to dislodge the tarp, could he fall through to the third floor? As long as he released her before he fell, she might be able to grab something to keep her balance. But would he release her?

He slapped her again and tightened his grip. "If I fall, you fall with me. Show me where to walk."

Fanny led Gabriel along the path to the front edge of the roof. Rain rolled down Fanny's hair and face and under her collar. Her clothes began to cling together and the weight of her drenched skirts and petticoats slowed her. If she tried to run away from Gabriel, would her rain-soaked clothes allow her to?

At the edge of the roof, she looked down toward Annunciation Street. It seemed that everyone in Wisdom Hall had spilled out onto the front lawn to witness the drama on the rooftop. Gabriel Boylan watched only the staircase opening.

Something whistled across the roof and then again. Gunshot! Fanny tried to crouch but Boylan kept her against his body, an arm about her waist, the other hand holding the long knife against her ribs. They watched together as Daniel Crenshaw stepped from the spiral staircase onto the rooftop. He held a gun in his right hand and as a bullet threaded across the roof he yelled over the rain, "Stop shooting!"

Fanny heard someone call out her name and struggled to see Lawrence just behind the detective. He looked about wildly before following the detective onto the rooftop.

"He killed Nora!" Fanny shouted to whoever could hear her.

To her surprise, she heard Terence Boylan yell out, "Gabriel! For God's sake, give yourself up!"

Daniel Crenshaw inched toward Gabriel and Fanny. Lawrence—who Fanny knew did not have a knife or gun—followed closely behind him. Even Terence Boylan emerged from the staircase opening and moved toward them.

Gabriel tightened his hold on Fanny and ran the knife up from her ribs to her throat. Fanny's breath shortened; sudden fear would not let her catch it. Gabriel meant to kill her. And his knife at her throat was quicker than Crenshaw's pistol. Fanny would have to save herself.

The timbers creaked and bent beneath Fanny. Gabriel Boylan lengthened his stance inch by inch, until his footing seemed stable. The timbers and tarpaulin shifted beneath him but he kept his balance.

Fanny cringed as she watched Lawrence slip, fall, and curse. He rose quickly, only to slip and curse again. Finally, he recovered to his hands and knees and attempted to crawl toward her, still slipping on the tarpaulin.

Gabriel tightened his hold about Fanny's waist until she could not breathe, would not be able to breathe ever again.

Another gunshot whistled past. Gabriel peered down at the lawn, watching as a policeman reloaded his shotgun. Fanny looked to Crenshaw, who was steps away from her. What would kill Fanny first? Gabriel's knife? Or the policeman's bullet?

Lightning crackled overhead in a violent burst and within seconds thunder shattered the sky. The entire roof seemed to shake and sway, as though it had been sent a fatal stroke of God's judgment. Fanny heard the sound of timber breaking. The framing underneath her quivered. Gabriel's muscles loosened and then tightened; he was just as fearful as Fanny. Even the knife wavered away from Fanny's throat.

Gabriel shivered as if he was going to leap away but Fanny's own muscles tensed with expectation. As one more stroke of lighting rent the night sky, Fanny jerked away from Gabriel's limp hold. She fell to the rooftop and within seconds found herself wrapped in the cocoon of Crenshaw's arms. She clutched his wet jacket and felt his heart beating as fiercely and loudly as her own. Crenshaw rolled her roughly until he lay on top of her, shielding her from Gabriel's reach. Thunder roared. The rafters swayed beneath them and then steadied.

The rain stopped suddenly, but the air was alive with unexploded electricity. From underneath the detective, Fanny realized that Terence Boylan had found his footing and reached Gabriel. The brothers clutched in a fierce bear hug until both men teetered on the edge of the rooftop.

An explosion of magnesium powder ripped from the front lawn and filtered toward the roof. Gabriel forced himself from his brother's grasp and tumbled backwards into the thin railing that protected the rooftop. Gabriel hung against the railing for a few seconds. In a sudden silence, Fanny heard the railing splinter. Then she watched as Gabriel gasped and thrashed as he fell backwards.

And then he was gone from her sight. She heard Gabriel smash onto the roof of the gallery two stories below and then crash on top of Sylvia's table of glass tumblers. As Fanny tensed within Daniel Crenshaw's arms, caught under the pressure of his shifting weight, another tray of Pierre deVille's magnesium powder exploded on the lawn.

42.

FANNY, SYLVIA, AND OLIVE MET LAWRENCE outside the Parish Prison on Friday morning. Fanny studied the two dozen men and women standing at the prison's perimeter. She was amazed. Three weeks ago, the people of New Orleans wanted to lynch Karl Schultz; now they waited to witness his release.

Sylvia tilted her parasol toward the warming sun and frowned at Liam, who was running around the grounds in excitement. "Will there be a speech?"

"I doubt it," replied Lawrence as he guided the women into the shadow of a large oak tree.

"There certainly won't be an apology," said Olive. "Even though they arrested the wrong man."

The door to the prison opened. A uniformed policeman walked through, followed by Daniel Crenshaw and then Karl. He was dressed in fresh clothing and attempts had been made to comb his hair and beard but still he looked exhausted. He stood in the open doorway, shying from the sunlight, head cast downward, as though waiting to be pushed out.

Two tidy women and a bear of a man emerged from the crowd and walked toward Karl.

"That's Karl's landlady," said Sylvia.

The women silently flanked Karl and walked him from the prison entrance toward the street. Clarence Halloway approached Karl but the bear growled at him. Clarence shrank back. Karl and his escorts passed the women and Lawrence without a word or a look. As they neared the street, Liam and others from the crowd joined in behind them.

"That's it?" said Sylvia.

"That's all it ever is," replied Lawrence as he stood next to Fanny. "Karl Schultz is free, Nora Keegan's murderer is dead, and you are all safe from harm."

"Daniel Crenshaw is the new hero of New Orleans; you forgot to mention that." Sylvia watched as the detective stepped toward them. "And the hero approaches." Sylvia took Olive's hand and led her toward Lawrence's carriage. She nodded at Fanny to join them but saw that Lawrence had entwined Fanny's arm with his.

Fanny understood Sylvia's irritation with Daniel Crenshaw. Fanny had sat with the detective Saturday night, carefully explaining the many steps that had led to her getting Gabriel to admit he murdered Nora. Crenshaw had been awestruck by the trio's detection, something that greatly satisfied Fanny. And Sylvia and Olive, when Fanny told them later that night.

As news of Gabriel's guilt and death spread throughout the city, Detective Daniel Crenshaw was hailed as a hero. Fanny was not surprised. Not really. New Orleans had lived in fear for weeks and now that the city was assured the murderer was dead, they needed someone to thank for freeing them from the terror of Jack the Ripper.

Certainly, no one would have believed that Fanny, Sylvia, and Olive could have injected themselves into a grisly murder, studied pornography, or visited a whorehouse *and* a prison. No lady could have attempted any of those social offenses.

Fanny had heard nothing from the detective since Saturday night, although Lawrence had reported back to Fanny throughout the week: Terence had buried his brother; Lester Adams had run from town; Detective Crenshaw was getting a promotion. And he (Lawrence) was readying the apartment above the law office for Fanny's return. As his wife.

Fanny had spent the week making peace with her typewriter. She could now type 40 words a minute and considered herself the mistress of the machine.

The detective removed his bowler as he reached Fanny and Lawrence. "A word alone with Miss Newcomb?"

Lawrence released his grip on Fanny slowly and returned to the carriages.

Fanny stood a few feet from the detective, unable to escape one of her strongest memories of Saturday night: when Daniel held Fanny tightly in his arms just after she escaped Gabriel's knife. Their bodies pulsed with excitement as they gulped for air. She had not tried to leave his embrace—he must have known it—and now, facing him in the merciless daylight, Fanny felt exposed and awkward.

Fanny steadied herself before asking, "It feels good, doesn't it? To see Karl released."

"It would be better if everyone knew the truth about who really got him released."

Crenshaw's jaw tightened as he studied Fanny. Perhaps he was also thinking of those moments when he held Fanny on the rooftop?

The detective said, "Look, I didn't mean for all of this publicity to fall on me. You and the other ladies found out Gabriel, and I want everyone to know that it was you. I'd like to make amends."

"But I don't want anyone to know about my involvement and Sylvia and Olive feel the same."

Truthfully, Fanny did not *need* anyone else to congratulate her. She had triumphed as an investigator. She had identified Nora's murderer and secured his confession. Fanny was as capable as any professional detective and no one could tell her that she wasn't.

"There is one thing you can tell me," Fanny had to admit. "Are you sure Lester Adams wrote that ugly letter to Sylvia?"

"Absolutely."

"And you're sure he's left town?"

"We've heard reports that he's starting up again redeeming women in Chicago. I don't have all of the facts about that, but I am sure that he's gone from New

Orleans. You and Miss Sylvia and Dr. Giddings are safe from his threats." The detective fingered the band of his hat. "Now, there's one thing you can tell me."

Fanny thrilled. Crenshaw was taking her seriously. They were speaking detective to detective. "Of course."

"Why did you leave me Lester's letter? And deVille's broadside? And leave that note asking me to find out exactly where deVille was the night of Nora's murder? It seems so unlike you."

"To ask for help? Is that what you mean?"

"Yes."

"It's not hard to explain." From their very first meeting when he arrested Karl at Wisdom Hall, Fanny had sensed a rapport with Daniel Crenshaw. She knew him to be a man of intelligence, persistence, and ability—qualities she cultivated in herself—and she trusted him because of it. "You wanted to help and we needed it. If you and your men hadn't arrived when you did, there's no telling what Gabriel Boylan could have done." A frown passed across Crenshaw's brow and, before he could reply, Fanny added, "You said earlier you'd like to make amends. I do have a request: Put Pierre deVille out of business. Pornographic business."

"Done. Anything else?"

"Nora's money?"

"Is going back home to her family in Ireland. Although her camera's staying at Mrs. O's. Seems that some of the girls have taken an interest in pictures. Nice pictures. And I wouldn't be surprised if you had two more students in your classes."

"Deirdre and Millie? They want schooling?"

"So, they said yesterday and it looks like they'll be allowed, one night a week."

"Good." Fanny smiled. Mrs. O had sent Fanny back her check but had mentioned nothing about Deirdre and Millie.

"Still...Halloway's right over there," Crenshaw nodded to the reporter, who was attempting to get

Sylvia to talk to him. "He'd be glad to get the true story. And I understand that you owe him."

"He told you that?"

"He tells me quite a lot. It's an arrangement we have."

Fanny paused, wondering just how much the detective and the reporter discussed about things. About Wisdom Hall. About her. Fanny watched as Lawrence shooed Clarence away from Sylvia and then assisted the women into their carriage. Duty completed, Lawrence stared at Fanny; it was time for her to say good-bye to the detective.

But Fanny could not relinquish her moment with Daniel Crenshaw. "I do owe Mr. Halloway but I don't think he'd appreciate the story I have to tell. My story's all about Nora and what she could have done with her life. And about Sylvia and Olive and their work at Wisdom Hall. I don't think anyone's much interested in that just now."

The detective caught a motion from Sergeant Flynn and turned from Fanny to meet him.

From under the shade of the oak tree, Fanny watched as the men conferred. Her gaze passed to the street, where Sylvia and Olive waited in the carriage and Liam and Thomas huddled on the driver's seat. Just beyond them was Lawrence, who'd been pulled into a discussion by a pair of attorneys. Finally, Fanny's sweep settled on Clarence Halloway, who stood in the bright sunlight a few yards away, gnawing on an apple. And staring at her.

Fanny stared right back at him.

Clarence Halloway knew what Fanny had done to find justice for Nora and Karl and he had kept her secrets. So far.

In fact, all of the people assembled about Fanny knew that she would flatter or lie or steal or pry to dislodge the truth. They all knew that Fanny could claim one triumphant success today and they expected her to cherish the memory for the rest of her life.

But Fanny Newcomb also knew that she was not finished with investigating or questioning or detecting. And that she would look for any opportunity to seek out justice again, with or without Sylvia and Olive's assistance. And she would look for that opportunity very, very soon.

Afterword

While it's been my pleasure to write Fanny Newcomb and the Irish Channel Ripper, researching late 19th century New Orleans has been my fascination for quite a while.

Here's a little information about Fanny Newcomb's fact and fiction: In 1889, New Orleans had a population of close to a quarter of a million people, including a handful of formidable, fierce, and energetic women.

The impressive roll call of real-life heroines includes Eliza Holbrook Nicholson, poet and editor of the Daily Picayune newspaper (and friend of the fictional Giddings sisters), Kate and Jean Gordon, child labor reformers and suffragists, and Kate Chopin, author of The Awakening and other writings about Creole Louisiana. These brilliant women challenged the status quo, fought for their beliefs, and bettered New Orleans. All the while wearing bustles and bonnets in humid 90 degree heat.

Fanny's character is lovingly cast from that same Steel Magnolia mold, and her last name honors the spirit and energy of New Orleans' now-dissolved Newcomb College, which opened in the 1880's to provide a liberal education to young white women.

Fanny's quest for justice and dreams of working as a lawyer were not entirely unrealistic. The first female lawyer was admitted to the Iowa bar in 1869, and Fanny could certainly hope that Louisiana would follow suit. Someday. And as the fictional female detectives of

Wilkie Collins, Katherine Anna Green, and Catherine Louisa Pirkis suggest, Fanny's spirited investigations are very much in sync with her times.

Many of the landmarks visited in the story still exist: the Irish Channel, Garden District, French Quarter, St. Alphonsus Catholic Church, and Metairie Cemetery are just as vibrant today as they were in 1889. But the Charity Hospital, Lee Circle, and the Parish Prison of 1889 are gone forever.

The Wisdom Hall Settlement House never existed in New Orleans. But Kingsley House—the New Orleans social settlement house launched by concerned citizens in 1896—did. Both Wisdom Hall and Kingsley House were inspired by London's Toynbee Hall, the world's first Social Settlement House, established in 1884.

Prostitution and pornography certainly existed in 1889 New Orleans, just as they do today. Storyville, the world-famous legalized prostitution district was not established until 1897, but I've located Mrs. O'Sullivan's House of Prostitution at the edge of the district.

Documentary photography—which captured the world as it truly existed, warts and all—had a huge moment in the late 19th century, and John Thomson and Jacob Riis (who titled his 1890 images of the poor How the Other Half Lives were especially celebrated for their photographic vision. My special thanks to the brilliant Paul Strand, whose photograph of a woman with a Blind tag inspired a scene in my book.

Tragically, Jack the Ripper did exist. Whether or not he escaped London for anywhere, the power of his evil murders and mutilations quickly took root in American lives. Fortunately for the real citizens of New Orleans 1889, the Irish Channel Ripper is entirely fictional.

For more information about books, articles, & websites about historic New Orleans and Gilded Age America, visit me at www.anabrazil.com.

Source Materials and Author Notes

It takes a woman...

The Diary of Beatrice Webb: Volume I: 1873 – 1892, Glitter Around and Darkness Within, Virago, 1986.

To craft the character of Fanny Newcomb, I went searching for a candid and intimate diary of a Gilded Age southern woman. I didn't find one. I did find the diaries of Englishwoman Beatrice Webb, a Victorian social reformer and labor historian. Both Fanny and Beatrice question authority, investigate thoroughly, meticulously organize facts, and fight for justice. And both Fanny and Beatrice fall in love with one of their partners-in-work. Perhaps more than once.

Twenty years at Hull House, Jane Addams, 1910.

Just like my fictional Sylvia Giddings, American Jane Addams visited London's Toynbee Hall in the late 1880's and came away energized and enthused. In 1889, Addams and Ellen Gates Star founded the Hull House Settlement in Chicago to provide educational and cultural opportunities to their immigrant neighbors. Addams' and

Star's work certainly encouraged the creation of New Orleans' Kingsley House Settlement (the inspiration for Wisdom Hall), and Addams was an admirer of Kingsley House head resident (and inspiration for Sylvia Giddings) Eleanor McMain.

Send Us a Lady Physician, Women Doctors in America, 1835-1920. Edited by Ruth J. Abram, 1985.

This fine history contains a broad range of primary source text and photography. I couldn't have understood Olive Giddings' skillful, forthright, and frosty character without it.

Women and New Orleans, A History, Mary Gehman and Nancy Ries, 1985.

Includes profiles and photographs of New Orleans' Gilded and Progressive Age social justice pioneers like Eleanor McMain, Eliza Nicholson, Sara Mayo, and the art students of Newcomb College.

The Path from the Parlor, Louisiana Women, 1879-1920, Carmen Lindig, 1986.

A very useful investigation of the state's pioneering and progressive reformers, writers, physicians, nurses, educators, and suffragettes.

The way it was…

New Orleans in the Gilded Age: Politics and Urban Progress, 1880-1896, Joy Jackson, 1969.

An incredible secondary source that provides a wealth of details about the political, social, and economic details of Gilded Age New Orleans.

New Orleans Daily Picayune, 1887-1889.

Just like Fanny and Sylvia, I became a voracious reader of the Daily Picayune.

"New Orleans, Our Southern Capital", Harper's New Monthly Magazine, Julian Ralph, February 1893.

Want to know how to read a death notice, where to shop on Canal Street, or what it takes to be a New Orleans policeman? Just read this article about "the biggest little city in the country."

New Orleans, The Place and the People, Grace King, 1896.

Grace King was a New Orleans native and "Southern Woman of Letters." Her book explores 200 years of Crescent City history and concludes with contemporary (for the Gilded Age) details about the French Quarter,

Mardi Gras celebrations, and Uptown living. Grace King was buried in Metairie Cemetery.

Practical common sense guide book through the World's Industrial and Cotton Centennial Exposition at New Orleans, 1885.

As the cover continues to explain…Giving in brief form the best things to be seen in each department, and just how and where to see them. Also, The Principal Places of Interest in and about the City. It's a fun read.

Let's hop a streetcar…

Historical Sketch Book and Guide to New Orleans and Environs, Edited and compiled by several leading writers of the New Orleans Press, Will H. Coleman, 1885.

Soard's Guide Book Illustrated, and Street Guide of New Orleans, 1885.
You may not want to know the exact addresses of the offices, hotels, hospitals, and prison that Fanny visits. But I do.

Lost New Orleans, Mary Cable, 1980.
One of the best sources for "what building used to be there."

New Orleans in Vintage Postcards, Scott Faragher, 1999.

I've been collecting and studying New Orleans postcards for decades, but I can still glean new information and ideas from these black and white images.

The Church of St. Alphonsus, Samuel Wilson, Jr., 1996.

A glorious celebration of the interior and exterior of this wondrous Irish Channel church. The church is now maintained by the Friends of St. Alphonsus, who regularly provide tours to the public.

New Orleans Architecture, Volume I: The Lower Garden District; Volume II: The American Sector (1998), Pelican Publishing Company, 1980s.

This series sets the bar for scholarly exploration of New Orleans architecture.

First, you make a roux...

La Cuisine Creole: A collection of culinary recipes from leading chefs and noted Creole housewives, who have made New Orleans famous for its cuisine, Lafcadio Hearn, 1885.

Elegant Entertaining Along St. Charles Avenue, Authentic Menus and 1890's Recipes from the Garden District of New Orleans, Susan R. Laudeman, 1994.

Crayfish Bisque. Pigeon pie. Roasted beefstakes. Sauce Piquant. Asparagus with cream. Okra and corn fricassee. Crullers. Lady Cake. Apple compote. Custard Cocoanut Pudding. Pop-Corn Balls. Oh my! Time to push away from the table!

Say "Prunes!"

Street Life in London, John Thomson (photos) and Adolphe Smith (text), 1876.

Thomson was the pioneering photographer of the harsh destitution of London street life and his images of the working poor still provoke disbelief and compassion. Terence Boylan would have approved.

Ernest J. Bellocq is the best-known photographer of New Orleans prostitutes, and his images of Storyville (a formal red light district that existed from 1897-1917) prostitutes were useful in creating Nora's story. Bellocq's photographs can be found online.

Finally…can any writer live without Wikipedia these days? Certainly not me!

A word about words....

Banquette (pronounced ban-ket) – A raised wooden sidewalk; very helpful in keeping your skirts dry when the streets flood.

Canal Street – A wide boulevard of large commercial buildings that separates the French Quarter from the "American" Uptown. Pierre deVille's studio is on Canal Street.

Carnival – A short season of parades, balls, and parties held throughout New Orleans just before the start of Lent (a season of fasting and prayer).

French Quarter – The first and oldest neighborhood in New Orleans and settled by the French. Cousin Charlotte lives and works in the French Quarter.

Rex – A socially prominent man who reigns as the "King of Carnival".

"The war" – This is, of course, the American Civil War (1861-1865). New Orleanians fought on the side of the south, and the city was captured and occupied in 1862. Federal troops did not leave New Orleans until 1877.

Uptown – The "American" commercial, residential, and industrial neighborhoods upriver from Canal Street and the French Quarter. Wisdom Hall, St. Alphonsus Catholic Church, Metairie Cemetery, and the Newcomb Decatur Law Offices are all Uptown.

Acknowledgments

Many people generously assisted me as I researched, wrote, and rewrote Fanny Newcomb and the Irish Channel Ripper. In somewhat chronological order, thanks to:

Drs. Valerie Jean Conner and Jean Bryant, whose classes in Women's & Gilded Age history at Florida State University prompted my lifelong pursuit of women's historical narratives.

The librarians and archivists at the New Orleans Public Library, Tulane University, and University of New Orleans, who enthusiastically assisted me as I researched.

Historian William J. (Bill) Murphy, who shared his love of St. Alphonsus Catholic Church with my husband and me.

My fabulous Florida & Mississippi friends—Elsa, Cheryl, Dean, Helene, Bruce, & Bill.

My longtime friend and editor Connie Hinckley, who provided superb editorial assistance and technical editing. On many drafts. Over many years.

My very thoughtful and helpful readers and supporters: Jeri, Bobbie, and Laura (Ladies of the Vicious

Circle); Margot Abbott and Penny Warner; Eileen and Lou; Dee and my brother Michael.

My former agent Nicholas Smith (aka "More Peril!") for believing in my work even when the New York publishers did not.

My many friends and fellow writers in the Historical Novel Society and Sisters in Crime (Hello GUPPIES!).

Tory Hartmann of Sand Hill Review Press for supporting Fanny Newcomb. Writing is very solitary work, and I very much appreciate the opportunity to have a publishing partner.

A huge, huge thanks to my husband Tim, who has lived with Fanny Newcomb and supported my writing and websites for such a long time.

Apologies if I've forgotten anyone; hopefully, I can rectify any oversight in the acknowledgment of a future Fanny Newcomb investigation.